D0673932

Also by

AGATHA CHRISTIE

★

MRS McGINTY'S
DEAD
and
THEY DO IT WITH
MIRRORS

" A blessed companion is a book "—JERROLD

MRS McGINTY'S DEAD

and

THEY DO IT WITH MIRRORS

*

AGATHA CHRISTIE

THE COMPANION BOOK CLUB
LONDON

Made and printed in Great Britain
for The Companion Book Club (Odhams Press Ltd.)
by Collins Clear-Type Press,
London and Glasgow
T. 154. VUA

MRS McGINTY'S DEAD

To
PETER SAUNDERS
in gratitude for his kindness
to authors

CHAPTER I

HERCULE POIROT came out of the *Vieille Grand'mère* restaurant into Soho. He turned up the collar of his overcoat through prudence, rather than necessity, since the night was not cold. "But at my age, one takes no risks," Poirot was wont to declare.

His eyes held a reflective sleepy pleasure. The *Escargots de la Vieille Grand'mère* had been delicious. A real find, this dingy little restaurant. Meditatively, like a well fed dog, Hercule Poirot curled his tongue round his lips. Drawing his handkerchief from his pocket, he dabbed his luxuriant moustaches.

Yes, he had dined well . . . And now what?

A taxi, passing him, slowed down invitingly. Poirot hesitated for a moment, but made no sign. Why take a taxi? He would in any case reach home too early to go to bed.

"Alas," murmured Poirot to his moustaches, "that one can only eat three times a day . . ."

For afternoon tea was a meal to which he had never become acclimatised. "If one partakes of the five o'clock, one does not," he explained, "approach the dinner with the proper quality of expectant gastric juices. And the dinner, let us remember, is the supreme meal of the day!"

Not for him, either, the mid-morning coffee. No, chocolate and *croissants* for breakfast, *Déjeuner* at twelve-thirty if possible but certainly not later than one o'clock, and finally the climax: *Le Dîner*!

These were the peak periods of Hercule Poirot's day. Always a man who had taken his stomach seriously, he was reaping his reward in old age. Eating was now not only a physical pleasure, it was also an intellectual research. For in between meals he spent quite a lot of time searching out and marking down possible sources of new and delicious food. *La Vieille Grand'mère* was the result of one of these quests, and *La Vieille Grand'mère* had just received the seal of Hercule Poirot's gastronomic approval.

9

But now, unfortunately, there was the evening to put in. Hercule Poirot sighed.

"If only," he thought, "*ce cher Hastings* were available . . ."

He dwelt with pleasure on his remembrances of his old friend.

"My first friend in this country—and still to me the dearest friend I have. True, often and often did he enrage me. But do I remember that now? No. I remember only his incredulous wonder, his open-mouthed appreciation of my talents—the ease with which I misled him without uttering an untrue word, his bafflement, his stupendous astonishment when he at last perceived the truth that had been clear to me all along. *Ce cher, cher ami!* It is my weakness, it has always been my weakness, to desire to show off. That weakness, Hastings could never understand. But indeed it is very necessary for a man of my abilities to admire himself—and for that one needs stimulation from outside. I cannot, truly I cannot, sit in a chair all day reflecting how truly admirable I am. One needs the human touch. One needs—as they say nowadays—the *stooge*."

Hercule Poirot sighed. He turned into Shaftesbury Avenue.

Should he cross it and go on to Leicester Square and spend the evening at a cinema? Frowning slightly, he shook his head. The cinema, more often than not, enraged him by the looseness of its plots—the lack of logical continuity in the argument—even the photography which, raved over by some, to Hercule Poirot seemed often no more than the portrayal of scenes and objects so as to make them appear totally different from what they were in reality.

Everything, Hercule Poirot decided, was too artistic nowadays. Nowhere was there the love of order and method that he himself prized so highly. And seldom was there any appreciation of subtlety. Scenes of violence and crude brutality were the fashion, and as a former police officer, Poirot was bored by brutality. In his early days, he had seen plenty of crude brutality. It had been more the rule than the exception. He found it fatiguing and unintelligent.

"The truth is," Poirot reflected as he turned his steps homeward, "I am not in tune with the modern world. And

10

I am, in a superior way, a slave as other men are slaves. My work has enslaved me just as their work enslaves them. When the hour of leisure arrives, they have nothing with which to fill their leisure. The retired financier takes up golf, the little merchant puts bulbs in his garden, me, I eat. But there it is, I come round to it again. *One can only eat three times a day.* And in between are the gaps."

He passed a newspaper-seller and scanned the bill.

"Result of McGinty Trial. Verdict."

It stirred no interest in him. He recalled vaguely a small paragraph in the papers. It had not been an interesting murder. Some wretched old woman knocked on the head for a few pounds. All part of the senseless crude brutality of these days.

Poirot turned into the courtyard of his block of flats. As always his heart swelled in approval. He was proud of his home. A splendid symmetrical building. The lift took him up to the third floor where he had a large luxury flat with impeccable chromium fittings, square armchairs, and severely rectangular ornaments. There could truly be said not to be a curve in the place.

As he opened the door with his latchkey and stepped into the square, white lobby, his manservant, George, stepped softly to meet him.

"Good evening, sir. There is a—gentleman waiting to see you."

He relieved Poirot deftly of his overcoat.

"Indeed?" Poirot was aware of that very slight pause before the word *gentleman*. As a social snob, George was an expert.

"What is his name?"

"A Mr. Spence, sir."

"Spence." The name, for the moment, meant nothing to Poirot. Yet he knew that it should do so.

Pausing for a moment before the mirror to adjust his moustaches to a state of perfection, Poirot opened the door of the sitting-room and entered. The man sitting in one of the big square armchairs got up.

"Hallo, M. Poirot, hope you remember me. It's a long time . . . Superintendent Spence."

"But of course." Poirot shook him warmly by the hand.

Superintendent Spence of the Kilchester Police. A very interesting case that had been . . . As Spence had said, a long time ago now . . .

Poirot pressed his guests with refreshments. A *Grenadine? Crème de Menthe? Benedictine? Crème de Cacao?* . . .

At this moment George entered with a tray on which was a whisky bottle and a siphon. "Or beer if you prefer it, sir?" he murmured to the visitor.

Superintendent Spence's large red face lightened.

"Beer for me," he said.

Poirot was left to wonder once more at the accomplishments of George. He himself had had no idea that there was beer in the flat and it seemed incomprehensible to him that it could be preferred to a sweet liqueur.

When Spence had his foaming tankard, Poirot poured himself out a tiny glass of gleaming green *crème de menthe*.

"But it is charming of you to look me up," he said. "Charming. You have come up from——?"

"Kilchester. I'll be retired in about six months. Actually, I was due for retirement eighteen months ago. They asked me to stop on and I did."

"You were wise," said Poirot with feeling. "You were very wise . . ."

"Was I? I wonder. I'm not so sure."

"Yes, yes, you were wise," Poirot insisted. "The long hours of *ennui*, you have no conception of them."

"Oh, I'll have plenty to do when I retire. Moved into a new house last year, we did. Quite a bit of garden and shamefully neglected. I haven't been able to get down to it properly yet."

"Ah yes, you are one of those who garden. Me, once, I decided to live in the country and grow vegetable marrows. It did not succeed. I have not the temperament."

"You should have seen one of my marrows last year," said Spence with enthusiasm. "Colossal! And my roses. I'm keen on roses. I'm going to have——"

He broke off.

"That's not what I came to talk about."

"No, no, you came to see an old acquaintance—it was kind. I appreciate it."

"There's more to it than that, I'm afraid, M. Poirot. I'll be honest. I want something."

Poirot murmured delicately:

"There is a mortgage, possibly, on your house? You would like a loan——"

Spence interrupted in a horrified voice:

"Oh, good lord, it's not *money*! Nothing of that kind."

Poirot waved his hands in graceful apology.

"I demand your pardon."

"I'll tell you straight out—it's damned cheek what I've come for. If you send me away with a flea in my ear I shan't be surprised."

"There will be no flea," said Poirot. "But continue."

"It's the McGinty case. You've read about it, perhaps?"

Poirot shook his head.

"Not with attention. Mrs. McGinty—an old woman in a shop or a house. She is dead, yes. How did she die?"

Spence stared at him.

"Lord!" he said. "That takes me back. Extraordinary. And I never thought of it until now."

"I beg your pardon?"

"Nothing. Just a game. Child's game. We used to play it when we were kids. A lot of us in a row. Question and answer all down the line. '*Mrs. McGinty's dead!*' '*How did she die?*' '*Down on one knee just like I.*' And then the next question, '*Mrs. McGinty's dead.*' '*How did she die?*' '*Holding her hand out just like I.*' And there we'd be, all kneeling and our right arms held out stiff. And then you *got* it! '*Mrs. McGinty's dead.*' '*How did she die?*' '*Like THIS!*' Smack, the top of the row would fall sideways and down we all went like a pack of ninepins!" Spence laughed uproariously at the remembrance. "Takes me back, it does!"

Poirot waited politely. This was one of the moments when even after half a lifetime in the country, he found the English incomprehensible. He himself had played at *Cache Cache* in his childhood, but he felt no desire to talk about it or even to think about it.

When Spence had overcome his own amusement, Poirot repeated with some slight weariness, "How *did* she die?"

The laughter was wiped off Spence's face. He was suddenly himself again.

"She was hit on the back of her head with some sharp, heavy implement. Her savings, about thirty pounds in cash, were taken after her room had been ransacked. She lived alone in a small cottage except for a lodger. Man of the name of Bentley. James Bentley."

"Ah yes, Bentley."

"The place wasn't broken into. No signs of any tampering with the windows or locks. Bentley was hard up, had lost his job, and owed two months' rent. The money was found hidden under a loose stone at the back of the cottage. Bentley's coat sleeve had blood on it and hair—same blood group and the right hair. According to his first statement he was never near the body—so it couldn't have come there by accident."

"Who found her?"

"The baker called with bread. It was the day he got paid. James Bentley opened the door to him and said he'd knocked at Mrs. McGinty's bedroom door, but couldn't get an answer. The baker suggested she might have been taken bad. They got the woman from next door to go up and see. Mrs. McGinty wasn't in the bedroom, and hadn't slept in the bed, but the room had been ransacked and the floorboards had been prised up. Then they thought of looking in the parlour. She was there, lying on the floor, and the neighbour fairly screamed her head off. Then they got the police, of course."

"And Bentley was eventually arrested and tried?"

"Yes. The case came on at the Assizes. Yesterday. Open and shut case. The jury were only out twenty minutes this morning. Verdict: Guilty. Condemned to death."

Poirot nodded.

"And then, after the verdict, you got in a train and came to London and came here to see me. Why?"

Superintendent Spence was looking into his beer glass. He ran his finger slowly round and round the rim.

"Because," he said, "I don't think he did it. . . ."

CHAPTER II

THERE was a moment or two of silence.

"You came to me——"

Poirot did not finish the sentence.

Superintendent Spence looked up. The colour in his face was deeper than it had been. It was a typical countryman's face, unexpressive, self-contained, with shrewd but honest eyes. It was the face of a man with definite standards who would never be bothered by doubts of himself or by doubts of what constituted right and wrong.

"I've been a long time in the Force," he said. "I've had a good deal of experience of this, that and the other. I can judge a man as well as any other could do. I've had cases of murder during my service—some of them straightforward enough, some of them not so straightforward. One case *you* know of, M. Poirot——"

Poirot nodded.

"Tricky, that was. But for you, we mightn't have seen clear. But we did see clear—and there wasn't any doubt. The same with the others you don't know about. There was Whistler, he got his—*and* deserved it. There were those chaps who shot old Guterman. There was Verall and his arsenic. Tranter got off—but he did it all right. Mrs. Courtland—she was lucky—her husband was a nasty perverted bit of work, and the jury acquitted her accordingly. Not justice—just sentiment. You've to allow for that happening now and again. Sometimes there isn't enough evidence—sometimes there's sentiment, sometimes a murderer manages to put it across the jury—that last doesn't happen often, but it can happen. Sometimes it's a clever bit of work by defending counsel—or a prosecuting counsel takes the wrong tack. Oh yes, I've seen a lot of things like that. But—but——"

Spence wagged a heavy forefinger.

"I haven't seen—not in *my* experience—an innocent man hanged for something he didn't do. It's a thing, M. Poirot, that I don't *want* to see.

"Not," added Spence, "in *this* country!"

15

Poirot gazed back at him.

"And you think you are going to see it now. But why——"
Spence interrupted him.

"I know some of the things you're going to say. I'll answer
them without you having to ask them. I was put on this case.
I was put on to get evidence of what happened. I went into
the whole business very carefully. I got the facts, all the facts
I could. All those facts pointed one way—pointed to one
person. When I'd got all the facts I took them to my superior
officer. After that it was out of my hands. The case went to
the Public Prosecutor and it was up to him. He decided to
prosecute—he couldn't have done anything else—not on the
evidence. And so James Bentley was arrested and committed
for trial, and was duly tried and has been found guilty. They
couldn't have found him anything else, not on the evidence.
And evidence is what a jury have to consider. Didn't have
any qualms about it either, I should say. No, I should say
they were all quite satisfied he *was* guilty."

"But you—are not?"

"No."

"Why?"

Superintendent Spence sighed. He rubbed his chin
thoughtfully with his big hand.

"I don't know. What I mean is, I can't give a reason—a
concrete reason. To the jury I dare say he looked like a
murderer—to me he didn't—and I know a lot more about
murderers than they do."

"Yes, yes, you are an expert."

"For one thing, you know, he wasn't *cocky*. Not cocky at
all. And in my experience they usually are. Always so
damned pleased with themselves. Always think they're
stringing you along. Always sure they've been so clever about
the whole thing. And even when they're in the dock and
must know they're for it, they're still in a queer sort of way
getting a kick out of it all. They're in the limelight. They're
the central figure. Playing the star part—perhaps for the
first time in their lives. They're—well—you know—*cocky!*"

Spence brought out the word with an air of finality.

"You'll understand what I mean by that, M. Poirot."

"I understand very well. And this James Bentley—he was
not like that?"

16

"No. He was—well, just scared stiff. Scared stiff from the start. And to some people that would square in with his being guilty. But not to me."

"No, I agree with you. What is he like, this James Bentley?"

"Thirty-three, medium height, sallow complexion, wears glasses——"

Poirot arrested the flow.

"No, I do not mean his physical characteristics. What sort of a personality?"

"Oh—that." Superintendent Spence considered. "Unprepossessing sort of fellow. Nervous manner. Can't look you straight in the face. Has a sly sideways way of peering at you. Worst possible sort of manner for a jury. Sometimes cringing and sometimes truculent. Blusters in an inefficient kind of way."

He paused and added in a conversational tone:

"Really a shy kind of chap. Had a cousin rather like that. If anything's awkward they go and tell some silly lie that hasn't a chance of being believed."

"He does not sound attractive, your James Bentley."

"Oh, he isn't. Nobody could *like* him. But I don't want to see him hanged for all that."

"And you think he will be hanged?"

"I don't see why not. His counsel may lodge an appeal—but if so it will be on very flimsy grounds—a technicality of some kind, and I don't see that it will have a chance of success."

"Did he have a good counsel?"

"Young Graybrook was allotted to him under the Poor Persons' Defence Act. I'd say he was thoroughly conscientious and put up the best show he could."

"So the man had a fair trial and was condemned by a jury of his fellow-men."

"That's right. A good average jury. Seven men, five women —all decent reasonable souls. Judge was old Stanisdale. Scrupulously fair—no bias."

"So—according to the law of the land—James Bentley has nothing to complain of?"

"If he's hanged for something he didn't do, he's got something to complain of!"

"A very just observation."

"And the case against him was *my* case—*I* collected the facts and put them together—and it's on that case and those facts that he's been condemned. And I don't like it, M. Poirot, I don't like it."

Hercule Poirot looked for a long time at the red agitated face of Superintendent Spence.

"*Eh bien*," he said. "What do you suggest?"

Spence looked acutely embarrassed.

"I expect you've got a pretty good idea of what's coming. The Bentley case is closed. I'm on another case already—embezzlement. Got to go up to Scotland to-night. I'm not a free man."

"And—I am?"

Spence nodded in a shame-faced sort of way.

"You've got it. Awful cheek, you'll think. But I can't think of anything else—of any other way. I did all I could at the time, I examined every possibility I could. And I didn't get anywhere. I don't believe I ever would get anywhere. But who knows, it may be different for you. You look at things in —if you'll pardon me for saying so—in a funny sort of way. Maybe that's the way you've got to look at them in this case. Because if James Bentley didn't kill her, then somebody else did. She didn't chop the back of her head in herself. You may be able to find something that I missed. There's no reason why you should do anything about this business. It's infernal cheek my even suggesting such a thing. But there it is. I came to you because it was the only thing I could think of. But if you don't want to put yourself out—and why should you——"

Poirot interrupted him.

"Oh, but indeed there are reasons. I have leisure—too much leisure. And you have intrigued me—yes, you have intrigued me very much. It is a challenge—to the little grey cells of my brain. And then, I have a regard for you. I see you, in your garden in six months' time, planting, perhaps, the rose bushes—and as you plant them it is not with the happiness you should be feeling, because behind everything there is an unpleasantness in your brain, a recollection that you try to push away, and I would not have you feel that, my friend. And finally——" Poirot sat upright and nodded his head vigorously, "there is the principle of the thing. If a man has not committed murder, he should not be hanged." He paused and then added, "But supposing that after all, he did kill her?"

"In that case I'd be only too thankful to be convinced of it."

"And two heads are better than one? *Voilà*, everything is settled. I precipitate myself upon the business. There is, that is clear, no time to be lost. Already the scent is cold. Mrs. McGinty was killed—when?"

"Last November, 22nd."

"Then let us at once get down to the brass tacks."

"I've got my notes on the case which I'll pass over to you."

"Good. For the moment, we need only the bare outline. If James Bentley did not kill Mrs. McGinty, who did?"

Spence shrugged his shoulders and said heavily:

"There's nobody, so far as I can see."

"But that answer we do not accept. Now, since for every murder there must be a motive, what, in the case of Mrs. McGinty, could the motive be? Envy, revenge, jealousy, fear, money? Let us take the last and the simplest? Who profited by her death?"

"Nobody very much. She had two hundred pounds in the Savings Bank. Her niece gets that."

"Two hundred pounds is not very much—but in certain circumstances it could be enough. So let us consider the niece. I apologise, my friend, for treading in your footsteps. You too, I know, must have considered all this. But I have to go over with you the ground already traversed."

Spence nodded his large head.

"We considered the niece, of course. She's thirty-eight, married. Husband is employed in the building and decorating trade—a painter. He's got a good character, steady employment, sharp sort of fellow, no fool. She's a pleasant young woman, a bit talkative, seemed fond of her aunt in a mild sort of way. Neither of them had any urgent need for two hundred pounds, though quite pleased to have it, I dare say."

"What about her cottage? Do they get that?"

"It was rented. Of course, under the Rent Restriction Act the landlord couldn't get the old woman out. But now she's

19

dead, I don't think the niece could have taken over—anyway she and her husband didn't want to. They've got a small modern council house of their own of which they are extremely proud." Spence sighed. "I went into the niece and her husband pretty closely—they seemed the best bet, as you'll understand. But I couldn't get hold of anything."

"*Bien*. Now let us talk about Mrs. McGinty herself. Describe her to me—and not only in physical terms, if you please."

Spence grinned.

"Don't want a police description? Well, she was sixty-four. Widow. Husband had been employed in the drapery department of Hodges in Kilchester. He died about seven years ago. Pneumonia. Since then, Mrs. McGinty has been going out daily to various houses round about. Domestic chores. Broadhinny's a small village which has lately become residential. One or two retired people, one of the partners in an engineering works, a doctor, that sort of thing. There's quite a good bus and train service to Kilchester, and Cullenquay which, as I expect you know, is quite a large summer resort, is only eight miles away, but Broadhinny itself is still quite pretty and rural—about a quarter of a mile off the main Drymouth and Kilchester road."

Poirot nodded.

"Mrs. McGinty's cottage was one of four that form the village proper. There is the post office and village shop, and agricultural labourers live in the others."

"And she took in a lodger?"

"Yes. Before her husband died, it used to be summer visitors, but after his death she just took one regular. James Bentley had been there for some months."

"So we come to—James Bentley?"

"Bentley's last job was with a house agent's in Kilchester. Before that, he lived with his mother in Cullenquay. She was an invalid and he looked after her and never went out much. Then she died, and an annuity she had died with her. He sold the little house and found a job. Well-educated man, but no special qualifications or aptitudes, and, as I say, an unprepossessing manner. Didn't find it easy to get anything. Anyway, they took him on at Breather & Scuttle's. Rather a second-rate firm. I don't think he was particularly efficient or successful. They cut down staff and he was the one to go. He couldn't get another job, and his money ran out. He usually paid Mrs. McGinty every month for his room. She gave him breakfast and supper and charged him three pounds a week—quite reasonable, all things considered. He was two months behind in paying her, and he was nearly at the end of his resources. He hadn't got another job and she was pressing him for what he owed her."

"And he knew that she had thirty pounds in the house? Why did she have thirty pounds in the house, by the way, since she had a Savings Bank account?"

"Because she didn't trust the Government. Said they'd got two hundred pounds of her money, but they wouldn't get any more. She'd keep that where she could lay her hand on it any minute. She said that to one or two people. It was under a loose board in her bedroom floor—a very obvious place. James Bentley admitted he knew it was there."

"Very obliging of him. And did niece and husband know that too?"

"Oh yes."

"Then we have now arrived back at my first question to you. How did Mrs. McGinty die?"

"She died on the night of November 22nd. Police surgeon put the time of death as being between 7 and 10 p.m. She'd had her supper—a kipper and bread and margarine, and according to all accounts, she usually had that about half-past six. If she adhered to that on the night in question, then by the evidence of digestion she was killed about eight-thirty or nine o'clock. James Bentley, by his own account, was out walking that evening from seven-fifteen to about nine. He went out and walked most evenings after dark. According to his own story he came in at about nine o'clock (he had his own key) and went straight upstairs to his room. Mrs. McGinty had had wash-basins fixed in the bedrooms because of summer visitors. He read for about half an hour and then went to bed. He heard and noticed nothing out of the way. Next morning he came downstairs and looked into the kitchen, but there was no one there and no signs of breakfast being prepared. He says he hesitated a bit and then knocked on Mrs. McGinty's door, but got no reply.

"He thought she must have overslept, but didn't like to go

21

on knocking. Then the baker came and James Bentley went up and knocked again, and after that, as I told you, the baker went next door and fetched in a Mrs. Elliot, who eventually found the body and went off the deep end. Mrs. McGinty was lying on the parlour floor. She'd been hit on the back of the head with something rather in the nature of a meat chopper with a very sharp edge. She'd been killed instantaneously. Drawers were pulled open and things strewn about, and the loose board in the floor in her bedroom had been prised up and the *cache* was empty. All the windows were closed and shuttered on the inside. No signs of anything being tampered with or of being broken into from outside."

"Therefore," said Poirot, "either James Bentley must have killed her, or else she must have admitted her killer herself whilst Bentley was out?"

"Exactly. It wasn't any hold-up or burglar. Now who would she be likely to let in? One of the neighbours, or her niece, or her niece's husband. It boils down to that. We eliminated the neighbours. Niece and husband were at the pictures that night. It is possible—just possible, that one or other of them left the cinema unobserved, bicycled three miles, killed the old woman, hid the money outside the house, and got back into the cinema unnoticed. We looked into that possibility, but we didn't find any confirmation of it. And why hide the money outside McGinty's house if so? Difficult place to pick it up later. Why not somewhere along the three miles back? No, the only reason for hiding it where it was hidden——"

Poirot finished the sentence for him.

"Would be because you were living in that house, but didn't want to hide it in your room or anywhere inside. In fact: James Bentley."

"That's right. Everywhere, every time, you came up against Bentley. Finally there was the blood on his cuff."

"How did he account for that?"

"Said he remembered brushing up against a butcher's shop the previous day. Baloney! It wasn't animal blood."

"And he stuck to that story?"

"Not likely. At the trial he told a completely different tale. You see, there was a hair on the cuff as well—a blood-stained

22

hair, and the hair was identical with Mrs. McGinty's hair. That had got to be explained away. He admitted then that he had gone into the room the night before when he came back from his walk. He'd gone in, he said, after knocking, and found her there, on the floor, dead. He'd bent over and touched her, he said, to make sure. And then he'd lost his head. He'd always been very much affected by the sight of blood, he said. He went to his room in a state of collapse and more or less fainted. In the morning he couldn't bring himself to admit he knew what had happened."

"A very fishy story," commented Poirot.

"Yes, indeed. And yet, you know," said Spence thoughtfully, "it might well be true. It's not the sort of thing that an ordinary man—or a jury—can believe. But I've come across people like that. I don't mean the collapse story. I mean people who are confronted by a demand for responsible action and who simply can't face up to it. Shy people. He goes in, say, and finds her. He knows that he ought to do something—get the police—go to a neighbour—do the right thing whatever it is. And he funks it. He thinks 'I don't need to know anything about it. I needn't have come in here to-night. I'll go to bed just as if I hadn't come in here at all. . . .' Behind it, of course, there's fear—fear that he may be suspected of having a hand in it. He thinks he'll keep himself out of it as long as possible, and so the silly juggins goes and puts himself into it—up to his neck."

Spence paused.

"It *could* have been that way."

"It could," said Poirot thoughtfully.

"Or again, it may have been just the best story his counsel could think up for him. But I don't know. The waitress in the café in Kilchester where he usually had lunch said that he always chose a table where he could look into a wall or a corner and not see people. He was that kind of a chap—just a bit screwy. But not screwy enough to be a killer. He'd no persecution complex or anything of that kind."

Spence looked hopefully at Poirot—but Poirot did not respond—he was frowning.

The two men sat silent for a while.

CHAPTER III

AT LAST Poirot roused himself with a sigh.

"*Eh bien*," he said. "We have exhausted the motive of money. Let us pass to other theories. Had Mrs. McGinty an enemy? Was she afraid of anyone?"

"No evidence of it."

"What did her neighbours have to say?"

"Not very much. They wouldn't to the police, perhaps, but I don't think they were holding anything back. She kept herself to herself, they said. But that's regarded as natural enough. Our villages, you know, M. Poirot, aren't friendly. Evacuees found that during the war. Mrs. McGinty passed the time of the day with the neighbours but they weren't intimate."

"How long had she lived there?"

"Matter of eighteen or twenty years, I think."

"And the forty years before that?"

"There's no mystery about her. Farmer's daughter from North Devon. She and her husband lived near Ilfracombe for a time, and then moved to Kilchester. Had a cottage the other side of it—but found it damp, so they moved to Broadhinny. Husband seems to have been a quiet, decent man, delicate—didn't go to the pub much. All very respectable and aboveboard. No mysteries anywhere, nothing to hide."

"And yet she was killed?"

"And yet she was killed."

"The niece didn't know of anyone who had a grudge against her aunt?"

"She says not."

Poirot rubbed his nose in an exasperated fashion.

"You comprehend, my dear friend, it would be so much easier if Mrs. McGinty was *not* Mrs. McGinty, so to speak. If she could be what is called a Mystery Woman—a woman with a past."

"Well, she wasn't," said Spence stolidly. "She was just Mrs. McGinty, a more or less uneducated woman, who let rooms

24

and went out charring. Thousands of them all over England."

"But they do not all get murdered."

"No. I grant you that."

"So why should Mrs. McGinty get murdered? The obvious answer we do not accept. What remains? A shadowy and improbable niece. An even more shadowy and improbable stranger. Facts? Let us stick to facts. What are the facts? An elderly charwoman is murdered. A shy and uncouth young man is arrested and convicted of the murder. Why was James Bentley arrested?"

Spence stared.

"The evidence against him. I've told you——"

"Yes. Evidence. But tell me, my Spence, was it real evidence or was it contrived?"

"Contrived?"

"Yes. Granted the premises that James Bentley is innocent, two possibilities remain. The evidence was manufactured, deliberately, to throw suspicion upon him. Or else he was just the unfortunate victim of circumstances."

Spence considered.

"Yes. I see what you're driving at."

"There is nothing to show that the former was the case. But again there is nothing to show that it was not so. The money was taken and hidden outside the house in a place easily found. To have actually hidden it in his room would have been a little too much for the police to swallow. The murder was committed at a time when Bentley was taking a lonely walk, as he often did. Did the bloodstain come on his sleeve as he said it did at his trial, or was that, too, contrived? Did someone brush against him in the darkness and smear tell-tale evidence on his sleeve?"

"I think that's going a bit far, M. Poirot."

"Perhaps, perhaps. But we have got to go far. I think that in this case we have got to go so far that the imagination cannot as yet see the path clearly. . . . For, you see, *mon cher Spence*, if Mrs. McGinty is just an ordinary charwoman—it is the *murderer* who must be extraordinary. Yes—that follows clearly. It is in the murderer and not the murdered that the interest of this case lies. That is not the case in most crimes. Usually it is in the personality of the murdered person that the crux of the situation lies. It is the silent dead in whom I am usually interested. Their hates, their loves, their actions. And when you really know the murdered victim, then the victim speaks, and those dead lips utter a name— the name you want to know."

Spence looked rather uncomfortable.

"These foreigners!" he seemed to be saying to himself.

"But here," continued Poirot, "it is the opposite. Here we guess at a veiled personality—a figure still hidden in darkness. How did Mrs. McGinty die? Why did she die? The answer is not to be found in studying the life of Mrs. McGinty. The answer is to be found in the personality of the murderer. You agree with me there?"

"I suppose so," said Superintendent Spence cautiously.

"Someone who wanted—what? To strike down Mrs. McGinty? *Or to strike down James Bentley?*"

The Superintendent gave a doubtful "H'm!"

"Yes—yes, that is one of the first points to be decided. Who is the real victim? Who was intended to be the victim?"

Spence said incredulously: "You really think someone would bump off a perfectly inoffensive old woman in order to get someone else hanged for murder?"

"One cannot make an omelette, they say, without breaking eggs. Mrs. McGinty, then, may be the egg, and James Bentley is the omelette. So let me hear, now, what you know of James Bentley."

"Nothing much. Father was a doctor—died when Bentley was nine years old. He went to one of the smaller public schools, unfit for the Army, had a weak chest, was in one of the Ministries during the war and lived with a possessive mother."

"Well," said Poirot, "there are certain possibilities there . . . More than there are in the life history of Mrs. McGinty."

"Do you seriously believe what you are suggesting?"

"No, I do not believe anything as yet. But I say that there are two distinct lines of research, and that we have to decide, very soon, which is the right one to follow."

"How are you going to set about things, M. Poirot? Is there anything I can do?"

"First, I should like an interview with James Bentley."

26

"That can be managed. I'll get on to his solicitors."

"After that and subject, of course, to the result, if any—I am not hopeful—of that interview, I shall go to Broadhinny. There, aided by your notes, I shall, as quickly as possible, go over that same ground where you have passed before me."

"In case I've missed anything," said Spence with a wry smile.

"In case, I would prefer to say, that some circumstance should strike me in a different light to the one in which it struck you. Human reactions vary and so does human experience. The resemblance of a rich financier to a soap boiler whom I had known in Liége once brought about a most satisfactory result. But no need to go into that. What I should like to do is to eliminate one or other of the trails I indicated just now. And to eliminate the Mrs. McGinty trail—trail No. 1—will obviously be quicker and easier than to attack trail No. 2. Where, now, can I stay in Broadhinny? Is there an inn of moderate comfort?"

"There's the Three Ducks—but it doesn't put people up. There's the Lamb in Cullavon three miles away—or there is a kind of a Guest House in Broadhinny itself. It's not really a Guest House, just a rather decrepit country house where the young couple who own it take in paying guests. I don't think," said Spence dubiously, "that it's very comfortable."

Hercule Poirot closed his eyes in agony.

"If I suffer, I suffer," he said. "It has to be."

"I don't know what you'll go there as," continued Spence doubtfully as he eyed Poirot. "You might be some kind of an opera singer. Voice broken down. Got to rest. That might do."

"I shall go," said Hercule Poirot, speaking with accents of royal blood, "as myself."

Spence received this pronouncement with pursed lips.

"D'you think that's advisable?"

"I think it is *essential*! But yes, essential. Consider, *cher ami*, it is *time* we are up against. What do we know? Nothing. So the hope, the best hope, is to go pretending that I know a great deal. I am Hercule Poirot. I am the great, the unique Hercule Poirot. And I, Hercule Poirot, am not satisfied about the verdict in the McGinty case. I, Hercule

Poirot, have a very shrewd suspicion of *what really happened.* There is a circumstance that I, alone, estimate at its true value. You see?"

"And then?"

"And then, having made my effect, I observe the reactions. For there should be reactions. Very definitely, there should be reactions."

Superintendent Spence looked uneasily at the little man.

"Look here, M. Poirot," he said. "Don't go sticking out your neck. I don't want anything to happen to you."

"But if it does, you would be proved right beyond the shadow of a doubt, is it not so?"

"I don't want it proved the hard way," said Superintendent Spence.

CHAPTER IV

WITH great distaste, Hercule Poirot looked round the room in which he stood. It was a room of gracious proportions but there its attraction ended. Poirot made an eloquent grimace as he drew a suspicious finger along the top of a book case. As he had suspected—dust! He sat down gingerly on a sofa and its broken springs sagged depressingly under him. The two faded armchairs were, as he knew, little better. A large fierce-looking dog whom Poirot suspected of having mange growled from his position on a moderately comfortable fourth chair.

The room was large, and had a faded Morris wallpaper. Steel engravings of unpleasant subjects hung crookedly on the walls with one or two good oil paintings. The chair-covers were both faded and dirty, the carpet had holes in it and had never been of a pleasant design. A good deal of miscellaneous bric-a-brac was scattered haphazard here and there. Tables rocked dangerously owing to absence of castors. One window was open, and no power on earth could, apparently, shut it again. The door, temporarily shut, was not likely to remain so. The latch did not hold, and with every gust of wind it burst open and whirling gusts of cold wind eddied round the room.

"I suffer," said Hercule Poirot to himself in acute self-pity. "Yes, I suffer."

The door burst open and the wind and Mrs. Summerhayes came in together. She looked round the room, shouted "What?" to someone in the distance and went out again.

Mrs. Summerhayes had red hair and an attractively freckled face and was usually in a distracted state of putting things down, or else looking for them.

Hercule Poirot sprang to his feet and shut the door.

A moment or two later it opened again and Mrs. Summerhayes reappeared. This time she was carrying a large enamel basin and a knife.

A man's voice from some way away called out:

"Maureen, that cat's been sick again. What shall I do?"

Mrs. Summerhayes called: "I'm coming, darling. Hold everything."

She dropped the basin and the knife and went out again. Poirot got up again and shut the door. He said:

"Decidedly, I suffer."

A car drove up, the large dog leaped from the chair and raised its voice in a crescendo of barking. He jumped on a small table by the window and the table collapsed with a crash.

"Enfin," said Hercule Poirot. "C'est insupportable!"

The door burst open, the wind surged round the room, the dog rushed out, still barking. Maureen's voice came, upraised loud and clear.

"Johnnie, why the hell did you leave the back door open! Those bloody hens are in the larder."

"And for this," said Hercule Poirot with feeling, "I pay seven guineas a week!"

The door banged to with a crash. Through the window came the loud squawking of irate hens.

Then the door opened again and Maureen Summerhayes came in and fell upon the basin with a cry of joy.

"Couldn't think where I'd left it. Would you mind frightfully, Mr. Er—hum—I mean, would it bother you if I sliced the beans in here? The smell in the kitchen is too frightful."

"Madame, I should be enchanted."

It was not, perhaps, the exact phrase, but it was near enough. It was the first time in twenty-four hours that Poirot

29

had seen any chance of a conversation of more than six seconds' duration.

Mrs. Summerhayes flung herself down in a chair and began slicing beans with frenzied energy and considerable awkwardness.

"I do hope," she said, "that you're not too frightfully uncomfortable? If there's anything you want altered, do say so."

Poirot had already come to the opinion that the only thing in Long Meadows he could even tolerate was his hostess.

"You are too kind, madame," he replied politely. "I only wish it were within my powers to provide you with suitable domestics."

"Domestics!" Mrs. Summerhayes gave a squeal. "What a hope! Can't even get hold of a *daily*. Our really good one was murdered. Just my luck."

"That would be Mrs. McGinty," said Poirot quickly.

"Mrs. McGinty it was. God, how I miss that woman! Of course it was all a big thrill at the time. First murder we've ever had right in the family, so to speak, but as I told Johnnie, it was a downright bit of bad luck for us. Without McGinty I just can't cope."

"You were attached to her?"

"My dear man, she was *reliable*. She *came*, Monday afternoons and Thursday mornings—just like a clock. Now I have that Burp woman from up by the station. Five children and a husband. Naturally she's never here. Either her husband's taken queer, or the old mother, or the children have some foul disease or other. With old McGinty, at least it was only she herself who came over queer, and I must say she hardly ever did."

"And you found her always reliable and honest? You had trust in her?"

"Oh, she'd never pinch anything—not even food. Of course she snooped a bit. Had a look at one's letters and all that. But one expects that sort of thing. I mean they must live such awfully drab lives, mustn't they?"

"Had Mrs. McGinty had a drab life?"

"Ghastly, I expect," said Mrs. Summerhayes vaguely. "Always on your knees scrubbing. And then piles of other people's washing up waiting for you on the sink when you arrive in the morning. If I had to face that every day, I'd be positively relieved to be murdered. I really would."

The face of Major Summerhayes appeared at the window. Mrs. Summerhayes sprang up, upsetting the beans, and rushed across to the window, which she opened to the fullest extent.

"That damned dog's eaten the hens' food again, Maureen."

"Oh damn, now *he'll* be sick!"

"Look here," John Summerhayes displayed a colander full of greenery, "is this enough spinach?"

"Of course not."

"Seems a colossal amount to me."

"It'll be about a teaspoonful when it's cooked. Don't you know by now what spinach is like?"

"Oh lord!"

"Has the fish come?"

"Not a sign of it."

"Hell, we'll have to open a tin of something. You might do that, Johnnie. One of the ones in the corner cupboard. That one we thought was a bit bulged. I expect it's quite all right really."

"What about the spinach?"

"I'll get that."

She leapt through the window, and husband and wife moved away together.

"*Nom d'un nom d'un nom!*" said Hercule Poirot. He crossed the room and closed the window as nearly as he could. The voice of Major Summerhayes came to him borne on the wind.

"What about this new fellow, Maureen? Looks a bit peculiar to me. What's his name again?"

"I couldn't remember it just now when I was talking to him. Had to say Mr. Er-um. Poirot—that's what it is. He's French."

"You know, Maureen, I seem to have seen that name some-where."

"Home Perm, perhaps. He looks like a hairdresser." Poirot winced.

"N-no. Perhaps it's pickles. I don't know. I'm sure it's familiar. Better get the first seven guineas out of him, quick."

The voices died away.

Hercule Poirot picked up the beans from the floor where they had scattered far and wide. Just as he finished doing so, Mrs. Summerhayes came in again through the door.

He presented them to her politely.

"*Voici, madame.*"

"Oh thanks awfully. I say, these beans look a bit black. We store them, you know, in crocks, salted down. But these seem to have gone wrong. I'm afraid they won't be very nice."

"I, too, fear that . . . You permit that I shut the door? There is a decided draught."

"Oh yes, do. I'm afraid I always leave doors open."

"So I have noticed."

"Anyway, that door never stays shut. This house is practically falling to pieces. Johnnie's father and mother lived here and they were very badly off, poor dears, and they never did a thing to it. And then when we came home from India to live here, we couldn't afford to do anything either. It's fun for the children in the holidays, though, lots of room to run wild in, and the garden and everything. Having paying guests here just enables us to keep going, though I must say we've had a few rude shocks."

"Am I your only guest at present?"

"We've got an old lady upstairs. Took to her bed the day she came and has been there ever since. Nothing the matter with her that I can see. But there she is, and I carry up four trays a day. Nothing wrong with her appetite. Anyway, she's going to-morrow to some niece or other."

Mrs. Summerhayes paused for a moment before resuming in a slightly artificial voice.

"The fishman will be here in a minute. I wonder if you'd mind—er—forking out the first week's rent. You are staying a week, aren't you?"

"Perhaps longer."

"Sorry to bother you. But I've not got any cash in the house and you know what these people are like—always dunning you."

"Pray do not apologise, madame." Poirot took out seven pound notes and added seven shillings. Mrs. Summerhayes gathered the money up with avidity.

"Thanks a lot."

"I should, perhaps, madame, tell you a little more about myself. *I am Hercule Poirot.*"

The revelation left Mrs. Summerhayes unmoved.

"What a lovely name," she said kindly. "Greek, isn't it?"

"I am, as you may know," said Poirot, "a detective." He tapped his chest. "Perhaps the most famous detective there is."

Mrs. Summerhayes screamed with amusement.

"I see you're a great practical joker, M. Poirot. What are you detecting? Cigarette ash and footprints?"

"I am investigating the murder of Mrs. McGinty," said Poirot. "And I do not joke."

"Ouch," said Mrs. Summerhayes. "I've cut my hand."

She raised a finger and inspected it.

Then she stared at Poirot.

"Look here," she said. "Do you mean it? What I mean is, it's over, all that. They arrested that poor half-wit who lodged there and he's been tried and convicted and everything. He's probably been hanged by now."

"No, madame," said Poirot. "He has not been hanged—yet. And it is not 'over'—the case of Mrs. McGinty. I will remind you of the line from one of your poets. 'A question is never settled until it is settled—right.' "

"Oo," said Mrs. Summerhayes, her attention diverted from Poirot to the basin on her lap. "I'm bleeding over the beans. Not too good as we've got to have them for lunch. Still it won't matter really because they'll go into boiling water. Things are always all right if you boil them, aren't they? Even tins."

"I think," said Hercule Poirot quietly, "that I shall not be in for lunch."

CHAPTER V

"I DON'T know, I'm sure," said Mrs. Burch.

She had said that three times already. Her natural distrust of foreign-looking gentlemen with black moustaches, wearing large fur-lined coats was not to be easily overcome.

"Very unpleasant it's been," she went on. "Having poor auntie murdered and the police and all that. Tramping round everywhere, and ferreting about and asking questions. With the neighbours all agog. I didn't feel at first we'd ever live it down. And my husband's mother's been downright nasty about it. Nothing of that kind ever happened in *her* family, she kept saying. And 'poor Joe' and all that. What about poor me? She was *my* aunt, wasn't she? But really I did think it was all over now."

"And supposing that James Bentley is innocent, after all?"

"Nonsense," snapped Mrs. Burch. "Of course he isn't innocent. He did it all right. I never did like the looks of him. Wandering about muttering to himself. Said to auntie, I did: 'You oughtn't to have a man like that in the house. Might go off his head,' I said. But she said he was quiet and obliging and didn't give trouble. No drinking, she said, and he didn't even smoke. Well, she knows better now, poor soul."

Poirot looked thoughtfully at her. She was a big, plump woman with a healthy colour and a good-humoured mouth. The small house was neat and clean and smelt of furniture polish and brasso. A faint appetising smell came from the direction of the kitchen.

A good wife who kept her house clean and took the trouble to cook for her man. He approved. She was prejudiced and obstinate but, after all, why not? Most decidedly, she was not the kind of woman one could imagine using a meat chopper on her aunt, or conniving at her husband's doing so. Spence had not thought her that kind of woman, and rather reluctantly, Hercule Poirot agreed with him. Spence had gone into the financial background of the

Burches and had found no motive there for murder, and Spence was a very thorough man.

He sighed, and persevered with his task, which was the breaking down of Mrs. Burch's suspicion of foreigners. He led the conversation away from murder and focused on the victim of it. He asked questions about "poor auntie," her health, her habits, her preferences in food and drink, her politics, her late husband, her attitude to life, to sex, to sin, to religion, to children, to animals.

Whether any of this irrelevant matter would be of use, he had no idea. He was looking through a haystack to find a needle. But, incidentally, he was learning something about Bessie Burch.

Bessie did not really know very much about her aunt. It had been a family tie, honoured as such, but without intimacy. Now and again, once a month or so, she and Joe had gone over on a Sunday to have midday dinner with auntie, and more rarely, auntie had come over to see them. They had exchanged presents at Christmas. They'd known that auntie had a little something put by, and that they'd get it when she died.

"But that's not to say we were needing it," Mrs. Burch explained with rising colour. "We've got something put by ourselves. And we buried her beautiful. A real nice funeral it was. Flowers and everything."

Auntie had been fond of knitting. She didn't like dogs, they messed up a place, but she used to have a cat—a ginger. It strayed away and she hadn't had one since, but the woman at the post office had been going to give her a kitten. Kept her house very neat and didn't like litter. Kept brass a treat and washed down the kitchen floor every day. She made quite a nice thing of going out to work. One shilling and tenpence an hour—two shillings from Holmeleigh, that was Mr. Carpenter's of the Works' house. Rolling in money, the Carpenters were. Tried to get auntie to come more days in the week, but auntie wouldn't disappoint her other ladies because she'd gone to them before she went to Mr. Carpenter's, and it wouldn't have been right.

Poirot mentioned Mrs. Summerhayes at Long Meadows.

Oh yes, auntie went to her—two days a week. They'd come back from India where they'd had a lot of native servants and Mrs. Summerhayes didn't know a thing about a house. They tried to market-garden, but they didn't know anything about that, either. When the children came home for the holidays, the house was just pandemonium. But Mrs. Summerhayes was a nice lady and auntie liked her.

So the portrait grew. Mrs. McGinty knitted, and scrubbed floors and polished brass, she liked cats and didn't like dogs. She liked children, but not very much. She kept herself to herself.

She attended church on Sunday, but didn't take part in any church activities. Sometimes, but rarely, she went to the pictures. She didn't hold with goings on—and had given up working for an artist and his wife when she had discovered they weren't properly married. She didn't read books, but she enjoyed the Sunday paper and she liked old magazines when her ladies gave them to her. Although she didn't go much to the pictures, she was interested in hearing about film stars and their doings. She wasn't interested in politics, but voted Conservative like her husband had always done. Never spent much on clothes, but got quite a lot given her from her ladies, and was of a saving disposition.

Mrs. McGinty was, in fact, very much the Mrs. McGinty that Poirot had imagined she would be. And Bessie Burch, her niece, was the Bessie Burch of Superintendent Spence's notes.

Before Poirot took his leave, Joe Burch came home for the lunch hour. A small, shrewd man, less easy to be sure about than his wife. There was a faint nervousness in his manner. He showed less signs of suspicion and hostility than his wife. Indeed he seemed anxious to appear co-operative. And that, Poirot reflected, was very faintly out of character. For why should Joe Burch be anxious to placate an importunate foreign stranger? The reason could only be that that stranger had brought with him a letter from Superintendent Spence of the County Police.

So Joe Burch was anxious to stand in well with the police? Was it that he couldn't afford, as his wife could, to be critical of the police?

A man, perhaps, with an uneasy conscience. Why was that conscience uneasy? There could be so many reasons—none of them connected with Mrs. McGinty's death. Or was it that, somehow or other, the cinema alibi had been cleverly faked, and that it was Joe Burch who had knocked on the door of the cottage, had been admitted by auntie and who had struck down the unsuspecting old woman. He would pull out the drawers and ransack the rooms to give the appearance of robbery, he might hide the money outside, cunningly, to incriminate James Bentley, the money that was in the Savings Bank was what he was after. Two hundred pounds coming to his wife which, for some reason unknown, he badly needed. The weapon, Poirot remembered, had never been found. Why had that not also been left on the scene of the crime? Any moron knew enough to wear gloves or rub off fingerprints. Why then had the weapon, which much have been a heavy one with a sharp edge, been removed? Was it because it could easily be identified as belonging to the Burch ménage? Was that same weapon, washed and polished, here in the house now? Something in the nature of a meat chopper the police surgeon had said —but not, it seemed, actually a meat chopper. Something, perhaps a little unusual ... a little out of the ordinary, easily identified. The police had hunted for it, but not found it. They had searched woods, dragged ponds. There was nothing missing from Mrs. McGinty's kitchen, and nobody could say that James Bentley had had anything of that kind in his possession. They had never traced any purchase of a meat chopper or any such implement to him. A small, but negative point in his favour. Ignored in the weight of other evidence. But still a point ...

Poirot cast a swift glance round the rather overcrowded little sitting-room in which he was sitting.

Was the weapon here, somewhere, in this house? Was that why Joe Burch was uneasy and conciliatory?

Poirot did not know. He did not really think so. But he was not absolutely sure. ...

CHAPTER VI

I

IN THE offices of Messrs. Breather & Scuttle, Poirot was shown, after some demur, into the room of Mr. Scuttle himself.

Mr. Scuttle was a brisk, bustling man, with a hearty manner.

"Good morning. Good morning." He rubbed his hands. "Now, what can we do for you?"

His professional eye shot over Poirot, trying to place him, making, as it were, a series of marginal notes.

Foreign. Good quality clothes. Probably rich. Restaurant proprietor? Hotel manager? Films?

"I hope not to trespass on your time unduly. I wanted to talk to you about your former employee, James Bentley."

Mr. Scuttle's expressive eyebrows shot up an inch and dropped.

"James Bentley. James Bentley?" He shot out a question. "Press?"

"No."

"And you wouldn't be police?"

"No. At least—not of this country."

"Not of this country." Mr. Scuttle filed this away rapidly as though for future reference. "What's it all about?"

Poirot, never hindered by a pedantic regard for truth, launched out into speech.

"I am opening a further inquiry into James Bentley's case—at the request of certain relatives of his."

"Didn't know he had any. Anyway, he's been found guilty, you know, and condemned to death."

"But not yet executed."

"While there's life, there's hope, eh?" Mr. Scuttle shook his head. "Should doubt it, though. Evidence was strong. Who are these relations of his?"

"I can tell you only this, they are both rich and powerful. Immensely rich."

"You surprise me." Mr. Scuttle was unable to help thawing slightly. The words "immensely rich" had an attractive and hypnotic quality. "Yes, you really do surprise me."

"Bentley's mother, the late Mrs. Bentley," explained Poirot, "cut herself and her son off completely from her family."

"One of these family feuds, eh? Well, well. And young Bentley without a farthing to bless himself with. Pity these relations didn't come to the rescue before."

"They have only just become aware of the facts," explained Poirot. "They have engaged me to come with all speed to this country and do everything possible."

Mr. Scuttle leaned back, relaxing his businesslike manner.

"Don't know what you can do. I suppose there's insanity? A bit late in the day—but if you got hold of the big medicos. Of course I'm not up in these things myself."

Poirot leaned forward.

"Monsieur, James Bentley worked here. You can tell me about him."

"Precious little to tell—precious little. He was one of our junior clerks. Nothing against him. Seemed a perfectly decent young fellow, quite conscientious and all that. But no idea of salesmanship. He just couldn't put a project over. That's no good in this job. If a client comes to us with a house he wants to sell, we're there to sell it for him. And if a client wants a house, we find him one. If it's a house in a lonely place with no amenities, we stress its antiquity, call it a period piece—and don't mention the plumbing! And if a house looks straight into the gasworks, we talk about amenities and facilities and don't mention the view. Hustle your client into it—that's what you're here to do. All sorts of little tricks there are. 'We advise you, madam, to make an immediate offer. There's a Member of Parliament who's very keen on it—very keen indeed. Going out to see it again this afternoon.' They fall for that every time—a Member of Parliament is always a good touch. Can't think why! No member ever lives away from his constituency. It's just the good solid sound of it." He laughed suddenly displayed gleaming dentures. "Psychology—that's what it is—just psychology."

Poirot leaped at the word.

"Psychology. How right you are. I see that you are a judge of men."

"Not too bad. Not too bad," said Mr. Scuttle modestly.

"So I ask you again what was your impression of James Bentley? Between ourselves—strictly between ourselves—you think he killed the old woman?"

Scuttle stared.

"Of course."

"And you think, too, that it was a likely thing for him to do—psychologically speaking?"

"Well—if you put it like that—no, not really. Shouldn't have thought he had the guts. Tell you what, if you ask me, he was barmy. Put it that way, and it works. Always a bit soft in the head, and what with being out of a job and worrying and all that, he just went right over the edge."

"You had no special reason for discharging him?"

Scuttle shook his head.

"Bad time of year. Staff hadn't enough to do. We sacked the one who was least competent. That was Bentley. Always would be, I expect. Gave him a good reference and all that. He didn't get another job, though. No pep. Made a bad impression on people."

It always came back to that, Poirot thought, as he left the office. James Bentley made a bad impression on people. He took comfort in considering various murderers he had known whom most people had found full of charm.

I I

"Excuse me, do you mind if I sit down here and talk to you for a moment?"

Poirot, ensconced at a small table in the Blue Cat, looked up from the menu he was studying with a start. It was rather dark in the Blue Cat, which specialised in an old-world effect of oak and leaded panes, but the young woman who had just sat down opposite to him stood out brightly from her dark background.

She had determinedly golden hair, and was wearing an electric blue jumper suit. Moreover, Hercule Poirot was conscious of having noticed her somewhere only a short time previously.

She went on:

"I couldn't help, you see, hearing something of what you were saying to Mr. Scuttle."

Poirot nodded. He had realised that the partitions in the offices of Breather & Scuttle were made for convenience rather than privacy. That had not worried him, since it was chiefly publicity that he desired.

"You were typing," he said, "to the right of the back window."

She nodded. Her teeth shone white in an acquiescing smile. A very healthy young woman, with a full buxom figure that Poirot approved. About thirty-three or four, he judged, and by nature dark-haired, but not one to be dictated to by nature.

"About Mr. Bentley," she said.

"What about Mr. Bentley?"

"Is he going to appeal? Does it mean that there's new evidence? Oh, I'm so glad. I couldn't—I just couldn't believe he did it."

Poirot's eyebrows rose.

"So you never thought he did it," he said slowly.

"Well, not at first. I thought it must be a mistake. But then the evidence——" she stopped.

"Yes, the evidence," said Poirot.

"There just didn't seem anyone else who could have done it. I thought perhaps he'd gone a little mad."

"Did he ever seem to you a little—what shall I say—queer?"

"Oh no. Not queer in that way. He was just shy and awkward as anyone might be. The truth was, he didn't make the best of himself. He hadn't confidence in himself."

Poirot looked at her. She certainly had confidence in herself. Possibly she had enough confidence for two.

"You liked him?" he asked.

She flushed.

"Yes, I did. Amy—that's the other girl in the office—used to laugh at him and call him a drip, but I liked him very much. He was gentle and polite—and he knew a lot really. Things out of books, I mean."

41

"Ah yes, things out of books."

"He missed his mother. She'd been ill for years, you know. At least, not really ill, but not strong, and he'd done everything for her."

Poirot nodded. He knew those mothers.

"And of course she'd looked after him, too. I mean taken care of his health and his chest in winter and what he ate and all that."

Again he nodded. He asked:

"You and he were friends?"

"I don't know—not exactly. We used to talk sometimes. But after he left here, he—I—I didn't see much of him. I wrote to him once in a friendly way, but he didn't answer."

Poirot said gently:

"But you like him?"

She said rather defiantly:

"Yes, I do . . ."

"That is excellent," said Poirot.

His mind switched back to the day of his interview with the condemned prisoner. . . . He saw James Bentley clearly. The mouse-coloured hair, the thin awkward body, the hands with their big knuckles and wrists, the Adam's apple in the lean neck. He saw the furtive, embarrassed—almost sly glance. Not straightforward, not a man whose word could be trusted—a secretive, sly deceitful fellow with an ungracious, muttering way of talking. . . . That was the impression James Bentley would give to most superficial observers. It was the impression he had given in the dock. The sort of fellow who would tell lies, and steal money, and hit an old woman over the head. . . .

But on Superintendent Spence, who knew men, he had not made that impression. Nor on Hercule Poirot. . . . And now here was this girl.

"What is your name, mademoiselle?" he asked.

"Maude Williams. Is there anything I could do—to help?"

"I think there is. There are people who believe, Miss Williams, that James Bentley is innocent. They are working to prove that fact. I am the person charged with that investigation, and I may tell you that I have already made considerable progress—yes, considerable progress."

He uttered that lie without a blush. To his mind it was

42

a very necessary lie. Someone, somewhere, had got to be made uneasy. Maude Williams would talk, and talk was like a stone in a pond, it made a ripple that went on spreading outwards.

He said: "You tell me that you and James Bentley talked together. He told you about his mother and his home life. Did he ever mention anyone with whom he, or perhaps his mother, was on bad terms?"

Maude Williams reflected.

"No—not what you'd call bad terms. His mother didn't like young women much, I gather."

"Mothers of devoted sons never like young women. No, I mean more than that. Some family feud, some enmity. Someone with a grudge?"

She shook her head.

"He never mentioned anything of that kind."

"Did he ever speak of his landlady, Mrs. McGinty?"

She shivered slightly.

"Not by name. He said once that she gave him kippers much too often—and once he said his landlady was upset because she had lost her cat."

"Did he ever—you must be honest, please—mention that he knew where she kept her money?"

Some of the colour went out of the girl's face, but she threw up her chin defiantly.

"Actually, he did. We were talking about people being distrustful of banks—and he said his old landlady kept her spare money under a floorboard. He said: 'I could help myself any day to it when she's out.' Not quite as a joke, he didn't joke, more as though he were really worried by her carelessness."

"Ah," said Poirot. "That is good. From my point of view, I mean. When James Bentley thinks of stealing, it presents itself to him as an action that is done behind someone's back. He might have said, you see, 'Some day someone will knock her on the head for it.'"

"But either way, he wouldn't be meaning it."

"Oh no. But talk, however light, however idle, gives away, inevitably, the sort of person you are. The wise criminal would never open his mouth, but criminals are seldom wise

43

and usually vain and they talk a good deal—and so most criminals are caught."

Maude Williams said abruptly:

"But *someone* must have killed the old woman."

"Naturally."

"Who did? Do you know? Have you any idea?"

"Yes," said Hercule Poirot mendaciously. "I think I have a very good idea. But we are only at the beginning of the road."

The girl glanced at her watch.

"I must get back. We're only supposed to take half an hour. One-horse place, Kilchester—I've always had jobs in London before. You'll let me know if there's anything I can do—really *do*, I mean?"

Poirot took out one of his cards. On it he wrote Long Meadows and the telephone number.

"That is where I am staying."

His name, he noted with chagrin, made no particular impression on her. The younger generation, he could not but feel, were singularly lacking in knowledge of notable celebrities.

III

Hercule Poirot caught a bus back to Broadhinny feeling slightly more cheerful. At any rate there was one person who shared his belief in James Bentley's innocence. Bentley was not so friendless as he had made himself out to be.

His mind went back again to Bentley in prison. What a dispiriting interview it had been. There had been no hope aroused, hardly a stirring of interest.

"Thank you," Bentley had said dully, "but I don't suppose there is anything anyone can do."

No, he was sure he had not got any enemies.

"When people barely notice you're alive, you're not likely to have any enemies."

"Your mother? Did she have an enemy?"

"Certainly not. Everyone liked and respected her."

There was a faint indignation in his tone.

"What about your friends?"

44

And James Bentley had said, or rather muttered, "I haven't any friends . . ."

But that had not been quite true. For Maude Williams was a friend.

"What a wonderful dispensation it is of Nature's," thought Hercule Poirot, "that every man, however superficially unattractive, should be some woman's choice."

For all Miss Williams's sexy appearance, he had a shrewd suspicion that she was really the maternal type.

She had the qualities that James Bentley lacked, the energy, the drive, the refusal to be beaten, the determination to succeed.

He sighed.

What monstrous lies he had told that day! Never mind— they were necessary.

"For somewhere," said Poirot to himself, indulging in an absolute riot of mixed metaphors, "there is in the hay a needle, and among the sleeping dogs there is one on whom I shall put my foot, and by shooting the arrows into the air, one will come down and hit a glass-house!"

CHAPTER VII

I

THE COTTAGE where Mrs. McGinty had lived was only a few steps from the bus stop. Two children were playing on the doorstep. One was eating a rather wormy-looking apple and the other was shouting and beating on the door with a tin tray. They appeared quite happy. Poirot added to the noise by beating hard on the door himself.

A woman looked round the corner of the house. She had on a coloured overall and her hair was untidy.

"Stop it, Ernie," she said.

"Sha'n't," said Ernie and continued.

Poirot deserted the doorstep and made for the corner of the house.

"Can't do anything with children, can you?" the woman said.

45

Poirot thought you could, but forbore to say so.

He was beckoned round to the back door.

"I keep the front bolted up, sir. Come in, won't you?"

Poirot passed through a very dirty scullery into an almost more dirty kitchen.

"She wasn't killed here," said the woman. "In the parlour."

Poirot blinked slightly.

"That's what you're down about, isn't it? You're the foreign gentleman from up at Summerhayes?"

"So you know all about me, Mrs.——" said Poirot. He beamed. "Yes, indeed, Mrs.——"

"Kiddle. My husband's a plasterer. Moved in four months ago, we did. Been living with Bert's mother before . . . Some folks said: 'You'd never go into a house where there's been a murder, surely?'—but what I said was, a house is a house, and better than a back sitting-room and sleeping on two chairs. Awful, this 'ousing shortage, isn't it? And anyway *we've* never been troubled 'ere. Always say they *walk* if they've been murdered, but she doesn't! Like to see where it happened?"

Feeling like a tourist being taken on a conducted tour, Poirot assented.

Mrs. Kiddle led him into a small room over-burdened with a heavy Jacobean suite. Unlike the rest of the house, it showed no signs of ever having been occupied.

"Down on the floor she was and the back of her head split open. Didn't half give Mrs. Elliot a turn. She's the one what found her—she and Larkin who comes from the Co-op with the bread. But the money was took from upstairs. Come along up and I'll show you where."

Mrs. Kiddle led the way up the staircase and into a bedroom which contained a large chest of drawers, a big brass bed, some chairs, and a fine assembly of baby clothes, wet and dry.

"Right here it was," said Mrs. Kiddle proudly.

Poirot looked round him. Hard to visualise that this rampant stronghold of haphazard fecundity was once the well-scrubbed domain of an elderly woman who was house-proud. Here Mrs. McGinty had lived and slept.

"I suppose this isn't her furniture?"

46

"Oh no. Her niece over in Cullavon took away all that."

There was nothing left here of Mrs. McGinty. The Kiddles had come and conquered. Life was stronger than death.

From downstairs the loud fierce wail of a baby arose.

"That's the baby woken up," said Mrs. Kiddle unnecessarily.

She plunged down the stairs and Poirot followed her.

There was nothing here for him.

He went next door.

II

"Yes, sir, it was me found her."

Mrs. Elliot was dramatic. A neat house, this, neat and prim. The only drama in it was Mrs. Elliot's, a tall gaunt dark-haired woman, recounting her one moment of glorious living.

"Larkin, the baker, he came and knocked at the door. 'It's Mrs. McGinty,' he said, 'we can't make her hear. Seems she might have been taken bad.' And indeed I thought she might. She wasn't a young woman, not by any means. And palpitations she'd had, to my certain knowledge. I thought she might have had a stroke. So I hurried over, seeing as there were only the two men, and naturally they wouldn't like to go into the bedroom."

Poirot accepted this piece of propriety with an assenting murmur.

"Hurried up the stairs, I did. *He* was on the landing, pale as death he was. Not that I ever thought at the time—well, of course, then I didn't know what had happened. I knocked on the door loud and there wasn't any answer, so I turned the handle and I went in. The whole place messed about— and the board in the floor up. 'It's robbery,' I said. 'But where's the poor soul herself?' And then we thought to look in the sitting-room. *And there she was* . . . Down on the floor with her poor head stove in. Murder! I saw at once what it was—murder! Couldn't be anything else! Robbery and murder! Here in Broadhinny. I screamed and I screamed! Quite a job they had with me. Came over all faint, I did. They had to go and get me brandy from the Three Ducks.

47

And even then I was all of a shiver for hours and hours. 'Don't you take on so, mother,' that's what the sergeant said to me when he came. 'Don't you take on so. You go home and make yourself a nice cup of tea.' And so I did. And when Elliot came home, 'Why, whatever's happened?' he says, staring at me. Still all of a tremble I was. Always was sensitive from a child."

Poirot dexterously interrupted this thrilling personal narrative.

"Yes, yes, one can see that. And when was the last time you had seen poor Mrs. McGinty?"

"Must have been the day before, when she'd stepped out into the back garden to pick a bit of mint. I was just feeding the chickens."

"Did she say anything to you?"

"Just good afternoon and were they laying any better."

"And that's the last time you saw her? You didn't see her on the day she died?"

"No. I saw *Him* though." Mrs. Elliot lowered her voice. "About eleven o'clock in the morning. Just walking along the road. Shuffling his feet the way he always did."

Poirot waited, but it seemed that there was nothing to add. He asked:

"Were you surprised when the police arrested him?"

"Well, I was and I wasn't. Mind you, I'd always thought he was a bit daft. And no doubt about it, these daft ones do turn nasty, sometimes. My uncle had a feeble-minded boy, and he could go very nasty sometimes—as he grew up, that was. Didn't know his strength. Yes, that Bentley was daft all right, and I shouldn't be surprised if they don't hang him when it comes to it, but sends him to the asylum instead. Why, look at the place he hid the money. No one would hide money in a place like that unless he wanted it to be found. Just silly and simple like, that's what he was."

"Unless he wanted it found," murmured Poirot. "You did not, by any chance, miss a chopper—or an axe?"

"No, sir, I did *not*. The police asked me that. Asked all of us in the cottages here. It's a mystery still what he killed her with."

48

Hercule Poirot walked towards the post office.

The murderer had wanted the money found, but he had not wanted the weapon to be found. For the money would point to James Bentley and the weapon would point to—whom?

He shook his head. He had visited the other two cottages. They had been less exuberant than Mrs. Kiddle and less dramatic than Mrs. Elliot. They had said in effect that Mrs. McGinty was a very respectable woman who kept herself to herself, that she had a niece over at Cullavon, that nobody but the said niece ever came to see her, that nobody, so far as they knew, disliked her or bore a grudge against her, that was it true that there was a petition being got up for James Bentley and would they be asked to sign it?

"I get nowhere—nowhere," said Poirot to himself. "There is nothing—no little gleam. I can well understand the despair of Superintendent Spence. But it should be different for *me*. Superintendent Spence, he is a very good and painstaking police officer, but me, I am Hercule Poirot. For *me*, there should be illumination!"

One of his patent leather shoes slopped into a puddle and he winced.

He was the great, the unique Hercule Poirot, but he was also a very old man and his shoes were tight.

He entered the post office.

The right-hand side was given to the business of Her Majesty's mails. The left-hand side displayed a rich assortment of varied merchandise, comprising sweets, groceries, toys, hardware, stationery, birthday cards, knitting wool and children's underclothes.

Poirot proceeded to a leisurely purchase of stamps.

The woman who bustled forward to attend to him was middle-aged with sharp, bright eyes.

"Here," said Poirot to himself, "is undoubtedly the brains of the village of Broadhinny."

Her name, not inappropriately, was Mrs. Sweetiman.

"And twelve pennies," said Mrs. Sweetiman, deftly extracting them from a large book. "That's four and tenpence altogether. Will there be anything more, sir?"

She fixed a bright eager glance on him. Through the door at the back a girl's head showed listening avidly. She had untidy hair and a cold in the head.

"I am by way of being a stranger in these parts," said Poirot solemnly.

"That's right, sir," agreed Mrs. Sweetiman. "Come down from London, haven't you?"

"I expect you know my business here as well as I do," said Poirot with a slight smile.

"Oh no, sir, I've really no idea," said Mrs. Sweetiman in a wholly perfunctory manner.

"Mrs. McGinty," said Poirot.

Mrs. Sweetiman shook her head.

"That was a sad business—a shocking business."

"I expect you knew her well?"

"Oh I did. As well as anyone in Broadhinny, I should say. She'd always pass the time of day with me when she came in here for any little thing. Yes, it was a terrible tragedy. And not settled yet, or so I've heard people say."

"There is a doubt—in some quarters—as to James Bentley's guilt."

"Well," said Mrs. Sweetiman, "it wouldn't be the first time the police got hold of the wrong man—though I wouldn't say they had in this case. Not that I should have thought it of him really. A shy awkward sort of fellow, but not dangerous or so you'd think. But there, you never know, do you?"

Poirot hazarded a request for notepaper.

"Of course, sir. Just come across the other side, will you?"

Mrs. Sweetiman bustled round to take her place behind the left-hand counter.

"What's difficult to imagine is, who it could have been if it wasn't Mr. Bentley," she remarked as she stretched up to a top shelf for notepaper and envelopes. "We do get some nasty tramps along here sometimes, and it's possible one of these might have found a window unfastened and got in that way. But he wouldn't go leaving the money behind him, would he? Not after doing murder to get it—and pound notes anyway, nothing with numbers or marked. Here you are, sir, that's a nice blue Bond, and envelopes to match."

Poirot made his purchase.

"Mrs. McGinty never spoke of being nervous of anyone, or afraid, did she?" he asked.

"Not to me, she didn't. She wasn't a nervous woman. She'd stay late sometimes at Mr. Carpenter's—that's Holmeleigh at the top of the hill. They often have people to dinner and stopping with them, and Mrs. McGinty would go there in the evening sometimes to help wash up, and she'd come down the hill in the dark, and that's more than I'd like to do. Very dark it is—coming down that hill."

"Do you know her niece at all—Mrs. Burch?"

" I know her just to speak to. She and her husband come over sometimes."

"They inherited a little money when Mrs. McGinty died."

The piercing dark eyes looked at him severely.

"Well, that's natural enough, isn't it, sir? You can't take it with you, and it's only right your own flesh and blood should get it."

"Oh yes, oh yes, I am entirely in agreement. Was Mrs. McGinty fond of her niece?"

"Very fond of her, I think, sir. In a quiet way."

"And her niece's husband?"

An evasive look appeared in Mrs. Sweetiman's face.

"As far as I know."

"When did you see Mrs. McGinty last?"

Mrs. Sweetiman considered, casting her mind back.

"Now let me see, when was it, Edna?" Edna, in the doorway, sniffed unhelpfully. "Was it the day she died? No, it was the day before—or the day before that again? Yes, it was a Monday. That's right. She was killed on the Wednesday. Yes, it was Monday. She came in to buy a bottle of ink."

"She wanted a bottle of ink?"

"Expect she wanted to write a letter," said Mrs. Sweetiman brightly.

"That seems probable. And she was quite her usual self, then? She did not seem different in any way?"

"N-no, I don't think so."

The sniffing Edna shuffled through the door into the shop and suddenly joined in the conversation.

51

"She was different," she asserted. "Pleased about something—well—not pleased quite—excited."

"Perhaps you're right," said Mrs. Sweetiman. "Not that I noticed it at the time. But now that you say so—sort of spry, she was."

"Do you remember anything she said on that day?"

"I wouldn't ordinarily. But what with her being murdered and the police and everything, it makes things stand out. She didn't say anything about James Bentley, that I'm quite sure. Talked about the Carpenters a bit and Mrs. Upward—places where she worked, you know."

"Oh yes, I was going to ask you whom exactly she worked for here."

"Mondays and Thursdays she went to Mrs. Summerhayes at Long Meadow. That's where you are staying, isn't it?"

"Yes." Poirot sighed. "I suppose there is not anywhere else to stay?"

"Not right in Broadhinny, there isn't. I suppose you aren't very comfortable at Long Meadows? Mrs. Summerhayes is a nice lady but she doesn't know the first thing about a house. These ladies don't who come back from foreign parts. Terrible mess there always was there to clean up, or so Mrs. McGinty used to say. Yes, Monday afternoons and Thursday mornings Mrs. Summerhayes, then Tuesday mornings Dr. Rendell's and afternoons Mrs. Upward at Laburnums. Wednesday was Mrs. Wetherby at Hunter's Close and Friday Mrs. Selkirk—Mrs. Carpenter she is now. Mrs. Upward's an elderly lady who lives with her son. They've got a maid, but she's getting on, and Mrs. McGinty used to go once a week to give things a good turn out. Mr. and Mrs. Wetherby never seem to keep any help long—she's rather an invalid. Mr. and Mrs. Carpenter have a beautiful home and do a lot of entertaining. They're all very nice people."

It was with this final pronouncement on the population of Broadhinny that Poirot went out into the street again.

He walked slowly up the hill towards Long Meadows. He hoped devoutly that the contents of the bulged tin and the bloodstained beans had been duly eaten for lunch and had not been saved for a supper treat for him. But possibly there were other doubtful tins. Life at Long Meadows certainly had its dangers.

It had been, on the whole, a disappointing day.

What had he learned?

That James Bentley had a friend. That neither he nor Mrs. McGinty had had any enemies. That Mrs. McGinty had looked excited two days before her death and had bought a bottle of ink——

Poirot stopped dead . . . Was that a fact, a tiny fact at last?

He had asked idly, what Mrs. McGinty should want with a bottle of ink, and Mrs. Sweetiman had replied, quite seriously, that she supposed she wanted to write a letter.

There was significance there—a significance that had nearly escaped him because to him, as to most people, writing a letter was a common everyday occurrence.

But it was not so to Mrs. McGinty. Writing a letter was to Mrs. McGinty such an uncommon occurrence that she had to go out and buy a bottle of ink if she wanted to do so.

Mrs. McGinty, then, hardly ever wrote letters. Mrs. Sweetiman, who was the postmistress, was thoroughly cognisant of that fact. But Mrs. McGinty had written a letter two days before her death. To whom had she written and why?

It might be quite unimportant. She might have written to her niece—to an absent friend. Absurd to lay such stress on a simple thing like a bottle of ink.

But it was all he had got and he was going to follow it up.

A bottle of ink . . .

CHAPTER VIII

I

"A LETTER?" Bessie Burch shook her head. "No, I didn't get any letter from auntie. What should she write to me about?"

Poirot suggested: "There might have been something she wanted to tell you."

"Auntie wasn't much of a one for writing. She was getting on for seventy, you know, and when she was young they didn't get much schooling."

"But she could read and write?"

"Oh, of course. Not much of a one for reading, though she liked her *News of the World* and her *Sunday Comet*. But writing came a bit difficult always. If she'd anything to let me know about, like putting us off from coming to see her, or saying she couldn't come to us, she'd usually ring up Mr. Benson, the chemist next door, and he'd send the message in. Very obliging that way, he is. You see, we're in the area, so it only cost twopence. There's a call-box at the post office in Broadhinny."

Poirot nodded. He appreciated the fact that twopence was better than twopence ha'penny. He already had a picture of Mrs. McGinty as the spare and saving kind. She had been, he thought, very fond of money.

He persisted gently.

"But your aunt did write to you sometimes, I suppose?"

"Well, there were cards at 'Xmas."

"And perhaps she had friends in other parts of England to whom she wrote?"

"I don't know about that. There was her sister-in-law, but she died two years ago and there was a Mrs. Birdlip— but she's dead too."

"So, if she wrote to someone, it would be most likely in answer to a letter she had received?"

Again Bessie Burch looked doubtful.

"I don't know who'd be writing to her, I'm sure. . . . Of course," her face brightened, "there's always the Government."

Poirot agreed that in these days, communications from what Bessie loosely referred to as "the Government" were the rule, rather than the exception.

"And a lot of fandangle it usually is," said Mrs. Burch. "Forms to fill in, and a lot of impertinent questions as shouldn't be asked of any decent body."

"So Mrs. McGinty might have got some Government communication that she had to answer?"

"If she had, she'd have brought it along to Joe, so as he could help her with it. Those sort of things fussed her and she always brought them to Joe."

"Can you remember if there were any letters among her personal possessions?"

"I couldn't rightly say. I don't remember anything. But then the police took over at first. It wasn't for quite a while they let me pack her things and take them away."

"What happened to those things?"

"That chest over there is hers—good solid mahogany, and there's a wardrobe upstairs, and some good kitchen stuff. The rest we sold because we'd no room for them."

"I meant her own personal things." He added: "Such things as brushes and combs, photographs, toilet things, clothes . . ."

"Oh, them. Well, tell you the truth, I packed them in a suitcase and it's still upstairs. Didn't rightly know what to do with them. Thought I'd take the clothes to the jumble sale at 'Xmas, but I forgot. Didn't seem nice to take them to one of those nasty second-hand clothes people."

"I wonder—might I see the contents of that suitcase?"

"Welcome, I'm sure. Though I don't think you'll find anything to help you. The police went through it all, you know."

"Oh I know. But, all the same——"

Mrs. Burch led him briskly into a minute back bedroom, used, Poirot judged, mainly for home dressmaking. She pulled out a suitcase from under the bed and said:

"Well, here you are, and you'll excuse me stopping, but I've got the stew to see to."

Poirot gratefully excused her, and heard her thumping downstairs again. He drew the suitcase towards him and opened it.

With a feeling of pity, he lifted out the contents, so eloquent in their revelation of a woman who was dead. A rather worn long black coat. Two woollen jumpers. A coat and skirt. Stockings. No underwear (presumably Bessie Burch had taken those for her own wear). Two pairs of shoes wrapped up in newspaper. A brush and comb, worn but clean. An old dented silver-backed mirror. A photograph in a leather frame of a wedding pair dressed in the style of thirty years ago—a picture of Mrs. McGinty and her husband presumably. Two picture post-cards of Margate. A china dog. A recipe torn out of a paper for making vegetable marrow jam. Another piece dealing with "Flying Saucers" on a sensational note. A third clipping dealt with Mother

55

Shipton's prophecies. There was also a Bible and a Prayer Book.

There were no handbags, or gloves. Presumably Bessie Burch had taken these, or given them away. The clothes here, Poirot judged, would have been too small for the buxom Bessie. Mrs. McGinty had been a thin, spare woman.

He unwrapped one of the pairs of shoes. They were of quite good quality and not much worn. Decidedly on the small side for Bessie Burch.

He was just about to wrap them up neatly again when his eye was caught by the heading on the piece of newspaper.

It was the *Sunday Comet* and the date was November 19th. Mrs. McGinty had been killed on November 22nd.

This then was the paper she had bought on the Sunday preceding her death. It had been lying in her room and Bessie Burch had used it in due course to wrap up her aunt's things.

Sunday, November 19th. And on *Monday* Mrs. McGinty had gone into the post office to buy a bottle of ink. . . .

Could that be because of something she had seen in Sunday's newspaper?

He unwrapped the other pair of shoes. They were wrapped in the *News of the World* of the same date.

He smoothed out both papers and took them over to a chair where he sat down to read them. And at once he made a discovery. On one page of the *Sunday Comet,* something had been cut out. It was a rectangular piece out of the middle page. The space was too big for any of the clippings he had found.

He looked through both newspapers, but could find nothing else of interest. He wrapped them round the shoes again and packed the suitcase tidily.

Then he went downstairs.

Mrs. Burch was busy in the kitchen.

"Don't suppose you found anything?" she said.

"Alas, no." He added in a casual voice : "You do not remember if there was a cutting from a newspaper in your aunt's purse or in her handbag, was there?"

"Can't remember any. Perhaps the police took it."

But the police had not taken it. That Poirot knew from his study of Spence's notes. The contents of the dead woman's handbag had been listed, no newspaper cutting was among them.

"*Eh bien,*" said Hercule Poirot to himself. "The next step is easy. It will be either the wash-out—or else, at last, I advance."

Sitting very still, with the dusty files of newspaper in front of him, Poirot told himself that his recognition of the significance of the bottle of ink had not played him false.

The *Sunday Comet* was given to romantic dramatisations of past events.

The paper at which Poirot was looking was the *Sunday Comet* of Sunday, November 19th.

At the top of the middle page were these words in big type:

WOMEN VICTIMS OF BYGONE TRAGEDIES
WHERE ARE THESE WOMEN NOW?

Below the caption were four very blurred reproductions of photographs clearly taken many years ago.

The subjects of them did not look tragic. They looked actually, rather ridiculous, since nearly all of them were dressed in the style of a bygone day, and nothing is more ridiculous than the fashions of yesterday—though in another thirty years or so their charm may have reappeared, or at any rate be once more apparent.

Under each photo was a name.

Eva Kane, the "other woman" in the famous Craig case.

Janice Courtland, the "tragic wife" whose husband was a fiend in human form.

Little Lily Gamboll, tragic child product of our overcrowded age.

Vera Blake, unsuspecting wife of a killer.

And then came the question in bold type again:

WHERE ARE THESE WOMEN NOW?

Poirot blinked and set himself to read meticulously the

somewhat romantic prose which gave the life stories of these dim and blurry heroines.

The name of Eva Kane he remembered, for the Craig Case had been a very celebrated one. Alfred Craig had been Town Clerk of Parminster, a conscientious, rather nondescript little man, correct and pleasant in his behaviour. He had had the misfortune to marry a tiresome and temperamental wife. Mrs. Craig ran him into debt, bullied him, nagged him, and suffered from nervous maladies that unkind friends said were entirely imaginary. Eva Kane was the young nursery governess in the house. She was nineteen, pretty, helpless and rather simple. She fell desperately in love with Craig and he with her. Then one day the neighbours heard that Mrs. Craig had been "ordered abroad" for her health. That had been Craig's story. He took her up to London, the first stage of the journey, by car late one evening, and "saw her off" to the South of France. Then he returned to Parminster and at intervals mentioned how his wife's health was no better by her accounts of it in letters. Eva Kane remained behind to housekeep for him, and tongues soon started wagging. Finally, Craig received news of his wife's death abroad. He went away and returned a week later, with an account of the funeral.

In some ways, Craig was a simple man. He made the mistake of mentioning where his wife had died, a moderately well-known resort on the French Riviera. It only remained for someone who had a relative or friend living there to write to them, discover that there had been no death or funeral of anyone of that name and, after a period of rank gossip, to communicate with the police.

Subsequent events can be briefly summarised.

Mrs. Craig had not left for the Riviera. She had been cut in neat pieces and buried in the Craig cellar. And the autopsy of the remains showed poisoning by a vegetable alkaloid.

Craig was arrested and sent for trial. Eva Kane was originally charged as an accessory, but the charge was dropped, since it appeared clear that she had throughout been completely ignorant of what had occurred. Craig in the end made a full confession and was sentenced and executed.

Eva Kane, who was expecting a child, left Parminster and,

in the words of the *Sunday Comet*: *Kindly relatives in the New World offered her a home. Changing her name, the pitiful young girl, seduced in her trusting youth by a cold-blooded murderer, left these shores for ever, to begin a new life and to keep for ever locked in her heart and concealed from her daughter the name of her father.*

"My daughter shall grow up happy and innocent. Her life shall not be tainted by the cruel past. That I have sworn. My tragic memories shall remain mine alone."

Poor frail trusting Eva Kane. To learn, so young, the villainy and infamy of man. Where is she now? Is there, in some Mid-western town, an elderly woman, quiet and respected by her neighbours, who has, perhaps, sad eyes . . . And does a young woman, happy and cheerful, with children, perhaps, of her own, come and see "Momma," telling her of all the little rubs and grievances of daily life—with no idea of what past sufferings her mother has endured?

"Oh la la!" said Hercule Poirot. And passed on to the next Tragic Victim.

Janice Courtland, the "tragic wife," had certainly been unfortunate in her husband. His peculiar practices, referred to in such a guarded way as to rouse instant curiosity, had been suffered by her for eight years. Eight years of martyrdom, the *Sunday Comet* said firmly. Then Janice made a friend. An idealistic and unworldly young man who, horrified by a scene between husband and wife that he had witnessed by accident, had thereupon assaulted the husband with such vigour that the latter had crashed in his skull on a sharply-edged marble fire surround. The jury had found that provocation had been intense, that the young idealist had had no intention of killing, and a sentence of five years for manslaughter was given.

The suffering Janice, horrified by all the publicity the case had brought her, had gone abroad "to forget."

Has she forgotten? asked the *Sunday Comet. We hope so. Somewhere, perhaps, is a happy wife and mother to whom those years of nightmare suffering silently endured, seem now only like a dream. . . .*

"Well, well," said Hercule Poirot and passed on to Lily Gamboll, the tragic child product of our overcrowded age.

Lily Gamboll had, it seemed, been removed from her overcrowded home. An aunt had assumed responsibility for Lily's life. Lily had wanted to go to the pictures, aunt had said "No." Lily Gamboll had picked up the meat chopper which was lying conveniently on the table and had aimed a *blow at her aunt with it. The aunt, though autocratic, was* small and frail. The blow killed her. Lily was a well-developed and muscular child for her twelve years. An approved school had opened its doors and Lily had disappeared from the everyday scene.

By now she is a woman, free again to take her place in our civilisation. Her conduct, during her years of confinement and probation, is said to have been exemplary. Does not this show that it is not the child, but the system, that we must blame? Brought up in ignorance, in slum conditions, little Lily was the victim of her environment.

Now, having atoned for her tragic lapse, she lives somewhere, happily, we hope, a good citizen and a good wife and mother. Poor little Lily Gamboll.

Poirot shook his head. A child of twelve who took a swing at her aunt with a meat chopper and hit her hard enough to kill her was not, in his opinion, a nice child. His sympathies were, in this case, with the aunt.

He passed on to Vera Blake.

Vera Blake was clearly one of those women with whom everything goes wrong. She had first taken up with a boyfriend who turned out to be a gangster wanted by the police for killing a bank watchman. She had then married a respectable tradesman who turned out to be a receiver of stolen goods. Her two children had likewise, in due course, attracted the attention of the police. They went with mamma to department stores and did a pretty line in shoplifting. Finally, however, a "good man" had appeared on the scene. He had offered tragic Vera a home in the Dominions. She and her children should leave this effete country.

From henceforward a New Life awaited them. At last after long years of repeated blows from Fate, Vera's troubles are over.

"I wonder," said Poirot sceptically. "Very possibly she will find she has married a confidence trickster who works the liners!"

He leaned back and studied the four photographs. Eva

Kane with tousled curly hair over her ears and an enormous hat, held a bunch of roses up to her ear like a telephone receiver. Janice Courtland had a cloche hat pushed down over her ears and a waist round her hips. Lily Gamboll was a plain child with an adenoidal appearance of open mouth, hard breathing and thick spectacles. Vera Blake was so tragically black and white that no features showed.

For some reason Mrs. McGinty had torn out this feature, photographs and all. Why? Just to keep because the stories interested her? He thought not. Mrs. McGinty had kept very few things during her sixty-odd years of life. Poirot knew that from the police reports of her belongings.

She had torn this out on the Sunday and on the Monday she had bought a bottle of ink and the inference was that she, who never wrote letters, was about to write a letter. If it had been a business letter, she would probably have asked Joe Burch to help her. So it had not been business. It had been—what?

Poirot's eyes looked over the four photographs once again. *Where*, the *Sunday Comet* asked, *are these women now?*

One of them, Poirot thought, might have been in Broadhinny last November.

III

It was not until the following day that Poirot found himself *tête à tête* with Miss Pamela Horsefall.

Miss Horsefall couldn't give him long, because she had to rush away to Sheffield, she explained.

Miss Horsefall was tall, manly-looking, a hard drinker and smoker, and it would seem, looking at her, highly improbable that it was her pen which had dropped such treacly sentiment in the *Sunday Comet*. Nevertheless it was so.

"Cough it up, cough it up," said Miss Horsefall impatiently to Poirot. "I've got to be going."

"It is about your article in the *Sunday Comet*. Last November. The series about Tragic Women."

"Oh, *that* series. Pretty lousy, weren't they?"

Poirot did not express an opinion on that point. He said:

"I refer in particular to the article on Women Associated

61

with Crime that appeared on November 19th. It concerned
Eva Kane, Vera Blake, Janice Courtland and Lily Gamboll."

Miss Horsefall grinned.

"*Where are these tragic women now?* I remember."

"I suppose you sometimes get letters after the appearance
of these articles?"

"You bet I do! Some people seem to have nothing better
to do than write letters. Somebody 'once saw the murderer
Craig walking down the street.' Somebody would like to tell
me 'the story of her life, far more tragic than anything I
could ever imagine.'"

"Did you get a letter after the appearance of that article
from a Mrs. McGinty of Broadhinny?"

"My dear man, how on earth should I know? I get buckets
of letters. How should I remember one particular name?"

"I thought you might remember," said Poirot, "because
a few days later Mrs. McGinty was murdered."

"Now you're talking." Miss Horsefall forgot to be im-
patient to get to Sheffield, and sat down astride a chair.
"McGinty—McGinty . . . I do remember the name. Conked
on the head by her lodger. Not a very exciting crime from
the point of view of the public. No sex appeal about it. You
say the woman wrote to me?"

"She wrote to the *Sunday Comet*, I think."

"Same thing. It would come on to me. And with the
murder—and her name being in the news—surely I should
remember——" She stopped. "Look here—it wasn't from
Broadhinny. It was from Broadway."

"So you do remember?"

"Well, I'm not sure . . . But the name . . . Comic name,
isn't it? McGinty! Yes—atrocious writing and quite illi-
terate. If I'd only realised . . . But I'm sure it came from
Broadway."

Poirot said: "You say yourself the writing was bad.
Broadway and Broadhinny—they could look alike."

"Yes—might be so. After all, one wouldn't be likely to
know these queer rural names. McGinty—yes. I do remember definitely. Perhaps the murder fixed the name for me."

"Can you remember what she said in her letter?"

"Something about a photograph. She knew where there

was a photograph like in the paper—and would we pay her anything for it and how much?"

"And you answered?"

"My dear man, we don't want anything of that kind. We sent back the standard reply. Polite thanks but nothing doing. But as we sent it to Broadway—I don't suppose she'd ever get it."

"She knew where there was a photograph. . . ."

Into Poirot's mind there came back a remembrance. Maureen Summerhayes' careless voice saying, "Of course she snooped round a bit."

Mrs. McGinty had snooped. She was honest, but she liked to know about things. And people kept things—foolish, meaningless things from the past. Kept them for sentimental reasons, or just overlooked them and didn't remember they were there.

Mrs. McGinty had seen an old photograph and later she had recognised it reproduced in the *Sunday Comet*. And she had wondered if there was any money in it. . . .

He rose briskly. "Thank you, Miss Horsefall. You will pardon me, but those notes on the cases that you wrote, were they accurate? I notice, for instance, that the year of the Craig trial is given wrongly—it was actually a year later than you say. And in the Courtland case, the husband's name was Herbert, I seem to remember, not Hubert. Lily Gamboll's aunt lived in Buckinghamshire, not Berkshire."

Miss Horsefall waved a cigarette.

"My dear man. No point in accuracy. Whole thing was a romantic farrago from beginning to end. I just mugged up the facts a bit and then let fly with a lot of hou ha."

"What I am trying to say is that even the characters of your heroines are not, perhaps, quite as represented."

Pamela let out a neighing sound like a horse.

"Course they weren't. What do *you* think? I've no doubt that Eva Kane was a thorough little bitch, and not an injured innocent at all. And as for the Courtland woman, why did she suffer in silence for eight years with a sadistic pervert? Because he was rolling in money, and the romantic boy-friend hadn't any."

"And the tragic child, Lily Gamboll?"

63

"I wouldn't care to have her gambolling about *me* with a meat chopper."

Poirot ticked off on his fingers.

"They left the country—they went to the New World—abroad—'to the Dominions'—'to start a New Life.' And there is nothing to show, is there, that they did not, subsequently, come back to this country?"

"Not a thing," agreed Miss Horsefall. "And now—I really must fly——"

Later that night Poirot rang up Spence.

"I've been wondering about you, Poirot. Have you got anything? Anything at all?"

"I have made my inquiries," said Poirot grimly.

"Yes?"

"And the result of them is this: *The people who live in Broadhinny are all very nice people.*"

"What do you mean by that, M. Poirot?"

"Oh, my friend, consider. 'Very nice people.' That has been, before now, a motive for murder."

CHAPTER IX

I

"ALL VERY nice people," murmured Poirot as he turned in at the gate of Crossways, near the station.

A brass plate in the doorpost announced that Dr. Rendell, M.D., lived there.

Dr. Rendell was a large cheerful man of forty. He greeted his guest with definite *empressement*.

"Our quiet little village is honoured," he said, "by the presence of the great Hercule Poirot."

"Ah," said Poirot. He was gratified. "*You* have, then, heard of me?"

"Of course we have heard of you. Who hasn't?"

The answer to that would have been damaging to Poirot's self-esteem. He merely said politely: "I am fortunate to find you at home."

64

It was not particularly fortunate. It was, on the contrary, astute timing. But Dr. Rendell replied heartily:

"Yes. Just caught me. Surgery in a quarter of an hour. Now what can I do for you? I'm devoured with curiosity to know what you're doing down here. A rest cure? Or have we crime in our midst?"

"In the past tense—not the present."

"Past? I don't remember——"

"Mrs. McGinty."

"Of course. Of course. I was forgetting. But don't say you're concerned with that—at this late date?"

"If I may mention this to you in confidence, I am employed by the defence. Fresh evidence on which to lodge an appeal."

Dr. Rendell said sharply: "But what fresh evidence can there be?"

"That, alas, I am not at liberty to state——"

"Oh, quite—please forgive me."

"But I have come across certain things which are, I may say—very curious—very—how shall I put it?—suggestive? I came to you, Dr. Rendell, because I understand that Mrs. McGinty occasionally was employed here."

"Oh yes, yes—she was—— What about a drink? Sherry? Whisky? You prefer sherry? So do I." He brought two glasses and, sitting down by Poirot, he went on: "She used to come once a week to do extra cleaning. I've got a very good housekeeper—excellent—but the brasses—and scrubbing the kitchen floor—well, my Mrs. Scott can't get down on her knees very well. Mrs. McGinty was an excellent worker."

"Do you think that she was a truthful person?"

"Truthful? Well, that's an odd question. I don't think I could say—no opportunity of knowing. As far as I know she was quite truthful."

"If then she made a statement to anyone, you think that statement would probably be true?"

Dr. Rendell looked faintly disturbed.

"Oh, I wouldn't like to go as far as that. I really know so little about her. I could ask Mrs. Scott. She'd know better."

"No, no. It would be better not to do that."

"You're arousing my curiosity," said Dr. Rendell genially.

"What was it she was going around saying? Something a bit libellous, was it? Slanderous, I suppose I mean."

Poirot merely shook his head. He said : "You understand, all this is extremely hush hush at present. I am only at the very commencement of my investigation."

Dr. Rendell said rather dryly:

"You'll have to hurry a bit, won't you?"

"You are right. The time at my disposal is short."

"I must say you surprise me . . . We've all been quite sure down here that Bentley did it. There didn't seem any doubt possible."

"It seemed an ordinary sordid crime—not very interesting. That is what you would say?"

"Yes—yes, that sums it up very fairly."

"You knew James Bentley?"

"He came to see me professionally once or twice. He was nervous about his own health. Coddled by his mother, I fancy. One sees that so often. We've another case in point here."

"Ah, indeed?"

"Yes. Mrs. Upward. Laura Upward. Dotes upon that son of hers. She keeps him well tied to her apron-strings. He's a clever fellow—not quite as clever as he thinks himself, between you and me—but still definitely talented. By way of being a budding playwright is our Robin."

"They have been here long?"

"Three or four years. Nobody has been in Broadhinny very long. The original village was only a handful of cottages, grouped round Long Meadows. You're staying there, I understand?"

"I am," said Poirot without undue elation.

Dr. Rendell appeared amused.

"Guest House indeed," he said. "What that young woman knows about running a Guest House is just nothing at all. She's lived in India all her married life with servants running round all over the place. I bet you're uncomfortable. Nobody ever stays long. As for poor old Summerhayes, he'll never make anything of this market gardening stunt he's trying to run. Nice fellow—but not an idea of the commercial life—and the commercial life it's got to be nowadays if you want to keep your head above water. Don't run away

66

with the idea that I heal the sick. I'm just a glorified form-filler and signer of certificates. I like the Summerhayes, though. She's a charming creature, and though Summerhayes has a devilish temper and is inclined to be moody, he's one of the old gang. Out of the top drawer all right. You should have known old Colonel Summerhayes, a regular tartar, proud as the devil."

"That was Major Summerhayes' father?"

"Yes. There wasn't much money when the old boy died and of course there have been death duties to cripple these people, but they're determined to stick to the old place. One doesn't know whether to admire them, or whether to say 'Silly fools.'"

He looked at his watch.

"I must not keep you," said Poirot.

"I've got a few minutes still. Besides, I'd like you to meet my wife. I can't think where she is. She was immensely interested to hear you were down here. We're both very crime-minded. Read a lot about it."

"Criminology, fiction, or the Sunday papers?" asked Poirot smiling.

"All three."

"Do you descend as low as the *Sunday Comet*?"

Rendell laughed.

"What would Sunday be without it?"

"They had some interesting articles about five months ago. One in particular about women who had been involved in murder cases and the tragedy of their lives."

"Yes, I remember the one you mean. All a lot of hooey, though."

"Ah, you think that?"

"Well of course the Craig case I only know from reading about it, but one of the others—Courtland case, I can tell you *that* woman was no tragic innocent. Regular vicious bit of goods. I know because an uncle of mine attended the husband. He was certainly no beauty, but his wife wasn't much better. She got hold of that young greenhorn and egged him on to murder. Then he goes to prison for manslaughter and she goes off, a rich widow, and marries someone else."

"The *Sunday Comet* did not mention that. Do you remember whom she married?"

Rendell shook his head.

"Don't think I ever heard the name, but someone told me that she'd done pretty well for herself."

"One wondered in reading the article where those four women are now," mused Poirot.

"I know. One may have met one of them at a party last week. I bet they all keep their past pretty dark. You'd certainly never recognise any of 'em from those photographs. My word, they looked a plain lot."

The clock chimed and Poirot rose to his feet. "I must detain you no longer. You have been most kind."

"Not much help, I'm afraid. The mere man barely knows what his charlady looks like. But half a second, you must meet the wife. She'd never forgive me."

He preceded Poirot out into the hall, calling loudly:

"Shelagh—Shelagh——"

A faint answer came from upstairs.

"Come down here. I've got something for you."

A thin fair-haired pale woman ran lightly down the stairs.

"Here's M. Hercule Poirot, Shelagh. What do you think of that?"

"Oh," Mrs. Rendell appeared to be startled out of speaking. Her very pale blue eyes stared at Poirot apprehensively.

"Madame," said Poirot, bowing over her hand in his most foreign manner.

"We heard that you were here," said Shelagh Rendell. "But we didn't know——" She broke off. Her light eyes went quickly to her husband's face.

"It is from him she takes the Greenwich time," said Poirot to himself.

He uttered a few florid phrases and took his leave.

An impression remained with him of a genial Dr. Rendell and a tongue-tied, apprehensive Mrs. Rendell.

So much for the Rendells, where Mrs. McGinty had gone to work on Tuesday mornings.

Hunter's Close was a solidly built Victorian house approached by a long untidy drive overgrown with weeds. It had not originally been considered a big house, but was now big enough to be inconvenient domestically.

Poirot inquired of the foreign young woman who opened the door for Mrs. Wetherby.

She stared at him and then said: "I do not know. Please to come. Miss Henderson perhaps?"

She left him standing in the hall. It was in an estate agent's phrase "fully furnished"—with a good many curios from various parts of the world. Nothing looked very clean or well dusted.

Presently the foreign girl reappeared. She said: "Please to come," and showed him into a chilly little room with a large desk. On the mantelpiece was a big and rather evil-looking copper coffee pot with an enormous hooked spout like a large hooked nose.

The door opened behind Poirot and a girl came into the room.

"My mother is lying down," she said. "Can I do anything for you?"

"You are Miss Wetherby?"

"Henderson. Mr. Wetherby is my stepfather."

She was a plain girl of about thirty, large and awkward. She had watchful eyes.

"I was anxious to hear what you could tell me about a Mrs. McGinty who used to work here."

She stared at him.

"Mrs. McGinty? But she's dead."

"I know that," said Poirot gently. "Nevertheless, I would like to hear about her."

"Oh. Is it for insurance or something?"

"Not for insurance. It is a question of fresh evidence."

"Fresh evidence. You mean—her death?"

"I am engaged," said Poirot, "by the solicitors for the defence to make an inquiry on James Bentley's behalf."

Staring at him, she asked: "But didn't he do it?"

69

"The jury thought he did. But juries have been known to make a mistake."

"Then it was really somebody else who killed her?'

"It may have been."

She asked abruptly: "Who?"

"That," said Poirot softly, "is the question."

"I don't understand at all."

"No? But you can tell me something about Mrs. McGinty, can't you?"

She said rather reluctantly:

"I suppose so. . . . What do you want to know?"

"Well—to begin with—what did you think of her?"

"Why—nothing in particular. She was just like anybody else."

"Talkative or silent? Curious or reserved? Pleasant or morose? A nice woman, or—not a very nice woman?"

Miss Henderson reflected.

"She worked well—but she talked a lot. Sometimes she said rather funny things. . . . I didn't—really—like her very much."

The door opened and the foreign help said:

"Miss Deirdre, your mother say: please to bring."

"My mother wants me to take this gentleman upstairs to her?"

"Yes please, thank you."

Deirdre Henderson looked at Poirot doubtfully.

"Will you come up to my mother?"

"But certainly."

Deirdre led the way across the hall and up the stairs. She said inconsequently: "One does get so very tired of foreigners."

Since her mind was clearly running on her domestic help and not on the visitor, Poirot did not take offence. He reflected that Deirdre Henderson seemed a rather simple young woman—simple to the point of gaucheness.

The room upstairs was crowded with knick-knacks. It was the room of a woman who had travelled a good deal and who had been determined wherever she went to have a souvenir of the place. Most of the souvenirs were clearly made for the delight and exploitation of tourists. There were too many sofas and tables and chairs in the room, too little

70

air and too many draperies—and in the midst of it all was Mrs. Wetherby.

Mrs. Wetherby seemed a small woman—a pathetic small woman in a large room. That was the effect. But she was not really quite so small as she had decided to appear. The "poor little me" type can achieve its result quite well, even if really of medium height.

She was reclining very comfortably on a sofa and near her were books and some knitting and a glass of orange juice and a box of chocolates. She said brightly:

"You *must* forgive me not getting up, but the doctor does so insist on my resting every day, and everyone scolds me if I don't do what I'm told."

Poirot took her extended hand and bowed over it with the proper murmur of homage.

Behind him, uncompromising, Deirdre said: "He wants to know about Mrs. McGinty."

The delicate hand that had lain passively in his tightened and he was reminded for a moment of the talon of a bird. Not really a piece of delicate Dresden china—a scratchy predatory claw . . .

Laughing slightly, Mrs. Wetherby said:

"How ridiculous you are, Deirdre darling. Who is Mrs. McGinty?"

"Oh, Mummy—you do remember really. She worked for us. You know, the one who was murdered."

Mrs. Wetherby closed her eyes, and shivered.

"Don't, darling. It was all so horrid. I felt nervous for weeks afterwards. Poor old woman, but so *stupid* to keep money under the floor. She ought to have put it in the bank. Of course I remember all that—I'd just forgotten her *name*."

Deirdre said stolidly:

"He wants to know about her."

"Now do sit down, M. Poirot. I'm quite devoured by curiosity. Mrs. Rendell just rang up and she said we had a very famous criminologist down here, and she described you. And then, when that idiot Frieda described a visitor, I felt sure it must be you, and I sent down word for you to come up. Now tell me, what *is* all this?"

"It is as your daughter says, I want to know about Mrs. McGinty. She worked here. She came to you, I understand, on Wednesdays. And it was on a Wednesday she died. So she had been here that day, had she not?"

"I suppose so. Yes, I suppose so. I can't really tell now. It's so long ago."

"Yes. Several months. And she did not say anything that day—anything special?"

"That class of person always talks a lot," said Mrs. Wetherby with distaste. "One doesn't really listen. And anyway she couldn't tell she was going to be robbed and killed that night, could she?"

"There is cause and effect," said Poirot.

Mrs. Wetherby wrinkled her forehead.

"I don't see what you mean."

"Perhaps I do not see myself—not yet. One works through darkness towards light. . . . Do you take in the Sunday papers, Mrs. Wetherby?"

Her blue eyes opened very wide.

"Oh yes. Of course. We have the *Observer* and the *Sunday Times*. Why?"

"I wondered. Mrs. McGinty took the *Sunday Comet* and the *News of the World*."

He paused but nobody said anything. Mrs. Wetherby sighed and half closed her eyes. She said:

"It was all very upsetting. That horrible lodger of hers. I don't think really he can have been quite right in the head. Apparently he was quite an educated man, too. That makes it worse, doesn't it?"

"Does it?"

"Oh yes—I do think so. Such a brutal crime. A meat chopper. Ugh!"

"The police never found the weapon," said Poirot.

"I expect he threw it in a pond or something."

"They dragged the ponds," said Deirdre. "I saw them."

"Darling," her mother sighed, "don't be morbid. You know how I hate thinking of things like that. My head."

Fiercely the girl turned on Poirot.

"You mustn't go on about it," she said. "It's bad for her. She's frightfully sensitive. She can't even read detective stories."

"My apologies," said Poirot. He rose to his feet. "I have

72

only one excuse. A man is to be hanged in three weeks' time. If he did not do it——"

Mrs. Wetherby raised herself on her elbow. Her voice was shrill.

"But of course he did it," she cried. "Of course he did."

Poirot shook his head.

"I am not so sure."

He left the room quickly. As he went down the stairs, the girl came after him. She caught up with him in the hall.

"What do you mean?" she asked.

"What I said, mademoiselle."

"Yes, but——" She stopped.

Poirot said nothing.

Deirdre Henderson said slowly:

"You've upset my mother. She hates things like that— robberies and murders and—and violence."

"It must, then, have been a great shock to her when a woman who had actually worked here was killed."

"Oh yes—oh yes, it was."

"She was prostrated—yes?"

"She wouldn't hear anything about it. . . . We—I—we try to—to spare her things. All the beastliness."

"What about the war?"

"Luckily we never had any bombs near here."

"What was your part in the war, mademoiselle?"

"Oh, I did V.A.D. work in Kilchester. And some driving for the W.V.S. I couldn't have left home, of course. Mother needed me. As it was, she minded my being out so much. It was all very difficult. And then servants—naturally mother's never done any housework—she's not strong enough. And it was so difficult to get anyone at all. That's why Mrs. McGinty was such a blessing. That's when she began coming to us. She was a splendid worker. But of course nothing—anywhere—is like it used to be."

"And do you mind that so much, mademoiselle?"

"I? Oh no." She seemed surprised. "But it's different for mother. She—she lives in the past a lot."

"Some people do," said Poirot. His visual memory conjured up the room he had been in a short time before. There had been a bureau drawer half pulled out. A drawer full of odds and ends—a silk pin-cushion, a broken fan, a silver

73

coffee pot—some old magazines. The drawer had been too full to shut. He said softly: "And they keep things—memories of old days—the dance programme, the fan, the photographs of bygone friends, even the menu cards and the theatre programmes because, looking at these things, old memories revive."

"I suppose that's it," said Deirdre. "I can't understand it myself. I never keep anything."

"You look forwards, not back?"

Deirdre said slowly:

"I don't know that I look anywhere . . . I mean, to-day's usually enough, isn't it?"

The front door opened and a tall, spare, elderly man came into the hall. He stopped dead as he saw Poirot.

He glanced at Deirdre and his eyebrows rose in interrogation.

"This is my stepfather," said Deirdre. "I—I don't know your name?"

"I am Hercule Poirot," said Poirot with his usual embarrassed air of announcing a royal title.

Mr. Wetherby seemed unimpressed.

He said "Ah," and turned to hang up his coat.

Deirdre said:

"He came to ask about Mrs. McGinty."

Mr. Wetherby remained still for a second, then he finished his adjustment of the coat on the peg.

"That seems to me rather remarkable," he said. "The woman met her death some months ago and, although she worked here, we have no information concerning her or her family. If we had done we should already have given it to the police."

There was finality in his tone. He glanced at his watch.

"Lunch, I presume, will be ready in a quarter of an hour."

"I'm afraid it may be rather late to-day."

Mr. Wetherby's eyebrows rose again.

"Indeed? Why, may I ask?"

"Frieda has been rather busy."

"My dear Deirdre, I hate to remind you, but the task of running the household devolves on you. I should appreciate a little more punctuality."

Poirot opened the front door and let himself out. He glanced over his shoulder.

There was cold dislike in the gaze that Mr. Wetherby gave his stepdaughter. There was something very like hate in the eyes that looked back at him.

CHAPTER X

POIROT left his third call until after luncheon. Luncheon was under-stewed oxtail, watery potatoes, and what Maureen hoped optimistically might turn out to be pancakes. They were very peculiar.

Poirot walked slowly up the hill. Presently, on his right, he would come to Laburnums, two cottages knocked into one and remodelled to modern taste. Here lived Mrs. Upward and that promising young playwright, Robin Upward.

Poirot paused a moment at the gate to pass a hand over his moustaches. As he did so a car came twisting slowly down the hill and an apple core directed with force struck him on the cheek.

Startled, Poirot let out a yelp of protest. The car halted and a head came through the window.

"I'm so sorry. Did I hit you?"

Poirot paused in the act of replying. He looked at the rather noble face, the massive brow, the untidy billows of grey hair and a chord of memory stirred. The apple core, too, assisted his memory.

"But surely," he exclaimed, "it is Mrs. Oliver."

It was indeed that celebrated detective-story writer.

Exclaiming "Why, it's M. Poirot," the authoress attempted to extract herself from the car. It was a small car and Mrs. Oliver was a large woman. Poirot hastened to assist.

Murmuring in an explanatory voice, "Stiff after the long drive," Mrs. Oliver suddenly arrived out on the road, rather in the manner of a volcanic eruption.

Large quantities of apples came, too, and rolled merrily down the hill.

"Bag's burst," explained Mrs. Oliver.

She brushed a few stray pieces of half-consumed apple from the jutting shelf of her bust and then shook herself rather like a large Newfoundland dog. A last apple, concealed in the recesses of her person, joined its brothers and sisters.

"Pity the bag burst," said Mrs. Oliver. "They were Cox's. Still I suppose there will be lots of apples down here in the country. Or aren't there? Perhaps they all get sent away. Things are so odd nowadays, I find. Well, how are you, M. Poirot? You don't live here, do you? No, I'm sure you don't. Then I suppose it's murder? Not my hostess, I hope?"

"Who is your hostess?"

"In there," said Mrs. Oliver, nodding her head. "That's to say if that's a house called Laburnums, half-way down the hill on the left after you pass the church. Yes, that must be it. What's she like?"

"You do not know her?"

"No, I've come down professionally, so to speak. A book of mine is being dramatised—by Robin Upward. We're supposed to sort of get together over it."

"My felicitations, madame."

"It's not like that at all," said Mrs. Oliver. "So far it's pure *agony*. Why I ever let myself in for it I don't know. My books bring me in quite enough money—that is to say the bloodsuckers take most of it, and if I made more, they'd take more, so I don't overstrain myself. But you've no idea of the agony of having your characters taken and made to say things that they never would have said, and do things that they never would have done. And if you protest, all they say is that it's 'good theatre.' That's all Robin Upward thinks of. Everyone says he's very clever. If he's so clever I don't see why he doesn't write a play of his own and leave my poor unfortunate Finn alone. He's not even a Finn any longer. He's become a member of the Norwegian Resistance movement." She ran her hands through her hair. "What have I done with my hat?"

Poirot looked into the car.

"I think madame, that you must have been sitting on it."

"It does look like it," agreed Mrs. Oliver, surveying the wreckage. "Oh well," she continued cheerfully, "I never liked it much. But I thought I might have to go to church on

76

Sunday, and although the Archbishop has said one needn't, I still think that the more old-fashioned clergy expect one to wear a hat. But tell me about your murder or whatever it is. Do you remember *our* murder?"

"Very well indeed."

"Rather fun, wasn't it? Not the actual murder—I didn't like that at all. But afterwards. Who is it this time?"

"Not so picturesque a person as Mr. Shaitana. An elderly charwoman who was robbed and murdered five months ago. You may have read about it. Mrs. McGinty. A young man was convicted and sentenced to death——"

"And he didn't do it, but you know who did, and you're going to prove it," said Mrs. Oliver rapidly. "Splendid."

"You go too fast," said Poirot with a sigh. "I do not yet know who did it—and from there it will be a long way to prove it."

"Men are so slow," said Mrs. Oliver disparagingly. "I'll soon tell you who did it. Someone down here, I suppose? Give me a day or two to look round, and I'll spot the murderer. A woman's intuition—that's what you need. I was quite right over the Shaitana case, wasn't I?"

Poirot gallantly forbore to remind Mrs. Oliver of her rapid changes of suspicion on that occasion.

"You men," said Mrs. Oliver indulgently. "Now if a woman were the head of Scotland Yard——"

She left this well worn theme hanging in the air as a voice hailed them from the door of the cottage.

"Hallo," said the voice, an agreeable light tenor. "Is that Mrs. Oliver?"

"Here I am," called Mrs. Oliver. To Poirot she murmured: "Don't worry. I'll be very discreet."

"No, no, madame. I do not want you to be discreet. *On the contrary.*"

Robin Upward came down the path and through the gate. He was bareheaded and wore very old grey flannel trousers and a disreputable sports coat. But for a tendency to embonpoint, he would have been good looking.

"Ariadne, my precious!" he exclaimed and embraced her warmly.

He stood away, his hands on her shoulders.

"My dear, I've had the most marvellous idea for the second act."

"Have you?" said Mrs. Oliver without enthusiasm. "This is M. Hercule Poirot."

"Splendid," said Robin. "Have you got any luggage?"

"Yes, it's in the back."

Robin hauled out a couple of suitcases.

"Such a bore," he said. "We've no proper servants. Only old Janet. And we have to spare her all the time. That's such a nuisance don't you think? How heavy your cases are. Have you got bombs in them?"

He staggered up the path, calling out over his shoulder: "Come in and have a drink."

"He means you," said Mrs. Oliver, removing her handbag, a book, and a pair of old shoes from the front seat. "Did you actually say just now that you wanted me to be *indiscreet*?"

"The more indiscreet the better."

"I shouldn't tackle it that way myself," said Mrs. Oliver, "but it's *your* murder. I'll help all I can."

Robin reappeared at the front door.

"Come in, come in," he called. "We'll see about the car later. Madre is dying to meet you."

Mrs. Oliver swept up the path and Hercule Poirot followed her.

The interior of Laburnums was charming. Poirot guessed that a very large sum of money had been spent on it, but the result was an expensive and charming simplicity. Each small piece of cottage oak was a genuine piece.

In a wheeled chair by the fireplace of the living-room Laura Upward smiled a welcome. She was a vigorous-looking woman of sixty-odd, with iron-grey hair and a determined chin.

"I'm delighted to meet you, Mrs. Oliver," she said. "I expect you hate people talking to you about your books, but they've been an enormous solace to me for years—and especially since I've been such a cripple."

"That's very nice of you," said Mrs. Oliver, looking uncomfortable and twisting her hands in a schoolgirlish way. "Oh, this is M. Poirot, an old friend of mine. We met by chance just outside here. Actually I hit him with an apple core. Like William Tell—only the other way about."

78

"How d'you do, M. Poirot. Robin."

"Yes, Madre?"

"Get some drinks. Where are the cigarettes?"

"On that table."

Mrs. Upward asked: "Are you a writer, too, M. Poirot?"

"Oh, no," said Mrs. Oliver. "He's a detective. You know. The Sherlock Holmes kind—deerstalkers and violins and all that. And he's come here to solve a murder."

There was a faint tinkle of broken glass. Mrs. Upward said sharply: "Robin, do be careful." To Poirot she said: "That's very interesting, M. Poirot."

"So Maureen Summerhayes was right," exclaimed Robin. "She told me some long rigmarole about having a detective on the premises. She seemed to think it was frightfully funny. But it's really quite serious, isn't it?"

"Of course it's serious," said Mrs. Oliver. "You've got a criminal in your midst."

"Yes, but look here, who's been murdered? Or is it someone that's been dug up and it's all frightfully hush hush?"

"It is not hush hush," said Poirot. "The murder, you know about it already."

"Mrs. Mc—something—a charwoman—last autumn," said Mrs. Oliver.

"Oh!" Robin Upward sounded disappointed. "But that's all over."

"It's not over at all," said Mrs. Oliver. "They arrested the wrong man, and he'll be hanged if M. Poirot doesn't find the real murderer in time. It's all frightfully exciting."

Robin apportioned the drinks.

"White Lady for you, Madre."

"Thank you, my dear boy."

Poirot frowned slightly. Robin handed drinks to Mrs. Oliver and to him.

"Well," said Robin, "here's to crime."

He drank.

"She used to work here," he said.

"Mrs. McGinty?" asked Mrs. Oliver.

"Yes. Didn't she, Madre?"

"When you say work here, she came one day a week."

"And odd afternoons sometimes."

"What was she like?" asked Mrs. Oliver.

79

"Terribly respectable," said Robin. "And maddeningly tidy. She had a ghastly way of tidying up everything and putting things into drawers so that you simply couldn't guess where they were."

Mrs. Upward said with a certain grim humour:

"If somebody didn't tidy things away at least one day a week, you soon wouldn't be able to move in this small house."

"I know, Madre, I know. But unless things are left where I put them, I simply can't work at all. My notes get all disarranged."

"It's annoying to be as helpless as I am," said Mrs. Upward. "We have a faithful old maid, but it's all she can manage just to do a little simple cooking."

"What is it?" asked Mrs. Oliver. "Arthritis?"

"Some form of it. I shall have to have a permanent nurse-companion soon, I'm afraid. Such a bore. I like being independent."

"Now, darling," said Robin. "Don't work yourself up."

He patted her arm.

She smiled at him with sudden tenderness.

"Robin's as good as a daughter to me," she said. "He does everything—and thinks of everything. No one could be more considerate."

They smiled at each other.

Hercule Poirot rose.

"Alas," he said. "I must go. I have another call to make and then a train to catch. Madame, I thank you for your hospitality. Mr. Upward, I wish all success to the play."

"And all success to you with your murder," said Mrs. Oliver.

"Is this really serious, M. Poirot?" asked Robin Upward. "Or is it a terrific hoax?"

"Of course it isn't a hoax," said Mrs. Oliver. "It's deadly serious. He won't tell me who the murderer is, but he knows, don't you?"

"No, no, madame," Poirot's protest was just sufficiently unconvincing. "I told you that as yet, no, I do not know."

"That's what you said, but I think you do know really. . . . But you're so frightfully secretive, aren't you?"

Mrs. Upward said sharply:

"Is this really true? It's not a joke?"

"It is not a joke, madame," said Poirot.

He bowed and departed.

As he went down the path he heard Robin Upward's clear tenor voice:

"But Ariadne, darling," he said, "it's all very well, but with that moustache and everything, how *can* one take him seriously? Do you really mean he's *good*?"

Poirot smiled to himself. Good indeed!

About to cross the narrow lane, he jumped back just in time.

The Summerhayes' station wagon, lurching and bumping, came racing past him. Summerhayes was driving.

"Sorry," he called. "Got to catch train." And faintly from the distance: "Covent Garden . . ."

Poirot also intended to take a train—the local train to Kilchester, where he had arranged a conference with Superintendent Spence.

He had time, before catching it, for just one last call.

He went to the top of the hill and through gates and up a well-kept drive to a modern house of frosted concrete with a square roof and a good deal of window. This was the home of Mr. and Mrs. Carpenter. Guy Carpenter was a partner in the big Carpenter Engineering Works—a very rich man who had recently taken to politics. He and his wife had only been married a short time.

The Carpenters' front door was not opened by foreign help, or an aged faithful. An imperturbable manservant opened the door and was loath to admit Hercule Poirot. In his view Hercule Poirot was the kind of caller who is left outside. He clearly suspected that Hercule Poirot had come to sell something.

"Mr. and Mrs. Carpenter are not at home."

"Perhaps, then, I might wait?"

"I couldn't say when they will be in."

He closed the door.

Poirot did not go down the drive. Instead he walked round the corner of the house and almost collided with a tall young woman in a mink coat.

"Hallo," she said. "What the hell do you want?"

Poirot raised his hat with gallantry.

"I was hoping," he said, "that I could see Mr. or Mrs. Carpenter. Have I the pleasure of seeing Mrs. Carpenter?"

"I'm Mrs. Carpenter."

She spoke ungraciously, but there was a faint suggestion of appeasement behind her manner.

"My name is Hercule Poirot."

Nothing registered. Not only was the great, the unique name unknown to her, but he thought that she did not even identify him as Maureen Summerhayes' latest guest. Here, then, the local grape-vine did not operate. A small but significant fact, perhaps.

"Yes?"

"I demand to see either Mr. or Mrs. Carpenter, but you, madame, will be the best for my purpose. For what I have to ask is of domestic matters."

"We've got a Hoover," said Mrs. Carpenter suspiciously.

Poirot laughed.

"No, no, you misunderstand. It is only a few questions that I ask about a domestic matter."

"Oh, you mean one of these domestic questionnaires. I do think it's absolutely idiotic——" She broke off. "Perhaps you'd better come inside."

Poirot smiled faintly. She had just stopped herself from uttering a derogatory comment. With her husband's political activities, caution in criticising Government activities was indicated.

She led the way through the hall and into a good-sized room giving on to a carefully tended garden. It was a very new-looking room, a large brocaded suite of sofa and two wing-chairs, three or four reproductions of Chippendale chairs, a bureau, a writing desk. No expense had been spared, the best firms had been employed, and there was absolutely no sign of individual taste. The bride, Poirot thought, had been what? Indifferent? Careful?

He looked at her appraisingly as she turned. An expensive and good-looking young woman. Platinum blonde hair, carefully applied make-up, but something more—wide cornflower blue eyes—eyes with a wide frozen stare in them—beautiful drowned eyes.

She said—graciously now, but concealing boredom:

"Do sit down."

He sat. He said:

"You are most amiable, madame. These questions now that I wish to ask you. They relate to a Mrs. McGinty who died—was killed that is to say—last November."

"Mrs. McGinty? I don't know what you mean."

She was glaring at him. Her eyes hard and suspicious.

"You remember Mrs. McGinty?"

"No, I don't. I don't know anything about her."

"You remember her murder? Or is murder so common here that you do not even notice it?"

"Oh, the *murder*? Yes, of course. I'd forgotten what the old woman's name was."

"Although she worked for you in this house?"

"She didn't. I wasn't living here then. Mr. Carpenter and I were only married three months ago."

"But she did work for you. On Friday mornings, I think it was. You were then Mrs. Selkirk and you lived in Rose Cottage."

She said sulkily:

"If you know the answers to everything I don't see why you need to ask questions. Anyway, what's it all about?"

"I am making an investigation into the circumstances of the murder."

"Why? What on earth for? Anyway, why come to me?"

"You might know something—that would help me."

"I don't know anything at all. Why should I? She was only a stupid old charwoman. She kept her money under the floor and somebody robbed and murdered her for it. It was quite disgusting—beastly, the whole thing. Like things you read in the Sunday papers."

Poirot took that up quickly.

"Like the Sunday papers, yes. Like the *Sunday Comet*. You read, perhaps, the *Sunday Comet*?"

She jumped up, and made her way, blunderingly, towards the opened french windows. So uncertainly did she go that she actually collided with the window frame. Poirot was reminded of a beautiful big moth, fluttering blindly against a lamp shade.

She called: "Guy—Guy!"

A man's voice a little way away answered:

"Eve?"

83

"Come here quickly."

A tall man of about thirty-five came into sight. He quickened his pace and came across the terrace to the window. Eve Carpenter said vehemently:

"There's a man here—a foreigner. He's asking me all sorts of questions about that horrid murder last year. Some old charwoman—you remember? I *hate* things like that. You know I do."

Guy Carpenter frowned and came into the drawing-room through the window. He had a long face like a horse, he was pale and looked rather supercilious. His manner was pompous.

Hercule Poirot found him unattractive.

"May I ask what all this is about?" he asked. "Have you been annoying my wife?"

Hercule Poirot spread out his hands.

"The last thing I should wish is to annoy so charming a lady. I hoped only that, the deceased woman having worked for her, she might be able to aid me in the investigations I am making."

"But—what are these investigations?"

"Yes, ask him that," urged his wife.

"A fresh inquiry is being made into the circumstances of Mrs. McGinty's death."

"Nonsense—the case is over."

"No, no, there you are in error. It is not over."

"A fresh inquiry, you say?" Guy Carpenter frowned. He said suspiciously: "By the police? Nonsense—you're nothing to do with the police."

"That is correct. I am working independently of the police."

"It's the Press," Eve Carpenter broke in. "Some horrid Sunday newspaper. He said so."

A gleam of caution came into Guy Carpenter's eye. In his position he was not anxious to antagonise the Press. He said, more amicably:

"My wife is very sensitive. Murders and things like that upset her. I'm sure it can't be necessary for you to bother her. She hardly knew this woman."

Eve said vehemently:

84

"She was only a stupid old charwoman. I told him so."
She added:

"And she was a frightful liar, too."

"Ah, that is interesting." Poirot turned a beaming face from one to the other of them. "So she told lies. That may give us a very valuable lead."

"I don't see how," said Eve sulkily.

"The establishment of motive," said Poirot. "That is the line I am following up."

"She was robbed of her savings," said Carpenter sharply. "That was the motive of the crime."

"Ah," said Poirot softly. "But was it?"

He rose like an actor who had just spoken a telling line.

"I regret if I have caused madame any pain," he said politely. "These affairs are always rather unpleasant."

"The whole business was distressing," said Carpenter quickly. "Naturally my wife didn't like being reminded of it. I'm sorry we can't help you with any information."

"Oh, but you have."

"I beg your pardon?"

Poirot said softly:

"*Mrs. McGinty told lies.* A valuable fact. What lies, exactly, did she tell, madame?"

He waited politely for Eve Carpenter to speak. She said at last:

"Oh, nothing particular. I mean—I can't remember."

Conscious perhaps, that both men were looking at her expectantly, she said:

"Stupid things—about people. Things that couldn't be true."

Still there was a silence, then Poirot said:

"I see—she had a dangerous tongue."

Eve Carpenter made a quick movement.

"Oh no—I didn't mean as much as that. She was just a gossip, that was all."

"Just a gossip," said Poirot softly.

He made a gesture of farewell.

Guy Carpenter accompanied him out into the hall.

"This paper of yours—this Sunday paper—which is it?"

"The paper I mentioned to madame," replied Poirot carefully, "was the *Sunday Comet.*"

He paused. Guy Carpenter repeated thoughtfully:

"The *Sunday Comet*. I don't very often see that, I'm afraid."

"It has interesting articles sometimes. And interesting illustrations. . . ."

Before the pause could be too long, he bowed, and said quickly:

"Au revoir, Mr. Carpenter. I am sorry if I have—disturbed you."

Outside the gate, he looked back at the house.

"I wonder," he said. "Yes, I wonder . . ."

CHAPTER XI

SUPERINTENDENT SPENCE sat opposite Hercule Poirot and sighed.

"I'm not saying you haven't got anything, M. Poirot," he said slowly. "Personally, I think you have. But it's thin. It's terribly thin!"

Poirot nodded.

"By itself it will not do. There must be more."

"My sergeant or I ought to have spotted that newspaper."

"No, no, you cannot blame yourself. The crime was so obvious. Robbery with violence. The room all pulled about, the money missing. Why should there be significance to you in a torn newspaper amongst the other confusion."

Spence repeated obstinately:

"I should have got that. And the bottle of ink——"

"I heard of that by the merest chance."

"Yet it meant something to you—why?"

"Only because of that chance phrase about writing a letter. You and I, Spence, we write so many letters—to us it is such a matter of course."

Superintendent Spence sighed. Then he laid out on the table four photographs.

"These are the photos you asked me to get—the original photos that the *Sunday Comet* used. At any rate they're a little clearer than the reproductions. But upon my word, they're not much to go upon. Old, faded—and with women

86

the hair-do makes a difference. There's nothing definite in any of them to go upon like ears or a profile. That *cloche* hat and that arty hair and the roses! Doesn't give you a chance."

"You agree with me that we can discard Vera Blake?"

"I should think so. If Vera Blake was in Broadhinny, everyone would know it—telling the sad story of her life seems to have been her speciality."

"What can you tell me about the others?"

"I've got what I could for you in the time. Eva Kane left the country after Craig was sentenced. And I can tell you the name she took. It was Hope. Symbolic, perhaps?"

Poirot murmured:

"Yes, yes—the romantic approach. *'Beautiful Evelyn Hope is dead.'* A line from one of your poets. I dare say she thought of that. Was her name Evelyn, by the way?"

"Yes, I believe it was. But Eva was what she was known as always. And by the way, M. Poirot, now that we're on the subject, the police opinion of Eva Kane doesn't quite square with this article here. Very far from it."

Poirot smiled.

"What the police think—it is not evidence. But it is usually a very sound guide. What did the police think of Eva Kane?"

"That she was by no means the innocent victim that the public thought her. I was quite a young chap at the time and remember hearing it discussed by my old Chief and Inspector Traill who was in charge of the case. Traill believed (no evidence, mind you) that the pretty little idea of putting Mrs. Craig out of the way was all Eva Kane's idea—and that she not only thought of it, but she did it. Craig came home one day and found his little friend had taken a short cut. She thought it would all pass off as natural death, I dare say. But Craig knew better. He got the wind up and disposed of the body in the cellar and elaborated the plan of having Mrs. Craig die abroad. Then, when the whole thing came out, he was frantic in his assertions that he'd done it alone, that Eva Kane had known nothing about it. Well," Superintendent Spence shrugged his shoulders, "nobody could prove anything else. The stuff was in the house. Either of them could have used it. Pretty Eva Kane was all innocence and

87

horror. Very well she did it, too: a clever little actress. Inspector Traill had his doubts—but there was nothing to go upon. I'm giving you that for what it's worth, M. Poirot. It's not evidence."

"But it suggests the possibility that one, at least, of these 'tragic women' was something more than a tragic woman— that she was a murderess and that, if the incentive was strong enough, she might murder again . . . And now the next one, Janice Courtland, what can you tell me about her?"

"I've looked up the files. A nasty bit of goods. If we hanged Edith Thompson we certainly ought to have hanged Janice Courtland. An unpleasant pair, she and her husband, nothing to choose between them, and she worked on that young man until she had him all up in arms. But all the time, mark you, there was a rich man in the background, and it was to marry him she wanted her husband out of the way."

"Did she marry him?"

Spence shook his head.

"No idea."

"She went abroad—and then?"

Spence shook his head.

"She was a free woman. She'd not been charged with anything. Whether she married, or what happened to her, we don't know."

"One might meet her at a cocktail party any day," said Poirot, thinking of Dr. Rendell's remark.

"Exactly."

Poirot shifted his gaze to the last photograph.

"And the child? Lily Gamboll?"

"Too young to be charged with murder. She was sent to an approved school. Good record there. Was taught short-hand and typing and was found a job under probation. Did well. Last heard of in Ireland. I think we could wash her out, you know, M. Poirot, same as Vera Blake. After all, she'd made good, and people don't hold it against a kid of twelve for doing something in a fit of temper. What about washing her out?"

"I might," said Poirot, "if it were not for the chopper. It is undeniable that Lily Gamboll used a chopper on her aunt,

and the unknown killer of Mrs. McGinty used something
that was said to be like a chopper."

"Perhaps you're right. Now, M. Poirot, let's have your side
of things. Nobody's tried to do you in, I'm glad to see."

"N-no," said Poirot with a momentary hesitation.

"I don't mind telling you I've had the wind up about you
once or twice since that evening in London. Now what are
the possibilities amongst the residents of Broadhinny?"

Poirot opened his little notebook.

"Eva Kane, if she is still alive, would be now approaching
sixty. Her daughter, of whose adult life our *Sunday Comet*
paints such a touching picture, would be now in the thirties.
Lily Gamboll would also be about that age. Janice Courtland would now be not far short of fifty."

Spence nodded agreement.

"So we come to the residents of Broadhinny, with especial
reference to those for whom Mrs. McGinty worked."

"That last is a fair assumption, I think."

"Yes, it is complicated by the fact that Mrs. McGinty did
occasional odd work here and there, but we will assume for
the time being that she saw whatever she did see, presumably
a photograph, at one of her regular 'houses.' "

"Agreed."

"Then as far as age goes, that gives us as possibles—first
the Wetherbys where Mrs. McGinty worked on the day of
her death. Mrs. Wetherby is the right age for Eva Kane
and she has a daughter of the right age to be Eva Kane's
daughter—a daughter said to be by a previous marriage."

"And as regards the photograph?"

"*Mon cher*, no positive identification from that is possible.
Too much time has passed, too much water, as you say, has
flowed from the waterworks. One can but say this: Mrs.
Wetherby has been, decidedly, a pretty woman. She has all
the mannerisms of one. She seems much too fragile and helpless to do murder, but then that was, I understand, the
popular belief about Eva Kane. How much actual physical
strength would have been needed to kill Mrs. McGinty is
difficult to say without knowing exactly what weapon was
used, its handle, the ease with which it could be swung, the
sharpness of its cutting edge, etcetera."

"Yes, yes. Why we never managed to find that—but go on."

"The only other remarks I have to make about the Wetherby household are that Mr. Wetherby could make himself, and I fancy does make himself, very unpleasant if he likes. The daughter is fanatically devoted to her mother. She hates her stepfather. I do not remark on these facts. I present them, only, for consideration. Daughter might kill to prevent mother's past coming to stepfather's ears. Mother might kill for same reason. Father might kill to prevent 'scandal' coming out. More murders have been committed for respectability than one would believe possible! The Wetherbys are 'nice people.' "

Spence nodded.

" If—I say if—there is anything in this *Sunday Comet* business, then the Wetherbys are clearly the best bet," he said.

"Exactly. The only other person in Broadhinny who would fit in age with Eva Kane is Mrs. Upward. There are two arguments against Mrs. Upward, as Eva Kane, having killed Mrs. McGinty. First, she suffers from arthritis, and spends most of her time in a wheeled chair——"

"In a book," said Spence enviously, "that wheeled chair business would be phoney, but in real life it's probably all according to Cocker."

"Secondly," continued Poirot, "Mrs. Upward seems of a dogmatic and forceful disposition, more inclined to bully than to coax, which does not agree with the accounts of our young Eva. On the other hand, people's characters do develop and self-assertiveness is a quality that often comes with age."

"That's true enough," conceded Spence. "Mrs. Upward—not impossible but unlikely. Now the other possibilities. Janice Courtland?"

"Can, I think, be ruled out. There is no one in Broadhinny the right age."

"Unless one of the younger women is Janice Courtland with her face lifted. Don't mind me—just my little joke."

"There are three women of thirty-odd. There is Deirdre Henderson. There is Dr. Rendell's wife, and there is Mrs. Guy Carpenter. That is to say, any one of these *could* be

Lily Gamboll or alternatively Eva Kane's daughter as far as age goes."

"And as far as possibility goes?"

Poirot sighed.

"Eva Kane's daughter may be tall or short, dark or fair—we have no guide to what she looks like. We have considered Deirdre Henderson in that role. Now for the other two. First of all I will tell you this: Mrs. Rendell is afraid of something."

"Afraid of you?"

"I think so."

"That might be significant," said Spence slowly. "You're suggesting that Mrs. Rendell might be Eva Kane's daughter or Lily Gamboll. Is she fair or dark?"

"Fair."

"Lily Gamboll was a fair-haired child."

"Mrs. Carpenter is also fair-haired. A most expensively made-up young woman. Whether she is actually good-looking or not, she has very remarkable eyes. Lovely wide-open dark-blue eyes."

"Now, Poirot——" Spence shook his head at his friend.

"Do you know what she looked like as she ran out of the room to call her husband? I was reminded of a lovely fluttering moth. She blundered into the furniture and stretched her hands out like a blind thing."

Spence looked at him indulgently.

"Romantic, that's what you are, M. Poirot," he said. "You and your lovely fluttering moths and wide-open blue eyes."

"Not at all," said Poirot. "My friend Hastings, he was romantic and sentimental, me never! Me, I am severely practical. What I am telling you is that if a girl's claims to beauty depend principally on the loveliness of her eyes, then, no matter how short-sighted she is, she will take off her spectacles and learn to feel her way round even if outlines are blurred and distances hard to judge."

And gently, with his forefinger, he tapped the photograph of the child Lily Gamboll in her thick disfiguring spectacles.

"So that's what you think? Lily Gamboll?"

"No, I speak only of what might be. At the time Mrs. McGinty died Mrs. Carpenter was not yet Mrs. Carpenter. She was a young war widow, very badly off, living in a labourer's cottage. She was engaged to be married to the rich man of the neighbourhood—a man with political ambitions and a great sense of his own importance. If Guy Carpenter had found out that he was about to marry, say, a child of low origin who had attained notoriety by hitting her aunt on the head with a chopper, or alternatively the daughter of Craig, one of the most notorious criminals of the century—prominently placed in your Chamber of Horrors —well, one asks would he have gone through with it? You say perhaps, if he loved the girl, *yes!* But he is not quite that kind of man. I would put him down as selfish, ambitious, and a man very nice in the manner of his reputation. I think that if young Mrs. Selkirk, as she was then, was anxious to achieve the match she would have been very very anxious that no hint of an unfortunate nature got to her fiancé's ears."

"I see, you think it's her, do you?"

"I tell you again, *mon cher, I do not know.* I examine only possibilities. Mrs. Carpenter was on her guard against me, watchful, alarmed."

"That looks bad."

"Yes, yes, but it is all very difficult. Once I stayed with some friends in the country and they went out to do the shooting. You know the way it goes? One walks with the dogs and the guns, and the dogs, they put up the game—it flies out of the woods, up into the air and you go bang bang. That is like us. It is not only one bird we put up, perhaps, there are other birds in the covert. Birds, perhaps, with which we have nothing to do. But the birds themselves do not know that. We must make very sure, *cher ami,* which is *our* bird. During Mrs. Carpenter's widowhood, there may have been indiscretions—no worse than that, but still inconvenient. Certainly there must be some reason why she says to me quickly that Mrs. McGinty was a liar!"

Superintendent Spence rubbed his nose.

"Let's get this clear, Poirot. What *do* you really think?"

"What I think does not matter. I must *know*. And as yet, the dogs have only just gone into the covert."

Spence murmured: "If we could get anything at all definite. One really suspicious circumstance. As it is, it's all theory and rather far-fetched theory at that. The whole thing's thin, you know, as I said. *Does* anyone really murder for the reasons we've been considering?"

"That depends," said Poirot. "It depends on a lot of family circumstances we do not know. But the passion for respectability is very strong. These are not artists or Bohemians. Very nice people live in Broadhinny. My postmistress said so. And nice people like to preserve their niceness. Years of happy married life, maybe, no suspicion that you were once a notorious figure in one of the most sensational murder trials, no suspicion that your child is the child of a famous murderer. One might say 'I would rather die than have my husband know!' Or 'I would rather die than have my daughter discover who she is!' And then you would go on to reflect that it would be better, perhaps, if Mrs. McGinty died. . . ."

Spence said quietly:

"So you think it's the Wetherbys."

"No. They fit the best, perhaps, but that is all. In actual character, Mrs. Upward is a more *likely* killer than Mrs. Wetherby. She has determination and willpower and she fairly dotes on her son. To prevent his learning of what happened before she married his father and settled down to respectable married bliss, I think she might go far."

"Would it upset him so much?"

"Personally I do not think so. Young Robin has a modern sceptical point of view, is thoroughly selfish, and in any case is less devoted, I should say, to his mother than she to him. He is not another James Bentley."

"Granting Mrs. Upward *was* Eva Kane, her son Robin wouldn't kill Mrs. McGinty to prevent that fact coming out?"

"Not for a moment, I should say. He would probably capitalise it. Use the fact for publicity for his plays! I can't see Robin Upward committing a murder for respectability, or devotion, or in fact for anything but a good solid gain to Robin Upward."

Spence sighed. He said: "It's a wide field. We may be able to get something on the past history of these people. But it will take time. The war has complicated things. Records destroyed—endless opportunities for people who want to cover their traces doing so by means of other people's identity cards, etc., especially after 'incidents' when nobody could know which corpse was which! If we could concentrate on just *one* lot, but you've got so many possibles, M. Poirot."

"We may be able to cut them down soon."

Poirot left the superintendent's office with less cheerfulness in his heart than he had shown in his manner. He was obsessed as Spence was, by the urge of time. If only he could have *time* . . .

And further back still was the one teasing doubt—was the edifice he and Spence had built up really sound? Supposing, after all, that James Bentley *was* guilty. . . .

He did not give in to that doubt, but it worried him.

Again and again he had gone over in his mind the interview he had had with James Bentley. He thought of it now whilst he waited on the platform of Kilchester for his train to come in. It had been market day and the platform was crowded. More crowds were coming in through the barriers.

Poirot leaned forward to look. Yes, the train was coming at last. Before he could right himself he felt a sudden hard purposeful shove in the small of his back. It was so violent and so unexpected that he was taken completely unawares. In another second he would have fallen on the line under the incoming train, but a man beside him on the platform caught hold of him in the nick of time, pulling him back.

"Why, whatever came over you?" he demanded. He was a big burly Army sergeant. "Taken queer? Man, you were nearly under the train."

"I thank you. I thank you a thousand times." Already the crowd was milling round them, boarding the train, others leaving it.

"All right now? I'll help you in."

Shaken, Poirot subsided on to a seat.

Useless to say "I was pushed," but he *had* been pushed. Up till that very evening he had gone about consciously on his guard, on the alert for danger. But after talking with Spence, after Spence's bantering inquiry as to whether any attempt on his life had been made, he had insensibly regarded the danger as over or unlikely to materialise.

But how wrong he had been! Amongst those he had interviewed in Broadhinny one interview had achieved a result. Somebody had been afraid. Somebody had sought to

94

put an end to his dangerous resuscitation of a closed case.

From a call-box in the station at Broadhinny, Poirot rang up Superintendent Spence.

"It is you, *mon ami*? Attend, I pray. I have news for you. Splendid news. *Somebody has tried to kill me. . . .*"

He listened with satisfaction to the flow of remarks from the other end.

"No, I am not hurt. But it was a very near thing. . . . Yes, under a train. No, I did not see who did it. But be assured, my friend, *I shall find out*. We know now—that we are on the right track."

CHAPTER XII

I

THE MAN who was testing the electric meter passed the time of day with Guy Carpenter's superior manservant, who was watching him.

"Electricity's going to operate on a new basis," he explained. "Graded flat rate according to occupancy."

The superior butler remarked sceptically:

"What you mean is it's going to cost more like everything else."

"That depends. Fair shares for all, that's what I say. Did you go in to the meeting in Kilchester last night?"

"No."

"Your boss, Mr. Carpenter, spoke very well, they say. Think he'll get in?"

"It was a near shave last time, I believe."

"Yes. A hundred and twenty-five majority, something like that. Do you drive him in to these meetings, or does he drive himself?"

"Usually drives himself. Likes driving. He's got a Rolls Bentley."

"Does himself well. Mrs. Carpenter drive too?"

"Yes. Drives a lot too fast, in my opinion."

"Women usually do. Was she at the meeting last night too? Or isn't she interested in politics?"

95

The superior butler grinned.

"Pretends she is, anyway. However, she didn't stick it out last night. Had a headache or something and left in the middle of the speeches."

"Ah!" The electrician peered into the fuse boxes. "Nearly done now," he remarked. He put a few more desultory questions as he collected his tools and prepared to depart.

He walked briskly down the drive, but round the corner from the gateway he stopped and made an entry in his pocket book.

"C. drove home alone last night. Reached home 10.30 (approx.). Could have been at Kilchester Central Station time indicated. Mrs. C. left meeting early. Got home only ten minutes before C. Said to have come home by train."

It was the second entry in the electrician's book. The first ran:

"Dr. R. called out on case last night. Direction of Kilchester. Could have been at Kilchester Central Station at time indicated. Mrs. R. alone all evening in house(?) After taking coffee in, Mrs. Scott, housekeeper, did not see her again that night. Has small car of her own."

11

At Laburnums, collaboration was in process.

Robin Upward was saying earnestly:

"You do see, don't you, what a wonderful line that is? And if we really get a feeling of sex antagonism between the chap and the girl it'll pep the whole thing up enormously!"

Sadly, Mrs. Oliver ran her hands through her windswept grey hair, causing it to look as though swept not by wind but by a tornado.

"You do see what I mean, don't you, Ariadne darling?"

"Oh, I see what you *mean*," said Mrs. Oliver gloomily.

"But the main thing is for you to feel really happy about it."

Nobody but a really determined self-deceiver could have thought that Mrs. Oliver looked happy.

Robin continued blithely:

"What I feel is, here's that wonderful young man, parachuted down——"

Mrs. Oliver interrupted:

"He's sixty."

"Oh *no*!"

"He is."

"I don't *see* him like that. Thirty-five—not a day older."

"But I've been writing books about him for thirty years, and he was at least thirty-five in the first one."

"But, darling, if he's sixty, you can't have the tension between him and the girl—what's her name? Ingrid. I mean, it would make him just a nasty old man!"

"It certainly would."

"So you see, he *must* be thirty-five," said Robin triumphantly.

"Then he can't be Sven Hjerson. Just make him a Norwegian young man who's in the Resistance Movement."

"But darling Ariadne, the whole *point* of the play is Sven Hjerson. You've got an enormous public who simply *adore* Sven Hjerson, and who'll flock to see Sven Hjerson. He's *box office*, darling!"

"But people who read my books *know* what he's like! You can't invent an entirely new young man in the Norwegian Resistance Movement and just *call* him Sven Hjerson."

"Ariadne darling, I *did* explain all that. It's not a *book*, darling, it's a *play*. And we've just got to have glamour! And if we get this tension, this antagonism between Sven Hjerson and this—what's-her-name?—Karen—you know, all against each other and yet really frightfully attracted——"

"Sven Hjerson never cared for women," said Mrs. Oliver coldly.

"But you *can't* have him a *pansy*, darling! Not for *this* sort of play. I mean it's not green bay trees or anything like *that*. It's thrills and murders and clean open-air fun."

The mention of open air had its effect.

"I think I'm going out," said Mrs. Oliver abruptly. "I need air. I need air *badly*."

"Shall I come with you?" asked Robin tenderly.

"No, I'd rather go alone."

"Just as you like, darling. Perhaps you're right. I'd better go and whip up an egg-nog for Madre. The poor sweet is feeling just a teeny weeny bit left out of things. She *does* like attention, you know. And you'll think about that scene in the cellar, won't you? The whole thing is coming really wonderfully well. It's going to be the most tremendous success. I *know* it is!"

Mrs. Oliver sighed.

"But the main thing," continued Robin, "is for you to feel happy about it!"

Casting a cold look at him, Mrs. Oliver threw a showy military cape which she had once bought in Italy about her ample shoulders and went out into Broadhinny.

She would forget her troubles, she decided, by turning her mind to the elucidation of real crime. Hercule Poirot needed help. She would take a look at the inhabitants of Broadhinny, exercise her woman's intuition which had never failed, and tell Poirot who the murderer was. Then he would only have to get the necessary evidence.

Mrs. Oliver started her quest by going down the hill to the post office and buying two pounds of apples. During the purchase, she entered into amicable conversation with Mrs. Sweetiman.

Having agreed that the weather was very warm for the time of year, Mrs. Oliver remarked that she was staying with Mrs. Upward at Laburnums.

"Yes, I know. You'll be the lady from London that writes the murder books? Three of them I've got here now in Penguins."

Mrs. Oliver cast a glance over the Penguin display. It was slightly overlaid by children's waders.

"*The Affair of the Second Goldfish,*" she mused, "that's quite a good one. *The Cat it was Who Died*—that's where I made a blowpipe a foot long and it's really *six* feet. Ridiculous that a blowpipe should be that size, but someone wrote from a museum to tell me so. Sometimes I think there are people who only read books in the hope of finding mistakes in them. What's the other one of them? Oh! *Death of a Débutante*—that's frightful tripe! It made sulphonal soluble

98

in water and it isn't, and the whole thing is wildly impossible from start to finish. At least eight people die before Sven Hjerson gets his brainwave."

"Very popular they are," said Mrs. Sweetiman, unmoved by this interesting self-criticism. "You wouldn't believe! I've never read any myself, because I don't really get time for reading."

"You had a murder of your own down here, didn't you?" said Mrs. Oliver.

"Yes, last November that was. Almost next door here, as you might say."

"I hear there's a detective down here, looking into it?"

"Ah, you mean the little foreign gentleman up at Long Meadows? He was in here only yesterday and——"

Mrs. Sweetiman broke off as another customer entered for stamps.

She bustled round to the post office side.

"Good morning, Miss Henderson. Warm for the time of year, to-day."

"Yes, it is."

Mrs. Oliver stared hard at the tall girl's back. She had a Sealyham with her on a lead.

"Means the fruit blossom will get nipped later!" said Mrs. Sweetiman, with gloomy relish. "How's Mrs. Wetherby keeping?"

"Fairly well, thank you. She hasn't been out much. There's been such an east wind lately."

"There's a very good picture on at Kilchester this week, Miss Henderson. You ought to go."

"I thought of going last night, but I couldn't really bother."

"It's Betty Grable next week—I'm out of 5s. books of stamps. Will two 2s. 6d. ones do you?"

As the girl went out, Mrs. Oliver said:

"Mrs. Wetherby's an invalid, isn't she?"

"That's as may be," Mrs. Sweetiman replied rather acidly. "There's *some* of us as hasn't the time to lay by."

"I do so agree with you," said Mrs. Oliver. "I tell Mrs. Upward that if she'd only make more of an effort to use her legs it would be better for her."

Mrs. Sweetiman looked amused.

"She gets about when she wants to—or so I've heard."

"Does she now?"

Mrs. Oliver considered the source of information.

"Janet?" she hazarded.

"Janet Groom grumbles a bit," said Mrs. Sweetiman. "And you can hardly wonder, can you? Miss Groom's not so young herself and she has the rheumatism cruel bad when the wind's in the east. But archititis, it's called, when it's the gentry has it, *and* invalid chairs and what not. Ah well, I wouldn't risk losing the use of my legs, I wouldn't. But there, nowadays even if you've got a chilblain you run to the doctor with it so as to get your money's worth out of the National Health. Too much of this health business we've got. Never did you any good thinking how bad you feel."

"I expect you're right," said Mrs. Oliver.

She picked up her apples and went out in pursuit of Deirdre Henderson. This was not difficult, since the Sealyham was old and fat and was enjoying a leisurely examination of tufts of grass and pleasant smells.

Dogs, Mrs. Oliver considered, were always a means of introduction.

"What a darling!" she exclaimed.

The big young woman with the plain face looked gratified.

"He *is* rather attractive," she said. "Aren't you, Ben?"

Ben looked up, gave a slight wiggle of his sausage-like body, resumed his nasal inspection of a tuft of thistles, approved it and proceeded to register approval in the usual manner.

"Does he fight?" asked Mrs. Oliver. "Sealyhams do very often."

"Yes, he's an awful fighter. That's why I keep him on the lead."

"I thought so."

Both women considered the Sealyham.

Then Deirdre Henderson said with a kind of rush:

"You're—you're Ariadne Oliver, aren't you?"

"Yes. I'm staying with the Upwards."

"I know. Robin told us you were coming. I must tell you how much I enjoy your books."

Mrs. Oliver, as usual, went purple with embarrassment.

"Oh," she murmured unhappily. "I'm very glad," she added gloomily.

"I haven't read as many of them as I'd like to, because we get books sent down from the Times Book Club and Mother doesn't like detective stories. She's frightfully sensitive and they keep her awake at night. But I adore them."

"You've had a real crime down here, haven't you?" said Mrs. Oliver. "Which house was it? One of these cottages?"

"That one there."

Deirdre Henderson spoke in a rather choked voice.

Mrs. Oliver directed her gaze on Mrs. McGinty's former dwelling, the front doorstep of which was at present occupied by two unpleasant little Kiddles who were happily torturing a cat. As Mrs. Oliver stepped forward to remonstrate, the cat escaped by a firm use of its claws.

The eldest Kiddle, who had been severely scratched, set up a howl.

"Serves you right," said Mrs. Oliver, adding to Deirdre Henderson: "It doesn't *look* like a house where there's been a murder, does it?"

"No, it doesn't."

Both women seemed to be in accord about that.

Mrs. Oliver continued:

"An old charwoman, wasn't it, and somebody robbed her?"

"Her lodger. She had some money—under the floor."

"I see."

Deirdre Henderson said suddenly.

"But perhaps it wasn't him after all. There's a funny little man down here—a foreigner. His name's Hercule Poirot——"

"Hercule Poirot? Oh yes, I know all about him."

"Is he really a detective?"

"My dear, he's frightfully celebrated. And terribly clever."

"Then perhaps he'll find out that he didn't do it after all."

"Who?"

"The—the lodger. James Bentley. Oh, I do hope he'll get off."

"Do you? Why?"

"Because I don't want it to be him. I never wanted it to be him."

Mrs. Oliver looked at her curiously, startled by the passion in her voice.

"Did you know him?"

"No," said Deirdre slowly, "I didn't *know* him. But once Ben got his foot caught in a trap and he helped me to get him free. And we talked a little. . . ."

"What was he like?"

"He was dreadfully lonely. His mother had just died. He was frightfully fond of his mother."

"And you are very fond of yours?" said Mrs. Oliver acutely.

"Yes. That made me understand. Understand what he felt, I mean. Mother and I—we've just got each other, you see."

"I thought Robin told me that you had a stepfather."

Deirdre said bitterly: "Oh yes, I've got a *step*father."

Mrs. Oliver said vaguely: "It's not the same thing, is it, as one's own father. Do you remember your own father?"

"No, he died before I was born. Mother married Mr. Wetherby when I was four years old. I—I've always hated him. And Mother——" She paused before saying: "Mother's had a very sad life. She's had no sympathy or understanding. My stepfather is a most unfeeling man, hard and cold."

Mrs. Oliver nodded, and then murmured:

"This James Bentley doesn't sound at all like a criminal."

"I never thought the police would arrest *him*. I'm sure it must have been some tramp. There are horrid tramps along this road sometimes. It must have been one of them."

Mrs. Oliver said consolingly:

"Perhaps Hercule Poirot will find out the truth."

"Yes, perhaps——"

She turned off abruptly into the gateway of Hunter's Close.

Mrs. Oliver looked after her for a moment or two, then drew a small notebook from her handbag. In it she wrote: "*Not* Deirdre Henderson," and underlined the *not* so firmly that the pencil broke.

Half-way up the hill she met Robin Upward coming down it with a handsome platinum-haired young woman.

Robin introduced them.

"This is the wonderful Ariadne Oliver, Eve," he said. "My dear, I don't know how she does it. Looks so benevolent, too, doesn't she? Not at all as though she wallowed in crime. This is Eve Carpenter. Her husband is going to be our next Member. The present one, Sir George Cartwright, is quite gaga, poor old man. He jumps out at young girls from behind doors."

"Robin, you mustn't invent such terrible lies. You'll discredit the Party."

"Well, why should *I* care? It isn't my Party. I'm a Liberal. That's the only Party it's possible to belong to nowadays, really small and select, and without a chance of getting in. I adore lost causes."

He added to Mrs. Oliver:

"Eve wants us to come in for drinks this evening. A sort of party for you, Ariadne. You know, meet the lion. We're all terribly terribly thrilled to have you here. Can't you put the scene of your next murder in Broadhinny?"

"Oh do, Mrs. Oliver," said Eve Carpenter.

"You can easily get Sven Hjerson down here," said Robin. "He can be like Hercule Poirot, staying at the Summerhayes' Guest House. We're just going there now because I told Eve Hercule Poirot is just as much a celebrity in his line as you are in yours, and she says she was rather rude to him yesterday, so she's going to ask him to the party too. But seriously, dear, do make your next murder happen in Broadhinny. We'd all be so thrilled."

"Oh do, Mrs. Oliver. It would be such fun," said Eve Carpenter.

"Who shall we have as murderer and who as victim?" asked Robin.

"Who's your present charwoman?" asked Mrs. Oliver.

"Oh my dear, not *that* kind of murder. So dull. No, I think Eve here would make rather a nice victim. Strangled, perhaps, with her own nylon stockings. No, that's been done."

"I think *you'd* better be murdered, Robin," said Eve. "The coming playwright, stabbed in country cottage."

"We haven't settled on a murderer yet," said Robin. "What about my Mamma? Using her wheeled chair so that there wouldn't be footprints. I think that would be lovely."

"She wouldn't want to stab you, though, Robin."

Robin considered.

"No, perhaps not. As a matter of fact I was considering her strangling *you*. She wouldn't mind doing that half as much."

"But I want *you* to be the victim. And the person who kills you can be Deirdre Henderson. The repressed plain girl whom nobody notices."

"There you are, Ariadne," said Robin. "The whole plot of your next novel presented to you. All you'll have to do is work in a few false clues, and—of course—do the actual writing. Oh, goodness, what terrible dogs Maureen does have."

They had turned in at the gate of Long Meadows, and two Irish wolfhounds had rushed forward, barking.

Maureen Summerhayes came out into the stableyard with a bucket in her hand.

"Down, Flyn. Come here, Cormic. Hallo. I'm just cleaning out Piggy's stable."

"We know that, darling," said Robin. "We can smell you from here. How's Piggy getting along?"

"We had a terrible fright about him yesterday. He was lying down and he didn't want his breakfast. Johnnie and I read up all the diseases in the Pig Book and couldn't sleep for worrying about him, but this morning he was frightfully well and gay and absolutely charged Johnnie when Johnnie came in with his food. Knocked him flat, as a matter of fact. Johnnie had to go and have a bath."

"What exciting lives you and Johnnie lead," said Robin.

Eve said: "Will you and Johnnie come in and have drinks with us this evening, Maureen?"

"Love to."

"To meet Mrs. Oliver," said Robin, "but actually you can meet her now. This is she."

"Are you really?" said Maureen. "How thrilling? You and Robin are doing a play together, aren't you?"

"It's coming along splendidly," said Robin. "By the way, Ariadne, I had a brainwave after you went out this morning. About casting."

"Oh, casting," said Mrs. Oliver in a relieved voice.

"I know just the right person to play Eric. Cecil Leech—he's playing in the Little Rep at Cullenquay. We'll run over and see the show one evening."

"We want your P.G.," said Eve to Maureen. "Is he about? I want to ask him to-night too."

"We'll bring him along," said Maureen.

"I think I'd better ask him myself. As a matter of fact I was a bit rude to him yesterday."

"Oh! Well, he's somewhere about," said Maureen vaguely. "In the garden, I think—Cormic—Flyn—those damned dogs——" She dropped the bucket with a clatter and ran in the direction of the duck pond, whence a furious quacking had arisen.

CHAPTER XIII

MRS. OLIVER, glass in hand, approached Hercule Poirot towards the end of the Carpenters' party. Up till that moment they had each of them been the centre of an admiring circle. Now that a good deal of gin had been consumed, and the party was going well, there was a tendency for old friends to get together and retail local scandal, and the two outsiders were able to talk to each other.

"Come out on the terrace," said Mrs. Oliver, in a conspirator's whisper.

At the same time she pressed into his hand a small piece of paper.

Together they stepped out through the french windows and walked along the terrace. Poirot unfolded the piece of paper.

"Dr. Rendell," he read.

He looked questioningly at Mrs. Oliver. Mrs. Oliver nodded vigorously, a large plume of grey hair falling across her face as she did so.

"He's the murderer," said Mrs. Oliver.

"You think so? Why?"

"I just know it," said Mrs. Oliver. "He's the *type*. Hearty and genial, and all that."

"Perhaps."

Poirot sounded unconvinced.

"But what would you say was his motive?"

"Unprofessional conduct," said Mrs. Oliver. "And Mrs. McGinty knew about it. But whatever the reason was, you can be quite sure it was him. I've looked at all the others, and he's the one."

In reply, Poirot remarked conversationally:

"Last night somebody tried to push me on to the railway line at Kilchester station."

"Good gracious. To kill you, do you mean?"

"I have no doubt that was the idea."

"And Dr. Rendell was out on a case, I know he was."

"I understand—yes—that Dr. Rendell *was* out on a case."

"Then that settles it," said Mrs. Oliver with satisfaction.

"Not quite," said Poirot. "Both Mr. and Mrs Carpenter were in Kilchester last night and came home separately. Mrs. Rendell may have sat at home all the evening listening to her wireless or she may not—no one can say. Miss Henderson often goes to the pictures in Kilchester."

"She didn't last night. She was at home. She told me so."

"You cannot believe all you are told," said Poirot reprovingly. "Families hang together. The foreign maid, Frieda, on the other hand, *was* at the pictures last night, so she cannot tell us who was or was not at home at Hunter's Close! You see, it is not so easy to narrow things down."

"I can probably vouch for our lot," said Mrs. Oliver. "What time did you say this happened?"

"At nine thirty-five exactly."

"Then at any rate Laburnums has got a clean bill of health. From eight o'clock to half-past ten, Robin, his mother, and I were playing poker patience."

"I thought possibly that you and he were closeted together doing the collaboration?"

"Leaving Mamma to leap on a motor bicycle concealed in the shrubbery?" Mrs. Oliver laughed. "No, Mamma was under our eye." She sighed as sadder thoughts came to her. "Collaboration," she said bitterly. "The whole thing's a nightmare! How would *you* like to see a big black moustache stuck on to Superintendent Battle and be told it was *you*."

Poirot blinked a little.

"But it is a nightmare, that suggestion!"

"Now you know what I suffer."

"I, too, I suffer," said Poirot. "The cooking of Madame Summerhayes', it is beyond description. It is not cooking at all. And the draughts, the cold winds, the upset stomachs of the cats, the long hairs of the dogs, the broken legs of the chairs, the terrible, terrible bed in which I sleep"—he shut his eyes in remembrance of agonies—"the tepid water in the bathroom, the holes in the stair carpet, and the coffee—words cannot describe to you the fluid which they serve to you as coffee. It is an affront to the stomach."

"Dear me," said Mrs. Oliver. "And yet, you know, she's awfully nice."

"Mrs. Summerhayes? She is charming. She is quite charming. That makes it much more difficult."

"Here she comes now," said Mrs. Oliver.

Maureen Summerhayes was approaching them.

There was an ecstatic look on her freckled face. She carried a glass in her hand. She smiled at them both with affection.

"I think I'm a bit tiddly," she announced. "Such lots of lovely gin. I do like parties! We don't often have one in Broadhinny. It's because of you both being so celebrated. I wish *I* could write books. The trouble with me is, I can't do *anything* properly."

"You are a good wife and mother, madame," said Poirot primly.

Maureen's eyes opened wide. Attractive hazel eyes in a small freckled face. Mrs. Oliver wondered how old she was. Not much more than thirty, she guessed.

"Am I?" said Maureen. "I wonder. I love them all terribly, but is that enough?"

Poirot coughed.

"If you will not think me presumptuous, madame. A wife who truly loves her husband should take great care of his stomach. It is important, the stomach."

Maureen looked slightly affronted.

"Johnnie's got a wonderful stomach," she said indignantly.

107

"Absolutely flat. Practically not a stomach at all."

"I was referring to what is put inside it."

"You mean my cooking," said Maureen. "I never think it matters much *what* one eats."

Poirot groaned.

"Or what one wears," said Maureen dreamily. "Or what one does. I don't think *things* matter—not really."

She was silent for a moment or two, her eyes alcoholically hazy, as though she was looking into the far distance.

"There was a woman writing in the paper the other day," she said suddenly. "A really stupid letter. Asking what was best to do—to let your child be adopted by someone who could give it every advantage—*every advantage,* that's what she said—and she meant a good education, and clothes and comfortable surroundings—or whether to keep it when you couldn't give it advantages of any kind. I think that's stupid —*really* stupid. If you can just give a child enough to eat— that's all that matters."

She stared down into her empty glass as though it were a crystal.

"*I* ought to know," she said. "I was an adopted child. My mother parted with me and I had every advantage, as they call it. And it's always hurt—always—always—to know that you weren't really wanted, that your mother could let you go."

"It was a sacrifice for your good, perhaps," said Poirot.

Her clear eyes met his.

"I don't think that's ever true. It's the way they put it to themselves. But what it boils down to is that they can, really, get on without you. . . . And it hurts. I wouldn't give up *my* children—not for all the advantages in the world!"

"I think you're quite right," said Mrs. Oliver.

"And I, too, agree," said Poirot.

"Then that's all right," said Maureen cheerfully. "What are we arguing about?"

Robin, who had come along the terrace to join them, said:

"Yes, what are you arguing about?"

"Adoption," said Maureen. "I don't like being adopted, do you?"

"Well, it's much better than being an orphan, don't you

108

think so, darling? I think we ought to go now, don't you? Ariadne?"

The guests left in a body. Dr. Rendell had already had to hurry away. They walked down the hall together talking gaily with that extra hilarity that a series of cocktails induces.

When they reached the gate of Laburnums, Robin insisted that they should all come in.

"Just to tell Madre all about the party. So boring for her, poor sweet, not to have been able to go because her leg was playing her up. But she so hates being left out of things."

They surged in cheerfully and Mrs. Upward seemed pleased to see them.

"Who else was there?" she asked. "The Wetherbys?"

"No, Mrs. Wetherby didn't feel well enough, and that dim Henderson girl wouldn't come without her."

"She's really rather pathetic, isn't she?" said Shelagh Rendell.

"I think almost pathological, don't you?" said Robin.

"It's that mother of hers," said Maureen. "Some mothers really do almost eat their young, don't they?"

She flushed suddenly as she met Mrs. Upward's quizzical eye.

"Do I devour you, Robin?" Mrs. Upward asked.

"Madre! Of course not!"

To cover her confusion Maureen hastily plunged into an account of her breeding experiences with Irish wolfhounds. The conversation became technical.

Mrs. Upward said decisively:

"You can't get away from heredity—in people as well as dogs."

Shelagh Rendell murmured:

"Don't you think it's environment?"

Mrs. Upward cut her short.

"No, my dear, I don't. Environment can give a veneer—no more. It's what's bred in people that counts."

Hercule Poirot's eyes rested curiously on Shelagh Rendell's flushed face. She said with what seemed unnecessary passion:

"But that's cruel—unfair."

Mrs. Upward said: "Life is unfair."

109

The slow lazy voice of Johnnie Summerhayes joined in. "I agree with Mrs. Upward. Breeding tells. That's been my creed always."

Mrs. Oliver said questioningly: "You mean things are handed down. Unto the third or fourth generation——"

Maureen Summerhayes said suddenly in her sweet high voice:

"But that quotation goes on: 'And show mercy unto thousands.'"

Once again everybody seemed a little embarrassed, perhaps at the serious note that had crept into the conversation.

They made a diversion by attacking Poirot.

"Tell us all about Mrs. McGinty, M. Poirot. Why didn't the dreary lodger kill her?"

"He used to mutter, you know," said Robin. "Walking about in the lanes. I've often met him. And really, definitely, he looked frightfully queer."

"You must have some reason for thinking he didn't kill her, M. Poirot. Do tell us."

Poirot smiled at them. He twirled his moustache.

"If he didn't kill her, who did?"

"Yes, who did?"

Mrs. Upward said dryly: "Don't embarrass the man. He probably suspects one of us."

"One of us? Oo!"

In the clamour Poirot's eyes met those of Mrs. Upward. They were amused and—something else—challenging?

"He suspects one of us," said Robin delightedly. "Now then, Maureen," he assumed the manner of a bullying K.C., "Where were you on the night of the—what night *was* it?"

"November 22nd," said Poirot.

"On the night of the 22nd?"

"Gracious, I don't know," said Maureen.

"Nobody could know after all this time," said Mrs. Rendell.

"Well, I can," said Robin. "Because I was broadcasting that night. I drove to Coalport to give a talk on Some Aspects of the Theatre. I remember because I discussed Galsworthy's charwoman in the Silver Box at great length and the next day Mrs. McGinty was killed and I wondered if the charwoman in the play had been like her."

110

"That's right," said Shelagh Rendell suddenly. "And I remember now because you said your mother would be all alone because it was Janet's night off, and I came down here after dinner to keep her company. Only unfortunately I couldn't make her hear."

"Let me think," said Mrs. Upward. "Oh! yes, of course. I'd gone to bed with a headache and my bedroom faces the back garden."

"And next day," said Shelagh, "when I heard Mrs. McGinty had been killed, I thought 'Oo I might have passed the murderer in the dark'—because at first we all thought it must have been some tramp who broke in."

"Well, I still don't remember what I was doing," said Maureen. "But I do remember the next morning. It was the baker told us. 'Old Mrs. McGinty's been done in,' he said. And there I was, wondering why she hadn't turned up as usual."

She gave a shiver.

"It's horrible really, isn't it?" she said.

Mrs. Upward was still watching Poirot.

He thought to himself: "She is a very intelligent woman —and a ruthless one. Also selfish. In whatever she did, she would have no qualms and no remorse. . . ."

A thin voice was speaking—urging, querulous.

"Haven't you got any clues, M. Poirot?"

It was Shelagh Rendell.

Johnnie Summerhayes' long dark face lit up enthusiastically.

"That's it, clues," he said. "That's what I like in detective stories. Clues that mean everything to the detective—and nothing to you—until the end when you fairly kick yourself. Can't you give us one little clue, M. Poirot?"

Laughing, pleading faces turned to him. A game to them all (or perhaps not to one of them?). But murder wasn't a game—murder was dangerous. You never knew.

With a sudden brusque movement, Poirot pulled out four photographs from his pocket.

"You want a clue?" he said. "*Voilà!*"

And with a dramatic gesture he tossed them down on the table.

They clustered round, bending over, and uttering ejaculations.

"*Look!*"

"What frightful frumps!"

"Just look at the roses. '*Rowses, rowses, all the way!*' "

"My dear, that *hat*!"

"What a frightful child!"

"But who are they?"

"Aren't fashions ridiculous?"

"That woman must really have been rather good-looking once."

"But why are they clues?"

"Who are they?"

Poirot looked slowly round at the circle of faces.

He saw nothing other than he might have expected to see.

"You do not recognise any of them?"

"Recognise?"

"You do not, shall I say, remember having seen any of those photographs before? But yes—Mrs. Upward? You recognise something, do you not?"

Mrs. Upward hesitated.

"Yes—I think——"

"Which one?"

Her forefinger went out and rested on the spectacled childlike face of Lily Gamboll.

"You have seen that photograph—when?"

"Quite recently. . . . Now where—no, I can't remember. But I'm sure I've seen a photograph just like that."

She sat frowning, her brows drawn together.

She came out of her abstraction as Mrs. Rendell came to her.

"Good-bye, Mrs. Upward. I do hope you'll come to tea with me one day if you feel up to it."

"Thank you, my dear. If Robin pushes me up the hill."

"Of course, Madre. I've developed the most tremendous muscles pushing that chair. Do you remember the day we went to the Wetherbys' and it was so muddy——"

"Ah!" said Mrs. Upward suddenly.

"What is it, Madre?"

"Nothing. Go on."

112

"Getting you up the hill again. First the chair skidded and then I skidded. I thought we'd never get home."

Laughing, they took their leave and trooped out.

Alcohol, Poirot thought, certainly loosens the tongue.

Had he been wise or foolish to display those photographs? Had that gesture also been the result of alcohol?

He wasn't sure.

But, murmuring an excuse, he turned back.

He pushed open the gate and walked up to the house. Through the open window on his left he heard the murmur of two voices. They were the voices of Robin and Mrs. Oliver. Very little of Mrs. Oliver and a good deal of Robin.

Poirot pushed the door open and went through the right-hand door into the room he had left a few moments before. Mrs. Upward was sitting before the fire. There was a rather grim look on her face. She had been so deep in thought that his entry startled her.

At the sound of the apologetic little cough he gave, she looked up sharply, with a start.

"Oh," she said. "It's you. You startled me."

"I am sorry, madame. Did you think it was someone else? Who did you think it was?"

She did not answer that, merely said:

"Did you leave something behind?"

"What I feared I had left was danger."

"Danger?"

"Danger, perhaps, to you. Because you recognised one of those photographs just now."

"I wouldn't say recognised. All old photographs look exactly alike."

"Listen, madame. Mrs. McGinty also, or so I believe, recognised one of those photographs. *And Mrs. McGinty is dead.*"

With an unexpected glint of humour in her eye, Mrs. Upward said:

"*Mrs. McGinty's dead. How did she die? Sticking her neck out just like I.* Is that what you mean?"

"Yes. If you know anything—anything at all, tell it to me now. It will be safer so."

"My dear man, it's not nearly so simple as that. I'm not at all sure that I do know anything—certainly nothing as definite as a *fact*. Vague recollections are very tricky things. One would have to have some idea of how and where and when, if you follow what I mean."

"But it seems to me that you already have that idea."

"There is more to it than that. There are various factors to be taken into consideration. Now it's no good your rushing me, M. Poirot. I'm not the kind of person who rushes into decisions. I've a mind of my own, and I take time to make it up. When I come to a decision, I act. But not till I'm ready."

"You are in many ways a secretive woman, madame."

"Perhaps—up to a point. Knowledge is power. Power must only be used for the right ends. You will excuse my saying that you don't perhaps appreciate the pattern of our English country life."

"In other words you say to me, 'You are only a damned foreigner.' "

Mrs. Upward smiled slightly.

"I shouldn't be as rude as that."

"If you do not want to talk to me, there is Superintendent Spence."

"My dear M. Poirot. Not the police. Not at this stage."

He shrugged his shoulders.

"I have warned you," he said.

For he was sure that by now Mrs. Upward remembered quite well exactly when and where she had seen the photograph of Lily Gamboll.

CHAPTER XIV

I

"DECIDEDLY," said Hercule Poirot to himself the following morning, "the spring is here."

His apprehensions of the night before seemed singularly groundless.

Mrs. Upward was a sensible woman who could take good care of herself.

Nevertheless in some curious way, she intrigued him. He

did not at all understand her reactions. Clearly she did not want him to. She had recognised the photograph of Lily Gamboll and she was determined to play a lone hand.

Poirot, pacing a garden path while he pursued these reflections, was startled by a voice behind him.

"M. Poirot."

Mrs. Rendell had come up so quietly that he had not heard her. Since yesterday he had felt extremely nervous.

"*Pardon*, madame. You made me jump."

Mrs. Rendell smiled mechanically. If he were nervous, Mrs. Rendell, he thought, was even more so. There was a twitching in one of her eyelids and her hands worked restlessly together.

"I—I hope I'm not interrupting you. Perhaps you're busy."

"But no, I am not busy. The day is fine. I enjoy the feeling of spring. It is good to be outdoors. In the house of Mrs. Summerhayes there is always, but always, the current of air."

"The current——"

"What in England you call a draught."

"Yes. Yes, I suppose there is."

"The windows, they will not shut and the doors they fly open all the time."

"It's rather a ramshackle house. And of course, the Summerhayes are so badly off they can't afford to do much to it. I'd let it go if I were them. I know it's been in their family for hundreds of years, but nowadays you just can't cling on to things for sentiment's sake."

"No, we are not sentimental nowadays."

There was a silence. Out of the corner of his eye, Poirot watched those nervous white hands. He waited for her to take the initiative. When she did speak it was abruptly.

"I suppose," she said, "that when you are, well, investigating a thing, you'd always have to have a pretext?"

Poirot considered the question. Though he did not look at her, he was perfectly aware of her eager sideways glance fixed on him.

"As you say, madame," he replied non-committally. "It is a convenience."

"To explain your being there, and—and asking things."

"It might be expedient."

115

"Why—why are you really here in Broadhinny, M. Poirot?"

He turned a mild surprised gaze on her.

"But, my dear lady, I told you—to inquire into the death of Mrs. McGinty."

Mrs. Rendell said sharply:

"I know that's what you say. But it's ridiculous."

Poirot raised his eyebrows.

"Is it?"

"Of course it is. Nobody believes it."

"And yet I assure you, it is simple fact."

Her pale blue eyes blinked and she looked away.

"You won't tell me."

"Tell you—what, madame?"

She changed the subject abruptly again, it seemed.

"I wanted to ask you—about anonymous letters."

"Yes," said Poirot encouragingly as she stopped.

"They're really always lies, aren't they?"

"They are sometimes lies," said Poirot cautiously.

"Usually," she persisted.

"I don't know that I would go as far as saying that."

Shelagh Rendell said vehemently:

"They're cowardly, treacherous, *mean* things!"

"All that, yes, I would agree."

"And you wouldn't ever believe what was said in one, would you?"

"That is a very difficult question," said Poirot gravely.

"I wouldn't. I wouldn't believe anything of that kind."

She added vehemently:

"I know why you're down here. And it isn't true, I tell you, it isn't true."

She turned sharply and walked away.

Hercule Poirot raised his eyebrows in an interested fashion.

"And now what?" he demanded of himself. "Am I being taken up the garden walk? Or is this the bird of a different colour?"

It was all, he felt, very confusing.

Mrs. Rendell professed to believe that he was down here for a reason other than that of inquiring into Mrs. McGinty's death. She had suggested that that was only a pretext.

116

Did she really believe that? Or was she, as he had just said to himself, leading him up the garden walk?

What had anonymous letters got to do with it?

Was Mrs. Rendell the original of the photograph that Mrs. Upward had said she had "seen recently"?

In other words, was Mrs. Rendell Lily Gamboll? Lily Gamboll, a rehabilitated member of society, had been last heard of in Eire. Had Dr. Rendell met and married his wife there, in ignorance of her history? Lily Gamboll had been trained as a stenographer. Her path and the doctor's might easily have crossed.

Poirot shook his head and sighed.

It was all perfectly possible. But he had to be sure.

A chilly wind sprang up suddenly and the sun went in.

Poirot shivered and retraced his steps to the house.

Yes, he had to be sure. If he could find the actual weapon of the murder——

And at that moment, with a strange feeling of certainty—he *saw* it.

II

Afterwards he wondered whether, subconsciously, he had seen and noted it much earlier. It had stood there, presumably, ever since he had come to Long Meadows . . .

There on the littered top of the bookcase near the window.

He thought: "Why did I never notice that before?"

He picked it up, weighed it in his hands, examined it, balanced it, raised it to strike——

Maureen came in through the door with her usual rush, two dogs accompanying her. Her voice, light and friendly, said:

"Hallo, are you playing with the sugar cutter?"

"Is that what it is? A sugar cutter?"

"Yes. A sugar cutter—or a sugar hammer—I don't know what exactly is the right term. It's rather fun, isn't it? So childish with the little bird on top."

Poirot turned the implement carefully in his hands. Made of much ornamented brass, it was shaped like an adze, heavy, with a sharp cutting edge. It was studded here and there with

coloured stones, pale blue and red. On top of it was a frivo-
lous little bird with turquoise eyes.

"Lovely thing for killing anyone, wouldn't it be?" said
Maureen conversationally.

She took it from him and aimed a murderous blow on a
point in space.

"Frightfully easy," she said. "What's that bit in the Idylls
of the King? ' "Mark's way," he said, and clove him to the
brain.' I should think you could cleave anyone to the brain
with this all right, don't you?"

Poirot looked at her. Her freckled face was serene and
cheerful.

She said:

"I've told Johnnie what's coming to him if I get fed up
with him. I call it the wife's best friend!"

She laughed, put the sugar hammer down and turned towards the door.

"What did I come in here for?" she mused. "I can't remember . . . Bother! I'd better go and see if that pudding
needs more water in the saucepan."

Poirot's voice stopped her before she got to the door.

"You brought this back with you from India, perhaps?"

"Oh no," said Maureen. "I got it at the B. and B. at
Christmas."

"B. and B.?" Poirot was puzzled.

"Bring and Buy," explained Maureen glibly. "At the
Vicarage. You bring things you don't want, and you buy
something. Something not too frightful, if you can find it.
Of course there's practically never anything you really want.
I got this and that coffee pot. I like the coffee pot's nose and
I liked the little bird on the hammer."

The coffee pot was a small one of beaten copper. It had
a big curving spout that struck a familiar note to Poirot.

"I think they come from Baghdad," said Maureen. "At
least I think that's what the Wetherbys said. Or it may have
been Persia."

"It was from the Wetherbys' house, then, that these
came?"

"Yes. They've got a most frightful lot of junk. I *must* go.
That pudding."

She went out. The door banged. Poirot picked up the sugar cutter again and took it to the window.

On the cutting edge were faint, very faint discolourations. Poirot nodded his head.

He hesitated for a moment, then he carried the sugar hammer out of the room and up to his bedroom. There he packed it carefully in a box, did the whole thing up neatly in paper and string, and going downstairs again, left the house.

He did not think that anyone would notice the disappearance of the sugar cutter. It was not a tidy household.

III

At Laburnums, collaboration was pursuing its difficult course.

"But I really don't feel it's right making him a vegetarian, darling," Robin was objecting. "Too faddy. And definitely not glamorous."

"I can't help it," said Mrs. Oliver obstinately. "He's *always* been a vegetarian. He takes round a little machine for grating raw carrots and turnips."

"But, Ariadne, precious, *why*?"

"How do I know?" said Mrs. Oliver crossly. "How do I know why I ever thought of the revolting man? I must have been mad! Why a Finn when I know nothing about Finland? Why a vegetarian? Why all the idiotic mannerisms he's got? These things just *happen*. You try something—and people seem to like it—and then you go on—and before you know where you are, you've got someone like that maddening Sven Hjerson tied to you for life. And people even write and say how fond you must be of him. Fond of him? If I met that bony, gangling, vegetable-eating Finn in real life, I'd do a better murder than any I've ever invented."

Robin Upward gazed at her with reverence.

"You know, Ariadne, that might be rather a marvellous idea. A real Sven Hjerson—and *you* murder him. You might make a Swan Song book of it—to be published after your death."

119

"No fear!" said Mrs. Oliver. "What about the money? Any money to be made out of murders I want now."

"Yes. Yes. There I couldn't agree with you more."

The harassed playwright strode up and down.

"This Ingrid creature is getting rather tiresome," he said. "And after the cellar scene which is really going to be marvellous, I don't quite see how we're going to prevent the next scene from being rather an anti-climax."

Mrs. Oliver was silent. Scenes, she felt, were Robin Upward's headache.

Robin shot a dissatisfied glance at her.

That morning, in one of her frequent changes of mood, Mrs. Oliver had disliked her windswept coiffure. With a brush dipped in water she had plastered her grey locks close to her skull. With her high forehead, her massive glasses, and her stern air, she was reminding Robin more and more of a school teacher who had awed his early youth. He found it more and more difficult to address her as darling, and even flinched at "Ariadne."

He said fretfully:

"You know, I don't feel a bit in the mood to-day. All that gin yesterday, perhaps. Let's scrap work and go into the question of casting. If we can get Denis Callory, of course it will be too marvellous, but he's tied up in films at the moment. And Jean Bellews for Ingrid would be just right—and she *wants* to play it which is so nice. Eric—as I say, I've had a brainwave for Eric. We'll go over to the Little Rep to-night, shall we? And you'll tell me what you think of Cecil for the part."

Mrs. Oliver agreed hopefully to this project and Robin went off to telephone.

"There," he said returning. "That's all fixed."

I V

The fine morning had not lived up to its promise. Clouds had gathered and the day was oppressive with a threat of rain. As Poirot walked through the dense shrubberies to the front door of Hunter's Close, he decided that he would not like to live in this hollow valley at the foot of the hill. The house itself was closed in by trees and its walls suffocated in ivy. It needed, he thought, the woodman's axe.

(The *axe*. The sugar cutter?)

He rang the bell and after getting no response, rang it again.

It was Deirdre Henderson who opened the door to him. She seemed surprised.

"Oh," she said, "it's you."

"May I come in and speak to you?"

"I—well, yes, I suppose so."

She led him into the small dark sitting-room where he had waited before. On the mantelpiece he recognised the big brother of the small coffee pot on Maureen's shelf. Its vast hooked nose seemed to dominate the small Western room with a hint of Eastern ferocity.

"I'm afraid," said Deirdre in an apologetic tone, "that we're rather upset to-day. Our help, the German girl—she's going. She's only been here a month. Actually it seems she just took this post to get over to this country because there was someone she wanted to marry. And now they've fixed it up, and she's going straight off to-night."

Poirot clicked his tongue.

"Most inconsiderate."

"It is, isn't it? My stepfather says it isn't legal. But even if it isn't legal, if she just goes off and gets married, I don't see what one can do about it. We shouldn't even have known she *was* going if I hadn't found her packing her clothes. She would just have walked out of the house without a word."

"It is, alas, not an age of consideration."

"No," said Deirdre dully. "I suppose it's not."

She rubbed her forehead with the back of her hand.

"I'm tired," she said. "I'm very tired."

"Yes," said Poirot gently. "I think you may be very tired."

"What was it you wanted, M. Poirot?"

"I wanted to ask you about a sugar hammer."

"A sugar hammer?"

Her face was blank, uncomprehending.

"An instrument of brass, with a bird on it, and inlaid with blue and red and green stones." Poirot enunciated the description carefully.

"Oh yes, I know."

Her voice showed no interest or animation.

"I understand it came from this house?"

"Yes. My mother bought it in the bazaar at Baghdad. It's one of the things we took to the Vicarage sale."

"The Bring and Buy sale, that is right?"

"Yes. We have a lot of them here. It's difficult to get people to give money, but there's usually something you can rake up and send."

"So it was here, in this house, until Christmas, and then you sent it to the Bring and Buy sale? Is that right?"

Deirdre frowned.

"Not the Christmas Bring and Buy. It was the one before. The Harvest Festival one."

"The Harvest Festival—that would be—when? October? September?"

"The end of September."

It was very quiet in the little room. Poirot looked at the girl and she looked back at him. Her face was mild, expressionless, uninterested. Behind the blank wall of her apathy, he tried to guess what was going on. Nothing, perhaps. Perhaps she was, as she had said, just tired. . . .

He said, quietly, urgently:

"You are quite sure it was the Harvest Festival Sale? Not the Christmas one?"

"Quite sure."

Her eyes were steady, unblinking.

Hercule Poirot waited. He continued to wait. . . .

But what he was waiting for did not come.

He said formally:

"I must not keep you any longer, mademoiselle."

She went with him to the front door.

Presently he was walking down the drive again.

Two divergent statements—statements that could not possibly be reconciled.

Who was right? Maureen Summerhayes or Deirdre Henderson?

If the sugar cutter had been used as he believed it had been used, the point was vital. The Harvest Festival had been the end of September. Between then and Christmas, on November 22nd, Mrs. McGinty had been killed. Whose property had the sugar cutter been at that time?

He went to the post office. Mrs. Sweetiman was always helpful and she did her best. She'd been to both sales, she said. She always went. You picked up many a nice bit there. She helped, too, to arrange things beforehand. Though most people brought things with them and didn't send them beforehand.

A brass hammer, rather like an axe, with coloured stones and a little bird? No, she couldn't rightly remember. There was such a lot of things, and so much confusion and some things snatched up at once. Well, perhaps she did remember something like that—priced at five shillings it had been, and with a copper coffee pot, but the pot had got a hole in the bottom—you couldn't use it, only for ornament. But she couldn't remember when it was—some time ago. Might have been Christmas, might have been before. She hadn't been noticing. . . .

She accepted Poirot's parcel. Registered? Yes.

She copied down the address; he noticed just a sharp flicker of interest in her keen black eyes as she handed him the receipt.

Hercule Poirot walked slowly up the hill, wondering to himself.

Of the two, Maureen Summerhayes, scatter-brained, cheerful, inaccurate, was the more likely to be wrong. Harvest or Christmas, it would be all one to her.

Deirdre Henderson, slow, awkward, was far more likely to be accurate in her identification of times and dates.

Yet there remained that irking question.

Why, after his questions, hadn't she asked him *why he wanted to know*? Surely a natural, an almost inevitable, question?

But Deirdre Henderson hadn't asked it.

CHAPTER XV

I

"Someone rang you up," called Maureen from the kitchen as Poirot entered the house.

"Rang me up? Who was that?"

He was slightly surprised.

"Don't know. But I jotted the number down on my ration book."

"Thank you, Madame."

He went into the dining-room and over to the desk. Amongst the litter of papers he found the ration book lying near the telephone and the words—Kilchester 350.

Raising the receiver of the telephone, he dialled the number.

Immediately a woman's voice said:

"Breather & Scuttle."

Poirot made a quick guess.

"Can I speak to Miss Maude Williams?"

There was a moment's interval and then a contralto voice said:

"Miss Williams speaking."

"This is Hercule Poirot. I think you rang me."

"Yes—yes, I did. It's about the property you were asking me about the other day."

"The property?" For a moment Poirot was puzzled. Then he realised that Maude's conversation was being overheard. Probably she had telephoned him before when she was alone in the office.

"I understand you, I think. It is the affair of James Bentley and Mrs. McGinty's murder."

"That's right. Can we do anything in the matter for you?"

"You want to help. You are not private where you are?"

"That's right."

"I understand. Listen carefully. You really want to help James Bentley?"

"Yes."

"Would you resign your present post?"

There was no hesitation.

"Yes."

"Would you be willing to take a domestic post? Possibly with not very congenial people."

"Yes."

"Could you get away at once? By to-morrow, for instance."

"Oh yes, M. Poirot. I think that could be managed."

"You understand what I want you to do. You would be a domestic help—to live in. You can cook?"

A faint amusement tinged the voice.

"Very well."

"*Bon Dieu*, what a rarity! Now listen, I am coming into Kilchester at once. I will meet you in the same café where I met you before, at lunch time."

"Yes, certainly."

Poirot rang off.

"An admirable young woman," he reflected. "Quick-witted, knows her own mind—perhaps, even, she can cook. . . ."

With some difficulty he disinterred the local telephone directory from under a treatise on pigkeeping and looked up the Wetherbys' number.

The voice that answered him was that of Mrs. Wetherby.

"'Allo? 'Allo? It is M. Poirot—you remember, madame——"

"I don't think I——"

"M. Hercule Poirot."

"Oh yes—of course—do forgive me. Rather a domestic upset to-day——"

"It is for that reason exactly I rang you up. I am desolated to learn of your difficulties."

"So ungrateful—these foreign girls. Her fare paid over here, and everything. I do so hate ingratitude."

"Yes, yes. I do indeed sympathise. It is monstrous—that is why I hasten to tell you that I have, perhaps, a solution. By the merest chance I know of a young woman wanting a domestic post. Not, I fear, fully trained."

"Oh, there's no such thing as training nowadays. Will she cook—so many of them won't cook."

"Yes—yes—she cooks. Shall I then send her to you—at least on trial? Her name is Maude Williams."

125

"Oh, please do, M. Poirot. It's most kind of you. Anything would be better than nothing. My husband is so particular and gets so annoyed with dear Deirdre when the household doesn't go smoothly. One can't expect men to understand how difficult everything is nowadays—I——"

There was an interruption. Mrs. Wetherby spoke to someone entering the room, and though she had placed her hand over the receiver Poirot could hear her slightly muffled words.

"It's the little detective man—knows of someone to come in to replace Frieda. No, not foreign—English, thank goodness. Very kind of him, really, he seems quite concerned about me. Oh, darling, don't make objections. What does it *matter*? You know the absurd way Roger goes on. Well, I think it's very kind—and I don't suppose she's too awful."

The asides over, Mrs. Wetherby spoke with the utmost graciousness.

"Thank you very much, M. Poirot. We are most grateful."

Poirot replaced the receiver and glanced at his watch.

He went to the kitchen.

"Madame, I shall not be in to lunch. I have to go to Kilchester."

"Thank goodness," said Maureen. "I didn't get to that pudding in time. It had boiled dry. I think it's really all right—just a little scorched perhaps. In case it tasted rather nasty I thought I would open a bottle of those raspberries I put up last summer. They seem to have a bit of mould on top but they say nowadays that that doesn't matter. It's really rather good for you—practically penicillin."

Poirot left the house, glad that scorched pudding and near-penicillin were not to be his portion to-day. Better—far better—eat macaroni and custard and plums at the Blue Cat than the improvisations of Maureen Summerhayes.

At Laburnums a little friction had arisen.

"Of course, Robin, you never seem to remember anything when you are working on a play."

Robin was contrite.

"Madre, I am most terribly sorry. I'd forgotten all about its being Janet's night out."

"It doesn't matter at all," said Mrs. Upward coldly.

"Of course it matters. I'll ring up the Rep and tell them we'll go to-morrow night instead."

"You'll do nothing of the sort. You've arranged to go to-night and you'll go."

"But really——"

"That's settled."

"Shall I ask Janet to go out another night?"

"Certainly *not*. She hates to have her plans disarranged."

"I'm sure she wouldn't really mind. Not if I put it to her——"

"You'll do nothing of the sort, Robin. Please don't go upsetting Janet. And don't go on about it. I don't care to feel I'm a tiresome old woman spoiling other people's pleasure."

"Madre—sweetest——"

"That's enough—you go and enjoy yourselves. I know who I'll ask to keep me company."

"Who?"

"That's my secret," said Mrs. Upward, her good humour restored. "Now stop fussing, Robin."

"I'll ring up Shelagh Rendell——"

"I'll do my own ringing up, thank you. It's all settled. Make the coffee before you go, and leave it by me in the percolator ready to switch on. Oh, and you might as well put out an extra cup—in case I have a visitor."

CHAPTER XVI

SITTING at lunch in the Blue Cat, Poirot finished outlining his instructions to Maude Williams.

"So you understand what it is you have to look for?"

Maude Williams nodded.

"You have arranged matters with your office?"

She laughed.

"My auntie's dangerously ill! I sent myself a telegram."

"Good. I have one more thing to say. Somewhere, in that

village, we have a murderer at large. That is not a very safe thing to have."

"Warning me?"

"Yes."

"I can take care of myself," said Maude Williams.

"That," said Hercule Poirot, "might be classed under the heading of Famous Last Words."

She laughed again, a frank amused laugh. One or two heads at near tables turned round to look at her.

Poirot found himself appraising her carefully. A strong, confident young woman, full of vitality, keyed up and eager to attempt a dangerous task. Why? He thought again of James Bentley, his gentle defeated voice, his lifeless apathy. Nature was indeed curious and interesting.

Maude said:

"You're *asking* me to do it, aren't you? Why suddenly try to put me off?"

"Because if one offers a mission, one must be exact about what it involves."

"I don't think I'm in any danger," said Maude confidently.

"I do not think so at the moment. You are unknown in Broadhinny?"

Maude considered.

"Ye-es. Yes, I should say so."

"You have been there?"

"Once or twice—for the firm, of course—only once recently—that was about five months ago."

"Who did you see? Where did you go?"

"I went to see an old lady—Mrs. Carstairs—or Carlisle—I can't remember her name for sure. She was buying a small property near here, and I went over to see her with some papers and some queries and a surveyor's report which we'd got for her. She was staying at that Guest House sort of place where you are."

"Long Meadows?"

"That was it. Uncomfortable-looking house with a lot of dogs."

Poirot nodded.

"Did you see Mrs. Summerhayes, or Major Summerhayes?"

"I saw Mrs. Summerhayes, I suppose it was. She took me up to the bedroom. The old pussy was in bed."

128

"Would Mrs. Summerhayes remember you?"

"Don't suppose so. Even if she did, it wouldn't matter, would it? After all, one changes one's job quite often these days. But I don't suppose she even looked at me. Her sort don't."

There was a faint bitterness in Maude Williams' voice.

"Did you see anyone else in Broadhinny?"

Maude said rather awkwardly:

"Well, I saw Mr. Bentley."

"Ah, you saw Mr. Bentley. By accident."

Maude wriggled a little in her chair.

"No, as a matter of fact, I'd sent him a p.c. Telling him I was coming that day. Asked him if he'd meet me as a matter of fact. Not that there was anywhere to go. Dead little hole. No café or cinema or anything. 'S a matter of fact we just talked in the bus stop. While I was waiting for my bus back."

"That was before the death of Mrs. McGinty?"

"Oh yes. But not much before, though. Because it was only a few days later that it was all in the newspapers."

"Did Mr. Bentley speak to you at all of his landlady?"

"I don't think so."

"And you spoke to no one else in Broadhinny?"

"Well—only Mr. Robin Upward. I've heard him talk on the wireless. I saw him coming out of his cottage and I recognised him from his pictures and I did ask him for his autograph."

"And he gave it you?"

"Oh yes, he was ever so nice about it. I hadn't my book with me, but I'd got an odd sheet of notepaper, and he whipped out his fountain pen and wrote it at once."

"Do you know any of the other people in Broadhinny by sight?"

"Well, I know the Carpenters, of course. They're in Kilchester a lot. Lovely car they've got, and she wears lovely clothes. She opened a Bazaar about a month ago. They say he's going to be our next M.P."

Poirot nodded. Then he took from his pocket the envelope that he always carried about with him. He spread the four protographs on the table.

"Do you recognise any of—what's the matter?"

"It was Mr. Scuttle. Just going out of the door. I hope he

didn't see you with me. It might seem a bit odd. People are talking about you, you know. Saying you've been sent over from Paris—from the Sooretay or some name like that."

"I am Belgian, not French, but no matter."

"What's this about these photographs?" She bent over, studying them closely. "Rather on the old-fashioned side, aren't they?"

"The oldest is thirty years ago."

"Awfully silly, old fashioned clothes look. Makes the women look such fools."

"Have you seen any of them before?"

"D'you mean do I recognise any of the women, or do you mean have I seen the pictures?"

"Either."

"I've an idea I've seen that one." Her finger rested against Janice Courtland in her cloche hat. "In some paper or other, but I can't remember when. That kid looks a bit familiar, too. But I can't remember when I saw them; some time ago."

"All those photographs appeared in the *Sunday Comet* on the Sunday before Mrs. McGinty died."

Maude looked at him sharply.

"And they've got something to do with it? That's why you want me to——"

She did not finish the sentence.

"Yes," said Hercule Poirot. "That is why."

He took something else from his pocket and showed it to her. It was the cutting from the *Sunday Comet*.

"You had better read that," he said.

She read it carefully. Her bright golden head bent over the flimsy bit of newsprint.

Then she looked up.

"So that's who they are? And reading this has given you ideas?"

"You could not express it more justly."

"But all the same I don't see——" She was silent a moment, thinking. Poirot did not speak. However pleased he might be with his own ideas, he was always ready to hear other people's ideas too.

"You think one or other of these people is in Broad-hinny?"

"It might be, might it not?"

130

"Of course. Anyone may be anywhere . . ." She went on, placing her finger on Eva Kane's pretty simpering face: "She'd be quite old now—about Mrs. Upward's age."

"About that."

"What I was thinking was—the sort of woman she was—there must be several people who'd have it in for her."

"That is a point of view," said Poirot slowly. "Yes, it is a point of view." He added: "You remember the Craig case?"

"Who doesn't?" said Maude Williams. "Why, he's in Madame Tussaud's! I was only a kid at the time, but the newspapers are always bringing him up and comparing the case with other cases. I don't suppose it will ever be forgotten, do you?"

Poirot raised his head sharply.

He wondered what brought that sudden note of bitterness into her voice.

CHAPTER XVII

FEELING completely bewildered, Mrs. Oliver was endeavouring to cower in the corner of a very minute theatrical dressing-room. Not being the figure to cower, she only succeeded in bulging. Bright young men, removing grease paint with towels, surrounded her and at intervals pressed warm beer upon her.

Mrs. Upward, her good humour completely restored, had speeded their departure with good wishes. Robin had been assiduous in making all arrangements for her comfort before departure, running back a couple of times after they were in the car to see that all was as it should be.

On the last occasion he came back grinning.

"Madre was just ringing off on the telephone, and the wicked old thing still won't tell me who she was ringing up. But I bet I know."

"I know, too," said Mrs. Oliver.

"Well, who do you say?"

"Hercule Poirot."

"Yes, that's my guess, too. She's going to pump him. Madre does like having her little secrets, doesn't she? Now darling,

131

about the play to-night. It's very important that you tell me honestly just what you think of Cecil—and whether he's your idea of Eric . . ."

Needless to say, Cecil Leech had not been at all Mrs. Oliver's idea of Eric. Nobody, indeed, could have been more unlike. The play itself she had enjoyed, but the ordeal of "going round afterwards" was fraught with its usual terrors.

Robin, of course, was in his element. He had Cecil (at least Mrs. Oliver supposed it was Cecil) pinned against the wall and was talking nineteen to the dozen. Mrs. Oliver had been terrified of Cecil and much preferred somebody called Michael who was talking to her kindly at the moment. Michael, at least, did not expect her to reciprocate, in fact Michael seemed to prefer a monologue. Somebody called Peter made occasional incursions on the conversation, but on the whole it resolved itself into a thin stream of faintly amusing malice by Michael.

"——too sweet of Robin," he was saying. "We've been urging him to come and see the show. But of course he's completely under that terrible woman's thumb, isn't he? Dancing attendance. And really Robin is brilliant, don't you think so? Quite quite brilliant. He shouldn't be sacrificed on a Matriarchal altar. Women can be awful, can't they? You know what she did to poor Alex Roscoff? All over him for nearly a year and then discovered that he wasn't a Russian émigré at all. Of course he had been telling her some very tall stories, but quite amusing, and we all knew it wasn't true, but after all why should one care?——and then when she found out he was just a little East End tailor's son, she dropped him, my dear. I mean, I do hate a snob, don't you? Really Alex was thankful to get away from her. He said she could be quite frightening sometimes—a little queer in the head, he thought. Her rages! Robin dear, we're talking about your wonderful Madre. Such a shame she couldn't come to-night. But it's marvellous to have Mrs. Oliver. All those delicious murders."

An elderly man with a deep bass voice grasped Mrs. Oliver's hand and held it in a hot, sticky grasp.

"How can I ever thank you?" he said in tones of deep melancholy. "You've saved my life—saved my life many a time."

Then they all came out into the fresh night air and went across to the Pony's Head, where there were more drinks and more stage conversation.

By the time Mrs. Oliver and Robin were driving homeward, Mrs. Oliver was quite exhausted. She leaned back and closed her eyes. Robin, on the other hand, talked without stopping.

"——and you do think that might be an idea, don't you?" he finally ended.

"What?"

Mrs. Oliver jerked open her eyes.

She had been lost in a nostalgic dream of home. Walls covered with exotic birds and foliage. A deal table, her typewriter, black coffee, apples everywhere . . . What bliss, what glorious and solitary bliss! What a mistake for an author to emerge from her secret fastness. Authors were shy, unsociable creatures, atoning for their lack of social aptitude by inventing their own companions and conversations.

"I'm afraid you're tired," said Robin.

"Not really. The truth is I'm not very good with people."

"I adore people, don't you?" said Robin happily.

"No," said Mrs. Oliver firmly.

"But you must. Look at all the people in your books."

"That's different. I think trees are much nicer than people, more restful."

"I need people," said Robin, stating an obvious fact. "They stimulate me."

He drew up at the gate of Laburnums.

"You go in," he said. "I'll put the car away."

Mrs. Oliver extracted herself with the usual difficulty and walked up the path.

"The door's not locked," Robin called.

It wasn't. Mrs. Oliver pushed it open and entered. There were no lights on, and that struck her as rather ungracious on her hostess's part. Or was it perhaps economy? Rich people were so often economical. There was a smell of scent in the hall, something rather exotic and expensive. For a moment Mrs. Oliver wondered if she were in the right house, then she found the light switch and pressed it down.

The light sprang up in the low oak-beamed square hall. The door into the sitting-room was ajar and she caught sight

133

of a foot and leg. Mrs. Upward, after all, had not gone to bed. She must have fallen asleep in her chair, and since no lights were on, she must have been asleep a long time.

Mrs. Oliver went to the door and switched on the lights in the sitting-room.

"We're back——" she began and then stopped.

Her hand went up to her throat. She felt a tight knot there, a desire to scream that she could not put into operation.

Her voice came out in a whisper:

"Robin—Robin . . ."

It was some time before she heard him coming up the path, whistling, and then she turned quickly and ran to meet him in the hall.

"Don't go in there—don't go in. Your mother—she—she's dead—I think—she's been killed . . ."

CHAPTER XVIII

I

"Quite a neat bit of work," said Superintendent Spence.

His red countryman's face was angry. He looked across to where Hercule Poirot sat gravely listening.

"Neat and ugly," he said. "She was strangled," he went on. "Silk scarf—one of her own silk scarves, one she'd been wearing that day—just passed around the neck and the ends crossed—and pulled. Neat, quick, efficient. The thugs did it that way in India. The victim doesn't struggle or cry out—pressure on the carotid artery."

"Special knowledge?"

"Could be—need not. If you were thinking of doing it, you could read up the subject. There's no practical difficulty. Especially with the victim quite unsuspicious—and she *was* unsuspicious."

Poirot nodded.

"Someone she knew."

"Yes. They'd had coffee together—a cup opposite her and one opposite the—guest. Prints had been wiped off the guest's cup very carefully but lipstick is more difficult—there were still faint traces of lipstick."

"A woman, then?"

"You expected a woman, didn't you?"

"Oh yes. Yes, that was indicated."

Spence went on:

"Mrs. Upward recognised one of those photographs—the photograph of Lily Gamboll. So it ties up with the McGinty murder."

"Yes," said Poirot. "It ties up with the McGinty murder."

He remembered Mrs. Upward's slightly amused expression as she had said:

> "Mrs. McGinty's dead. How did she die?
> Sticking her neck out, just like I."

Spence was going on:

"She took an opportunity that seemed good to her—her son and Mrs. Oliver were going off to the theatre. She rang up the person concerned and asked that person to come and see her. Is that how you figure it out? She was playing detective."

"Something like that. Curiosity. She kept her knowledge to herself, but she wanted to find out more. She didn't in the least realise what she was doing might be dangerous." Poirot sighed. "So many people think of murder as a game. It is not a game. I told her so. But she would not listen."

"No, we know that. Well, that fits in fairly well. When young Robin started off with Mrs. Oliver and ran back into the house his mother had just finished telephoning to someone. She wouldn't say who to. Played it mysterious. Robin and Mrs. Oliver thought it might be *you*."

"I wish it had been," said Hercule Poirot. "You have no idea to whom it was that she telephoned?"

"None whatever. It's all automatic round here, you know."

"The maid couldn't help you in any way?"

"No. She came in about half-past ten—she has a key to the back door. She went straight into her own room which leads off the kitchen and went to bed. The house was dark and she assumed that Mrs. Upward had gone to bed and that the others had not yet returned."

135

Spence added:

"She's deaf and pretty crotchety as well. Takes very little notice of what goes on—and I imagine does as little work as she can with as much grumbling as possible."

"Not really an old faithful?"

"Oh no! She's only been with the Upwards a couple of years."

A constable put his head round the door.

"There's a young lady to see you, sir," he said. "Says there's something perhaps you ought to know. About last night."

"About last night? Send her in."

Deirdre Henderson came in. She looked pale and strained and, as usual, rather awkward.

"I thought perhaps I'd better come," she said. "If I'm not interrupting you or anything," she added apologetically.

"Not at all, Miss Henderson."

Spence rose and pushed forward a chair. She sat down on it squarely in an ungainly schoolgirlish sort of way.

"Something about last night?" said Spence encouragingly. "About Mrs. Upward, you mean?"

"Yes, it's true, isn't it, that she was murdered? I mean the post said so and the baker. Mother said of course it couldn't be true——" She stopped.

"I'm afraid your mother isn't quite right there. It's true enough. Now, you wanted to make a—to tell us something?"

Deirdre nodded.

"Yes," she said. "You see, I was there."

A difference crept into Spence's manner. It was, perhaps, even more gentle, but an official hardness underlay it.

"You were there," he said. "At Laburnums. At what time?"

"I don't know exactly," said Deirdre. "Between half-past eight and nine, I suppose. Probably nearly nine. After dinner, anyway. You see, she telephoned to me."

"Mrs. Upward telephoned to you?"

"Yes. She said Robin and Mrs. Oliver were going to the theatre in Cullenquay and that she would be all alone and would I come along and have coffee with her."

"And you went?"

"Yes."

"And you—had coffee with her?"

136

Deirdre shook her head.

"No, I got there—and I knocked. But there wasn't any answer. So I opened the door and went into the hall. It was quite dark and I'd seen from outside that there was no light in the sitting-room. So I was puzzled. I called 'Mrs. Upward' once or twice but there was no answer. So I thought there must be some mistake."

"What mistake did you think there could have been?"

"I thought perhaps she'd gone to the theatre with them after all."

"Without letting you know?"

"That did seem queer."

"You couldn't think of any other explanation?"

"Well, I thought perhaps Frieda might have bungled the original message. She does get things wrong sometimes. She's a foreigner. She was excited herself last night because she was leaving."

"What did you do, Miss Henderson?"

"I just went away."

"Back home?"

"Yes—that is, I went for a little walk first. It was quite fine."

Spence was silent for a moment or two, looking at her. He was looking, Poirot noticed, at her mouth.

Presently he roused himself and said briskly:

"Well, thank you, Miss Henderson. You were quite right to come and tell us this. We're much obliged to you."

He got up and shook hands with her.

"I thought I ought to," said Deirdre. "Mother didn't want me to."

"Didn't she now?"

"But I thought I'd better."

"Quite right."

He showed her out and came back.

He sat down, drummed on the table and looked at Poirot.

"No lipstick," he said. "Or is that only this morning?"

"No, it is not only this morning. She never uses it."

"That's odd, nowadays, isn't it?"

"She is rather an odd kind of girl—undeveloped."

"And no scent, either, as far as I could smell. That Mrs. Oliver says there was a distinct smell of scent—expensive

137

scent, she says—in the house last night. Robin Upward confirms that. It wasn't any scent his mother uses."

"This girl would not use scent, I think," said Poirot.

"I shouldn't think so either," said Spence. "Looks rather like the hockey captain from an old-fashioned girls' school —but she must be every bit of thirty, I should say."

"Quite that."

"Arrested development, would you say?"

Poirot considered. Then he said it was not quite so simple as that.

"It doesn't fit," said Spence frowning. "No lipstick, no scent. And since she's got a perfectly good mother, and Lily Gamboll's mother was done in in a drunken brawl in Cardiff when Lily Gamboll was nine years old, I don't see how she can be Lily Gamboll. *But*—Mrs. Upward telephoned her to come there last night—you can't get away from that." He rubbed his nose. "It isn't straightforward going."

"What about the medical evidence?"

"Not much help there. All the police surgeon will say definitely is that she was probably dead by half-past nine."

"So she may have been dead when Deirdre Henderson came to Laburnums?"

"Probably was if the girl is speaking the truth. Either she *is* speaking the truth—or else she's a deep one. Mother didn't want her to come to us, she said. Anything there?"

Poirot considered.

"Not particularly. It is what mother would say. She is the type, you comprehend, that avoids unpleasantness."

Spence sighed.

"So we've got Deirdre Henderson—on the spot. Or else someone who came there before Deirdre Henderson. A woman. A woman who uses lipstick and expensive scent."

Poirot murmured: "You will inquire——"

Spence broke in.

"I'm inquiring! Just tactfully for the moment. We don't want to alarm anyone. What was Eve Carpenter doing last night? What was Shelagh Rendell doing last night? Ten to one they were just sitting at home. Carpenter, I know, had a political meeting."

"Eve," said Poirot thoughtfully. "The fashions in names
138

change, do they not. Hardly ever, nowadays, do you hear of an Eva. It has gone out. But Eve, it is popular."

"She can afford expensive scent," said Spence, pursuing his own train of thought.

He sighed.

"We've got to get at more of her background. It's so convenient to be a war widow. You can turn up anywhere looking pathetic and mourning some brave young airman. Nobody likes to ask you questions."

He turned to another subject.

"That sugar hammer or what-not you sent along—I think you've hit the bull's-eye. It's the weapon used in the McGinty murder. Doctor agrees it's exactly suitable for the type of blow. And there has been blood on it. It was washed, of course—but they don't realise nowadays that a microscopic amount of blood will give a reaction with the latest reagents. Yes, it's human blood all right. And that again ties up with the Wetherbys and the Henderson girl. Or doesn't it?"

"Deirdre Henderson was quite definite that the sugar hammer went to the Harvest Festival Bring and Buy."

"And Mrs. Summerhayes was equally positive it was the Christmas one?"

"Mrs. Summerhayes is never positive about anything," said Poirot gloomily. "She is a charming person, but she has no order or method in her composition. But I will tell you this—I who have lived at Long Meadows—the doors and the windows they are always open. Anyone—anyone at all, could come and take something away and later come and put it back and neither Major Summerhayes nor Mrs. Summerhayes would notice. If it is not there one day, she thinks that her husband has taken it to joint a rabbit or to chop wood—and he, he would think she had taken it to chop dogmeat. In that house nobody uses the right implements—they just seize what is at hand and leave it in the wrong place. And nobody remembers anything. If I were to live like that I should be in a continual state of anxiety—but they—they do not seem to mind."

Spence sighed.

"Well—there's one good thing about all this—they won't execute James Bentley until this business is all cleared up.

We've forwarded a letter to the Home Secretary's office. It gives us what we've been wanting—time."

"I think," said Poirot, "that I would like to see Bentley again—now that we know a little more."

11

There was little change in James Bentley. He was, perhaps, rather thinner, his hands were more restless—otherwise he was the same quiet, hopeless creature.

Hercule Poirot spoke carefully. There had been some fresh evidence. The police were re-opening the case. There was, therefore, hope . . .

But James Bentley was not attracted by hope.

He said:

"It will be all no good. What more can they find out?"

"Your friends," said Hercule Poirot, "are working very hard."

"My friends?" He shrugged his shoulders. "I have no friends."

"You should not say that. You have, at the very least, two friends."

"Two friends? I should like to know who they are."

His tone expressed no wish for the information, merely a weary disbelief.

"First, there is Superintendent Spence——"

"Spence? Spence? The police superintendent who worked up the case against me? That's almost funny."

"It is not funny. It is fortunate. Spence is a very shrewd and conscientious police officer. He likes to be very sure that he has got the right man."

"He's sure enough of that."

"Oddly enough, he is not. That is why, as I said, he is your friend."

"That kind of a friend!"

Hercule Poirot waited. Even James Bentley, he thought, must have some human attributes. Even James Bentley could not be completely devoid of ordinary human curiosity.

And true enough, presently James Bentley said:

"Well, who's the other?"

"The other is Maude Williams."

Bentley did not appear to react.

"Maude Williams? Who is she?"

"She worked in the office of Breather & Scuttle."

"Oh—that Miss Williams."

"*Précisément,* that Miss Williams."

"But what's it got to do with her?"

There were moments when Hercule Poirot found the personality of James Bentley so irritating that he heartily wished that he could believe Bentley guilty of Mrs. McGinty's murder. Unfortunately the more Bentley annoyed him, the more he came round to Spence's way of thinking. He found it more and more difficult to envisage Bentley's murdering anybody. James Bentley's attitude to murder would have been, Poirot felt sure, that it wouldn't be much good anyway. If cockiness, as Spence insisted, was a characteristic of murderers, Bentley was certainly no murderer.

Containing himself, Poirot said:

"Miss Williams interests herself in this affair. She is convinced you are innocent."

"I don't see what she can know about it."

"She knows *you.*"

James Bentley blinked. He said, grudgingly:

"I suppose she does, in a way, but not well."

"You worked together in the office, did you not? You had, sometimes, meals together?"

"Well—yes—once or twice. The Blue Cat Café, it's very convenient—just across the street."

"Did you never go for walks with her?"

"As a matter of fact we did, once. We walked up on the downs."

Hercule Poirot exploded.

"*Ma foi,* is it a crime that I seek to drag from you? To keep the company with a pretty girl, is it not natural? Is it not enjoyable? Can you not be pleased with yourself about it?"

"I don't see why," said James Bentley.

"At your age it is natural and right to enjoy the company of girls."

"I don't know many girls."

"*Ça se voit!* But you should be ashamed of that, not smug!

141

You knew Miss Williams. You worked with her and talked with her and sometimes had meals with her, and once went for a walk on the downs. And when I mention her, you do not even remember her name!"

James Bentley flushed.

"Well, you see—I've never had much to do with girls. And she isn't quite what you'd call a lady, is she? Oh very nice—and all that—but I can't help feeling that Mother would have thought her common."

"It is what *you* think that matters."

Again James Bentley flushed.

"Her hair," he said. "And the kind of clothes she wears—Mother, of course, was old-fashioned——"

He broke off.

"But you found Miss Williams—what shall I say—sympathetic?"

"She was always very kind," said James Bentley slowly. "But she didn't—really—*understand*. Her mother died when she was only a child, you see."

"And then you lost your job," said Poirot. "You couldn't get another. Miss Williams met you once at Broadhinny, I understand?"

James Bentley looked distressed.

"Yes—yes. She was coming over there on business and she sent me a post-card. Asked me to meet her. I can't think why. It isn't as if I knew her at all well."

"But you did meet her?"

"Yes. I didn't want to be rude."

"And you took her to the pictures or a meal?"

James Bentley looked scandalised.

"Oh no. Nothing of that kind. We—er—just talked whilst she was waiting for her bus."

"Ah, how amusing that must have been for the poor girl!"

James Bentley said sharply:

"I hadn't got any money. You must remember that. I hadn't any money at all."

"Of course. It was a few days before Mrs. McGinty was killed, wasn't it?"

James Bentley nodded. He said unexpectedly:

"Yes, it was on the Monday. She was killed on Wednesday."

142

"I'm going to ask you something else, Mr. Bentley. Mrs. McGinty took the *Sunday Comet*."

"Yes, she did."

"Did you ever see her *Sunday Comet*?"

"She used to offer it sometimes, but I didn't often accept. Mother didn't care for that kind of paper."

"So you didn't see that week's *Sunday Comet*?"

"No."

"And Mrs. McGinty didn't speak about it, or about anything in it?"

"Oh yes, she did," said James Bentley unexpectedly. "She was full of it!"

"Ah la la. So she was full of it. And what did she say? Be careful. This is important."

"I don't remember very well now. It was all about some old murder case. Craig, I think it was—no, perhaps it wasn't Craig. Anyway, she said somebody connected with the case was living in Broadhinny now. Full of it, she was. I couldn't see why it mattered to her."

"Did she say who it was—in Broadhinny?"

James Bentley said vaguely:

"I think it was that woman whose son writes plays."

"She mentioned her by name?"

"No—I—really it's so long ago——"

"I implore you—try to think. You want to be free again, do you not?"

"Free?" Bentley sounded surprised.

"Yes, free."

"I—yes—I suppose I do——"

"Then *think*! *What did Mrs. McGinty say?*"

"Well—something like—'so pleased with herself as she is and so proud. Not so much to be proud of if all's known.' And then, 'You'd never think it was the same woman to look at the photograph.' But of course it had been taken years ago."

"But what made you sure that it was Mrs. Upward of whom she was speaking?"

"I really don't know. . . . . I just formed the impression. She had been speaking of Mrs. Upward—and then I lost interest and didn't listen, and afterwards—well, now I come to think of it, I don't really know who she was speaking about. She talked a lot, you know."

Poirot sighed.

He said: "I do not think myself that it was Mrs. Upward of whom she spoke. I think it was somebody else. It is preposterous to reflect that if you are hanged it will be because you do not pay proper attention to the people with whom you converse. . . . Did Mrs. McGinty speak much to you of the houses where she worked, or the ladies of those houses?"

"Yes, in a way—but it's no good asking me. You don't seem to realise, M. Poirot, that I had my own life to think of at that time. I was in very serious anxiety."

"Not in so much serious anxiety as you are now! Did Mrs. McGinty speak of Mrs. Carpenter—Mrs. Selkirk she was then—or of Mrs. Rendell?"

"Carpenter has that new house at the top of the hill and a big car, hasn't he? He was engaged to Mrs. Selkirk—Mrs. McGinty was always very down on Mrs. Selkirk. I don't know why. 'Jumped up,' that's what she used to call her. I don't know what she meant by it."

"And the Rendells?"

"He's the doctor, isn't he? I don't remember her saying anything particular about them."

"And the Wetherbys?"

"I do remember what she said about them." James Bentley looked pleased with himself. " 'No patience with her fusses and her fancies,' that's what she said. And about him, 'Never a word, good or bad, out of him.' " He paused. "She said—it was an unhappy house."

Hercule Poirot looked up. For a second James Bentley's voice had held something that Poirot had not heard in it before. He was not repeating obediently what he could recall. His mind, for a very brief space, had moved out of its apathy. James Bentley was thinking of Hunter's Close, of the life that went on there, of whether or not it was an unhappy house. James Bentley was thinking objectively.

Poirot said softly:

"You knew them? The mother? The father? The daughter?"

"Not really. It was the dog. A Sealyham. It got caught in a trap. She couldn't get it undone. I helped her."

144

There was again something new in Bentley's tone. "I helped her," he had said, and in those words was a faint echo of pride.

Poirot remembered what Mrs. Oliver had told him of her conversation with Deirdre Henderson.

He said gently:

"You talked together?"

"Yes. She—her mother suffered a lot, she told me. She was very fond of her mother."

"And you told her about yours?"

"Yes," said James Bentley simply.

Poirot said nothing. He waited.

"Life is very cruel," said James Bentley. "Very unfair. Some people never seem to get any happiness."

"It is possible," said Hercule Poirot.

"I don't think she had had much. Miss Wetherby."

"Henderson."

"Oh yes. She told me she had a stepfather."

"Deirdre Henderson," said Poirot. "Deirdre of the Sorrows. A pretty name—but not a pretty girl, I understand?"

James Bentley flushed.

"I thought," he said, "she was rather good-looking . . ."

CHAPTER XIX

"Now just you listen to me," said Mrs. Sweetiman.

Edna sniffed. She had been listening to Mrs. Sweetiman for some time. It had been a hopeless conversation, going round in circles. Mrs. Sweetiman had said the same things several times, varying the phraseology a little, but even that not much. Edna had sniffed and occasionally blubbered and had reiterated her own two contributions to the discussion: first, that she couldn't ever! Second, that Dad would skin her alive, he would.

"That's as may be," said Mrs. Sweetiman, "but murder's murder, and what you saw you saw, and you can't get away from it."

Edna sniffed.

'And what you did ought to do——"

Mrs. Sweetiman broke off and attended to Mrs. Wetherby, who had come in for some knitting pins and another ounce of wool.

"Haven't seen you about for some time, ma'am," said Mrs. Sweetiman brightly.

"No, I've been very far from well lately," said Mrs. Wetherby. "My heart, you know." She sighed deeply. "I have to lie up a great deal."

"I heard as you've got some help at last," said Mrs. Sweetiman. "You'll want dark needles for this light wool."

"Yes. Quite capable as far as she goes, and cooks not at all badly. But her manners! And her appearance! Dyed hair and the most unsuitable tight jumpers."

"Ah," said Mrs. Sweetiman. "Girls aren't trained proper to service nowadays. My mother, she started at thirteen and she got up at a quarter to five every morning. Head housemaid she was when she finished, and three maids under her. And she trained them proper, too. But there's none of that nowadays—girls aren't trained nowadays, they're just educated, like Edna."

Both women looked at Edna, who leant against the post office counter, sniffing and sucking a peppermint, and looking particularly vacant. As an example of education, she hardly did the educational system credit.

"Terrible about Mrs. Upward, wasn't it?" continued Mrs. Sweetiman conversationally, as Mrs. Wetherby sorted through various coloured needles.

"Dreadful," said Mrs. Wetherby. "They hardly dared tell me. And when they did, I had the most frightful palpitations. I'm so sensitive."

"Shock to all of us, it was," said Mrs. Sweetiman. "As for young Mr. Upward, he took on something terrible. Had her hands full with him, the authoress lady did, until the doctor came and give him a seddytiff or something. He's gone up to Long Meadows now as a paying guest, felt he couldn't stay in the cottage—and I don't know as I blame him. Janet Groom, she's gone home to her niece and the police have got the key. The lady what writes the murder books has gone back to London, but she'll come down for the inquest."

Mrs. Sweetiman imparted all this information with relish.

She prided herself on being well informed. Mrs. Wetherby, whose desire for knitting needles had perhaps been prompted by a desire to know what was going on, paid for her purchase.

"It's most upsetting," she said. "It makes the whole village so *dangerous*. There must be a maniac about. When I think that my own dear daughter was out that night, that she herself might have been attacked, perhaps killed." Mrs. Wetherby closed both eyes and swayed on her feet. Mrs. Sweetiman watched her with interest, but without alarm. Mrs. Wetherby opened her eyes again, and said with dignity:

"This place should be patrolled. No young people should go about after dark. And all doors should be locked and bolted. You know that up at Long Meadows, Mrs. Summerhayes never locks *any* of her doors. Not even at *night*. She leaves the back door and the drawing-room window open so that the dogs and cats can get in and out. I myself consider that is absolute madness, but she says they've always done it and that if burglars want to get in, they always can."

"Reckon there wouldn't be much for a burglar to take up at Long Meadows," said Mrs. Sweetiman.

Mrs. Wetherby shook her head sadly and departed with her purchase.

Mrs. Sweetiman and Edna resumed their argument.

"It's no good your setting yourself up to know best," said Mrs. Sweetiman. "Right's right and murder's murder. Tell the truth and shame the devil. That's what I say."

"Dad would skin me alive, he would, for sure," said Edna.

"I'd talk to your dad," said Mrs. Sweetiman.

"I couldn't ever," said Edna.

"Mrs. Upward's dead," said Mrs. Sweetiman. "And you saw something the police don't know about. You're employed in the post office, aren't you? You're a Government servant. You've got to do your duty. You've got to go along to Bert Hayling——"

Edna's sobs burst out anew.

"Not to Bert, I couldn't. However could I go to Bert? It'd be all over the place."

Mrs. Sweetiman said rather hesitantly:

"There's that foreign gentleman——"

147

"Not a foreigner, I couldn't. Not a foreigner."

"No, maybe you're right there."

A car drew up outside the post office with a squealing of brakes.

Mrs. Sweetiman's face lit up.

"That's Major Summerhayes, that is. You tell it all to him and he'll advise you what to do."

"I couldn't ever," said Edna, but with less conviction.

Johnnie Summerhayes came into the post office, staggering under the burden of three cardboard boxes.

"Good morning, Mrs. Sweetiman," he said cheerfully. "Hope these aren't overweight?"

Mrs. Sweetiman attended to the parcels in her official capacity. As Summerhayes was licking the stamps, she spoke.

"Excuse me, sir, I'd like your advice about something."

"Yes, Mrs. Sweetiman?"

"Seeing as you belong here, sir, and will know best what to do."

Summerhayes nodded. He was always curiously touched by the lingering feudal spirit of English villages. The villagers knew little of him personally, but because his father and his grandfather and many great-great-grandfathers had lived at Long Meadows, they regarded it as natural that he should advise and direct when asked so to do.

"It's about Edna here," said Mrs. Sweetiman.

Edna sniffed.

Johnnie Summerhayes looked at Edna doubtfully. Never, he thought, had he seen a more unprepossessing girl. Exactly like a skinned rabbit. Seemed half-witted too. Surely she couldn't be in what was known officially as "trouble." But no, Mrs. Sweetiman would not have come to him for advice in that case.

"Well," he said kindly, "what's the difficulty?"

"It's about the murder, sir. The night of the murder. Edna saw something."

Johnnie Summerhayes transferred his quick dark gaze from Edna to Mrs. Sweetiman and back again to Edna.

"What did you see, Edna?" he said.

Edna began to sob. Mrs. Sweetiman took over.

"Of course we've been hearing this and that. Some's rumour and some's true. But it's said definite as that there

148

were a lady there that night who drank coffee with Mrs. Upward. That's so, isn't it, sir?"

"Yes, I believe so."

"I know as that's true, because we had it from Bert Hayling."

Albert Hayling was the local constable whom Summerhayes knew well. A slow-speaking man with a sense of his own importance.

"I see," said Summerhayes.

"But they don't know, do they, who the lady is? Well, Edna here *saw* her."

Johnnie Summerhayes looked at Edna. He pursed his lips as though to whistle.

"You saw her, did you, Edna? Going in—or coming out?"

"Going in," said Edna. A faint sense of importance loosened her tongue. "Across the road I was, under the trees. Just by the turn of the lane where it's dark. I saw her. She went in at the gate and up to the door and she stood there a bit, and then—and then she went in."

Johnnie Summerhayes' brow cleared.

"That's all right," he said. "It was Miss Henderson. The police know all about that. She went and told them."

Edna shook her head.

"It wasn't Miss Henderson," she said.

"It wasn't—then who was it?"

"I dunno. I didn't see her face. Had her back to me, she had, going up the path and standing there. But it wasn't Miss Henderson."

"But how do you know it wasn't Miss Henderson if you didn't see her face?"

"Because she had fair hair. Miss Henderson's is dark."

Johnnie Summerhayes looked disbelieving.

"It was a very dark night. You'd hardly be able to see the colour of anyone's hair."

"But I did, though. That light was on over the porch. Left like that, it was, because Mr. Robin and the detective lady had gone out together to the theatre. And she was standing right under it. A dark coat she had on, and no hat, and her hair was shining fair as could be. I saw it."

Johnnie gave a slow whistle. His eyes were serious now.

"What time was it?" he asked.

149

Edna sniffed.

"I don't rightly know."

"You know about what time," said Mrs. Sweetiman.

"It wasn't nine o'clock. I'd have heard the church. And it was after half-past eight."

"Between half-past eight and nine. How long did she stop?"

"I dunno, sir. Because I didn't wait no longer. And I didn't hear nothing. No groans or cries or nothing like that." Edna sounded slightly aggrieved.

But there would have been no groans and no cries. Johnnie Summerhayes knew that. He said gravely:

"Well, there's only one thing to be done. The police have got to hear about this."

Edna burst into long sniffling sobs.

"Dad'll skin me alive," she whimpered. "He will, for sure."

She cast an imploring look at Mrs. Sweetiman and bolted into the back room. Mrs. Sweetiman took over with competence.

"It's like this, sir," she said in answer to Summerhayes' inquiring glance. "Edna's been behaving very foolish like. Very strict her dad is, maybe a bit over strict, but it's hard to say what's best nowadays. There's a nice young fellow over to Cullavon and he and Edna have been going together nice and steady, and her dad was quite pleased about it, but Reg he's on the slow side, and you know what girls are. Edna's taken up lately with Charlie Masters."

"Masters? One of Farmer Cole's men, isn't he?"

"That's right, sir. Farm labourer. And a married man with two children. Always after the girls, he is, and a bad fellow in every way. Edna hasn't got any sense, and her dad, he put a stop to it. Quite right. So, you see, Edna was going into Cullavon that night to go to the pictures with Reg—at least that's what she told her dad. But really she went out to meet this Masters. Waited for him, she did, at the turn of the lane where it seems they used to meet. Well, he didn't come. Maybe his wife kept him at home, or maybe he's after another girl, but there it is. Edna waited but at last she gave up. But it's awkward for her, as you can see, explaining what she was doing there, when she ought to have taken the bus into Cullavon."

150

Johnnie Summerhayes nodded. Suppressing an irrelevant feeling of wonder that the unprepossessing Edna could have sufficient sex appeal to attract the attention of two men, he dealt with the practical aspect of the situation.

"She doesn't want to go to Bert Hayling about it," he said with quick comprehension.

"That's right, sir."

Summerhayes reflected rapidly.

"I'm afraid the police have got to know," he said gently.

"That's what I told her, sir," said Mrs. Sweetiman.

"But they will probably be quite tactful about—er—the circumstances. Possibly she mayn't have to give evidence. And what she tells them, they'll keep to themselves. I could ring up Spence and ask him to come over here—no, better still, I'll take young Edna into Kilchester with me in my car. If she goes to the police station there, nobody here need know anything about it. I'll just ring them up first and warn them we're coming."

And so, after a brief telephone call, the sniffing Edna, buttoned firmly into her coat and encouraged by a pat on the back from Mrs. Sweetiman, stepped into the station wagon and was driven rapidly away in the direction of Kilchester.

CHAPTER XX

HERCULE POIROT was in Superintendent Spence's office in Kilchester. He was leaning back in a chair, his eyes closed and the tips of his fingers just touching each other in front of him.

The superintendent received some reports, gave instructions to a sergeant, and finally looked across at the other man.

"Getting a brainwave, M. Poirot?" he demanded.

"I reflect," said Poirot. "I review."

"I forgot to ask you. Did you get anything useful from James Bentley when you saw him?"

Poirot shook his head. He frowned.

It was indeed of James Bentley he had been thinking.

It was annoying, thought Poirot with exasperation, that

on a case such as this where he had offered his services without reward, solely out of friendship and respect for an upright police officer, that the victim of circumstances should so lack any romantic appeal. A lovely young girl, now, bewildered and innocent, or a fine upstanding young man, also bewildered, but whose "head is bloody but unbowed," thought Poirot, who had been reading a good deal of English poetry in an anthology lately. Instead, he had James Bentley, a pathological case if there ever was one, a self-centred creature who had never thought much of anyone but himself. A man ungrateful for the efforts that were being made to save him—almost, one might say, uninterested in them.

Really, thought Poirot, one might as well let him be hanged since he does not seem to care. . . .

No, he would not go quite as far as that.

Superintendent Spence's voice broke into these reflections.

"Our interview," said Poirot, "was, if I might say so, singularly unproductive. Anything useful that Bentley might have remembered he did not remember—what he did remember is so vague and uncertain that one cannot build upon it. But at any rate it seems fairly certain that Mrs. McGinty was excited by the article in the *Sunday Comet* and spoke about it to Bentley with special reference to 'someone connected with the case,' living in Broadhinny."

"With which case?" asked Superintendent Spence sharply.

"Our friend could not be sure," said Poirot. "He said, rather doubtfully, the Craig case—but the Craig case being the only one he had ever heard of, it would, presumably, be the only one he could remember. But the 'someone' was a woman. He even quoted Mrs. McGinty's words. Somebody who had 'not so much to be proud of if all's known.'"

"*Proud?*"

"*Mais oui,*" Poirot nodded his appreciation. "A suggestive word, is it not?"

"No clue as to who the proud lady was?"

"Bentley suggested Mrs. Upward—but as far as I can see for no real reason!"

Spence shook his head.

"Probably because she was a proud masterful sort of woman—outstandingly so, I should say. But it couldn't have been Mrs. Upward, because Mrs. Upward's dead, and dead for the same reason as Mrs. McGinty died—because she recognised a photograph."

Poirot said sadly: "I warned her."

Spence murmured irritably:

"Lily Gamboll! So far as age goes, there are only two possibilities, Mrs. Rendell and Mrs. Carpenter. I don't count the Henderson girl—she's got a background."

"And the others have not?"

Spence sighed.

"You know what things are nowadays. The war stirred up everyone and everything. The approved school where Lily Gamboll was, and all its records, were destroyed by a direct hit. Then take people. It's the hardest thing in the world to check on people. Take Broadhinny—the only people in Broadhinny we know anything about are the Summerhayes family, who have been there for three hundred years, and Guy Carpenter, who's one of the engineering Carpenters. All the others are—what shall I say—fluid? Dr. Rendell's on the Medical Register and we know where he trained and where he's practised, but we don't know his home background. His wife came from near Dublin. Eve Selkirk, as she was before she married Guy Carpenter, was a pretty young war widow. Anyone can be a pretty young war widow. Take the Wetherbys—they seem to have floated round the world, here, there and everywhere. Why? Is there a reason? Did he embezzle from a bank? Or did they occasion a scandal? I don't say we can't dig up about people. We can—but it takes time. The people themselves won't help you."

"Because they have something to conceal—but it need not be murder," said Poirot.

"Exactly. It may be trouble with the law, or it may be a humble origin, or it may be common or garden scandal. But whatever it is, they've taken a lot of pains to cover up—and that makes it difficult to uncover."

"But not impossible."

"Oh no. Not impossible. It just takes time. As I say, if Lily Gamboll is in Broadhinny, she's *either* Eve Carpenter or Shelagh Rendell. I've questioned them—just routine—that's the way I put it. They say they were both at home—alone. Mrs. Carpenter was the wide-eyed innocent, Mrs.

Rendell was nervous—but then she's a nervous type, you can't go by that."

"Yes," said Poirot thoughtfully. "She is a nervous type."

He was thinking of Mrs. Rendell in the garden at Long Meadows. Mrs. Rendell had received an anonymous letter, or so she said. He wondered, as he had wondered before, about that statement.

Spence went on:

"And we have to be careful—because even if one of them *is* guilty, the other is innocent."

"And Guy Carpenter is a prospective Member of Parliament and an important local figure."

"That wouldn't help him if he was guilty of murder or accessory to it," said Spence grimly.

"I know that. But you have, have you not, to be *sure*?"

"That's right. Anyway you'll agree, won't you, that it lies between the two of them?"

Poirot sighed.

"No—no—I would not say that. There are other possibilities."

"Such as?"

Poirot was silent for a moment, then he said in a different, almost casual tone of voice:

"Why do people keep photographs?"

"Why? Goodness knows! Why do people keep all sorts of things—junk—trash, bits and pieces. They do—that's all there is to it!"

"Up to a point I agree with you. Some people keep things. Some people throw everything away as soon as they have done with it. That, yes, it is a matter of temperament. But I speak now especially of photographs. Why do people keep, in particular, *photographs*?"

"As I say, because they just don't throw things away. Or else because it reminds them——"

Poirot pounced on the words.

"Exactly. *It reminds them*. Now again we ask—why? *Why* does a woman keep a photograph of herself when young? And I say that the first reason is, essentially, vanity. She has been a pretty girl and she keeps a photograph of herself to remind her of what a pretty girl she was. It encourages her when her mirror tells her unpalatable things. She says, per-

154

haps, to a friend, 'That was me when I was eighteen . . .' and she sighs. . . . You agree?"

"Yes—yes, I should say that's true enough."

"Then that is reason No. 1. Vanity. Now reason No. 2. Sentiment."

"That's the same thing?"

"No, no, not quite. Because this leads you to preserve not only your own photograph but that of someone else. . . . A picture of your married daughter—when she was a child sitting on a hearthrug with tulle round her."

"I've seen some of those," Spence grinned.

"Yes. Very embarrassing to the subject sometimes, but mothers like to do it. And sons and daughters often keep pictures of their mothers, especially, say, if their mother died young. 'This was my mother as a girl.' "

"I'm beginning to see what you're driving at, Poirot."

"And there is, possibly, a *third* category. Not vanity, not sentiment, not love—perhaps *hate*—what do you say?"

"Hate?"

"Yes. To keep a desire for revenge alive. Someone who has injured you—you might keep a photograph to remind you. might you not?"

"But surely that doesn't apply in this case?"

"Does it not?"

"What are you thinking of?"

Poirot murmured:

"Newspaper reports are often inaccurate. The *Sunday Comet* stated that Eva Kane was employed by the Craigs as a nursery governess. Was that actually the case?"

"Yes, it was. But we're working on the assumption that it's Lily Gamboll we're looking for."

Poirot sat up suddenly very straight in his chair. He wagged an imperative forefinger at Spence.

"Look. Look at the photograph of Lily Gamboll. She is not pretty—no! Frankly, with those teeth and those spectacles she is hideously ugly. Then nobody has kept that photograph for the first of our reasons. No woman would keep that photo out of vanity. If Eve Carpenter or Shelagh Rendell, who are both good-looking women, especially Eve Carpenter, had this photograph of themselves, they would tear it in pieces quickly in case somebody should see it!"

155

"Well, there is something in that."

"So reason No. 1 is out. Now take sentiment. Did anybody love Lily Gamboll at that age? The whole point of Lily Gamboll is that they did not. She was an unwanted and unloved child. The person who liked her best was her aunt, and her aunt died under the chopper. So it was not sentiment that kept this picture. And revenge? Nobody hated her either. Her murdered aunt was a lonely woman without a husband and with no close friends. Nobody had hate for the little slum child—only pity."

"Look here, M. Poirot, what you're saying is that *nobody* would have kept that photo."

"Exactly—that is the result of my reflections."

"But somebody did. Because Mrs. Upward had seen it."

"*Had she?*"

"Dash it all. It was you who told me. She said so herself."

"Yes, she said so," said Poirot. "But the late Mrs. Upward was, in some ways, a secretive woman. She liked to manage things her own way. I showed the photographs and she recognised one of them. But then, for some reason, she wanted to keep the identification to herself. She wanted, let us say, to deal with a certain situation in the way she fancied. And so, being very quick-witted, she deliberately pointed to the *wrong* picture. Thereby keeping her knowledge to herself."

"But why?"

"Because, as I say, she wanted to play a lone hand."

"It wouldn't be blackmail? She was an extremely wealthy woman, you know, widow of a North Country manufacturer."

"Oh no, not blackmail. More likely beneficence. We'll say that she quite liked the person in question, and that she didn't want to give their secret away. But nevertheless she was *curious*. She intended to have a private talk with that person. And whilst doing so, to make up her mind whether or not that person had had anything to do with the death of Mrs. McGinty. Something like that."

"Then that leaves the other three photos in?"

"Precisely. Mrs. Upward meant to get in touch with the person in question at the first opportunity. That came when

156

her son and Mrs. Oliver went over to the Repertory Theatre at Cullenquay."

"*And she telephoned to Deirdre Henderson.* That puts Deirdre Henderson right back in the picture. *And* her mother!"

Superintendent Spence shook his head sadly at Poirot.

"You do like to make it difficult, don't you, M. Poirot?" he said.

CHAPTER XXI

MRS. WETHERBY walked back home from the post office with a gait surprisingly spry in one habitually reported to be an invalid.

Only when she had entered the front door did she once more shuffle feebly into the drawing-room and collapse on the sofa.

The bell was within reach of her hand and she rang it.

Since nothing happened she rang it again, this time keeping her finger on it for some time.

In due course Maude Williams appeared. She was wearing a flowered overall and had a duster in her hand.

"Did you ring, madam?"

"I rang twice. When I ring I expect someone to come at once. I might be dangerously ill."

"I'm sorry, madam. I was upstairs."

"I know you were. You were in my room. I heard you overhead. And you were pulling the drawers in and out. I can't think why. It's no part of your job to go prying into my things."

"I wasn't prying. I was putting some of the things you left lying about away tidily."

"Nonsense. All you people snoop. And I won't have it. I'm feeling very faint. Is Miss Deirdre in?"

"She took the dog for a walk."

"How stupid. She might know I would need her. Bring me an egg beaten up in milk and add a little brandy. The brandy is on the sideboard in the dining-room."

"There are only just the three eggs for breakfast tomorrow."

"Then someone will have to go without. Hurry, will you? Don't stand there looking at me. And you're wearing far too much make-up. It isn't suitable."

There was a bark in the hall and Deirdre and her Sealyham came in as Maude went out.

"I heard your voice," said Deirdre breathlessly. "What have you been saying to her?"

"Nothing."

"She looked like thunder."

"I put her in her place. Impertinent girl."

"Oh, Mummy darling, must you? It's so difficult to get anyone. And she does cook well."

"I suppose it's of no importance that she's insolent to *me*! Oh well, I shan't be with you much longer." Mrs. Wetherby rolled up her eyes and took some fluttering breaths. "I walked too far," she murmured.

"You oughtn't to have gone out, darling. Why didn't you tell me you were going?"

"I thought some air would do me good. It's so stuffy. It doesn't matter. One doesn't really want to live—not if one's only a trouble to people."

"You're not a trouble, darling. I'd die without you."

"You're a good girl—but I can see how I weary you and get on your nerves."

"You don't—you don't," said Deirdre passionately.

Mrs. Wetherby sighed and let her eyelids fall.

"I—can't talk much," she murmured. "I must just lie still."

"I'll hurry up Maude with the egg-nog."

Deirdre ran out of the room. In her hurry she caught her elbow on a table and a bronze god bumped to the ground.

"So clumsy," murmured Mrs. Wetherby to herself, wincing.

The door opened and Mr. Wetherby came in. He stood there for a moment. Mrs. Wetherby opened her eyes.

"Oh, it's you, Roger?"

"I wondered what all the noise was in here. It's impossible to read quietly in this house."

"It was just Deirdre, dear. She came in with the dog."

Mr. Wetherby stooped and picked up the bronze monstrosity from the floor.

"Surely Deirdre's old enough not to knock things down the whole time."

"She's just rather awkward."

"Well, it's absurd to be awkward at her age. And can't she keep that dog from barking?"

"I'll speak to her, Roger."

"If she makes her home here, she must consider our wishes and not behave as though the house belonged to her."

"Perhaps you'd rather she went away," murmured Mrs. Wetherby. Through half-closed eyes she watched her husband.

"No, of course not. Of course not. Naturally her home is with us. I only ask for a little more good sense and good manners." He added: "You've been out, Edith?"

"Yes. I just went down to the post office."

"No fresh news about poor Mrs. Upward?"

"The police still don't know who it was."

"They seem to be quite hopeless. Any motive? Who gets her money?"

"The son, I suppose."

"Yes—yes, then it really seems as though it must have been one of these tramps. You should tell this girl she's got to be careful about keeping the front door locked. And only to open it on the chain when it gets near dusk. These men are very daring and brutal nowadays."

"Nothing seems to have been taken from Mrs. Upward's."

"Odd."

"Not like Mrs. McGinty," said Mrs. Wetherby.

"Mrs. McGinty? Oh! the charwoman. What's Mrs. McGinty got to do with Mrs. Upward?"

"She did work for her, Roger."

"Don't be silly, Edith."

Mrs. Wetherby closed her eyes again. As Mr. Wetherby went out of the room she smiled to herself.

She opened her eyes with a start to find Maude standing over her, holding a glass.

"Your egg-nog, madam," said Maude.

Her voice was loud and clear. It echoed too resonantly in the deadened house.

Mrs. Wetherby looked up with a vague feeling of alarm.

How tall and unbending the girl was. She stood over Mrs.

159

Wetherby like—"like a figure of doom," Mrs. Wetherby thought to herself—and then wondered why such extraordinary words had come into her head.

She raised herself on her elbow and took the glass.

"Thank you, Maude," she said.

Maude turned and went out of the room.

Mrs. Wetherby still felt vaguely upset.

CHAPTER XXII

I

HERCULE POIROT took a hired car back to Broadhinny.

He was tired because he had been thinking. Thinking was always exhausting. And his thinking had not been entirely satisfactory. It was as though a pattern, perfectly visible, was woven into a piece of material and yet, although he was holding the piece of material, he could not see what the pattern was.

But it was all there. That was the point. It was all there. Only it was one of those patterns, self-coloured and subtle, that are not easy to perceive.

A little way out of Kilchester his car encountered the Summerhayes' station wagon coming in the opposite direction. Johnnie was driving and he had a passenger. Poirot hardly noticed them. He was still absorbed in thought.

When he got back to Long Meadows, he went into the drawing-room. He removed a colander full of spinach from the most comfortable chair in the room and sat down. From overhead came the faint drumming of a typewriter. It was Robin Upward, struggling with a play. Three versions he had already torn up, so he told Poirot. Somehow, he couldn't concentrate.

Robin might feel his mother's death quite sincerely, but he remained Robin Upward, chiefly interested in himself.

"Madre," he said solemnly, "would have wished me to go on with my work."

Hercule Poirot had heard many people say much the same thing. It was one of the most convenient assumptions, this knowledge of what the dead would wish. The bereaved had never any doubt about their dear ones' wishes and those wishes usually squared with their own inclinations.

In this case it was probably true. Mrs. Upward had had great faith in Robin's work and had been extremely proud of him.

Poirot leaned back and closed his eyes.

He thought of Mrs. Upward. He considered what Mrs. Upward had really been like. He remembered a phrase that he had once heard used by a police officer.

"We'll take him apart and see what makes him tick."

What had made Mrs. Upward tick?

There was a crash, and Maureen Summerhayes came in. Her hair was flapping madly.

"I can't think what's happened to Johnnie," she said. "He just went down to the post office with those special orders. He ought to have been back hours ago. I want him to fix the henhouse door."

A true gentleman, Poirot feared, would have gallantly offered to fix the henhouse door himself. Poirot did not. He wanted to go on thinking about two murders and about the character of Mrs. Upward.

"And I can't find that Ministry of Agriculture form," continued Maureen. "I've looked everywhere."

"The spinach is on the sofa," Poirot offered helpfully.

Maureen was not worried about spinach.

"The form came last week," she mused. "And I must have put it somewhere. Perhaps it was when I was darning that pullover of Johnnie's."

She swept over to the bureau and started pulling out the drawers. Most of the contents she swept on to the floor ruthlessly. It was agony to Hercule Poirot to watch her.

Suddenly she uttered a cry of triumph.

"Got it!"

Delightedly she rushed from the room.

Hercule Poirot sighed and resumed meditation.

To arrange, with order and precision——

He frowned. The untidy heap of objects on the floor by the bureau distracted his mind. What a way to look for things!

Order and method. That was the thing. Order and method.

Though he had turned sideways in his chair, he could still see the confusion on the floor. Sewing things, a pile of socks, letters, knitting wool, magazines, sealing wax, photographs, a pullover——

It was insupportable!

Poirot rose, went across to the bureau and with quick deft movements began to return the objects to the open drawers.

The pullover, the socks, the knitting wool. Then, in the next drawer, the sealing wax, the photographs, the letters.

The telephone rang.

The sharpness of the bell made him jump.

He went across to the telephone and lifted the receiver.

"'Allo, 'allo, 'allo," he said.

The voice that spoke to him was the voice of Superintendent Spence.

"Ah! it's you, M. Poirot. Just the man I want."

Spence's voice was almost unrecognisable. A very worried man had given place to a confident one.

"Filling me up with a lot of fandangle about the wrong photograph," he said with reproachful indulgence. "We've got some new evidence. Girl at the post office in Broadhinny. Major Summerhayes just brought her in. It seems she was standing practically opposite the cottage that night and she saw a woman go in. Sometime after eight-thirty and before nine o'clock. And it wasn't Deirdre Henderson. It was a woman with fair hair. That puts us right back where we were—it's definitely between the two of them—Eve Carpenter and Shelagh Rendell. The only question is—which?"

Poirot opened his mouth but did not speak. Carefully, deliberately, he replaced the receiver on the stand.

He stood there staring unseeingly in front of him.

The telephone rang again.

"'Allo! 'Allo! 'Allo!"

"Can I speak to M. Poirot, please?"

"Hercule Poirot speaking."

"Thought so. Maude Williams here. Post office in a quarter of an hour?"

"I will be there."

He replaced the receiver.

162

He looked down at his feet. Should he change his shoes? His feet ached a little. Ah well—no matter.

Resolutely Poirot clapped on his hat and left the house.

On his way down the hill he was hailed by one of Superintendent Spence's men just emerging from Laburnums.

"Morning, M. Poirot."

Poirot responded politely. He noticed that Sergeant Fletcher was looking excited.

"The Super sent me over to have a thorough check up," he explained. "You know—any little thing we might have missed. Never know, do you? We'd been over the desk, of course, but the Super got the idea there might be a secret drawer—must have been reading spy stuff. Well, there wasn't a secret drawer. But after that I got on to the books. Sometimes people slip a letter into a book they're reading. You know?"

Poirot said that he knew. "And you found something?" he asked politely.

"Not a letter or anything of that sort, no. But I found something interesting—at least *I* think it's interesting. Look here."

He unwrapped from a piece of newspaper an old and rather decrepit book.

"In one of the bookshelves it was. Old book, published years ago. But look here." He opened it and showed the flyleaf. Pencilled across it were the words: *Evelyn Hope*.

"Interesting, don't you think? That's the name, in case you don't remember——"

"The name that Eva Kane took when she left England. I do remember," said Poirot.

"Looks as though when Mrs. McGinty spotted one of those photos here in Broadhinny, it was our Mrs. Upward. Makes it kind of complicated, doesn't it?"

"It does," said Poirot with feeling. "I can assure you that when you go back to Superintendent Spence with this piece of information he will pull out his hair by the roots—yes, assuredly by the roots."

"I hope it won't be as bad as that," said Sergeant Fletcher.

Poirot did not reply. He went on down the hill. He had ceased to think. Nothing anywhere made sense.

He went into the post office. Maude Williams was there

looking at knitting patterns. Poirot did not speak to her. He went to the stamp counter. When Maude had made her purchase, Mrs. Sweetiman came over to him and he bought some stamps. Maude went out of the shop.

Mrs. Sweetiman seemed preoccupied and not talkative. Poirot was able to follow Maude out fairly quickly. He caught her up a short distance along the road and fell into step beside her.

Mrs. Sweetiman, looking out of the post office window, exclaimed to herself disapprovingly. "Those foreigners! All the same, every manjack of 'em. Old enough to be her grandfather, he is!"

I I

"*Eh bien,*" said Poirot, "you have something to tell me?"

"I don't know that it's important. There was somebody trying to get in at the window of Mrs. Wetherby's room."

"When?"

"This morning. *She'd* gone out, and the girl was out with the dog. Old frozen fish was shut up in his study as usual. I'd have been in the kitchen normally—it faces the other way like the study—but actually it seemed a good opportunity to—you understand?"

Poirot nodded.

"So I nipped upstairs and into Her Acidity's bedroom. There was a ladder against the window and a man was fumbling with the window catch. She's had everything locked and barred since the murder. Never a bit of fresh air. When the man saw me he scuttled down and made off. The ladder was the gardener's—he'd been cutting back the ivy and had gone to have his elevenses."

"Who was the man? Can you describe him?"

"I only got the merest glimpse. By the time I got to the window he was down the ladder and gone, and when I first saw him he was against the sun, so I couldn't see his face."

"You are sure it *was* a man?"

Maude considered.

"Dressed as a man—an old felt hat on. It *might* have been a woman, of course. . . ."

164

"It is interesting," said Poirot. "It is very interesting. . . . Nothing else?"

"Not yet. The junk that old woman keeps! Must be dotty! She came in without me hearing this morning and bawled me out for snooping. I shall be murdering her next. If anyone asks to be murdered that woman does. A really nasty bit of goods."

Poirot murmured softly:

"Evelyn Hope . . ."

"What's that?" She spun round on him.

"So you know that name?"

"Why—yes . . . It's the name Eva Whatsername took when she went to Australia. It—it was in the paper—the *Sunday Comet*."

"The *Sunday Comet* said many things, but it did not say that. The police found the name written in a book in Mrs. Upward's house."

Maude exclaimed:

"Then it *was* her—and she *didn't* die out there . . . Michael was right."

"Michael?"

Maude said abruptly:

"I can't stop. I'll be late serving lunch. I've got it all in the oven, but it will be getting dried up."

She started off at a run. Poirot stood looking after her.

At the post office window, Mrs. Sweetiman, her nose glued to the pane, wondered if that old foreigner had been making suggestions of a certain character. . . .

I I I

Back at Long Meadows, Poirot removed his shoes, and put on a pair of bedroom slippers. They were not *chic*, not in his opinion *comme il faut*—but there must be relief.

He sat down on the easy-chair again and began once more to think. He had by now a lot to think about.

There were things he had missed—little things.

The pattern was all there. It only needed cohesion.

Maureen, glass in hand, talking in a dreamy voice—asking a question. . . . Mrs. Oliver's account of her evening at the

Rep. Cecil? Michael? He was almost sure that she had mentioned a Michael—Eva Kane, nursery governess to the Craigs——

Evelyn Hope . . .

Of course! Evelyn Hope!

CHAPTER XXIII

1

EVE CARPENTER came into the Summerhayes' house in the casual way that most people did, using any door or window that was convenient.

She was looking for Hercule Poirot and when she found him she did not beat about the bush.

"Look here," she said. "You're a detective and you're supposed to be good. All right, I'll hire you."

"Suppose I am not for hire. *Mon Dieu,* I am not a taxi-cab!"

"You're a private detective and private detectives get paid, don't they?"

"It is the custom."

"Well, that's what I'm saying. I'll pay you. I'll pay you well."

"For what? What do you want me to do."

Eve Carpenter said sharply:

"Protect me against the police. They're crazy. They seem to think I killed the Upward woman. And they're nosing around, asking me all sorts of questions—ferreting out things. I don't like it. It's driving me mental."

Poirot looked at her. Something of what she said was true. She looked many years older than when he had first seen her a few weeks ago. Circles under her eyes spoke of sleepless nights. There were lines from her mouth to her chin, and her hand, when she lit a cigarette, shook badly.

"You've got to stop it," she said. "You've got to."

"Madame, what can I do?"

"Fend them off somehow or other. Damned cheek! If Guy

166

was a man he'd stop all this. He wouldn't let them persecute me."

"And—he does nothing?"

She said sullenly:

"I've not told him. He just talks pompously about giving the police all the assistance possible. It's all right for *him*. He was at some ghastly political meeting that night."

"And you?"

"I was just sitting at home. Listening to the radio actually."

"But, if you can prove that——"

"How can I prove it? I offered the Crofts a fabulous sum to say they'd been in and out and seen me there—the damned swine refused."

"That was a very unwise move on your part."

"I don't see why. It would have settled the business."

"You have probably convinced your servants that you did commit the murder."

"Well—I'd paid Croft anyway for——"

"For what?"

"Nothing."

"Remember—you want my help."

"Oh! it was nothing that matters. But Croft took the message from her."

"From Mrs. Upward?"

"Yes. Asking me to go down and see her that night."

"And you say you didn't go?"

"Why should I go? Damned dreary old woman. Why should I go and hold her hand? I never dreamed of going for a moment."

"When did this message come?"

"When I was out. I don't know exactly when—between five and six, I think. Croft took it."

"And you gave him money to forget he had taken that message. Why?"

"Don't be idiotic. I didn't want to get mixed up in it all."

"And then you offer him money to give you an alibi? What do you suppose he and his wife think?"

"Who cares what they think!"

"A jury may care," said Poirot gravely.

She stared at him.

"You're not serious?"

"I am serious."

"They'd listen to servants—and not to me?"

Poirot looked at her.

Such crass rudeness and stupidity! Antagonising the people who might have been helpful. A short-sighted stupid policy. Short-sighted——

Such lovely wide blue eyes.

He said quietly:

"Why don't you wear glasses, madame? You need them."

"What? Oh, I do sometimes. I did as a child."

"And you had then a plate for your teeth."

She stared.

"I did, as a matter of fact. Why all this?"

"The ugly duckling becomes the swan?"

"I was certainly ugly enough."

"Did your mother think so?"

She said sharply:

"I don't remember my mother. What the hell are we talking about anyway? Will you take on the job?"

"I regret I cannot."

"Why can't you?"

"Because in this affair I act for James Bentley."

"James Bentley? Oh, you mean that half-wit who killed the charwoman. What's he got to do with the Upwards?"

"Perhaps—nothing."

"Well, then! Is it a question of money? How much?"

"That is your great mistake, madame. You think always in terms of money. You have money and you think that only money counts."

"I haven't always had money," said Eve Carpenter.

"No," said Poirot. "I thought not." He nodded his head gently. "That explains a good deal. It excuses some things. . . ."

II

Eve Carpenter went out the way she had come, blundering a little in the light as Poirot remembered her doing before.

Poirot said softly to himself: "Evelyn Hope . . ."

168

So Mrs. Upward had rung up both Deirdre Henderson *and* Evelyn Carpenter. Perhaps she had rung up someone else. Perhaps——

With a crash Maureen came in.

"It's my scissors now. Sorry lunch is late. I've got three pairs and I can't find one of them."

She rushed over to the bureau and the process with which Poirot was well acquainted was repeated. This time, the objective was attained rather sooner. With a cry of joy, Maureen departed.

Almost automatically, Poirot stepped over and began to replace the things in the drawer. Sealing wax, notepaper, a work basket, photographs——

Photographs . . .

He stood staring at the photograph he held in his hand.

Footsteps rushed back along the passage.

Poirot could move quickly in spite of his age. He had dropped the photograph on the sofa, put a cushion on it, and had himself sat on the cushion, by the time that Maureen re-entered.

"Where the hell I've put a colander full of spinach——"

"But it is there, madame."

He indicated the colander as it reposed beside him on the sofa.

"So that's where I left it." She snatched it up. "Everything's behindhand to-day . . ." Her glance took in Hercule Poirot sitting bolt upright.

"What on earth do you want to sit there for? Even on a cushion, it's the most uncomfortable seat in the room. All the springs are broken."

"I know, madame. But I am—I am admiring that picture on the wall."

Maureen glanced up at the oil painting of a naval officer complete with telescope.

"Yes—it's good. About the only good thing in the house. We're not sure that it isn't a Gainsborough." She sighed. "Johnnie won't sell it, though. It's his great-great and I think a few more greats, grandfather and he went down with his ship or did something frightfully gallant. Johnnie's terribly proud of it."

169

"Yes," said Poirot gently. "Yes, he has something to be proud about, your husband!"

I I I

It was three o'clock when Poirot arrived at Dr. Rendell's house.

He had eaten rabbit stew and spinach and hard potatoes and a rather peculiar pudding, not scorched this time. Instead, "The water got in," Maureen had explained. He had drunk half a cup of muddy coffee. He did not feel well.

The door was opened by the elderly housekeeper Mrs. Scott, and he asked for Mrs. Rendell.

She was in the drawing-room with the radio on and started up when he was announced.

He had the same impression of her that he had had the first time he saw her. Wary, on her guard, frightened of him, or frightened of what he represented.

She seemed paler and more shadowy than she had done. He was almost certain that she was thinner.

"I want to ask you a question, madame."

"A question? Oh? Oh yes?"

"Did Mrs. Upward telephone to you on the day of her death?"

She stared at him. She nodded.

"At what time?"

"Mrs. Scott took the message. It was about six o'clock, I think."

"What was the message? To ask you to go there that evening?"

"Yes. She said that Mrs. Oliver and Robin were going into Kilchester and she would be all alone as it was Janet's night out. Could I come down and keep her company."

"Was any time suggested?"

"Nine o'clock or after."

"And you went?"

"I meant to. I really meant to. But I don't know how it was, I fell asleep after dinner that night. It was after ten when I woke up. I thought it was too late."

"You did not tell the police about Mrs. Upward's call?"

Her eyes widened. They had a rather innocent childlike stare.

"Ought I to have done? Since I didn't go, I thought it didn't matter. Perhaps, even, I felt rather guilty. If I'd gone, she might have been alive now." She caught her breath suddenly. "Oh, I hope it wasn't like that."

"Not quite like that," said Poirot.

He paused and then said:

"*What are you afraid of, madame?*"

She caught her breath sharply.

"Afraid? I'm not afraid."

"But you are."

"What nonsense. What—what should I be afraid of?"

Poirot paused for a moment before speaking.

"I thought perhaps you might be afraid of *me* . . ."

She didn't answer. But her eyes widened. Slowly, defiantly, she shook her head.

CHAPTER XXIV

I

"THIS WAY to Bedlam," said Spence.

"It is not as bad as that," said Poirot soothingly.

"That's what you say. Every single bit of information that comes in makes things more difficult. Now you tell me that Mrs. Upward rang up *three* women. Asked them to come that evening. Why three? Didn't she know herself which of them was Lily Gamboll? Or isn't it a case of Lily Gamboll at all? Take that book with the name of Evelyn Hope in it. It suggests, doesn't it, that Mrs. Upward and Eva Kane are one and the same."

"Which agrees exactly with James Bentley's impression of what Mrs. McGinty said to him."

"I thought he wasn't sure."

"He was not sure. It would be impossible for James Bentley to be sure of anything. He did not listen properly to what Mrs. McGinty was saying. Nevertheless, if James Bentley had an impression that Mrs. McGinty was talking

171

about Mrs. Upward, it may very well be true. Impressions often are."

"Our latest information from Australia (it was Australia she went to, by the way, not America) seems to be to the effect that the 'Mrs. Hope' in question died out there twenty years ago."

"I have already been told that," said Poirot.

"You always know everything, don't you, Poirot?"

Poirot took no notice of this gibe. He said:

"At the one end we have 'Mrs. Hope' deceased in Australia —and at the other?"

"At the other end we have Mrs. Upward, the widow of a rich North Country manufacturer. She lived with him near Leeds, and had a son. Soon after the son's birth, her husband died. The boy was inclined to be tubercular and since her husband's death she lived mostly abroad."

"And when does this saga begin?"

"The saga begins four years after Eva Kane left England. Upward met his wife somewhere abroad and brought her home after the marriage."

"So actually Mrs. Upward *could* be Eva Kane. What was her maiden name?"

"Hargraves, I understand. But what's in a name?"

"What indeed. Eva Kane, or Evelyn Hope, may have died in Australia—but she may have arranged a convenient decease and resuscitated herself as Hargraves and made a wealthy match."

"It's all a long time ago," said Spence. "But supposing that it's true. Supposing she kept a picture of herself and supposing that Mrs. McGinty saw it—then one can only assume that *she* killed Mrs. McGinty."

"That could be, could it not? Robin Upward was broadcasting that night. Mrs. Rendell mentions going to the cottage that evening, remember, and not being able to make herself heard. According to Mrs. Sweetiman, Janet Groom told her that Mrs. Upward was not really as crippled as she made out."

"That's all very well, Poirot, but the fact remains that *she herself* was killed—after recognising a photograph. Now you want to make out that the two deaths are not connected."

"No, no. I do not say that. They are connected all right."

172

"I give it up."

"Evelyn Hope. There is the key to the problem."

"Evelyn Carpenter? Is that your idea? *Not* Lily Gamboll —but Eva Kane's daughter! But surely she wouldn't kill her own mother."

"No, no. This is not matricide."

"What an irritating devil you are, Poirot. You'll be saying next that Eva Kane and Lily Gamboll, and Janice Courtland *and* Vera Blake are *all* living in Broadhinny. All four suspects."

"We have more than four. Eva Kane was the Craigs' nursery governess, remember."

"What's that got to do with it?"

"Where there is a nursery governess, there must be children—or at least a child. What happened to the Craig children?"

"There was a girl and a boy, I believe. Some relative took them."

"So there are two more people to take into account. Two people who might have kept a photograph for the third reason I mentioned—revenge."

"I don't believe it," said Spence.

Poirot sighed.

"It has to be considered, all the same. I think I know the truth—though there is one fact that baffles me utterly."

"I'm glad something baffles you," said Spence.

"Confirm one thing for me, *mon cher* Spence. Eva Kane left the country before Craig's execution, that is right?"

"Quite right."

"And she was, at that time, expecting a child?"

"Quite right."

"*Bon Dieu*, how stupid I have been," said Hercule Poirot. "The whole thing is simple, is it not?"

It was after that remark that there was very nearly a third murder—the murder of Hercule Poirot by Superintendent Spence in Kilchester Police Headquarters.

173

"I want," said Hercule Poirot, "a personal call. To Mrs. Ariadne Oliver."

A personal call to Mrs. Oliver was not achieved without difficulties. Mrs. Oliver was working and could not be disturbed. Poirot, however, disregarded all denials. Presently he heard the authoress's voice.

It was cross and rather breathless.

"Well, what is it?" said Mrs. Oliver. "Have you got to ring me up just now? I've thought of a most wonderful idea for a murder in a draper's shop. You know, the old-fashioned kind that sells combinations and funny vests with long sleeves."

"I do not know," said Poirot. "And anyway what I have to say to you is far more important."

"It couldn't be," said Mrs. Oliver. "Not to *me*, I mean. Unless I get a rough sketch of my idea jotted down, it will *go*!"

Hercule Poirot paid no attention to this creative agony. He asked sharp imperative questions to which Mrs. Oliver replied somewhat vaguely.

"Yes—yes—it's a little Repertory Theatre—I don't know its name. . . . Well, one of them was Cecil Something, and the one I was talking to was Michael."

"Admirable. That is all I need to know."

"But why Cecil and Michael?"

"Return to the combinations and the long-sleeved vests, madame."

"I can't think why you don't arrest Dr. Rendell," said Mrs. Oliver. "I would, if I were the head of Scotland Yard."

"Very possibly. I wish you luck with the murder in the draper's shop."

"The whole idea has gone now," said Mrs. Oliver. "You've ruined it."

Poirot apologised handsomely.

He put down the receiver and smiled at Spence.

"We go now—or at least I will go—to interview a young actor whose Christian name is Michael and who plays the less important parts in the Cullenquay Repertory Theatre. I pray only that he is the right Michael."

"Why on earth——"

Poirot dexterously averted the rising wrath of Superintendent Spence.

"Do you know, *cher ami*, what is a *secret de Polichinelle*?"

"Is this a French lesson?" demanded the superintendent wrathfully.

"A *secret de Polichinelle* is a secret that everyone can know. For this reason the people who do not know it never hear about it—for if everyone thinks you know a thing, nobody tells you."

"How I manage to keep my hands off you I don't know," said Superintendent Spence.

CHAPTER XXV

THE INQUEST was over—a verdict had been returned of murder by a person or persons unknown.

After the inquest, at the invitation of Hercule Poirot, those who had attended it came to Long Meadows.

Working diligently, Poirot had induced some semblance of order in the long drawing-room. Chairs had been arranged in a neat semi-circle, Maureen's dogs had been excluded with difficulty, and Hercule Poirot, a self-appointed lecturer, took up his position at the end of the room and initiated proceedings with a slightly self-conscious clearing of the throat.

"Messieurs et Mesdames——"

He paused. His next words were unexpected and seemed almost farcical.

" Mrs. McGinty's dead. How did she die?
Down on her knees just like I.
Mrs. McGinty's dead. How did she die?
Holding her hand out just like I.
Mrs. McGinty's dead. How did she die?
Like this . . ."

Seeing their expressions, he went on:

"No, I am not mad. Because I repeat to you the childish rhyme of a childish game, it does not mean that I am in my second childhood. Some of you may have played that game as children. Mrs. Upward had played it. Indeed she repeated it to me—with a difference. She said: *'Mrs. McGinty's dead. How did she die? Sticking her neck out just like I.'* That is what she said—and that is what she did. She stuck her neck out—and so she also, like Mrs. McGinty, died. . . .

"For our purpose we must go back to the beginning—to Mrs. McGinty—down on her knees scrubbing other people's houses. Mrs. McGinty was killed, and a man, James Bentley, was arrested, tried and convicted. For certain reasons, Superintendent Spence, the officer in charge of the case, was not convinced of Bentley's guilt, strong though the evidence was. I agreed with him. I came down here to answer a question. 'How did Mrs. McGinty die? *Why* did she die?'

"I will not make you the long and complicated histories. I will say only that as simple a thing as a bottle of ink gave me a clue. In the *Sunday Comet,* read by Mrs. McGinty on the Sunday before her death, four photographs were published. You know all about those photographs by now, so I will only say that Mrs. McGinty recognised one of those photographs as a photograph she had seen in one of the houses where she worked.

"She spoke of this to James Bentley though he attached no importance to the matter at the time, nor indeed afterwards. Actually he barely listened. But he had the impression that Mrs. McGinty had seen the photograph in Mrs. Upward's house and that when she referred to a woman who need not be so proud if all was known, she was referring to Mrs. Upward. We cannot depend on that statement of his, but she certainly used that phrase about pride and there is no doubt that Mrs. Upward *was* a proud and imperious woman.

"As you all know—some of you were present and the others will have heard—I produced those four photographs at Mrs. Upward's house. I caught a flicker of surprise and recognition in Mrs. Upward's expression and taxed her with it. She had to admit it. She said that she 'had seen one of the photographs somewhere but she couldn't remember where.' When asked which photograph, she pointed to a photograph of the child Lily Gamboll. But that, let me tell you, *was not the truth*. For reasons of her own, Mrs. Upward wanted to keep her recognition to herself. She pointed to the wrong photograph to put me off.

"But one person was not deceived—the *murderer*. One person *knew* which photograph Mrs. Upward had recognised. And here I will not beat to and fro about the bush—the photograph in question was that of Eva Kane—a woman who was accomplice, victim or possibly leading spirit in the famous Craig Murder Case.

"On the next evening Mrs. Upward was killed. She was killed for the same reason that Mrs. McGinty was killed. Mrs. McGinty stuck her hand out, Mrs. Upward stuck her neck out—the result was the same.

"Now before Mrs. Upward died, three women received telephone calls. Mrs. Carpenter, Mrs. Rendell, and Miss Henderson. All three calls were a message from Mrs. Upward asking the person in question to come and see her that evening. It was her servant's night out and her son and Mrs. Oliver were going into Cullenquay. It would seem, therefore, that she wanted a private conversation with each of these three women.

"Now why *three* women? Did Mrs. Upward know *where* she had seen the photograph of Eva Kane? Or did she know she had seen it but could not remember where? Had these three women anything in common? Nothing, it would seem, but their *age*. They were all, roughly, in the neighbourhood of thirty.

"You have, perhaps, read the article of the *Sunday Comet*. There is a truly sentimental picture in it of Eva Kane's daughter in years to come. The women asked by Mrs. Upward to come and see her were all of the right age to be Eva Kane's daughter.

"So it would seem that living in Broadhinny was a young woman who was the daughter of the celebrated murderer Craig and of his mistress Eva Kane, and it would also seem that that young woman would go to any lengths to prevent that fact being known. Would go, indeed, to the length of twice committing murder. For when Mrs. Upward was found dead, there were two coffee cups on the table, both used, and on the visitor's cup faint traces of lipstick.

"Now let us go back to the three women who received telephone messages. Mrs. Carpenter got the message but says she did not go to Laburnums that night. Mrs. Rendell meant to go, but fell asleep in her chair. Miss Henderson *did* go to Laburnums but the house was dark and she could not make anyone hear and she came away again.

"That is the story these three women tell—but there is conflicting evidence. There is that second coffee cup with lipstick on it, and an outside witness, the girl Edna, states positively that she saw a fair-haired woman go *in* to the house. There is also the evidence of scent—an expensive and exotic scent which Mrs. Carpenter uses alone of those concerned."

There was an interruption. Eve Carpenter cried out:

"It's a lie. It's a wicked cruel lie. It wasn't me! I never went there! I never went near the place. Guy, can't you do something about these lies?"

Guy Carpenter was white with anger.

"Let me inform you, M. Poirot, that there is a law of slander and all these people present are witnesses."

"Is it slander to say that your wife uses a certain scent—and also, let me tell you, a certain lipstick?"

"It's ridiculous," cried Eve. "Absolutely ridiculous! *Anyone* could go splashing my scent about."

Unexpectedly Poirot beamed on her.

"*Mais oui*, exactly! Anyone could. An obvious, not very subtle thing to do. Clumsy and crude. So clumsy that as far as I was concerned, it defeated its object. It did more. It gave me ideas, as the phrase goes, yes it gave me ideas.

"Scent—and traces of lipstick on a cup. But it is so easy to remove lipstick from a cup—I assure you every trace can be wiped off quite easily. Or the cups themselves could be removed and washed. Why not? There was no one in the house. But that was not done. I asked myself why? And the answer seemed to be a deliberate stress on femininity, an underlining of the fact that it was a *woman's* murder. I reflected on the telephone calls to those three women—all of them had been *messages*. In no case had the recipient herself spoken to Mrs. Upward. So perhaps it was *not* Mrs. Upward who had telephoned. It was someone who was anxious to involve a *woman*—*any* woman—in the crime. Again I asked

178

why? And there can be only one answer—that it was not a woman who killed Mrs. Upward—but a *man*."

He looked round on his audience. They were all very still. Only two people responded.

Eve Carpenter said with a sigh: "Now you're talking sense!"

Mrs. Oliver, nodding her head vigorously, said: "Of course."

"So I have arrived at this point—a *man* killed Mrs. Upward and a *man* killed Mrs. McGinty! What man? The reason for the murder must still be the same—it all hinges on a photograph. In whose possession was that photograph? That is the first question? And why was it kept?

"Well, that is perhaps not so difficult. Say that it was kept originally for sentimental reasons. Once Mrs. McGinty is—removed, the photograph need not be destroyed. But after the second murder, it is different. This time the photograph has definitely been connected with the murder. The photograph is now a dangerous thing to keep. Therefore you will all agree, it is sure to be destroyed."

He looked round at the heads that nodded agreement.

"But, for all that, the photograph was *not* destroyed! No, it was not destroyed! I know that—because I found it. I found it a few days ago. I found it in this house. In the drawer of the bureau that you see standing against the wall. I have it here."

He held out the faded photograph of a simpering girl with roses.

"Yes," said Poirot. "It is Eva Kane. And on the back of it are written two words in pencil. Shall I tell you what they are? '*My mother*' . . ."

His eyes, grave and accusing, rested on Maureen Summerhayes. She pushed back the hair from her face and stared at him with wide bewildered eyes.

"I don't understand. I never——"

"No, Mrs. Summerhayes, you do not understand. There can be only two reasons for keeping this photograph after the second murder. The first of them is an innocent sentimentality. *You* had no feeling of guilt and so you could keep the photograph. You told us yourself, at Mrs. Carpenter's house one day, that you were an adopted child. I doubt whether you have ever known what your real mother's name was. But somebody else knew. Somebody who has all the pride of family—a pride that makes him cling to his ancestral home, a pride in his ancestors and his lineage. That man would rather die than have the world—and his children—know that Maureen Summerhayes is the daughter of the murderer Craig and of Eva Kane. That man, I have said, would rather die. But that would not help, would it? So instead let us say that we have here a man who is prepared to kill."

Johnnie Summerhayes got up from his seat. His voice, when he spoke, was quiet, almost friendly.

"Rather a lot of nonsense you're talkin', aren't you? Enjoying yourself spouting out a lot of theories? Theories, that's all they are! Saying things about my wife——"

His anger broke suddenly in a furious tide.

"You damned filthy swine——"

The swiftness of his rush across the floor took the room unawares. Poirot skipped back nimbly and Superintendent Spence was suddenly between Poirot and Summerhayes.

"Now, now, Major Summerhayes, take it easy—take it easy——"

Summerhayes recovered himself, shrugged, said:

"Sorry. Ridiculous really! After all—*anyone* can stick a photograph in a drawer."

"Precisely," said Poirot. "And the interesting thing about this photograph is that it has no fingerprints on it."

He paused, then nodded his head gently.

"But it should have had," he said. "If Mrs. Summerhayes kept it, she would have kept it innocently, and so her fingerprints *should* have been on it."

Maureen exclaimed:

"I think you're mad. I've never seen that photograph in my life—except at Mrs. Upward's that day."

"It is fortunate for you," said Poirot, "that I know that you are speaking the truth. The photograph was put into that drawer *only a few minutes before I found it there*. Twice that morning the contents of that drawer were tumbled on to the ground, twice I replaced them; the first time the photograph was *not* in the drawer, the second time

180

it *was*. It had been placed there during that interval—*and I know by whom.*"

A new note crept into his voice. He was no longer a ridiculous little man with an absurd moustache and dyed hair, he was a hunter very close to his quarry.

"The crimes were committed by a *man*—they were committed for the simplest of all reasons—for money. In Mrs. Upward's house there was a book found and on the flyleaf of that book is written *Evelyn Hope*. Hope was the name Eva Kane took when she left England. If her real name was Evelyn then in all probability she gave the name of Evelyn to her child when it was born. *But Evelyn is a man's name as well as a woman's.* Why had we assumed that Eva Kane's child was a girl? Roughly because the *Sunday Comet* said so! But actually the *Sunday Comet* had not said so in so many words, it had assumed it because of a romantic interview with Eva Kane. But Eva Kane left England *before* her child was born—so nobody could say what the sex of the child would be.

"That is where I let myself be misled. By the romantic inaccuracy of the Press.

"Evelyn Hope, Eva Kane's *son*, comes to England. He is talented and he attracts the attention of a very rich woman who knows nothing about his origin—only the romantic story he chooses to tell her. (A very pretty little story it was —all about a tragic young ballerina dying of tuberculosis in Paris!)

"She is a lonely woman who has recently lost her own son. The talented young playwright takes her name by deed poll.

"But your real name is Evelyn Hope, isn't it, Mr. Upward?"

Robin Upward cried out shrilly:

"Of course it isn't! I don't know what you're talking about."

"You really cannot hope to deny it. There are people who know you under that name. The name Evelyn Hope, written in the book, is in your handwriting—the same handwriting as the words 'my mother' on the back of this photograph. Mrs. McGinty saw the photograph and the writing on it when she was tidying your things away. She spoke to you about it after reading the *Sunday Comet*. Mrs. McGinty assumed that it was a photograph of *Mrs. Upward* when young, since she had no idea Mrs. Upward was not your real mother. But you knew that if once she mentioned the matter so that it came to Mrs. Upward's ears, it would be the end. Mrs. Upward had quite fanatical views on the subject of heredity. She would not tolerate for a moment an adopted son who was the son of a famous murderer. Nor would she forgive your lies on the subject.

'So Mrs. McGinty had at all costs to be silenced. You promised her a little present, perhaps, for being discreet. You called on her the next evening on your way to broadcast—and you killed her! *Like this . . .*"

With a sudden movement, Poirot seized the sugar hammer from the shelf and whirled it round and down as though to bring it crashing down on Robin's head.

So menacing was the gesture that several of the circle cried out.

Robin Upward screamed. A high terrified scream.

He yelled: "Don't . . . don't . . . It was an accident. I swear it was an accident. I didn't mean to kill her. I lost my head. I swear I did."

"You washed off the blood and put the sugar hammer back in this room where you had found it. But there are new scientific methods of determining blood stains—and of bringing up latent fingerprints."

"I tell you I never meant to kill her. . . . It was all a mistake. . . . And anyway it isn't my fault. . . . I'm not responsible. It's in my blood. I can't help it. You can't hang me for something that isn't my fault. . . ."

Under his breath Spence muttered: "Can't we? You see if we don't!"

Aloud he spoke in a grave official voice:

"I must warn you, Mr. Upward, that anything you say . . ."

CHAPTER XXVI

"I REALLY don't see, M. Poirot, how ever you came to suspect Robin Upward."

Poirot looked complacently at the faces turned towards him.

He always enjoyed explanations.

"I ought to have suspected him much sooner. The clue, such a simple clue, was the sentence uttered by Mrs. Summerhayes at the cocktail party that day. She said to Robin Upward: 'I don't like being adopted, do you?' Those were the revealing two words. *Do you?* They meant—they could only mean—that Mrs. Upward was not Robin's own mother."

"Mrs. Upward was morbidly anxious herself that no one should know that Robin was not her own son. She had probably heard too many ribald comments on brilliant young men who live with and upon elderly women. And very few people did know—only the small theatrical *coterie* where she had first come across Robin. She had few intimate friends in this country, having lived abroad so long, and she chose in any case to come and settle down here far away from her own Yorkshire. Even when she met friends of the old days, she did not enlighten them when they assumed that this Robin was the same Robin they had known as a little boy.

"But from the very first something had struck me as not quite natural in the household at Laburnums. Robin's attitude to Mrs. Upward was not that of either a spoiled child, or of a devoted son. It was the attitude of a protégé to a *patron*. The rather fanciful title of Madre had a theatrical touch. And Mrs. Upward, though she was clearly very fond of Robin, nevertheless unconsciously treated him as a prized possession that she had bought and paid for.

"So there is Robin Upward, comfortably established with 'Madre's' purse to back his ventures, and then into his assured world comes Mrs. McGinty who has recognised the photograph that he keeps in a drawer—the photograph with 'my mother' written on the back of it. His mother, whom he has told Mrs. Upward was a talented young ballet dancer who died of tuberculosis! Mrs. McGinty, of course, thinks that the photograph is of Mrs. Upward when young, since she assumes as a matter of course that Mrs. Upward is Robin's own mother. I do not think that actual blackmail ever entered Mrs. McGinty's mind, but she did hope, perhaps, for a 'nice little present,' as a reward for holding her tongue about a piece of bygone gossip which would not have been pleasant for a 'proud' woman like Mrs. Upward.

"But Robin Upward was taking no chances. He purloins the sugar hammer, laughingly referred to as a perfect weapon for murder by Mrs. Summerhayes, and on the following evening, he stops at Mrs. McGinty's cottage on his way to broadcast. She takes him into the parlour, quite unsuspicious, and he kills her. He knows where she keeps her savings—everyone in Broadhinny seems to know—and he fakes a burglary, hiding the money outside the house. Bentley is suspected and arrested. Everything is now safe for clever Robin Upward.

"But then, suddenly, I produce four photographs, and Mrs. Upward recognises the one of Eva Kane as being identical with a photograph of Robin's ballerina mother! She needs a little time to think things out. Murder is involved. Can it be possible that Robin——? No, she refuses to believe it.

"What action she would have taken in the end we do not know. But Robin was taking no chances. He plans the whole *mise en scène*. The visit to the Rep on Janet's night out, the telephone calls, the coffee cup carefully smeared with lipstick taken from Eve Carpenter's bag, he even buys a bottle of her distinctive perfume. The whole thing was a theatrical scene setting with prepared props. Whilst Mrs. Oliver waited in the car, Robin ran back twice into the house. The murder was a matter of seconds. After that there was only the swift distribution of the 'props.' And with Mrs. Upward dead, he inherited a large fortune by the terms of her will, and no suspicion could attach to him since it would seem quite certain that a *woman* had committed the crime. With three women visiting the cottage that night, one of them was almost sure to be suspected. And that, indeed, was so.

"But Robin, like all criminals, was careless and over confident. Not only was there a book in the cottage with his original name scribbled in it, but he also kept, for purposes of his own, the fatal photograph. It would have been much safer for him if he had destroyed it, but he clung to the belief that he could use it to incriminate someone else at the right moment.

"He probably thought then of Mrs. Summerhayes. That may be the reason he moved out of the cottage and into Long Meadows. After all, the sugar hammer was hers, and Mrs. Summerhayes was, he knew, an adopted child and might find it hard to prove she was not Eva Kane's daughter.

"However, when Deirdre Henderson admitted having been on the scene of the crime, he conceived the idea of planting the photograph amongst *her* possessions. He tried to do so, using a ladder that the gardener had left against the window. But Mrs. Wetherby was nervous and had insisted on all the windows being kept locked, so Robin did not succeed in his purpose. He came straight back here and put the photograph in a drawer which, unfortunately for him, I had searched only a short time before.

"I knew, therefore, that the photograph had been planted, and I knew by whom—by the only other person in the house —that person who was typing industriously over my head.

"Since the name Evelyn Hope had been written on the flyleaf of the book from the cottage, Evelyn Hope must be either Mrs. Upward—or Robin Upward. . . .

"The name Evelyn had led me astray—I had connected it with Mrs. Carpenter since her name was Eve. *But Evelyn was a man's name as well as a woman's.*

"I remembered the conversation Mrs. Oliver had told me about at the Little Rep in Cullenquay. The young actor who had been talking to her was the person I wanted to confirm my theory—the theory that Robin was not Mrs. Upward's own son. For by the way he had talked, it seemed clear that he knew the real facts. And his story of Mrs. Upward's swift retribution on a young man who had deceived her as to his origins was suggestive.

"The truth is that I ought to have seen the whole thing very much sooner. I was handicapped by a serious error. I believed that I had been deliberately pushed with the intention of sending me on to a railway line—and that the person who had done so was the murderer of Mrs. McGinty. Now Robin Upward was practically the only person in Broadhinny who could *not* have been at Kilchester station at that time."

There was a sudden chuckle from Johnnie Summerhayes.

"Probably some old market woman with a basket. They do shove."

Poirot said:

"Actually, Robin Upward was far too conceited to fear me at all. It is a characteristic of murderers. Fortunately, perhaps. For in this case there was very little evidence."

Mrs. Oliver stirred.

"Do you mean to say," she demanded incredulously, "that Robin murdered his mother whilst I sat outside in the car, and that I hadn't the least idea of it? There wouldn't have been time!"

"Oh yes, there would. People's ideas of time are usually ludicrously wrong. Just notice sometime how swiftly a stage can be reset. In this case it was mostly a matter of props."

"Good theatre," murmured Mrs. Oliver mechanically.

"Yes, it was pre-eminently a theatrical murder. All very much contrived."

"And I sat there in the car—and hadn't the least idea!"

"I am afraid," murmured Poirot, "that your woman's intuition was taking a day off. . . ."

CHAPTER XXVII

"I'm NOT going back to Breather & Scuttle," said Maude Williams. "They're a lousy firm anyway."

"And they have served their purpose."

"What do you mean by that, M. Poirot?"

"Why did you come to this part of the world?"

"I suppose being Mr. Knowall, you think you know?"

"I have a little idea."

"And what is this famous idea?"

Poirot was looking meditatively at Maude's hair.

"I have been very discreet," he said. "It has been assumed that the woman who went into Mrs. Upward's house, the fair-haired woman that Edna saw, was Mrs. Carpenter, and that she has denied being there simply out of fright. Since it was Robin Upward who killed Mrs. Upward, her presence has no more significance than that of Miss Henderson. But all the same I do not think she *was* there. I think, Miss Williams, that the woman Edna saw was *you*."

"Why me?"

Her voice was hard.

Poirot countered with another question.

"Why were you so interested in Broadhinny? Why, when you went over there, did you ask Robin Upward for an autograph—you are not the autograph-hunting type. What did you know about the Upwards? Why did you come to this part of the world in the first place? How did you know that Eva Kane died in Australia and the name she took when she left England?"

"Good at guessing, aren't you? Well, I've nothing to hide, not really."

She opened her handbag. From a worn notecase she pulled out a small newspaper cutting frayed with age. It showed the face that Poirot by now knew so well, the simpering face of Eva Kane.

Written across it were the words, *She killed my mother.*

Poirot handed it back to her.

"Yes, I thought so. Your real name is Craig?"

"I was brought up by some cousins—very decent they were. But I was old enough when it all happened not to forget. I used to think about it a good deal. About *her*. She was a nasty bit of goods all right—children know! My father was just—weak. And besotted by her. But he took the rap. For something, I've always believed, that *she* did. Oh yes, I know he's an accessory after the fact—but it's not quite the same thing, is it? I always meant to find out what had become of *her*. When I was grown up, I got detectives on to it. They traced her to Australia and finally reported that she was dead. She'd left a son—Evelyn Hope he called himself.

"Well, that seemed to close the account. But then I got pally with a young actor chap. He mentioned someone called Evelyn Hope who'd come from Australia, but who now called himself Robin Upward and who wrote plays. I was interested. One night Robin Upward was pointed out to me

—and he was with his *mother*. So I thought that, after all, Eva Kane *wasn't* dead. Instead, she was queening it about with a packet of money.

"I got myself a job down here. I was curious—and a bit more than curious. All right, I'll admit it, I thought I'd like to get even with her in some way. . . . When you brought up all this business about James Bentley, I jumped to the conclusion that it was Mrs. Upward who'd killed Mrs. McGinty. Eva Kane up to her tricks again. I happened to hear from Michael West that Robin Upward and Mrs. Oliver were coming over to this show at the Cullenquay Rep. I decided to go to Broadhinny and beard the woman. I meant—I don't quite know what I meant. I'm telling you everything—I took a little pistol I had in the war with me. To frighten her? Or more? Honestly, I don't know . . .

"Well, I got there. There was no sound in the house. The door was unlocked. I went in. You know how I found her. Sitting there dead, her face all purple and swollen. All the things I'd been thinking seemed silly and melodramatic. I knew that I'd never, really, want to kill anyone when it came to it. . . . But I did realise that it might be awkward to explain what I'd been doing in the house. It was a cold night and I'd got gloves on, so I knew I hadn't left any fingerprints, and I didn't think for a moment anyone had seen me. That's all." She paused and added abruptly: "What are you going to do about it?"

"Nothing," said Hercule Poirot. "I wish you good luck in life, that is all."

EPILOGUE

HERCULE POIROT and Superintendent Spence were celebrating at the *La Vieille Grand'mère*.

As coffee was served Spence leaned back in his chair and gave a deep sigh of repletion.

"Not at all bad grub here," he said approvingly. "A bit frenchified, perhaps, but after all where *can* you get a decent steak and chips nowadays?"

"I had been dining here on the evening you first came to me," said Poirot reminiscently.

"Ah, a lot of water under the bridge since then. I've got to hand it to you, M. Poirot. You did the trick all right." A slight smile creased his wooden countenance. "Lucky that young man didn't realise how very little evidence we'd really got. Why, a clever counsel would have made mincemeat of it! But he lost his head completely, and gave the show away. Spilt the beans and incriminated himself up to the hilt. Lucky for us!"

"It was not entirely luck," said Poirot reprovingly. "I played him, as you play the big fish! He thinks I take the evidence against Mrs. Summerhayes seriously—when it is not so, he suffers the reaction and goes to pieces. And besides, he is a coward. I whirl the sugar hammer and he thinks I mean to hit him. Acute fear always produces the truth."

"Lucky you didn't suffer from Major Summerhayes' reaction," said Spence with a grin. "Got a temper, he has, *and* quick on his feet. I only got between you just in time. Has he forgiven you yet?"

"Oh yes, we are the firmest friends. And I have given Mrs. Summerhayes a cookery book and have also taught her personally how to make an omelette. *Bon Dieu*, what I suffered in that house!"

He closed his eyes.

"Complicated business, the whole thing," ruminated Spence, uninterested in Poirot's agonised memories. "Just shows how true the old saying is that everyone's got something to hide. Mrs. Carpenter, now, had a narrow squeak of being arrested for murder. If ever a woman acted guilty, she did, and all for what?"

"*Eh bien*, what?" asked Poirot curiously.

"Just the usual business of a rather unsavoury past. She had been a taxi dancer—and a bright girl with plenty of men friends! She wasn't a war widow when she came and settled down in Broadhinny. Only what they call nowadays an 'unofficial wife.' Well, of course all that wouldn't do for a stuffed shirt like Guy Carpenter, so she'd spun him a very different sort of tale. And she was frantic lest the whole thing would come out once we started poking round into people's origins."

He sipped his coffee, and then gave a low chuckle.

"Then take the Wetherbys. Sinister sort of house. Hate and malice. Awkward frustrated sort of girl. And what's behind that? Nothing sinister. Just money! Plain £. s. d."

"As simple as that!"

"The girl has the money—quite a lot of it. Left her by an aunt. So mother keeps tight hold of her in case she should want to marry. And stepfather loathes her because *she* has the dibs and pays the bills. I gather he himself has been a failure at anything he's tried. A mean cuss—and as for Mrs. W., she's pure poison dissolved in sugar."

"I agree with you." Poirot nodded his head in a satisfied fashion. "It is fortunate that the girl has money. It makes her marriage to James Bentley much more easy to arrange."

Superintendent Spence looked surprised.

"Going to marry James Bentley? Deirdre Henderson? Who says so?"

"I say so," said Poirot. "I occupy myself with the affair. I have, now that our little problem is over, too much time on my hands. I shall employ myself in forwarding this marriage. As yet, the two concerned have no idea of such a thing. But they are attracted. Left to themselves, nothing would happen—but they have to reckon with Hercule Poirot. You will see! The affair will march."

Spence grinned.

"Don't mind sticking your fingers in other people's pies, do you?"

"*Mon cher*, that does not come well from you," said Poirot reproachfully.

"Ah, you've got me there. All the same, James Bentley is a poor stick."

"Certainly he is a poor stick! At the moment he is positively aggrieved because he is not going to be hanged."

"He ought to be down on his knees with gratitude to you," said Spence.

"Say, rather, to you. But apparently he does not think so."

"Queer cuss."

"As you say, and yet at least two women have been prepared to take an interest in him. Nature is very unexpected."

"I thought it was Maude Williams you were going to pair off with him."

"He shall make his choice," said Poirot. "He shall—how do you say it?—award the apple. But I think that it is Deirdre Henderson that he will choose. Maude Williams has too much energy and vitality. With her he would retire even farther into his shell."

"Can't think why either of them should want him!"

"The ways of Nature are indeed inscrutable."

"All the same, you'll have your work cut out. First bringing him up to the scratch—and then prising the girl loose from poison puss mother—she'll fight you tooth and claw!"

"Success is on the side of the big battalions."

"On the side of the big moustaches, I suppose you mean."

Spence roared. Poirot stroked his moustache complacently and suggested a brandy.

"I don't mind if I do, M. Poirot."

Poirot gave the order.

"Ah," said Spence, "I knew there was something else I had to tell you. You remember the Rendells?"

"Naturally."

"Well, when we were checking up on him, something rather odd came to light. It seems that when his first wife died in Leeds where his practice was at that time, the police there got some rather nasty anonymous letters about him. Saying, in effect, that he'd poisoned her. Of course people do say that sort of thing. She'd been attended by an outside doctor, reputable man, and he seemed to think her death was quite above board. There was nothing to go upon except the fact that they'd mutually insured their lives in each other's favour, and people do do that. . . . Nothing for us to go upon, as I say, and yet—I wonder? What do *you* think?"

Poirot remembered Mrs. Rendell's frightened air. Her mention of anonymous letters, and her insistence that she did not believe anything they said. He remembered, too, her certainty that his inquiry about Mrs. McGinty was only a pretext.

He said, "I should imagine that it was not only the police who got anonymous letters."

"Sent them to her, too?"

"I think so. When I appeared in Broadhinny, she thought I was on her husband's track, and that the McGinty business was a pretext. Yes—and he thought so, too. . . . That explains it! It was Dr. Rendell who tried to push me under the train that night!"

"Think he'll have a shot at doing this wife in, too?"

"I think she would be wise not to insure her life in his favour," said Poirot dryly. "But if he believes we have an eye on him he will probably be prudent."

"We'll do what we can. We'll keep an eye on our genial doctor, and make it clear we're doing so."

Poirot raised his brandy glass.

"To Mrs. Oliver," he said.

"What put her into your head suddenly?"

"Woman's intuition," said Poirot.

There was silence for a moment, then Spence said slowly: "Robin Upward is coming up for trial next week. You know, Poirot, I can't help feeling doubtful——"

Poirot interrupted him with horror.

"*Mon Dieu!* You are not now doubtful about Robin Upward's guilt, are you? Do not say you want to start over again."

"Good lord, no. *He's* a murderer all right!" He added: "Cocky enough for anything!"

THE END

THEY DO IT WITH MIRRORS

O.C.P. 21/709

To
MATHEW PRICHARD

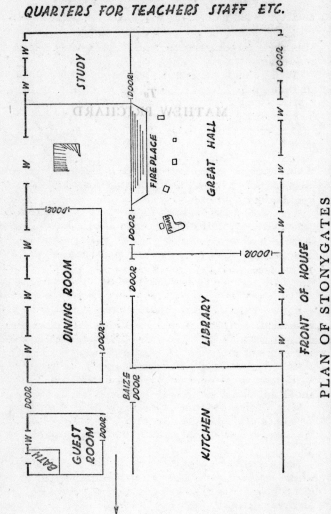

PLAN OF STONYGATES

CHAPTER I

Mrs. Van Rydock moved a little back from the mirror and sighed.

"Well, That'll have to do," she murmured. "Think it's all right, Jane?"

Miss Marple eyed the Lanvanelli creation appraisingly.

"It seems to me a very beautiful gown," she said.

"The gown's all right," said Mrs. Van Rydock and sighed.

"Take it off, Stephanie," she said.

The elderly maid with the grey hair and the small pinched mouth eased the gown carefully up over Mrs. Van Rydock's upstretched arms.

Mrs. Van Rydock stood in front of the glass in her peach satin slip. She was exquisitely corseted. Her still shapely legs were encased in fine nylon stockings. Her face, beneath a layer of cosmetics and constantly toned up by massage, appeared almost girlish at a slight distance. Her hair was less grey than tending to hydrangea blue and was perfectly set. It was practically impossible when looking at Mrs. Van Rydock to imagine what she would be like in a natural state. Everything that money could do had been done for her—reinforced by diet, massage, and constant exercises.

Ruth Van Rydock looked humorously at her friend.

"Do you think most people would guess, Jane, that you and I are practically the same age?"

Miss Marple responded loyally.

"Not for a moment, I'm sure," she said reassuringly. "I'm afraid, you know, that *I* look every minute of *my* age!"

Miss Marple was white-haired, with a soft pink and white wrinkled face and innocent china blue eyes. She looked a very sweet old lady. Nobody would have called Mrs. Van Rydock a sweet old lady.

"I guess you do, Jane," said Mrs. Van Rydock. She grinned suddenly, "And so do I. Only not in the same

way. 'Wonderful how that old hag keeps her figure.'
That's what they say of me. But they know I'm an old
hag all right! And, my God, do I feel like one!"

She dropped heavily on to the satin quilted chair.

"That's all right, Stephanie," she said. "You can go."
Stephanie gathered up the dress and went out.

"Good old Stephanie," said Ruth Van Rydock. "She's
been with me for over thirty years now. She's the only
woman who knows what I really look like! Jane, I want
to talk to you."

Miss Marple leant forward a little. Her face took on a
receptive expression. She looked, somehow, an incongruous figure in the ornate bedroom of the expensive
hotel suite. She was dressed in rather dowdy black, carried
a large shopping bag and looked every inch a lady.

"I'm worried, Jane. About Carrie Louise."

"Carrie Louise?" Miss Marple repeated the name
musingly. The sound of it took her a long way back.

The pensionnat in Florence. Herself, the pink and
white English girl from a Cathedral Close. The two
Martin girls, Americans, exciting to the English girl
because of their quaint ways of speech and their forthright
manner and vitality. Ruth, tall, eager, on top of the world;
Carrie Louise, small, dainty, wistful.

"When did you see her last, Jane?"

"Oh! not for many many years. It must be twenty-five
at least. Of course we still send cards at Christmas."

Such an odd thing, friendship! She, young Jane Marple,
and the two Americans. Their ways diverging almost at
once, and yet the old affection persisting; occasional
letters, remembrances at Christmas. Strange that Ruth
whose home—or rather homes—had been in America
should be the sister whom she had seen the more often
of the two. No, perhaps not strange. Like most Americans
of her class, Ruth had been cosmopolitan, every year or
two she had come over to Europe, rushing from London
to Paris, on to the Riviera, and back again, and always
keen to snatch a few moments wherever she was with her
old friends. There had been many meetings like this one.
In Claridges, or the Savoy, or the Berkeley, or the
Dorchester. A *recherché* meal, affectionate reminiscences,

and a hurried and affectionate good-bye. Ruth had never had time to visit St. Mary Mead. Miss Marple had not, indeed, ever expected it. Everyone's life has a *tempo*. Ruth's was *presto* whereas Miss Marple's was content to be *adagio*.

So it was American Ruth whom she had seen most of, whereas Carrie Louise who lived in England, she had not now seen for over twenty years. Odd, but quite natural, because when one lives in the same country there is no need to arrange meetings with old friends. One assumes that, sooner or later, one will see them without contrivance. Only, if you move in different spheres, that does not happen. The paths of Jane Marple and Carrie Louise did not cross. It was as simple as that.

"Why are you worried about Carrie Louise, Ruth?" asked Miss Marple.

"In a way that's what worries me most! I just don't know."

"She's not ill?"

"She's very delicate—always has been. I wouldn't say she'd been any worse than usual—considering that she's getting on just as we all are."

"Unhappy?"

"Oh *no*."

No, it wouldn't be that, thought Miss Marple. It would be difficult to imagine Carrie Louise unhappy—and yet there were times in her life when she must have been. Only—the picture did not come clearly. Bewildered—yes—incredulous—yes—but violent grief—no.

Mrs. Van Rydock's words came appositely.

"Carrie Louise," she said, "has always lived right out of this world. She doesn't know what it's like. Maybe it's *that* that worries me."

"Her circumstances," began Miss Marple, then stopped, shaking her head. "No," she said.

"No, it's she herself," said Ruth Van Rydock. "Carrie Louise was always the one of us who had ideals. Of course it was the fashion when we were young to have ideals—we all had them, it was the proper thing for young girls. You were going to nurse lepers, Jane, and I was going to be a nun. One gets over all that nonsense. Marriage, I suppose one might say, knocks it out of one. Still, take it by and large, I haven't done badly out of marriage."

Miss Marple thought that Ruth was expressing it mildly. Ruth had been married three times, each time to an extremely wealthy man, and the resultant divorces had increased her bank balance without in the least souring her disposition.

"Of course," said Mrs. Van Rydock, "I've always been tough. Things don't get me down. I've not expected too much of life and certainly not expected too much of men —and I've done very well out of it—and no hard feelings. Tommy and I are still excellent friends, and Julius often asks me my opinion about the market." Her face darkened. "I believe that's what worries me about Carrie Louise—she's always had a tendency, you know, to marry *cranks*."

"Cranks?"

"People with ideals. Carrie Louise was always a push-over for ideals. There she was, as pretty as they make them, just seventeen and listening with her eyes as big as saucers to old Gulbrandsen holding forth about his plans for the human race. Over fifty, and she married him, a widower with a family of grown-up children—all because of his philanthropic ideas. She used to sit listening to him spellbound. Just like Desdemona and Othello. Only fortunately there was no Iago about to mess things up—and anyway Gulbrandsen wasn't coloured. He was a Swede or a Norwegian or something."

Miss Marple nodded thoughtfully. The name of Gulbrandsen had an international significance. A man who with shrewd business acumen and perfect honesty had built up a fortune so colossal that really philanthropy had been the only solution to the disposal of it. The name still held significance. The Gulbrandsen Trust, the Gubrandsen Research Fellowships, the Gulbrandsen Administrative Almhouses, and best known of all the vast educational College for the sons of working men.

"She didn't marry him for his money, you know," said Ruth, "*I* should have if I'd married him at all. But not Carrie Louise. I don't know what would have happened if he hadn't died when she was thirty-two. Thirty-two's a very nice age for a widow. She's got experience, but she's still adaptable."

The spinster listening to her, nodded gently whilst her mind reviewed, tentatively, widows she had known in the village of St. Mary Mead.

"I was really happiest about Carrie Louise when she was married to Johnnie Restarick. Of course *he* married her for her money—or if not exactly that, at any rate he wouldn't have married her if she hadn't had any. Johnnie was a selfish, pleasure-loving, lazy hound, but that's so much safer than a crank. All Johnnie wanted was to live soft. He wanted Carrie Louise to go to the best dressmakers and have yachts and cars and enjoy herself with him. That kind of man is so very *safe*. Give him comfort and luxury and he'll purr like a cat and be absolutely charming to you. I never took that scene designing and theatrical stuff of his very seriously. But Carrie Louise was thrilled by it—saw it all as Art with a capital A and really forced him back into those surroundings, and then that dreadful Yugoslavian woman got hold of him and just swept him off with her. He didn't really want to go. If Carrie Louise had waited and been sensible, he would have come back to her."

"Did she care very much?" asked Miss Marple.

"That's the funny thing. I don't really believe she did. She was absolutely sweet about it all—but then she would be. She *is* sweet. Quite anxious to divorce him so that he and that creature could get married. And offering to give those two boys of his by his first marriage a home with her because it would be more settled for them. So there poor Johnnie was—he *had* to marry the woman and she led him an awful six months and then drove him over a precipice in a car in a fit of rage. They *said* it was an accident, but *I* think it was just temper!"

Mrs. Van Rydock paused, took up a mirror and gazed at her face searchingly. She picked up her eyebrow tweezers and pulled out a hair.

"And what does Carrie Louise do next but marry this man Lewis Serrocold. Another crank! Another man with ideals! Oh, I don't say he isn't devoted to her—I think he is—but he's bitten by that same bug of wanting to improve everybody's lives for them. And really, you know, nobody can do that but yourself."

"I wonder," said Miss Marple.

"Only, of course, there's a fashion in these things, just like there is in clothes. (My dear, have you seen what Christian Dior is trying to make us wear in the way of skirts?) Where was I? Oh yes, Fashion. Well, there's a fashion in philanthropy too. It used to be education in Gulbrandsen's day. But that's out of date now. The State has stepped in. Everyone expects education as a matter of right—and doesn't think much of it when they get it! Juvenile Delinquency—that's what is the rage nowadays. All these young criminals and potential criminals. Everyone's mad about them. You should see Lewis Serrocold's eyes sparkle behind those thick glasses of his. Crazy with enthusiasm! One of those men of enormous will power who like living on a banana and a piece of toast and put all their energies into a Cause. And Carrie Louise eats it up—just as she always did. But I don't like it, Jane. They've had meetings of the Trustees and the whole place has been turned over to this new idea. It's a training establishment now for these juvenile criminals, complete with psychiatrists and psychologists and all the rest of it. There Lewis and Carrie Louise are, living there, surrounded by these boys—who aren't perhaps quite normal. And the place stiff with occupational therapists and teachers and enthusiasts, half of *them* quite mad. Cranks, all the lot of them, and my little Carrie Louise in the middle of it all!"

She paused—and stared helplessly at Miss Marple.

Miss Marple said in a faintly puzzled voice:

"But you haven't told me yet, Ruth, what you are really afraid of."

"I tell you, I don't *know*! And *that's* what worries me. I've just been down there—for a flying visit. And I felt all along that there was something wrong. In the atmosphere—in the house—I know I'm not mistaken. I'm sensitive to atmosphere, always have been. Did I ever tell you how I urged Julius to sell out of Amalgamated Cereals before the crash came? And wasn't I right? Yes, something is *wrong* down there. But I don't know why or what—if it's these dreadful young jailbirds—or if it's nearer home. I can't say what it is. There's Lewis just living for his ideas and not noticing anything else, and Carrie Louise, bless her, never seeing or hearing or thinking anything except what's a lovely sight, or a lovely sound, or a lovely thought. It's sweet but it isn't *practical*. There *is* such a thing as evil —and I want you, Jane, to go down there right away and find out just exactly what's the matter."

"*Me?*" exclaimed Miss Marple. "Why me?"

"Because you've got a nose for that sort of thing. You always had. You've always been a sweet innocent-looking creature, Jane, and all the time underneath nothing has ever surprised you, you always believe the worst."

"The worst is so often true," murmured Miss Marple.

"Why you have such a poor idea of human nature, I can't think—living in that sweet peaceful village of yours, so old world and pure."

"You have never lived in a village, Ruth. The things that go on in a pure peaceful village would probably surprise you."

"Oh I daresay. My point is that they don't surprise *you*. So you *will* go down to Stonygates and find out what's wrong, won't you?"

"But, Ruth dear, that would be a most difficult thing to do."

"No, it wouldn't. I've thought it all out. If you won't be absolutely mad at me, I've prepared the ground already."

Mrs. Van Rydock paused, eyed Miss Marple rather uneasily, lighted a cigarette, and plunged rather nervously into explanation.

"You'll admit, I'm sure, that things have been difficult in this country since the war, for people with small fixed incomes—for people like you, that is to say, Jane."

"Oh yes, indeed. But for the kindness, the really great kindness of my nephew Raymond, I don't know really where I should be."

"Never mind your nephew," said Mrs. Van Rydock. "Carrie Louise knows nothing about your nephew—or if she does, she knows him as a writer and has no idea that he's your nephew. The point, as I put it to Carrie Louise, is that it's just too bad about dear Jane. Really sometimes hardly enough to eat, and of course far too proud ever to appeal to old friends. One couldn't, I said, suggest *money*—but a nice long rest in lovely surroundings, with an old friend and with plenty of nourishing food, and no cares or worries"—Ruth Van Rydock paused and then added defiantly, "Now go on—be mad at me if you want to be."

Miss Marple opened her china blue eyes in gentle surprise.

"But why should I be mad at you, Ruth? A very ingenious and plausible approach. I'm sure Carrie Louise responded."

"She's writing to you. You'll find the letter when you get back. Honestly, Jane, you don't feel that I've taken an unpardonable liberty? You won't mind——"

She hesitated and Miss Marple put her thoughts deftly into words:

"Going to Stonygates as an object of charity—more or less under false pretences? Not in the least—if it is *necessary*. You think it is necessary—and I am inclined to agree with you."

Mrs. Van Rydock stared at her.

"But why? What have you heard?"

"I haven't heard anything. It's just your conviction. You're not a fanciful woman, Ruth."

"No, but I haven't anything definite to go upon."

"I remember," said Miss Marple thoughtfully, "one Sunday morning at church—it was the second Sunday in Advent—sitting behind Grace Lamble and feeling more and more worried about her. Quite sure, you know, that something was wrong—badly wrong—and yet being quite unable to say why. A most disturbing feeling and very very definite."

"And was there something wrong?"

"Oh yes. Her father, the old Admiral, had been *very* peculiar for some time, and the very next day he went for her with the coal hammer, roaring out that she was Antichrist masquerading as his daughter. He nearly killed her. They took him away to the asylum and she eventually recovered after months in hospital—but it was a very near thing."

"And you'd actually had a premonition that day in church?"

"I wouldn't call it a premonition. It was founded on *fact* —these things usually are, though one doesn't always recognise it at the time. She was wearing her Sunday hat the wrong way round. Very significant, really, because Grace Lamble was a most precise woman, not at all vague of absent-minded—and the circumstances under which she would not notice which way her hat was put on to go to church were really extremely limited. Her father, you see, had thrown a marble paperweight at her and it had shattered the looking-glass. She had caught up her hat, put it on, and hurried out of the house. Anxious to keep up appearances and for the servants not to hear anything. She put down these actions, you see, to 'dear Papa's Naval temper,' she didn't realise that his mind was definitely unhinged. Though she ought to have realised it clearly enough. He was always complaining to her of being spied upon and of enemies—all the usual symptoms, in fact."

Mrs. Van Rydock gazed respectfully at her friend.

"Maybe, Jane," she said, "that St. Mary Mead of yours isn't quite the idyllic retreat that I've always imagined it."

"Human nature, dear, is very much the same everywhere. It is more difficult to observe it closely in a city that is all."

"And you'll go to Stonygates?"

"I'll go to Stonygates. A little unfair, perhaps, on my nephew Raymond. To let it be thought that he does not assist me, I mean. Still, the dear boy is in Mexico for six months. And by that time it should all be over."

"What should all be over?"

"Carrie Louise's invitation will hardly be for an indefinite stay. Three weeks, perhaps—a month. That should be ample."

"For you to find out what is wrong?"

"For me to find out what is wrong."

"My, Jane," said Mrs. Van Rydock, "you've got a lot of confidence in yourself, haven't you?"

Miss Marple looked faintly reproachful.

"*You* have confidence in me, Ruth. Or so you say . . . . I can only assure you that I shall endeavour to justify your confidence."

CHAPTER II

BEFORE catching her train back to St. Mary Mead (Wednesday special cheap day return), Miss Marple, in a precise and businesslike fashion, collected certain data.

"Carrie Louise and I have corresponded after a fashion, but it has largely been a matter of Christmas cards or calendars. It's just the facts I should like, Ruth dear—and also some idea as to whom exactly I shall encounter in the household at Stonygates."

"Well, you know about Carrie Louise's marriage to Gulbrandsen. There were no children and Carrie Louise took that very much to heart. Gulbrandsen was a widower, and had three grown-up sons. Eventually they adopted a child. Pippa, they called her—a lovely little creature. She was just two years old when they got her."

"Where did she come from? What was her background?"

"Really, now, Jane, I can't remember—if I ever heard, that is. An Adoption Society, maybe? Or some unwanted child that Gulbrandsen had heard about. Why? Do you think it's important?"

"Well, one always likes to know the background, so to speak. But please go on."

"The next thing that happened was that Carrie Louise found that she was going to have a baby after all. I understand from doctors that that quite often happens."

Miss Marple nodded.

"I believe so."

"Anyway, it did happen, and in a funny kind of way, Carrie Louise was almost disconcerted, if you can understand what I mean. Earlier, of course, she'd have been wild with joy. As it was, she'd given such a devoted love to Pippa that she felt quite apologetic to Pippa for putting her nose out of joint, so to speak. And then Mildred, when she arrived, was really a very unattractive child. Took after the Gulbrandsens—who were solid and worthy—but definitely homely. Carrie Louise was always so anxious to make no difference between the adopted child and her own child that I think she rather tended to over indulge Pippa and pass over Mildred. Sometimes I think that Mildred resented it. However I didn't see them often. Pippa grew up a very beautiful girl and Mildred grew up a plain one. Eric Gulbrandsen died when Mildred was fifteen and Pippa eighteen. At twenty Pippa married an Italian, the Marchese di San Severiano—oh, quite a genuine Marchese—not an adventurer, or anything like that. She was by way of being an heiress (naturally, or San Severiano wouldn't have married her—you know what Italians are!). Gulbrandsen left an equal sum in trust for both his own and his adopted daughter. Mildred married a Canon Strete—a nice man but given to colds in the head. About ten or fifteen years older than she was. Quite a happy marriage, I believe.

"He died a year ago and Mildred has come back to Stonygates to live with her mother. But that's getting on too fast, I've skipped a marriage or two. I'll go back to them. Pippa married her Italian. Carrie Louise was quite pleased about the marriage. Guido had beautiful manners and was very handsome, and he was a fine sportsman. A year later Pippa had a daughter and died in childbirth. It was a terrible tragedy and Guido San Severiano was very cut up. Carrie Louise went to and fro between Italy and England a good deal, and it was in Rome that she met Johnnie Restarick and married him. The Marchese married again and he was quite willing for his little daughter to be brought up in England by her exceedingly wealthy grandmother. So they all settled down at Stonygates, Johnnie Restarick and Carrie Louise, and Johnnie's two boys, Alexis and Stephen (Johnnie's first wife was a Russian) and the baby Gina. Mildred married her Canon soon afterwards. Then came all this business of Johnnie and the Yugoslavian woman and the divorce. The boys still came to Stonygates for their holidays and were devoted to Carrie Louise, and then in 1938, I think it was, Carrie Louise married Lewis."

Mrs. Van Rydock paused for breath.

"You've not met Lewis?"

Miss Marple shook her head.

"No, I think I last saw Carrie Louise in 1928. She very sweetly took me to Covent Garden—to the Opera."

"Oh yes. Well, Lewis was a very suitable person for her

to marry. He was the head of a very celebrated firm of chartered accountants. I think he met her first over some question of the finances of the Gulbrandsen Trust and the College. He was well off, just about her own age, and a man of absolutely upright life. But he *was* a crank. He was absolutely rabid on the subject of the redemption of young criminals."

Ruth Van Rydock sighed.

"As I said just now, Jane, there are fashions in philanthropy. In Gulbrandsen's time it was education. Before that it was soup kitchens——"

Miss Marple nodded.

"Yes, indeed, Port wine jelly and calf's head broth taken to the sick. My mother used to do it."

"That's right. Feeding the body gave way to feeding the mind. Everyone went mad on educating the lower classes. Well, that's passed. Soon, I expect, the fashionable thing to do will be not to educate your children, preserve their illiteracy carefully until they're eighteen. Anyway, the Gulbrandsen Trust and Education Fund was in some difficulties because the State was taking over its functions. Then Lewis came along with his passionate enthusiasm about constructive training for juvenile delinquents. His attention had been drawn to the subject first in the course of his profession—auditing accounts where ingenious young men had perpetrated frauds. He was more and more convinced that juvenile delinquents were not subnormal—that they had excellent brains and abilities and only needed right direction."

"There is something in that," said Miss Marple. "But it is not entirely true. I remember——"

She broke off and glanced at her watch.

"Oh dear—I mustn't miss the 6.30."

Ruth Van Rydock said urgently:

"And you will go to Stonygates?"

Gathering up her shopping bag and her umbrella Miss Marple said:

"If Carrie Louise asks me——"

"She will ask you. You'll go? Promise, Jane?"

Jane Marple promised.

MISS MARPLE got out of the train at Market Kindle station. A kindly fellow passenger handed out her suitcase after her, and Miss Marple, clutching a string bag, a faded leather handbag and some miscellaneous wraps, uttered appreciative twitters of thanks.

"So kind of you, I'm sure. . . . So difficult nowadays—not many porters. I get so flustered when I travel."

The twitters were drowned by the booming noise of the station announcer saying loudly but indistinctly that the 3.18 was standing at Platform 1, and was about to proceed to various unidentifiable stations.

Market Kindle was a large empty windswept station with hardly any passengers or railway staff to be seen on it. Its claim to distinction lay in having six platforms and a bay where a very small train of one carriage was puffing importantly.

Miss Marple, rather more shabbily dressed than was her custom (so lucky that she hadn't given away the old speckledy), was peering around her uncertainly when a young man came up to her.

"Miss Marple?" he said. His voice had an unexpectedly dramatic quality about it, as though the utterance of her name were the first words of a part he was playing in amateur theatricals. "I've come to meet you—from Stonygates."

Miss Marple looked gratefully at him, a charming helpless looking old lady with, if he had chanced to notice it, very shrewd blue eyes. The personality of the young man did not quite match his voice. It was less important, one might almost say insignificant. His eyelids had a trick of fluttering nervously.

"Oh thank you," said Miss Marple. "There's just this suitcase."

She noticed that the young man did not pick up her suitcase himself. He flipped a finger at a porter who was trundling some packing case past on a trolley.

"Bring it out, please," he said, and added importantly, "for Stonygates."

The porter said cheerfully:

"Rightyho. Shan't be long."

Miss Marple fancied that her new acquaintance was not too pleased about this. It was as if Buckingham Palace had been dismissed as no more important that 3 Laburnum Road.

He said, "The railways get more impossible every day!"

Guiding Miss Marple towards the exit, he said: "I'm Edgar Lawson. Mrs. Serrocold asked me to meet you. I help Mr. Serrocold in his work."

There was again the faint insinuation that a busy and important man had, very charmingly, put important affairs on one side out of chivalry to his employer's wife.

And again the impression was not wholly convincing— it had a theatrical flavour.

Miss Marple began to wonder about Edgar Lawson.

They came out of the station and Edgar guided the old lady to where a rather elderly Ford V. 8 was standing.

He was just saying "Will you come in front with me, or would you prefer the back?" when there was a diversion.

A new gleaming two-seater Rolls Bentley came purring into the station yard and drew up in front of the Ford. A very beautiful young woman jumped out of it and came across to them. The fact that she wore dirty corduroy slacks and a simple shirt open at the neck seemed somehow to enhance the fact that she was not only beautiful but expensive.

"There you are, Edgar. I thought I wouldn't make it in time. I see you've got Miss Marple. I came to meet her." She smiled dazzlingly at Miss Marple, showing a row of lovely teeth in a sunburnt southern face. "I'm Gina," she said. "Carrie Louise's granddaughter. What was your journey like? Simply foul? What a nice string bag. I *love* string bags. I'll take it and the coats and then you can get in better."

Edgar's face flushed. He protested.

"Look here, Gina, I came to meet Miss Marple. It was all arranged . . ."

Again the teeth flashed in that wide lazy smile.

"Oh I know, Edgar, but I suddenly thought it would be nice if I came along. I'll take her with me and you can wait and bring her cases up."

She slammed the door on Miss Marple, ran round to the other side, jumped in the driving seat, and they purred swiftly out of the station.

Looking back, Miss Marple noticed Edgar Lawson's face.

"I don't think, my dear," she said, "that Mr. Lawson is very pleased."

Gina laughed.

"Edgar's a frightful idiot," she said. "Always so pompous about things. You'd really think he *mattered*!"

Miss Marple asked, "Doesn't he matter?"

"Edgar?" There was an unconscious note of cruelty in Gina's scornful laugh. "Oh, he's bats anyway."

"Bats?"

"They're all bats at Stonygates," said Gina. "I don't mean Lewis and Grandam and me and the boys—and not Miss Bellever, of course. But the others. Sometimes I feel *I'm* going a bit bats myself living there. Even Aunt Mildred goes out on walks and mutters to herself all the time—and you don't expect a Canon's widow to do that, do you?"

They swung out of the station approach and accelerated up the smooth surfaced empty road. Gina shot a swift sideways glance at her companion.

"You were at school with Grandam, weren't you? It seems so queer."

Miss Marple knew perfectly what she meant. To youth it seems very odd to think that age was once young and pigtailed and struggled with decimals and English literature.

"It must," said Gina with awe in her voice, and obviously not meaning to be rude, "have been a *very* long time ago."

"Yes, indeed," said Miss Marple. "You feel that more with me than you do with your grandmother, I expect?"

Gina nodded. "It's cute of you saying that. Grandam, you know, gives one a curiously ageless feeling."

"It is a long time since I've seen her. I wonder if I shall find her much changed."

"Her hair's grey, of course," said Gina vaguely. "And she walks with a stick because of her arthritis. It's got much

211

worse lately. I suppose that——" She broke off, and then asked: "Have you been to Stonygates before?"

"No, never. I've heard a great deal about it, of course."

"It's pretty ghastly, really," said Gina cheerfully. "A sort of Gothic monstrosity. What Steve calls Best Victorian Lavatory period. But it's fun, too, in a way. Only of course everything's madly earnest, and you tumble over psychiatrists everywhere underfoot. Enjoying themselves madly. Rather like Scout-masters, only worse. The young criminals are rather pets, some of them. One showed me how to diddle locks with a bit of wire and one angelic faced boy gave me a lot of points about coshing people."

Miss Marple considered this information thoughtfully.

"It's the thugs I like best," said Gina. "I don't fancy the queers so much. Of course Lewis and Dr. Maverick think they're *all* queers—I mean they think it's repressed desires and disordered home life and their mothers getting off with soldiers and all that. I don't really see it myself because some people have had awful home lives and yet have managed to turn out quite all right."

"I'm sure it is all a very difficult problem," said Miss Marple.

Gina laughed, again showing her magnificent teeth.

"It doesn't worry me much. I suppose some people have these sort of urges to make the world a better place. Lewis is quite dippy about it all—he's going to Aberdeen next week because there's a case coming up in the police court —a boy with five previous convictions."

"The young man who met me at the station? Mr. Lawson. He helps Mr. Serrocold, he told me. Is he his secretary?"

"Oh Edgar hasn't brains enough to be a secretary. He's a *case*, really. He used to stay at hotels and pretend he was a V.C. or a fighter pilot and borrow money and then do a flit. I think he's just a rotter. But Lewis goes through a routine with them all. Makes them feel one of the family and gives them jobs to do and all that to encourage their sense of responsibility. I daresay we shall be murdered by one of them one of these days." Gina laughed merrily.

Miss Marple did not laugh.

They turned in through some imposing gates where a Commissionaire was standing on duty in a military manner and drove up a drive flanked with rhododendrons. The drive was badly kept and the grounds seemed neglected.

Interpreting her companion's glance, Gina said, "No gardeners during the war, and since we haven't bothered. But it does look rather terrible."

They came round a curve and Stonygates appeared in its full glory. It was, as Gina had said, a vast edifice of Victorian Gothic—a kind of temple to Plutocracy. Philanthropy had added to it in various wings and outbuildings which, while not positively dissimilar in style, had robbed the structure as a whole of any cohesion or purpose.

"Hideous, isn't it?" said Gina affectionately. "There's Grandam on the terrace. I'll stop here and you can go and meet her."

Miss Marple advanced along the terrace towards her old friend.

From a distance, the slim little figure looked curiously girlish in spite of the stick on which she leaned and her slow and obviously rather painful progress. It was as though a young girl was giving an exaggerated imitation of old age. "Jane," said Mrs. Serrocold.

"Dear Carrie Louise."

Yes, unmistakably Carrie Louise. Strangely unchanged, strangely youthful still, although, unlike her sister, she used no cosmetics or artificial aids to youth. Her hair was grey, but it had always been of a silvery fairness and the colour had changed very little. Her skin had still a rose leaf pink and white appearance, though now it was a crumpled rose leaf. Her eyes had still their starry innocent glance. She had the slender youthful figure of a girl and her head kept its eager birdlike tilt.

"I do blame myself," said Carrie Louise in her sweet voice, "for letting it be so long. *Years* since I saw you, Jane dear. It's just lovely that you've come at last to pay us a visit here."

From the end of the terrace Gina called:

"You ought to come in, Grandam. It's getting cold—and Jolly will be furious."

Carrie Louise gave her little silvery laugh.

"They all fuss about me so," she said. "They rub it in that I'm an old woman."

213

"And you don't feel like one."

"No, I don't, Jane. In spite of all my aches and pains—and I've got plenty. Inside I go on feeling just a chit like Gina. Perhaps everyone does. The glass shows them how old they are and they just don't believe it. It seems only a few months ago that we were at Florence. Do you remember Fraulein Schweich and her boots?"

The two elderly women laughed together at events that had happened nearly half a century ago.

They walked together to a side door. In the doorway a gaunt elderly lady met them. She had an arrogant nose, a short haircut and wore stout well-cut tweeds.

She said fiercely:

"It's absolutely crazy of you, Cara, to stay out so late. You're absolutely incapable of taking care of yourself. What will Mr. Serrocold say?"

"Don't scold me, Jolly," said Carrie Louise pleadingly. She introduced Miss Bellever to Miss Marple.

"This is Miss Bellever, who is simply everything to me. Nurse, dragon, watchdog, secretary, housekeeper and very faithful friend."

Juliet Bellever sniffed, and the end of her big nose turned rather pink, a sign of emotion.

"I do what I can," she said gruffly. "This is a crazy household. You simply can't arrange any kind of planned routine."

"Darling Jolly, of course you can't. I wonder why you ever try. Where are you putting Miss Marple?"

"In the Blue Room. Shall I take her up?" asked Miss Bellever.

"Yes, please do, Jolly. And then bring her down to tea. It's in the library to-day, I think."

The Blue Room had heavy curtains of a rich faded blue brocade that must have been, Miss Marple thought, about fifty years old. The furniture was mahogany, big and solid, and the bed was a vast mahogany four poster. Miss Bellever opened a door into a connecting bathroom. This was unexpectedly modern, orchid in colouring and with much dazzling chromium.

She observed grimly:

"John Restarick had ten bathrooms put into the house

214

when he married Cara. The plumbing is about the only thing that's ever been modernised. He wouldn't hear of the rest being altered—said the whole place was a perfect Period Piece. Did you ever know him at all?"

"No, I never met him. Mrs. Serrocold and I have met very seldom though we have always corresponded."

"He was an agreeable fellow," said Miss Bellever. "No good, of course! A complete rotter. But pleasant to have about the house. Great charm. Women liked him far too much. That was his undoing in the end. Not really Cara's type."

She added with a brusque resumption of her practical manner:

"The housemaid will unpack for you. Do you want a wash before tea?"

Receiving an affirmative answer, she said that Miss Marple would find her waiting at the top of the stairs.

Miss Marple went into the bathroom and washed her hands and dried them a little nervously on a very beautiful orchid coloured face towel. Then she removed her hat and patted her soft white hair into place.

Opening her door, she found Miss Bellever waiting for her, and was conducted down the big gloomy staircase and across a vast dark hall and into a room where bookshelves went up to the ceiling and a big window looked out over an artificial lake.

Carrie Louise was standing by the window and Miss Marple joined her.

"What a very imposing house this is," said Miss Marple. "I feel quite lost in it."

"Yes, I know. It's ridiculous, really. It was built by a prosperous iron master—or something of that kind. He went bankrupt not long after. I don't wonder really. There were about fourteen living-rooms—all enormous. I've never seen what people *can* want with more than one sitting-room. And all those huge bedrooms. Such a lot of unnecessary space. Mine is terribly overpowering—and quite a long way to walk from the bed to the dressing table. And great heavy dark crimson curtains."

"You haven't had it modernised and redecorated?"

Carrie Louise looked vaguely surprised.

"No. On the whole it's very much as it was when I first lived here with Eric. It's been repainted, of course, but they always do it the same colour. Those things don't really matter, do they? I mean I shouldn't have felt justified in spending a lot of money on that kind of thing when there are so many things that are so much more important."

"Have there been no changes at all in the house?"

"Oh yes—heaps of them. We've just kept a kind of block in the middle of the house as it was—the Great Hall and the rooms off and over. They're the best ones and Johnnie —my second husband—was lyrical over them and said they should never be touched or altered—and of course he was an artist and a designer and he knew about these things. But the East and West wings have been completely remodelled. All the rooms partitioned off and divided up, so that we have offices, and bedrooms for the teaching staff, and all that. The boys are all in the College building—you can see it from here."

Miss Marple looked out towards where large red brick buildings showed through a belt of sheltering trees. Then her eyes fell on something nearer at hand, and she smiled a little.

"What a very beautiful girl Gina is," she said.

Carrie Louise's face lit up.

"Yes, isn't she?" she said softly. "It's so lovely to have her back here again. I sent her to America at the beginning of the war—to Ruth. Did Ruth talk about her at all?"

"No. At least she did just mention her."

Carrie Louise sighed.

"Poor Ruth! She was frightfully upset over Gina's marriage. But I've told her again and again that I don't blame her in the least. Ruth doesn't realise, as I do, that the old barriers and class shibboleths are gone—or at any rate are going.

"Gina was doing her war work—and she met this young man. He was a Marine and had a very good war record. And a week later they were married. It was all far too quick, of course, no time to find out if they were really suited to each other—but that's the way of things nowadays. Young people belong to their generation. We may think they're unwise in many of their doings, but we have to accept their decisions. Ruth, though, was terribly upset."

"She didn't consider the young man suitable?"

"She kept saying that one didn't know anything about him. He came from the Middle West and he hadn't any money—and naturally no profession. There are hundreds of boys like that everywhere—but it wasn't Ruth's idea of what was right for Gina. However, the thing was done. I was so glad when Gina accepted my invitation to come over here with her husband. There's so much going on here —jobs of every kind, and if Walter wants to specialise in medicine or get a degree or anything he could do it in this country. After all, this is Gina's home. It's delightful to have her back, to have someone so warm and gay and alive in the house."

Miss Marple nodded and looked out of the window again at the two young people standing near the lake.

"They're a remarkably handsome couple, too," she said. "I don't wonder Gina fell in love with him!"

"Oh, but that—that isn't Wally." There was, quite suddenly, a touch of embarrassment, or restraint, in Mrs. Serrocold's voice. "That's Steve—the younger of Johnnie Restarick's two boys. When Johnnie—when he went away, he'd no place for the boys in the holidays, so I always had them here. They look on this as their home. And Steve's here permanently now. He runs our dramatic branch. We have a theatre, you know, and plays—we encourage all the artistic instincts. Lewis says that so much of this juvenile crime is due to exhibitionism, most of the boys have had such a thwarted unhappy home life, and these hold-ups and burglaries make them feel heroes. We urged them to write their own plays and act in them and design and paint their own scenery. Steve is in charge of the theatre. He's so keen and enthusiastic. It's wonderful what life he's put into the whole thing."

"I see," said Miss Marple slowly.

Her long distance sight was good (as many of her neighbours knew to their cost in the village of St. Mary Mead) and she saw very clearly the dark handsome face of Stephen Restarick as he stood facing Gina, talking eagerly. Gina's face she could not see, since the girl had her back to them,

217

but there was no mistaking the expression in Stephen Restarick's face.

"It isn't any business of mine," said Miss Marple, "but I suppose you realise, Carrie Louise, that he's in love with her."

"Oh no——" Carrie Louise looked troubled. "Oh no, I do hope not."

"You were always up in the clouds, Carrie Louise. There's not the least doubt about it."

CHAPTER IV

Before Mrs. Serrocold could say anything, her husband came in from the hall carrying some open letters in his hand.

Lewis Serrocold was a short man, not particularly impressive in appearance, but with a personality that immediately marked him out. Ruth had once said of him that he was more like a dynamo than a human being. He usually concentrated entirely on what was immediately occupying his attention and paid no attention to the objects or persons who were surrounding them.

"A bad blow, dearest," he said. "That boy, Jackie Flint. Back at his tricks again. And I really did think he meant to go straight this time if he got a proper chance. He was most earnest about it. You know we found he'd always been keen on railways—and both Maverick and I thought that if he got a job on the railways he'd stick to it and make good. But it's the same story. Petty thieving from the parcels office. Not even stuff he could want or sell. That shows that it *must* be psychological. We haven't really got to the root of the trouble. But I'm not giving up."

"Lewis—this is my old friend, Jane Marple."

"Oh how d'you do," said Mr. Serrocold absently. "So glad —they'll prosecute, of course. A nice lad, too, not too many brains, but a really nice boy. Unspeakable home he came from. I——"

He suddenly broke off, and the dynamo was switched on to the guest.

218

"Why, Miss Marple, I'm so delighted you've come to stay with us for a while. It will make such a great difference to Caroline to have a friend of old days with whom she can exchange memories. She has in many ways a grim time here —so much sadness in the stories of these poor children. We do hope you'll stay with us a very long time."

Miss Marple felt the magnetism and realised how attractive it would have been to her friend. That Lewis Serrocold was a man who would always put causes before people she did not doubt for a moment. It might have irritated some women, but not Carrie Louise.

Lewis Serrocold sorted out another letter.

"At any rate we've *some* good news. This is from the Wiltshire and Somerset Bank. Young Morris is doing extremely well. They're thoroughly satisfied with him and in fact are promoting him next month. I always knew that all he needed was responsibility—that, and a thorough grasp of the handling of money and what it means."

He turned to Miss Marple.

"Half these boys don't *know* what money is. It represents to them going to the pictures or to the dogs, or buying cigarettes—and they're clever with figures and find it exciting to juggle them round. Well, I believe in—what shall I say?—rubbing their noses in the stuff—train them in accountancy, in figures—show them the whole inner romance of money, so to speak. Give them skill and then responsibility—let them handle it officially. Our greatest successes have been that way—only two out of thirty-eight have let us down. One's head cashier in a firm of druggists— a really responsible position——"

He broke off to say: "Tea's in, dearest," to his wife.

"I thought we were having it here. I told Jolly."

"No, it's in the Hall. The others are there."

"I thought they were all going to be out."

Carrie Louise linked her arm through Miss Marple's and they went into the Great Hall. Tea seemed a rather incongruous meal in its surroundings. The tea things were piled haphazard on a tray—white utility cups mixed with the remnants of what had been Rockingham and Spode tea services. There was a loaf of bread, two pots of jam, and some cheap and unwholesome-looking cakes.

A plump middle-aged woman with grey hair sat behind the tea table and Mrs. Serrocold said:

"This is Mildred, Jane. My daughter Mildred. You haven't seen her since she was a tiny girl."

Mildred Strete was the person most in tune with the house that Miss Marple had so far seen. She looked prosperous and dignified. She had married late in her thirties a Canon of the Church of England and was now a widow. She looked exactly like a Canon's widow, respectable and slightly dull. She was a plain woman with a large unexpressive face and dull eyes. She had been, Miss Marple reflected, a very plain little girl.

"And this is Wally Hudd—Gina's husband."

Wally was a big young man with hair brushed up on his head and a sulky expression. He nodded awkwardly and went on cramming cake into his mouth.

Presently Gina came in with Stephen Restarick. They were both very animated.

"Gina's got a wonderful idea for that backcloth," said Stephen. "You know, Gina, you've got a very definite flair for theatrical designing."

Gina laughed and looked pleased. Edgar Lawson came in and sat down by Lewis Serrocold. When Gina spoke to him, he made a pretence of not answering.

Miss Marple found it all a little bewildering and was glad to go to her room and lie down after tea.

There were more people still at dinner, a young Dr. Maverick who was either a psychiatrist or a psychologist— Miss Marple was rather hazy about the difference—and whose conversation, dealing almost entirely with the jargon of his trade, was practically unintelligible to her. There were also two spectacled young men who held posts on the teaching side, and a Mr. Baumgarten, who was an occupational therapist, and three intensely bashful youths who were doing their "house guest" week. One of them, a fair-haired lad with very blue eyes was, Gina informed her in a whisper, the expert with the "cosh."

The meal was not a particularly appetising one. It was indifferently cooked and indifferently served. A variety of costumes were worn. Miss Bellever wore a high black dress, Mildred Strete wore evening dress and a woollen cardigan over it. Carrie Louise had on a short dress of grey wool—Gina was resplendent in a kind of peasant get up. Wally had not changed, nor had Stephen Restarick, Edgar Lawson had on a neat dark blue suit. Lewis Serrocold wore the conventional dinner jacket. He ate very little and hardly seemed to notice what was on his plate.

After dinner Lewis Serrocold and Dr. Maverick went away to the latter's office. The occupational therapist and the schoolmasters went away to some lair of their own. The three "cases" went back to the college. Gina and Stephen went to the theatre to discuss Gina's idea for a set. Mildred knitted an indeterminate garment and Miss Bellever darned socks. Wally sat in a chair gently tilted backwards and stared into space. Carrie Louise and Miss Marple talked about old days. The conversation seemed strangely unreal.

Edgar Lawson alone seemed unable to find a niche. He sat down and then got up restlessly.

"I wonder if I ought to go to Mr. Serrocold," he said rather loudly. "He may need me."

Carrie Louise said gently, "Oh I don't think so. He was going to talk over one or two points with Dr. Maverick this evening."

"Then I certainly won't butt in! I shouldn't dream of going where I wasn't wanted. I've already wasted time to-day going down to the station when Mrs. Hudd meant to go herself."

"She ought to have told you," said Carrie Louise. "But I think she just decided at the last moment."

"You do realise, Mrs. Serrocold, that she made me look a complete fool! A complete fool!"

"No, no," said Carrie Louise, smiling. "You mustn't have these ideas."

"I know I'm not needed or wanted. . . . I'm perfectly aware of *that*. If things had been different—if I'd had my proper place in life it would be very different. Very different indeed. It's no fault of mine that I haven't got my proper place in life."

"Now, Edgar," said Carrie Louise. "Don't work yourself up about nothing. Jane thinks it was very kind of you to meet her. Gina always has these sudden impulses—she didn't mean to upset you."

221

"Oh yes, she did. It was done on purpose—to humiliate me——"

"Oh Edgar——"

"You don't know half of what's going on, Mrs. Serrocold. Well, I won't say any more now except good night."

Edgar went out, shutting the door with a slam behind him.

Miss Bellever snorted:

"Atrocious manners."

"He's so sensitive," said Carrie Louise vaguely.

Mildred Strete clicked her needles and said sharply:

"He really is a most odious young man. You shouldn't put up with such behaviour, Mother."

"Lewis says he can't help it."

Mildred said sharply:

"Everyone can help behaving rudely. Of course I blame Gina very much. She's so completely scatter-brained in everything she undertakes. She does nothing but make trouble. One day she encourages the young man and the next day she snubs him. What can you expect?"

Wally Hudd spoke for the first time that evening.

He said:

"That guy's crackers. That's all there is to it! Crackers!"

II

In her bedroom that night Miss Marple tried to review the pattern of Stonygates, but it was as yet too confused. There were currents and cross-currents here—but whether they could account for Ruth Van Rydock's uneasiness it was impossible to tell. It did not seem to Miss Marple that Carrie Louise was affected in any way by what was going on round her. Stephen was in love with Gina. Gina might or might not be in love with Stephen. Walter Hudd was clearly not enjoying himself. These were incidents that might and did occur in all places and at most times. There was, unfortunately, nothing exceptional about them. They ended in the divorce court and everybody hopefully started again—when fresh tangles were created. Mildred Strete was clearly jealous of Gina and disliked her. That, Miss Marple thought, was very natural.

She thought over what Ruth Van Rydock had told her. Carrie Louise's disappointment at not having a child—the adoption of little Pippa—and then the discovery that, after all, a child was on the way.

"Often happens like that," Miss Marple's doctor had told her. "Relief of tension, maybe, and then Nature can do its work."

He had added that it was usually hard lines on the adopted child.

But that had not been so in this case. Both Gulbrandsen and his wife had adored little Pippa. She had made her place too firmly in their hearts to be lightly set aside. Gulbrandsen was already a father. Paternity meant nothing new to him. Carrie Louise's maternal yearnings had been assuaged by Pippa. Her pregnancy had been uncomfortable and the actual birth difficult and prolonged. Possibly Carrie Louise, who had never cared for reality, did not enjoy her first brush with it.

There remained two little girls growing up, one pretty and amusing, the other plain and dull. Which again, Miss Marple thought, was quite natural. For when people adopt a baby girl, they choose a pretty one. And though Mildred might have been lucky and taken after the Martins who had produced handsome Ruth and dainty Carrie Louise, Nature elected that she should take after the Gulbrandsens, who were large and stolid and uncompromisingly plain.

Moreover, Carrie Louise was determined that the adopted child should never feel her position, and in making sure of this she was over-indulgent to Pippa and sometimes less than fair to Mildred.

Pippa had married and gone away to Italy, and Mildred for a time had been the only daughter of the house. But then Pippa had died and Carrie Louise had brought Pippa's baby back to Stonygates, and once more Mildred had been out of it. There had been the new marriage—the Restarick boys. In 1934 Mildred had married Canon Strete, a scholarly antiquarian about fifteen years her senior and had gone away to live in the South of England. Presumably she had been happy—but one did not really know. There had been

223

no children. And now here she was, back again in the same house where she had been brought up. And once again, Miss Marple thought, not particularly happy in it.

Gina, Stephen, Wally, Mildred, Miss Bellever who liked an ordered routine and was unable to enforce it. Lewis Serrocold who was clearly blissfully and wholeheartedly happy; an idealist able to translate his ideals into practical measures. In none of these personalities did Miss Marple find what Ruth's words had led her to believe she might find. Carrie Louise seemed secure, remote at the heart of the whirlpool—as she had been all her life. What then, in that atmosphere, had Ruth felt to be wrong . . .? Did she, Jane Marple, feel it also?

What of the outer personalities of the whirlpool—the occupational therapists, the schoolmasters, earnest, harmless young men, confident young Dr. Maverick, the three pink-faced innocent-eyed young delinquents—Edgar Lawson . . .

And here, just before she fell asleep, Miss Marple's thoughts stopped and revolved speculatively round the figure of Edgar Lawson. Edgar Lawson reminded her of someone or something. There *was* something a little wrong about Edgar Lawson—perhaps more than a little. Edgar Lawson was maladjusted—that was the phrase, wasn't it? But surely that didn't, and couldn't touch Carrie Louise?

Mentally, Miss Marple shook her head.

What worried her was something more than that.

CHAPTER V

I

GENTLY eluding her hostess the next morning, Miss Marple went out into the gardens. Their condition distressed her. They had once been an ambitiously set out achievement. Clumps of rhododendrons, smooth slopes of lawns, massed borders of herbaceous plants, clipped boxhedges surrounding a formal rose garden. Now all was largely derelict, the lawns raggedly mown, the borders full of weeds with tangled flowers struggling through them, the paths moss-covered and neglected. The kitchen gardens, on the other hand, enclosed by red brick walls, were prosperous and well stocked. That, presumably, was because they had a utility value. So, also, a large portion of what had once been lawn and flower garden, was now fenced off and laid out in tennis courts and a bowling green.

Surveying the herbaceous border, Miss Marple clicked her tongue vexedly and pulled up a flourishing plant of groundsel.

As she stood with it in her hand, Edgar Lawson came into view. Seeing Miss Marple, he stopped and hesitated. Miss Marple had no mind to let him escape. She called him briskly. When he came, she asked him if he knew where any gardening tools were kept.

Edgar said vaguely that there was a gardener somewhere who would know.

"It's such a pity to see this border so neglected," twittered Miss Marple. "I'm so fond of gardens." And since it was not her intention that Edgar should go in search of any necessary implement she went on quickly:

"It's about all an old and useless woman can find to do. Now I don't suppose *you* ever bother your head about gardens, Mr. Lawson. You have so much real and important work to do. Being in a responsible position here, with Mr. Serrocold. You must find it all most interesting."

He answered quickly, almost eagerly:

"Yes—yes—it is interesting."

"And you must be of the greatest assistance to Mr. Serrocold."

His face darkened.

"I don't know. I can't be sure. It's what's *behind* it all——"

He broke off. Miss Marple watched him thoughtfully. A pathetic undersized young man in a neat dark suit. A young man that few people would look at twice, or remember if they did look . . . .

There was a garden seat nearby and Miss Marple drifted towards it and sat. Edgar stood frowning in front of her.

"I'm sure," said Miss Marple brightly, "that Mr. Serrocold relies on you a *great* deal."

"I don't know," said Edgar. "I really don't know." He frowned and almost absently sat down beside her. "I'm in a very difficult position."

"Yes?" said Miss Marple.

The young man Edgar sat staring in front of him.

"This is all highly confidential," he said suddenly.

"Of course," said Miss Marple.

"If I had my rights——"

"Yes?"

"I might as well tell you. . . . You won't let it go any further I'm sure?"

"Oh no." She noticed he did not wait for her disclaimer.

"My father—actually, my father is a very important man."

This time there was no need to say anything. She had only to listen.

"Nobody knows except Mr. Serrocold. You see, it might prejudice my father's position if the story got out." He turned to her. He smiled. A sad dignified smile. "You see, *I'm Winston Churchill's son.*"

"Oh," said Miss Marple. "I *see.*"

And she did see. She remembered a rather sad story in St. Mary Mead—and the way it had gone.

Edgar Lawson went on, and what he said had the familiarity of a stage scene.

"There were reasons. My mother wasn't free. Her own husband was in an asylum—there could be no divorce—no question of marriage. I don't really blame them. At least, I think I don't. . . . He's done, always, everything he could. Discreetly, of course. And that's where the trouble has arisen. He's got enemies—and they're against me, too. They've managed to keep us apart. They watch me. Wherever I go, they spy on me. And they make things go wrong for me."

Miss Marple shook her head.

"Dear, dear," she said.

"In London I was studying to be a doctor. They tampered with my exams—they altered the answers. They *wanted* me to fail. They followed me about the streets. They told things about me to my landlady. They hound me wherever I go."

"Oh, but you can't be sure of that," said Miss Marple soothingly.

"I tell you I *know*! Oh they're very cunning. I never get a glimpse of them or find out who they are. But I shall find out. . . . Mr. Serrocold took me away from London and brought me down here. He was kind—very kind. But even here, you know, I'm not *safe*. They're here, too. Working against me. Making the others dislike me. Mr. Serrocold says that isn't true—but Mr. Serrocold doesn't know. Or else—I wonder—sometimes I've thought——"

He broke off. He got up.

"This is all confidential," he said. "You do understand that, don't you? But if you notice anyone *following* me—*spying*, I mean—you might let me know *who it is*!"

He went away, then—neat, pathetic, insignificant. Miss Marple watched him and wondered . . .

A voice spoke.

"Nuts," it said. "Just nuts."

Walter Hudd was standing beside her. His hands were thrust deep in his pockets and he was frowning as he stared after Edgar's retreating figure.

"What kind of a joint is this, anyway?" he said. "They're all bughouse, the whole lot of them."

Miss Marple said nothing and Walter went on:

"That Edgar guy—what do you make of him? Says his father's really Lord Montgomery. Doesn't seem likely to me? Not *Monty*! Not from all I've heard about him."

"No," said Miss Marple. "It doesn't seem very likely."

"He told Gina something quite different—some bunk about being really the heir to the Russian throne—said he was some Grand Duke's son or other. Hell, doesn't the chap know who his father really was?"

"I should imagine not," said Miss Marple. "That is probably just the trouble."

Walter sat down beside her, dropping his body on to the seat with a slack movement. He repeated his former statement.

"They're all bughouse here."

"You don't like being at Stonygates?"

The young man frowned.

"I simply don't *get* it—that's all! I don't get it. Take this place—the house—the whole set-up. They're rich, these people. They don't need dough—they've got it. And look

227

at the way they live. Cracked antique china and cheap plain stuff all mixed up. No proper upper-class servants—just some casual hired help. Tapestries and drapes and chair-covers all satin and brocade and stuff—and it's falling to pieces! Big silver tea urns and what do you know—all yellow and tarnished for want of cleaning. Mrs. Serrocold just doesn't care. Look at that dress she had on last night. Darned under the arms, nearly worn out—and yet she could go to a store and order what she liked. Bond Street or wherever it is. Dough? They're rolling in dough."

He paused and sat, deliberating.

"I understand being poor. There's nothing much wrong with it. If you're young and strong and ready to work. I never had much money, but I was all set to get where I wanted. I was going to open a garage. I'd got a bit of money put by. I talked to Gina about it. She listened. She seemed to understand, I didn't know much about her. All those girls in uniform, they look about the same. I mean you can't tell from looking at them who's got dough and who hasn't. I thought she was a cut above me, perhaps, education and all that. But it didn't seem to matter. We fell for each other. We got married. I'd got my bit put by and Gina had some too, she told me. We were going to set up a gas station back home—Gina was willing. Just a couple of crazy kids we were—mad about each other. Then that snooty aunt of Gina's started making trouble. . . . And Gina wanted to come here to England to see her grandmother. Well, that seemed fair enough. It was her home, and I was curious to see England anyway. I'd heard a lot about it. So we came. Just a visit—that's what I thought."

The frown became a scowl.

"But it hasn't turned out like that. We're caught up in this crazy business. Why don't we stay here—make our home here—that's what they say? Plenty of jobs for me. Jobs! I don't want a job feeding candy to gangster kids and helping them play at kids' games . . . what's the sense of it all? This place could be swell—*really* swell. Don't people who've got money understand their luck? Don't they understand that most of the world can't have a swell place like this and that they've got one? Isn't it plain crazy to kick your luck when you've got it? I don't mind working

if I've got to. But I'll work the way I like and at what I like
—and I'll work to get somewhere. This place makes me feel
I'm tangled up in a spider's web. And Gina—I can't make
Gina out. She's not the same girl I married over in the
States. I can't—dang it all—I can't even *talk* to her now.
Oh hell!"

Miss Marple said gently:

"I quite see your point of view."

Wally shot a swift glance at her.

"You're the only one I've shot my mouth off to so far.
Most of the time I shut up like a clam. Don't know what it
is about you—you're English right enough, really English
—but in the durndest way you remind me of my Aunt Betsy
back home."

"Now that's very nice."

"A lot of sense she had," Wally continued reflectively.
"Looked as frail as though you could snap her in two,
but actually she was tough—yes, sir, I'll say she was tough."

He got up.

"Sorry talking to you this way," he apologised. For the
first time, Miss Marple saw him smile. It was a very attractive smile, and Wally Hudd was suddenly transfigured from
an awkward sulky boy into a handsome and appealing
young man. "Had to get things off my chest, I suppose.
But too bad picking on you."

"Not at all, my dear boy," said Miss Marple. "I have a
nephew of my own—only, of course, a great deal older than
you are."

Her mind dwelt for a moment on the sophisticated
modern writer Raymond West. A greater contrast to Walter
Hudd could not have been imagined.

"You've got other company coming," said Walter Hudd.
"That dame doesn't like me. So I'll quit. So long, ma'am.
Thanks for the talk."

He strode away and Miss Marple watched Mildred Strete
coming across the lawn to join her.

11

"I see you've been victimised by that terrible young man,"

229

said Mrs. Strete, rather breathlessly, as she sank down on the seat. "What a tragedy that is."

"A tragedy?"

"Gina's marriage. It all came about from sending her off to America. I told mother at the time it was most unwise. After all, this is quite a quiet district. We had hardly any raids here. I do so dislike the way many people gave way to panic about their families—and themselves, too, very often."

"It must have been difficult to decide what was right to do," said Miss Marple thoughtfully. "Where children were concerned, I mean. With the prospect of possible invasion, it might have meant their being brought up under a German regime—as well as the danger of bombs."

"All nonsense," said Mrs. Strete. "I never had the least doubt that we should win. But mother has always been quite unreasonable where Gina is concerned. The child was always spoilt and indulged in every way. There was absolutely no need to take her away from Italy in the first place."

"Her father raised no objection, I understand?"

"Oh San Severiano! You know what Italians are. Nothing matters to them but money. He married Pippa for her money, of course."

"Dear me. I always understood he was very devoted to her and was quite inconsolable at her death."

"He pretended to be, no doubt. Why mother ever countenanced her marrying a foreigner, I can't imagine. Just the usual American pleasure in a title, I suppose."

Miss Marple said mildly:

"I have always thought that dear Carrie Louise was almost too unworldly in her attitude to life."

"Oh, I know. I've no patience with it. Mother's fads and whims and idealistic projects. You've no idea, Aunt Jane, of all that it has meant. I can speak with knowledge, of course. I was brought up in the middle of it all."

It was with a very faint shock that Miss Marple heard herself addressed as Aunt Jane. And yet that had been the convention of those times. Her Christmas presents to Carrie Louise's children were always labelled "With love from Aunt Jane," and as "Aunt Jane" they thought of her, when they thought of her at all. Which was not, Miss Marple supposed, very often.

She looked thoughtfully at the middle-aged woman sitting beside her. At the pursed tight mouth, the deep lines from the nose down, the hands tightly pressed together.

She said gently:

"You must have had—a difficult childhood."

Mildred Strete turned eager grateful eyes to her.

"Oh I'm so glad that somebody appreciates that. People don't really know what children go through. Pippa, you see, was the pretty one. She was older than I was, too. It was always she who got all the attention. Both father and mother encouraged her to push herself forward—not that she needed any encouragement—to show off. I was always the quiet one. I was shy—Pippa didn't know what shyness was. A child can suffer a great deal, Aunt Jane."

"I know that," said Miss Marple.

"'Mildred's so stupid'—that's what Pippa used to say. But I was younger than she was. Naturally I couldn't be expected to keep up with her in lessons. And it's very unfair on a child when her sister is always put in front of her.

"'What a lovely little girl,' people used to say to Mamma. They never noticed *me*. And it was Pippa that Papa used to joke and play with. Someone ought to have seen how hard it was on *me*. All the notice and attention going to her. I wasn't old enough to realise that it's *character* that matters."

Her lips trembled, then hardened again.

"And it was unfair—really unfair—I was their own child. Pippa was only adopted. *I* was the daughter of the house. She was—nobody."

"Probably they were extra indulgent to her on that account," said Miss Marple.

"They liked her best," said Mildred Strete. And added: "A child whose own parents didn't want her—or more probably illegitimate."

She went on:

"It's come out in Gina. There's bad blood there. Blood will tell. Lewis can have what theories he likes about environment. Bad blood does tell. Look at Gina."

"Gina is a very lovely girl," said Miss Marple.

231

"Hardly in behaviour," said Mrs. Strete. "Everyone but mother notices how she is carrying on with Stephen Restarick. Quite disgusting, I call it. Admittedly she made a very unfortunate marriage, but marriage is marriage and one should be prepared to abide by it. After all, she chose to marry that dreadful young man."

"Is he so dreadful?"

"Oh dear Aunt Jane! He really looks to me quite like a gangster. And so surly and rude. He hardly opens his mouth. And he always looks so raw and uncouth."

"He is unhappy, I think," said Miss Marple mildly.

"I really don't know why he should be—apart from Gina's behaviour, I mean. Everything has been done for him here. Lewis has suggested several ways in which he could try to make himself useful—but he prefers to skulk about doing nothing."

She burst out: "Oh this whole place is impossible—quite impossible. Lewis thinks of nothing but these horrible young criminals. And mother thinks of nothing but him. Everything Lewis does is right. Look at the state of the garden—the weeds—the overgrowth. And the house—nothing properly done. Oh I know a domestic staff is difficult nowadays, but it can be got. It's not as though there were any shortage of money. It's just that nobody *cares*. If it were *my* house——" She stopped.

"I'm afraid," said Miss Marple, "that we have all to face the fact that conditions are different. These large establishments are a great problem. It must be sad for you, in a way, to come back here and find everything so different. Do you really prefer living here to—well—somewhere of your own?"

Mildred Strete flushed.

"After all, it's my home," she said. "It was my father's house. Nothing can alter that. I've a right to be here if I choose. And I do choose. If only mother were not so impossible! She won't even buy herself proper clothes. It worries Jolly a lot."

"I was going to ask you about Miss Bellever."

"Such a comfort having her here. She adores mother. She's been with her a long time now—she came in John Restarick's time. And was wonderful, I believe, during the

232

whole sad business. I expect you heard that he ran away with a dreadful Yugoslavian woman—a most abandoned creature. She's had any amount of lovers, I believe. Mother was very fine and dignified about it all. Divorced him as quietly as possible. Even went so far as to have the Restarick boys for their holidays—quite unnecessary, really, other arrangements could have been made. It would have been unthinkable of course, to have let them go to their father and that woman. Anyway, mother had them here. . . . And Miss Bellever stood by all through things and was a tower of strength. I sometimes think she makes mother even more vague than she need be, by doing all the practical things herself. But I really don't know what mother would do without her."

She paused and then remarked in a tone of surprise:

"Here is Lewis. How odd. He seldom comes out in the garden."

Mr. Serrocold came towards them in the same single-minded way that he did everything. He appeared to notice Mildred, because it was only Miss Marple who was in his mind.

"I'm so sorry," he said. "I wanted to take you round our institution and show you everything. Caroline asked me to. Unfortunately I have to go off to Liverpool. The case of that boy and the railway parcels office. But Maverick will take you. He'll be here in a few minutes. I shan't be back until the day after to-morrow. It will be splendid if we can get them not to prosecute."

Mildred Strete got up and walked away. Lewis Serrocold did not notice her go. His earnest eyes gazed at Miss Marple through thick glasses.

"You see," he said, "the Magistrates nearly always take the wrong view. Sometimes they're too severe, but sometimes they're too lenient. If these boys get a sentence of a few months it's no deterrent—they get a kind of a kick out of it, even. Boast about it to their girl friends. But a severe sentence often sobers them. They realise that the game isn't worth it. Or else it's better not to serve a prison sentence at all. Corrective training—constructional training like we have here——"

Miss Marple interrupted him.

"Mr. Serrocold," she said. "Are you quite satisfied about young Mr. Lawson. Is he—is he quite normal?"

A disturbed expression appeared on Lewis Serrocold's face.

"I do hope he's not relapsing. What has he been saying?"

"He told me that he was Winston Churchill's son——"

"Of course—of course. The usual statements. He's illegitimate, as you've probably guessed, poor lad, and of very humble beginnings. He was a case recommended to me by a Society in London. He'd assaulted a man in the street who he said was spying on him. All very typical—Dr. Maverick will tell you. I went into his case history. Mother was of a poor class but a respectable family in Plymouth. Father a sailor—she didn't even know his name. . . . Child brought up in difficult circumstances. Started romancing about his father and later about himself. Wore uniform and decorations he wasn't entitled to—all quite typical. But Maverick considers the prognosis hopeful. If we can give him confidence in himself. I've given him responsibility here, tried to make him appreciate that it's not a man's birth that matters but what he *is*. I've tried to give him confidence in his own ability. The improvement was marked. I was very happy about him. And now you say——"

He shook his head.

"Mightn't he be dangerous, Mr. Serrocold?"

"Dangerous? I don't think he has shown any suicidal tendencies."

"I wasn't thinking of suicide. He talked to me of enemies —of persecution. Isn't that, forgive me—a dangerous sign?"

"I don't really think it has reached such a pitch. But I'll speak to Maverick. So far, he has been hopeful—very hopeful."

He looked at his watch.

"I must go. Ah, here is our dear Jolly. She will take charge of you."

Miss Bellever, arriving briskly, said, "The car is at the door, Mr. Serrocold. Dr. Maverick rang through from the Institute. I said I would bring Miss Marple over. He will meet us at the gates."

"Thank you. I must go. My brief case?"

"In the car, Mr. Serrocold."

Lewis Serrocold hurried away. Looking after him, Miss Bellever said:

"Someday that man will drop dead in his tracks. It's against human nature never to relax or rest. He only sleeps four hours a night."

"He is very devoted to this cause," said Miss Marple.

"Never thinks of anything else," said Miss Bellever grimly. "Never dreams of looking after his wife or considering her in any way. She's a sweet creature, as you know, Miss Marple, and she ought to have love and attention. But nothing's thought of or considered here except a lot of whining boys and young men who want to live easily and dishonestly and don't care about the idea of doing a little hard work. What about the decent boys from decent homes? Why isn't something done for them? Honesty just isn't interesting to cranks like Mr. Serrocold and Dr. Maverick and all the bunch of half-baked sentimentalists we've got here. I and my brothers were brought up the hard way, Miss Marple, and we weren't encouraged to whine. Soft, that's what the world is nowadays!"

They had crossed the garden and passed through a palisaded gate and had come to the arched gate which Eric Gulbrandsen had erected as an entrance to his College, a sturdily built, hideous, red brick building.

Dr. Maverick, looking, Miss Marple decided, distinctly abnormal himself, came out to meet them.

"Thank you, Miss Bellever," he said. "Now, Miss—er—oh yes, Miss Marple—I'm sure you're going to be interested in what we're doing here. In our splendid approach to this great problem. Mr. Serrocold is a man of great insight—great vision. And we've got Sir John Stillwell behind us—my old chief. He was at the Home Office until he retired and his influence turned the scales in getting this started. It's a *medical* problem—that's what we've got to get the legal authorities to understand. Psychiatry came into its own in the war. The one positive good that did come out of it—— Now first of all I want you to see our initial approach to the problem. Look up——"

Miss Marple looked up at the words carved over the large arched doorway:

RECOVER HOPE ALL YE WHO ENTER HERE

"Isn't that splendid? Isn't that just the right note to strike. You don't want to scold these lads—or punish them. That's what they're hankering after half the time, punishment. We want to make them feel what fine fellows they are."

"Like Edgar Lawson?" said Miss Marple.

"Interesting case, that. Have you been talking to him?"

"He has been talking to me," said Miss Marple. She added apologetically, "I wondered if, perhaps, he isn't a little *mad*?"

Dr. Maverick laughed cheerfully.

"We're all mad, dear lady," he said as he ushered her in through the door. "That's the secret of existence. We're all a little mad."

CHAPTER VI

ON THE whole it was rather an exhausting day.

Enthusiasm in itself can be extremely wearing, Miss Marple thought. She felt vaguely dissatisfied with herself and her own reactions. There was a pattern here—perhaps several patterns, and yet she herself could obtain no clear glimpse of it or them. Any vague disquietude she felt centred round the pathetic but inconspicuous personality of Edgar Lawson. If she could only find in her memory the right parallel.

Painstakingly she rejected the curious behaviour of Mr. Selkirk's delivery van—the absent-minded postman—the gardener who worked on Whit Monday—and that very curious affair of the summer weight combinations.

Something that she could not quite put her finger on was wrong about Edgar Lawson—something that went beyond the observed and admitted facts. But for the life of her, Miss Marple did not see how that wrongness, whatever it was, affected her friend Carrie Louise. In the confused patterns of life as Stonygates people's troubles and desires impinged on each other. But none of them (again as far as she could see) impinged on Carrie Louise.

Carrie Louise . . . Suddenly Miss Marple realised that it was she alone, except for the absent Ruth, who used that name. To her husband, she was Caroline. To Miss Bellever, Cara. Stephen Restarick usually addressed her as Madonna. To Wally she was formally Mrs. Serrocold, and Gina elected to address her as Grandam—a mixture, she had explained, of Grande Dame and Grandmamma.

Was there some significance, perhaps, in the various names that were found for Caroline Louise Serrocold? Was she to all of them a symbol and not quite a real person?

When on the following morning Carrie Louise, dragging her feet a little as she walked, came and sat down on the garden seat beside her friend and asked her what she was thinking about, Miss Marple replied promptly:

"You, Carrie Louise."

"What about me?"

"Tell me honestly—is there anything here that worries you?"

"Worries me?" The other woman raised wondering clear blue eyes. "But Jane, what should worry me?"

"Well, most of us have worries." Miss Marple's eyes twinkled a little. "I have. Slugs, you know—and the difficulty of getting linen properly darned—and not being able to get sugar candy for making my damson gin. Oh, lots of little things—it seems unnatural that you shouldn't have any worries at all."

"I suppose I must have really," said Mrs. Serrocold vaguely. "Lewis works too hard, and Stephen forgets his meals slaving at the theatre, and Gina is very jumpy—but I've never been able to alter people—I don't see how you can. So it wouldn't be any good worrying, would it?"

"Mildred's not very happy, either, is she?"

"Oh no," said Carrie Louise. "Mildred never is happy. She wasn't as a child. Quite unlike Pippa, who was always radiant."

"Perhaps," suggested Miss Marple, "Mildred had cause not to be happy?"

Carrie Louise said quietly:

"Because of being jealous? Yes, I daresay. But people

237

don't really need a cause for feeling what they do feel. They're just made that way. Don't you think so, Jane?"

Miss Marple thought briefly of Miss Moncrieff, a slave to a tyrannical invalid mother. Poor Miss Moncrieff who longed for travel and to see the world. And of how St. Mary Mead in a decorous way had rejoiced when Mrs. Moncrieff was laid in the churchyard and Miss Moncrieff, with a nice little income, was free at last. And of how Miss Moncrieff, starting on her travels, had got no farther than Hyères where, calling to see one of "mother's oldest friends," she had been so moved by the plight of an elderly hypochondriac that she had cancelled her travel reservations and taken up her abode in the villa to be bullied, overworked, and to long wistfully, once more, for the joys of a wider horizon.

Miss Marple said:

"I expect you're right, Carrie Louise."

"Of course my being so free from cares is partly due to Jolly. Dear Jolly. She came to me when Johnnie and I were just married and was wonderful from the first. She takes care of me as though I were a baby and quite helpless. She'd do anything for me. I feel quite ashamed sometimes. I really believe Jolly would murder someone for me, Jane. Isn't that an awful thing to say?"

"She's certainly very devoted," agreed Miss Marple.

"She gets so indignant." Mrs. Serrocold's silvery laugh rang out. "She'd like me to be always ordering wonderful clothes, and surrounding myself with luxuries, and she thinks everybody ought to put me first and to dance attendance on me. She's the one person who's absolutely unimpressed by Lewis's enthusiasm. All our poor boys are in her view pampered young criminals and not worth taking trouble over. She thinks this place is damp and bad for my rheumatism, and that I ought to go to Egypt or somewhere warm and dry."

"Do you suffer much from rheumatism?"

"It's got much worse lately. I find it difficult to walk. Horrid cramps in my legs. Oh well——" again there came that bewitching elfin smile, "age must tell."

Miss Bellever came out of the french windows and hurried across to them.

238

"A telegram, Cara, just come over the telephone. *Arriving this afternoon, Christian Gulbrandsen.*"

"Christian?" Carrie Louise looked very surprised. "I'd no idea he was in England."

"The oak suite, I suppose?"

"Yes, please, Jolly. Then there will be no stairs."

Miss Bellever nodded and turned back to the house.

"Christian Gulbrandsen is my stepson," said Carrie Louise. "Eric's eldest son. Actually he's two years older than I am. He's one of the trustees of the Institute—the principal trustee. How very annoying that Lewis is away. Christian hardly ever stays longer than one night. He's an immensely busy man. And there are sure to be so many things they would want to discuss."

Christian Gulbrandsen arrived that afternoon in time for tea. He was a big heavy-featured man, with a slow methodical way of talking. He greeted Carrie Louise with every sign of affection.

"And how is our little Carrie Louise? You do not look a day older. Not a day."

His hands on her shoulders—he stood smiling down at her. A hand tugged his sleeve.

"Christian!"

"Ah," he turned—"it is Mildred? How are you, Mildred?"

"I've not really been at all well lately."

"That is bad. That is bad."

There was a strong resemblance between Christian Gulbrandsen and his half sister Mildred. There was nearly thirty years' difference in age and they might easily have been taken for father and daughter. Mildred herself seemed particularly pleased by his arrival. She was flushed and talkative, and had talked repeatedly during the day of "my brother," "my brother Christian," "my brother, Mr. Gulbrandsen."

"And how is little Gina?" said Gulbrandsen, turning to that young woman. "You and your husband are still here, then?"

"Yes. We've quite settled down, haven't we, Wally?"

"Looks like it," said Wally.

Gulbrandsen's small shrewd eyes seemed to sum up Wally quickly. Wally, as usual, looked sullen and unfriendly.

"So here I am with all the family again," said Gulbrandsen.

His voice displayed a rather determined geniality—but in actual fact, Miss Marple thought, he was not feeling particularly genial. There was a grim set to his lips and a certain preoccupation in his manner.

Introduced to Miss Marple, he swept a keen look over her as though measuring and appraising this newcomer.

"We'd no idea you were in England, Christian," said Mrs. Serrocold.

"No, I came over rather unexpectedly."

"It is too bad that Lewis is away. How long can you stay?"

"I meant to go to-morrow. When will Lewis be back?"

"To-morrow afternoon or evening."

"It seems then that I must stay another night."

"If you'd only let us know——"

"My dear Carrie Louise, my arrangements, they were made very suddenly."

"You will stay to see Lewis?"

"Yes, it is necessary that I see Lewis."

Miss Bellever said to Miss Marple: "Mr. Gulbrandsen and Mr. Serrocold are both trustees of the Gulbrandsen Institute. The others are the Bishop of Cromer and Mr. Gilroy."

Presumably, then, it was on business concerned with the Gulbrandsen Institute that Christian Gulbrandsen had come to Stonygates. It seemed to be assumed so by Miss Bellever and everyone else. And yet Miss Marple wondered.

Once or twice the old man cast a thoughtful puzzled look at Carrie Louise when she was not aware of it—a look that puzzled Carrie Louise's watching friend. From Carrie Louise he shifted his gaze to the others, examining them one and all with a kind of covert appraisal that seemed distinctly odd.

After tea, Miss Marple withdrew tactfully from the others to the library, but rather to her surprise when she had settled herself with her knitting, Christian Gulbrandsen came in and sat down beside her.

"You are a very old friend, I think, of our dear Carrie Louise?" he said.

240

"We were at school together in Italy, Mr. Gulbrandsen. Many many years ago."

"Ah yes. And you are fond of her?"

"Yes, indeed," said Miss Marple warmly.

"So, I think, is everyone. Yes, I truly think that. It should be so. For she is a very dear and enchanting person. Always, since my father married her, I and my brothers have loved her very much. She has been to us like a very dear sister. She was a faithful wife to my father and loyal to all his ideas. She has never thought of herself, but put the welfare of others first."

"She has always been an idealist," said Miss Marple.

"An idealist? Yes. Yes, that is so. And therefore it may be that she does not truly appreciate the evil that there is in the world."

Miss Marple looked at him, surprised. His face was very stern.

"Tell me," he said. "How is her health?"

Again Miss Marple felt surprised.

"She seems to me very well—apart from arthritis—or rheumatism."

"Rheumatism? Yes. And her heart? Her heart is good?"

"As far as I know." Miss Marple was still more surprised. "But until yesterday I had not seen her for many years. If you want to know the state of her health, you should ask somebody in the house here. Miss Bellever, for instance."

"Miss Bellever—— Yes, Miss Bellever. Or Mildred?"

"Or, as you say, Mildred."

Miss Marple was faintly embarrassed.

Christian Gulbrandsen was staring at her very hard.

"There is not between the mother and daughter a very great sympathy, would you say?"

"No, I don't think there is."

"I agree. It is a pity—her only child, but there it is. Now this Miss Bellever, you think, is really attached to her?"

"Very much so."

"And Carrie Louise leans on this Miss Bellever?"

"I think so."

Christian Gulbrandsen was frowning. He spoke as though more to himself than to Miss Marple.

"There is the little Gina—but she is so young. It is

difficult——" He broke off. "Sometimes," he said simply, "it is hard to know what is best to be done. I wish very much to act for the best. I am particularly anxious that no harm and no unhappiness should come to that dear lady. But it is not easy—not easy at all."

Mrs. Strete came into the room at that moment.

"Oh, there you are, Christian. We were wondering where you were. Dr. Maverick wants to know if you would like to go over anything with him."

"That is the new young doctor here? No—no, I will wait until Lewis returns."

"He's waiting in Lewis's study. Shall I tell him——"

"I will have a word with him myself."

Gulbrandsen hurried out. Mildred Strete stared after him and then stared at Miss Marple.

"I wonder if anything is wrong. Christian is very unlike himself. . . . Did he say anything——"

"He only asked me about your mother's health."

"Her health? Why should he ask you about that?"

Mildred spoke sharply, her large square face flushing unbecomingly.

"I really don't know."

"Mother's health is perfectly good. Surprisingly so for a woman of her age. Much better than mine as far as that goes." She paused a moment before saying: "I hope you told him so?"

"I don't really know anything about it," said Miss Marple. "He asked me about her heart."

"Her *heart*?"

"Yes."

"There's nothing wrong with mother's heart. Nothing at all!"

"I'm delighted to hear you say so, my dear."

"What on earth put all these queer ideas into Christian's head?"

"I've no idea," said Miss Marple.

242

CHAPTER VII

I

THE NEXT day passed uneventfully to all appearances, yet to Miss Marple it seemed that there were signs of an inner tension. Christian Gulbrandsen spent his morning with Dr. Maverick in going round the Institute and in discussing the general results of the Institute's policy. In the early afternoon Gina took him for a drive, and after that Miss Marple noticed that he induced Miss Bellever to show him something in the gardens. It seemed to her that it was a pretext for ensuring a *tête-à-tête* with that grim woman. And yet, if Christian Gulbrandsen's unexpected visit had only to do with business matters, why this wish for Miss Bellever's company, since the latter dealt only with the domestic side of Stonygates.

But in all this, Miss Marple could tell herself that she was being fanciful. The one really disturbing incident of the day happened about four o'clock. She had rolled up her knitting and had gone out in the garden to take a little stroll before tea. Rounding a straggling rhododendron she came upon Edgar Lawson, who was striding along muttering to himself and who nearly ran into her.

He said, "I beg your pardon," hastily, but Miss Marple was startled by the queer staring expression of his eyes.

"Aren't you feeling well, Mr. Lawson?"

"Well? How should I be feeling well? I've had a shock —a terrible shock."

"What kind of a shock?"

The young man gave a swift glance past her, and then a sharp uneasy glance to either side. His doing so gave Miss Marple a nervous feeling.

"Shall I tell you?" He looked at her doubtfully. "I don't know. I don't really *know*. I've been so spied upon."

Miss Marple made up her mind. She took him firmly by the arm.

"If we walk down this path. . . . There, now, there are no trees or bushes near. Nobody can overhear."

"No—no, you're right." He drew a deep breath, bent his head and almost whispered his next words. "I've made a discovery. A terrible discovery."

"What kind of a discovery?"

Edgar Lawson began to shake all over. He was almost weeping.

"To have trusted someone! To have believed . . . and it was lies—all lies. Lies to keep me from finding out the truth. I can't bear it. It's too wicked. You see, he was the one person I trusted, and now to find out that all the time he's been at the bottom of it all. It's *he* who's been my enemy! It's *he* who has been having me followed about and spied upon. But he can't get away with it any more. I shall speak out. I shall tell him I know what he has been doing."

"Who is '*he*'?" demanded Miss Marple.

Edgar Lawson drew himself up to his full height. He might have looked pathetic and dignified. But actually he only looked ridiculous.

"I'm speaking of my father."

"Viscount Montgomery—or do you mean Winston Churchill?"

Edgar threw her a glance of scorn.

"They let me think that—just to keep me from guessing the truth. But I know now. I've got a friend—a real friend. A friend who tells me the truth and lets me know just how I've been deceived. Well, my father will have to reckon with *me*. I'll throw his lies in his face! I'll challenge him with the truth. We'll see what he's got to say to that."

And suddenly breaking away, Edgar went of at a run and disappeared in the park.

Her face grave, Miss Marple went back to the house.

"We're all a little mad, dear lady," Dr. Maverick had said.

But it seemed to her that in Edgar's case it went rather further than that.

11

Lewis Serrocold arrived back at six-thirty. He stopped the car at the gates and walked to the house through the park. Looking out of her window, Miss Marple saw Christian Gulbrandsen go out to meet him and the two men, having greeted one another, turned and paced to and fro up and down the terrace.

Miss Marple had been careful to bring her bird glasses with her. At this moment she brought them into action. Was there, or was there not, a flight of siskins by that far clump of trees?

She noted as the glasses swept down before rising that both men were looking seriously disturbed. Miss Marple leant out a little farther. Scraps of conversation floated up to her now and then. If either of the men should look up, it would be quite clear that an enraptured bird watcher had her attention fixed on a point far removed from their conversation.

". . . how to spare Carrie Louise the knowledge——" Gulbrandsen was saying.

The next time they passed below, Lewis Serrocold was speaking.

"—If it *can* be kept from her. I agree that it is she who must be considered . . ."

Other faint snatches came to the listener.

"—Really serious—" "—not justified—" "—too big a responsibility to take—" "—we should, perhaps, take outside advice—"

Finally Miss Marple heard Christian Gulbrandsen say: "Ach, it grows cold. We must go inside."

Miss Marple drew her head in through the window with a puzzled expression. What she had heard was too fragmentary to be easily pieced together—but is served to confirm that vague apprehension that had been gradually growing upon her and about which Ruth Van Rydock had been so positive.

Whatever was wrong at Stonygates, it definitely affected Carrie Louise.

III

Dinner that evening was a somewhat constrained meal. Both Gulbrandsen and Lewis were absent-minded and absorbed in their own thoughts. Walter Hudd glowered

even more than usual, and for once Gina and Stephen
seemed to have little to say either to each other or to the
company at large. Conversation was mostly sustained by
Dr. Maverick, who had a lengthy technical discussion with
Mr. Baumgarten, one of the Occupational Therapists.

When they moved into the Hall after dinner, Christian
Gulbrandsen excused himself almost at once. He said he
had an important letter to write.

"So if you will forgive me, dear Carrie Louise, I will go
now to my room."

"You have all you want there? Jolly?"

"Yes, yes. Everything. A typewriter, I asked, and one has
been put there. Miss Bellever has been most kind and
attentive."

He left the Great Hall by the door on the left which led
past the foot of the main staircase and along a corridor,
at the end of which was a suite of bedroom and bathroom.

When he had gone out Carrie Louise said:

"Not going down to the theatre to-night, Gina?"

The girl shook her head. She went over and sat by the
window overlooking the front drive and the court.

Stephen glanced at her, then strolled over to the big
grand piano. He sat down at it and strummed very softly
—a queer melancholy little tune. The two Occupational
Therapists, Mr. Baumgarten and Mr. Lacy, and Dr.
Maverick, said good night and left. Walter turned on the
switch of a reading lamp and with a crackling noise half
the lights in the Hall went out.

He growled.

"That darned switch is always faulty. I'll go and put a
new fuse in."

He left the Hall and Carrie Louise murmured, "Wally's
so clever with electrical gadgets and things like that. You
remember how he fixed that toaster?"

"It seems to be all he does do here," said Mildred Strete.
"Mother, have you taken your tonic?"

Miss Bellever looked annoyed.

"I declare I completely forgot to-night." She jumped up
and went into the dining-room, returning presently with
a small glass containing a little rose-coloured fluid.

Smiling a little, Carrie Louise held out an obedient hand.

246

"Such horrid stuff and nobody lets me forget it," she said, making a wry face.

And then, rather unexpectedly, Lewis Serrocold said: "I don't think I should take it to-night, my dear. I'm not sure it really agrees with you."

Quietly, but with that controlled energy always so apparent in him, he took the glass from Miss Bellever and put it down on the big oak Welsh dresser.

Miss Bellever said sharply:

"Really, Mr. Serrocold, I can't agree with you there. Mrs. Serrocold has been very much better since——"

She broke off and turned sharply.

The front door was pushed violently open and allowed to swing to with a crash. Edgar Lawson came into the big dim Hall with the air of a star performer making a triumphal entry.

He stood in the middle of the floor and struck an attitude. It was almost ridiculous—but not quite ridiculous.

Edgar said theatrically:

"So I have found you, O mine enemy!"

He said it to Lewis Serrocold.

Mr. Serrocold looked mildly astonished.

"Why, Edgar, what is the matter?"

"You can say that to me—you! You know what's the matter. You've been deceiving me, spying on me, working with my enemies against me."

Lewis took him by the arm.

"Now, now, my dear lad, don't excite yourself. Tell me all about it quietly. Come into my office."

He led him across the Hall and through a door on the right, closing it behind him. After he had done so, there was another sound, the sharp sound of a key being turned in the lock.

Miss Bellever looked at Miss Marple, the same idea in both their minds. *It was not Lewis Serrocold who had turned the key.*

Miss Bellever said sharply: "That young man is just about to go off his head in my opinion. It isn't safe."

Mildred said: "He's a most unbalanced young man—and absolutely ungrateful for everything that's been done for him—you ought to put your foot down, Mother."

With a faint sigh Carrie Louise murmured:

"There's no harm in him really. He's fond of Lewis. He's very fond of him."

Miss Marple looked at her curiously. There had been no fondness in the expression that Edgar had turned on Lewis Serrocold a few moments previously, very far from it. She wondered, as she had wondered before, if Carrie Louise deliberately turned her back on reality.

Gina said sharply:

"He had something in his pocket. Edgar, I mean. Playing with it."

Stephen murmured as he took his hands from the keys:

"In a film it would certainly have been a revolver."

Miss Marple coughed.

"I think, you know," she said apologetically, "it *was* a revolver."

From behind the closed door of Lewis's office the sound of voices had been plainly discernible. Now, suddenly, they became clearly audible. Edgar Lawson shouted whilst Lewis Serrocold's voice kept its even reasonable note.

"Lies—lies—lies, all lies. *You're* my father. I'm *your* son. You've deprived me of my rights. *I* ought to own this place. You hate me—you want to get rid of me!"

There was a soothing murmur from Lewis and then the hysterical voice rose still higher. It screamed out foul epithets. Edgar seemed rapidly losing control of himself. Occasional words came from Lewis—"calm—just be calm —you know none of this is true——" But they seemed not to soothe, but on the contrary to enrage the young man still further.

Insensibly everyone in the Hall was silent, listening intently to what went on behind the locked door of Lewis's study.

"I'll make you listen to me," yelled Edgar. "I'll take that supercilious expression off your face. I'll have revenge, I tell you. Revenge for all you've made me suffer."

The other voice came curtly, unlike Lewis's usual unemotional tones.

"Put that revolver down!"

Gina cried sharply:

"Edgar will kill him. He's crazy. Can't we get the police or something?"

Carrie Louise, still unmoved, said softly:

"There's no need to worry, Gina. Edgar loves Lewis. He's just dramatising himself, that's all."

Edgar's voice sounded through the door in a laugh that Miss Marple had to admit sounded definitely insane.

"Yes, I've got a revolver—and it's loaded. No, don't speak, don't move. You're going to hear me out. It's you who started this conspiracy against me and now you're going to pay for it."

What sounded like the report of a firearm made them all start, but Carrie Louise said:

"It's all right, it's outside—in the park somewhere."

Behind the locked door, Edgar was raving in a high screaming voice.

"You sit there looking at me—looking at me—pretending to be unmoved. Why don't you get down on your knees and beg for mercy? I'm going to shoot, I tell you. I'm going to shoot you dead! I'm your son—your unacknowledged despised son—you wanted me hidden away, out of the world altogether, perhaps. You set your spies to follow me—to hound me down—you plotted against me. You, my father! My father. I'm only a bastard, aren't I? Only a bastard. You went on filling me up with lies. Pretending to be kind to me, and all the time—all the time. . . . You're not fit to live. I won't let you live."

Again there came a stream of obscene profanity. Somewhere during the scene Miss Marple was conscious of Miss Bellever saying:

"We must *do* something," and leaving the Hall.

Edgar seemed to pause for breath and then he shouted out:

"You're going to die—to *die*. You're going to die *now*. Take *that*, you devil, and *that*!"

Two sharp cracks rang out—not in the park this time, but definitely behind the locked door.

Somebody, Miss Marple thought it was Mildred, cried out:

"Oh God, what shall we do?"

There was a thud from inside the room and then a sound,

almost more terrible than what had gone before, the sound of slow heavy sobbing.

Somebody strode past Miss Marple and started shaking and rattling the door.

It was Stephen Restarick.

"Open the door. Open the door," he shouted.

Miss Bellever came back into the Hall. In her hand she held an assortment of keys.

"Try some of these," she said breathlessly.

At that moment the fused lights came on again. The Hall sprang into life again after its eerie dimness.

Stephen Restarick began trying the keys.

They heard the inside key fall out as he did so.

Inside that wild desperate sobbing went on.

Walter Hudd, coming lazily back into the Hall, stopped dead and demanded:

"Say, what's going on round here?"

Mildred said tearfully:

"That awful crazy young man has shot Mr. Serrocold."

"Please." It was Carrie Louise who spoke. She got up and came across to the study door. Very gently she pushed Stephen Restarick aside. "Let me speak to him."

She called—very softly—"Edgar . . . Edgar . . . let me in, will you? Please, Edgar."

They heard the key fitted into the lock. It turned and the door was slowly opened.

But it was not Edgar who opened it. It was Lewis Serrocold. He was breathing hard as though he had been running, but otherwise he was unmoved.

"It's all right, dearest," he said. "Dearest, it's quite all right."

"We thought you'd been shot," said Miss Bellever gruffly.

Lewis Serrocold frowned. He said with a trifle of asperity:

"Of course I haven't been shot."

They could see into the study by now. Edgar Lawson had collapsed by the desk. He was sobbing and gasping. The revolver lay on the floor where it had dropped from his hand.

"But we heard the shots," said Mildred.

"Oh yes, he fired twice."

250

"And he missed you?"

"Of course he missed me," snapped Lewis.

Miss Marple did not consider that there was any of course about it. The shots must have been fired at fairly close range.

Lewis Serrocold said irritably:

"Where's Maverick? It's Maverick we need."

Miss Bellever said:

"I'll get him. Shall I ring up the police as well?"

"Police? Certainly not."

"Of course we must ring up the police," said Mildred. "He's dangerous."

"Nonsense," said Lewis Serrocold. "Poor lad. Does he look dangerous?"

At the moment he did not look dangerous. He looked young and pathetic and rather repulsive.

His voice had lost its carefully acquired accent.

"I didn't mean to do it," he groaned. "I dunno what came over me—talking all that stuff—I must have been mad."

Mildred sniffed.

"I really must have been mad. I didn't mean to. Please, Mr. Serrocold, I really didn't mean to."

Lewis Serrocold patted him on the shoulder.

"That's all right, my boy. No damage done."

"I might have killed you, Mr. Serrocold."

Walter Hudd walked across the room and peered at the wall behind the desk.

"The bullets went in here," he said. His eye dropped to the desk and the chair behind it. "Must have been a near miss," he said grimly.

"I lost my head. I didn't rightly know what I was doing. I thought he'd done me out of my rights. I thought——"

Miss Marple put in the question she had been wanting to ask for some time.

"Who told you," she asked, "that Mr. Serrocold was your father?"

Just for a second a sly expression peeped out of Edgar's distracted face. It was there and gone in a flash.

"Nobody," he said. "I just got it into my head."

251

Walter Hudd was staring down at the revolver where it lay on the floor.

"Where the hell did you get that gun?" he demanded.

"Gun?" Edgar stared down at it.

"Looks mighty like my gun," said Walter. He stooped down and picked it up. "By heck, it *is*! You took it out of my room, you creeping louse, you."

Lewis Serrocold interposed between the cringing Edgar and the menacing American.

"All this can be gone into later," he said. "Ah, here's Maverick. Take a look at him, will you, Maverick?"

Dr. Maverick advanced upon Edgar with a kind of professional zest.

"This won't do, Edgar," he said. "This won't do, you know."

"He's a dangerous lunatic," said Mildred sharply. "He's been shooting off a revolver and raving. He only just missed my stepfather."

Edgar gave a little yelp and Dr. Maverick said reprovingly:

"Careful, please, Mrs. Strete."

"I'm sick of all this. Sick of the way you all go on here! I tell you this man's a lunatic."

With a bound Edgar wrenched himself away from Dr. Maverick and fell to the floor at Serrocold's feet.

"Help me. Help me. Don't let them take me away and shut me up. Don't let them . . ."

An unpleasing scene, Miss Marple thought.

Mildred said angrily, "I tell you he's——"

Her mother said soothingly:

"Please, Mildred. Not now. He's suffering."

Walter muttered:

"Suffering cripes! They're all cuckoo round here."

"I'll take charge of him," said Dr. Maverick. "You come with me, Edgar. Bed and a sedative—and we'll talk everything over in the morning. Now you trust me, don't you?"

Rising to his feet and trembling a little, Edgar looked doubtfully at the young doctor and then at Mildred Strete.

"She said—I was a lunatic."

"No, no, you're not a lunatic."

Miss Bellever's footsteps rang purposefully across the

Hall. She came in with her lips pursed together and a flushed face.

"I've telephoned the police," she said grimly. "They will be here in a few minutes."

Carrie Louise cried, "Jolly!" in tones of dismay.

Edgar uttered a wail.

Lewis Serrocold frowned angrily.

"I told you, Jolly, I did *not* want the police summoned. This is a medical matter."

"That's as may be," said Miss Bellever. "I've my own opinion. But I had to call the police. Mr. Gulbrandsen's been shot dead."

CHAPTER VIII

IT WAS a moment or two before anyone took in what she was saying.

Carrie Louise said incredulously:

"Christian shot? Dead? Oh, surely, that's impossible."

"If you don't believe me," said Miss Bellever, pursing her lips, and addressing not so much Carrie Louise, as the assembled company, "go and look for yourselves."

She was angry. And her anger sounded in the crisp sharpness of her voice.

Slowly, unbelievingly, Carrie Louise took a step towards the door. Lewis Serrocold put a hand on her shoulder.

"No, dearest, let me go."

He went out through the doorway. Dr. Maverick, with a doubtful glance at Edgar, followed him. Miss Bellever went with them.

Miss Marple gently urged Carrie Louise into a chair. She sat down, her eyes looking hurt and stricken.

"Christian—shot?" she said again.

It was the bewildered hurt tone of a child.

Walter Hudd remained close by Edgar Lawson, glowering down at him. In his hand he held the gun that he had picked up from the floor.

Mrs. Serrocold said in a wondering voice:

"But who could possibly want to shoot *Christian*?"

It was not a question that demanded an answer.

Walter muttered under his breath:

"Nuts! The whole lot of them."

Stephen had moved protectively closer to Gina. Her young startled face was the most vivid thing in the room.

Suddenly the front door opened and a rush of cold air together with a man in a big overcoat came in.

The heartiness of his greeting seemed incredibly shocking.

"Hullo, everybody, what's going on to-night? A lot of fog on the road. I had to go dead slow."

For a startled moment, Miss Marple thought that she was seeing double. Surely the same man could not be standing by Gina and coming in by the door. Then she realised that it was only a likeness and not, when you looked closely, such a very strong likeness. The two men were clearly brothers with a strong family resemblance, but no more.

Where Stephen Restarick was thin to the point of emaciation the newcomer was sleek. The big coat with the astrakhan collar fitted the sleekness of body snugly. A handsome young man, and one who bore upon him the authority and good humour of success.

But Miss Marple noted one thing about him. His eyes, as he entered the hall, looked immediately at Gina.

He said, a little doubtfully:

"You *did* expect me? You got my wire?"

He was speaking now to Carrie Louise. He came towards her.

Almost mechanically, she put her hand out to him. He took it and kissed it gently. It was an affectionate act of homage, not a mere theatrical courtesy.

She murmured:

"Of course, Alex dear—of course. Only, you see—things have been happening——"

"Happening?"

Mildred gave the information, gave it with a kind of grim relish that Miss Marple found distasteful.

"Christian Gulbrandsen," she said. "My brother Christian Gulbrandsen has been found shot dead."

"Good God," Alex registered a more than life-size dismay. "Suicide, do you mean?"

Carrie Louise moved swiftly.

"Oh no," she said. "It couldn't be suicide. Not *Christian*! Oh no."

"Uncle Christian would never shoot himself, I'm sure," said Gina.

Alex Restarick looked from one person to the other. From his brother Stephen he received a short confirmative nod. Walter Hudd stared back at him with faint resentment. Alex's eyes rested on Miss Marple with a sudden frown. It was as though he had found some unwanted prop on a stage set.

He looked as though he would like her explained. But nobody explained her, and Miss Marple continued to look an old, fluffy and sweetly bewildered old lady.

"When?" asked Alex. "When did this happen, I mean?"

"Just before you arrived," said Gina. "About—oh three or four minutes ago, I suppose. Why, of course, we actually heard the shot. Only we didn't notice it—not really."

"Didn't notice it? Why not?"

"Well, you see, there were other things going on . . ." Gina spoke rather hesitantly.

"Sure were," said Walter with emphasis.

Juliet Bellever came into the Hall by the door from the library.

"Mr. Serrocold suggests that we should all wait in the library. It would be convenient for the police. Except for Mrs. Serrocold. You've had a shock, Cara. I've ordered some hot bottles to be put in your bed. I'll take you up and——"

Rising to her feet, Carrie Louise shook her head.

"I must see Christian first," she said.

"Oh no, dear. Don't upset yourself——"

Carrie Louise put her very gently to one side.

"Dear Jolly—you don't understand." She looked round and said, "Jane?"

Miss Marple had already moved towards her.

"Come with me, will you, Jane?"

They moved together towards the door. Dr. Maverick, coming in, almost collided with them.

Miss Bellever exclaimed:

"Dr. Maverick. Do stop her. So foolish."

Carrie Louise looked calmly at the young doctor. She even gave a tiny smile.

Dr. Maverick said: "You want to go and—see him?"

"I must."

"I see." He stood aside. "If you feel you must, Mrs. Serrocold. But afterwards, please go and lie down and let Miss Bellever look after you. At the moment you do not feel the shock, but I assure you that you will do so."

"Yes. I expect you are right. I will be quite sensible. Come, Jane."

The two women moved out through the door, past the foot of the main staircase and along the corridor, past the dining-room on the right and double doors leading to the kitchen quarters on the left, past the side door to the terrace and on to the door that gave admission to the Oak suite that had been allotted to Christian Gulbrandsen. It was a room furnished as a sitting-room more than a bedroom, with a bed in an alcove to one side and a door leading into a dressing-room and bathroom.

Carrie Louise stopped on the threshold. Christian Gulbrandsen had been sitting at the big mahogany desk with a small portable typewriter open in front of him. He sat there now, but slumped sideways in the chair. The high arms of the chair prevented him from slipping to the floor.

Lewis Serrocold was standing by the window. He had pulled the curtain a little aside and was gazing out into the night.

He looked round and frowned.

"My dearest, you shouldn't have come."

He came towards her and she stretched out a hand to him. Miss Marple retreated a step or two.

"Oh yes, Lewis. I had to—see him. One has to know just exactly how things are."

She walked slowly towards the desk.

Lewis said warningly:

"You mustn't touch anything. The police must have things left exactly as we found them."

"Of course. He was shot deliberately by someone, then?"

"Oh yes." Lewis Serrocold looked a little surprised that the question had even been asked. "I thought—you knew that?"

"I did really. Christian would not commit suicide, and he was such a competent person that it could not possibly have been an accident. That only leaves"—she hesitated a moment—"murder."

She walked up behind the desk and stood looking down at the dead man. There was sorrow and affection in her face.

"Dear Christian," she said. "He was always good to me." Softly, she touched the top of his head with her fingers. "Bless you and thank you, dear Christian," she said.

Lewis Serrocold said with something more like emotion than Miss Marple had ever seen in him before:

"I wish to God I could have spared you this, Caroline." His wife shook her head gently.

"You can't really spare anyone anything," she said. "Things always have to be faced sooner or later. And therefore it had better be sooner. I'll go and lie down now. I suppose you'll stay here, Lewis, until the police come?"

"Yes."

Carrie Louise turned away and Miss Marple slipped an arm round her.

CHAPTER IX

INSPECTOR CURRY and his entourage found Miss Bellever alone in the Great Hall when they arrived.

She came forward efficiently.

"I am Juliet Bellever, companion and secretary to Mrs. Serrocold."

"It was you who found the body and telephoned to us?"

"Yes. Most of the household are in the library—through that door there. Mr. Serrocold remained in Mr. Gulbrandsen's room to see that nothing was disturbed. Dr. Maverick, who first examined the body, will be here very shortly. He had to take a—case over to the other wing. Shall I lead the way?"

"If you please."

"Competent woman," thought the Inspector to himself. "Seems to have got the whole thing taped."

He followed her along the corridor.

For the next twenty minutes the routine of police procedure was duly set in motion. The photographer took the necessary pictures. The police surgeon arrived and was joined by Dr. Maverick. Half an hour later, the ambulance had taken away the mortal remains of Christian Gulbrandsen, and Inspector Curry started his official interrogation.

Lewis Serrocold took him into the library, and he glanced keenly round the assembled people, making brief notes in his mind. An old lady with white hair, a middle-aged lady, the good-looking girl he'd seen driving her car round the countryside, that sulky looking American husband of hers. A couple of young men who were mixed up in the outfit somewhere or other and the capable woman, Miss Bellever, who'd phoned him and met him on arrival.

Inspector Curry had already thought out a little speech and he now delivered it as planned.

"I'm afraid this is all very upsetting to you," he said, "and I hope not to keep you too long this evening. We can go into things more thoroughly to-morrow. It was Miss Bellever who found Mr. Gulbrandsen dead, and I'll ask Miss Bellever to give me an outline of the general situation as that will save too much repetition. Mr. Serrocold, if you want to go up to your wife, please do, and when I have finished with Miss Bellever, I should like to talk to you. Is that all quite clear? Perhaps there is some small room where——"

Lewis Serrocold said: "My office, Jolly?"

Miss Bellever nodded, and said: "I was just going to suggest it."

She led the way across the Great Hall, and Inspector Curry and his attendant Sergeant followed her.

Miss Bellever arranged them and herself suitably. It might have been she and not Inspector Curry who was in charge of the investigation.

The moment had come, however, when the initiative passed to him. Inspector Curry had a pleasant voice and manner. He looked quiet and serious and just a little apologetic. Some people made the mistake of underrating him. Actually he was as competent in his way as Miss

Bellever was in hers. But he preferred not to make a parade of the fact.

He cleared his throat.

"I've had the main facts from Mr. Serrocold. Mr. Christian Gulbrandsen was the eldest son of the late Eric Gulbrandsen, the founder of the Gulbrandsen Trust and Fellowships . . . and all the rest of it. He was one of the trustees of this place and he arrived here unexpectedly yesterday. That is correct?"

"Yes."

Inspector Curry was pleased by her conciseness. He went on:

"Mr. Serrocold was away in Liverpool. He returned this evening by the 6.30 train."

"Yes."

"After dinner this evening, Mr. Gulbrandsen announced his intention of working in his own room and left the rest of the party here after coffee had been served. Correct?"

"Yes."

"Now, Miss Bellever, please tell me in your own words how you came to discover him dead."

"There was a rather unpleasant incident this evening. A young man, a psychopathic case, became very unbalanced and threatened Mr. Serrocold with a revolver. They were locked into this room. The young man eventually fired the revolver—you can see the bullet holes in the wall there. Fortunately Mr. Serrocold was unhurt. After firing the shots, this young man went completely to pieces. Mr. Serrocold sent me to find Dr. Maverick. I got through on the house phone but he was not in his room. I found him with one of his colleagues and gave him the message and he came here at once. On my own way back I went to Mr. Gulbrandsen's room. I wanted to ask him if there was anything he would like—hot milk, or whisky, before settling for the night. I knocked, but there was no response, so I opened the door. I saw that Mr. Gulbrandsen was dead. I then rang you up."

"What entrances and exits are there to the house? And how are they secured? Could anyone have come in from outside without being heard or seen?"

"Anyone could have come in by the side door to the

terrace. That is not locked until we all go to bed, as people come in and out that way to go to the College buildings."

"And you have, I believe, between two hundred and two hundred and fifty juvenile delinquents in the College?"

"Yes. But the College buildings are well secured and patrolled. I should say it was most unlikely that anyone could leave the College unsponsored."

"We shall have to check up on that, of course. Had Mr. Gulbrandsen given any cause for—shall we say, rancour? Any unpopular decisions as to policy?"

Miss Bellever shook her head.

"Oh no, Mr. Gulbrandsen had nothing whatever to do with the running of the College, or with administrative matters."

"What was the purpose of his visit?"

"I have no idea."

"But he was annoyed to find Mr. Serrocold absent, and immediately decided to wait until he returned?"

"Yes."

"So his business here was definitely with Mr. Serrocold?"

"Yes. But it would be—because it would be almost certainly business to do with the Institute."

"Yes, presumably that is so. Did he have a conference with Mr. Serrocold?"

"No, there was no time. Mr. Serrocold only arrived just before dinner this evening?"

"But after dinner, Mr. Gulbrandsen said he had important letters to write and went away to do so. He didn't suggest a session with Mr. Serrocold?"

Miss Bellever hesitated.

"No. No, he didn't."

"Surely that was rather odd—if he had waited on at inconvenience to himself to see Mr. Serrocold?"

"Yes, it was odd."

The oddness of it seemed to strike Miss Bellever for the first time.

"Mr. Serrocold did not accompany him to his room?"

"No. Mr. Serrocold remained in the Hall."

"And you have no idea at what time Mr. Gulbrandsen was killed?"

260

"I think it is possible that we heard the shot. If so, it was at twenty-three minutes past nine."

"You heard a shot? And it did not alarm you?"

"The circumstances were peculiar."

She explained in rather more detail the scene between Lewis Serrocold and Edgar Lawson which had been in progress.

"So it occurred to no one that the shot might actually have come from within the house?"

"No. No, I certainly don't think so. We were all so relieved, you know, that the shot didn't come from in here."

Miss Bellever added rather grimly:

"You don't expect murder and attempted murder in the same house on the same night."

Inspector Curry acknowledged the truth of that.

"All the same," said Miss Bellever, suddenly, "you know, I believe that's what made me go along to Mr. Gulbrandsen's room later. I did mean to ask him if he would like anything, but it was a kind of excuse to reassure myself that everything was all right."

Inspector Curry stared at her for a moment.

"What made you think it mightn't be all right?"

"I don't know. I think it was the shot outside. It hadn't meant anything at the time. But afterwards it came back into my mind. I told myself that it was only a backfire from Mr. Restarick's car——"

"Mr. Restarick's car?"

"Yes. Alex Restarick. He arrived by car this evening—he arrived just after all this happened."

"I see. When you discovered Mr. Gulbrandsen's body, did you touch anything in the room?"

"Of course not." Miss Bellever sounded reproachful. "Naturally I knew that nothing must be touched or moved. Mr. Gulbrandsen had been shot through the head but there was no firearm to be seen, so I knew it was murder."

"And just now, when you took us into the room, everything was exactly as it had been when you found the body?"

Miss Bellever considered. She sat back screwing up her eyes. She had, Inspector Curry thought, one of those photographic memories.

"One thing was different," she said. "There was nothing in the typewriter."

"You mean," said Inspector Curry, "that when you first went in Mr. Gulbrandsen had been writing a letter on the typewriter, and that that letter had since been removed?"

"Yes, I'm almost sure that I saw the white edge of the paper sticking up."

"Thank you, Miss Bellever. Who else went into that room before we arrived?"

"Mr. Serrocold, of course. He remained there when I came to meet you. And Mrs. Serrocold and Miss Marple went there. Mrs. Serrocold insisted."

"Mrs. Serrocold and Miss Marple," said Inspector Curry. "Which is Miss Marple?"

"The old lady with white hair. She was a school friend of Mrs. Serrocold's. She came on a visit about four days ago."

"Well, thank you, Miss Bellever. All that you have told us is quite clear. I'll go into things with Mr. Serrocold now. Ah, but perhaps—Miss Marple's an old lady, isn't she? I'll just have a word with her first and then she can go off to bed. Rather cruel to keep an old lady like that up," said Inspector Curry virtuously. "This must have been a shock to her."

"I'll tell her, shall I?"

"If you please."

Miss Bellever went out. Inspector Curry looked at the ceiling.

"Gulbrandsen?" he said. "Why Gulbrandsen? Two hundred odd maladjusted youngsters on the premises. No reason any of them shouldn't have done it. Probably one of them did. But why Gulbrandsen? The stranger within the gates."

Sergeant Lake said: "Of course we don't know everything yet."

Inspector Curry said:

"So far, we don't know anything at all."

He jumped up and was gallant when Miss Marple came in. She seemed a little flustered and he hurried to put her at her ease.

"Now don't upset yourself, m'am." The old ones liked M'am, he thought. To them, police officers were definitely

262

of the lower classes and should show respect to their betters. "This is all very distressing, I know. But we've just got to get the facts clear. Get it all clear."

"Oh yes, I know," said Miss Marple. "So difficult, isn't it? To be clear about anything, I mean. Because if you're looking at one thing, you can't be looking at another. And one so often looks at the wrong thing, though whether because one happens to do so or because you're meant to, it's very hard to say. Misdirection, the conjurers call it. So clever, aren't they? And I never *have* known how they manage with a bowl of goldfish—because really that cannot fold up small, can it?"

Inspector Curry blinked a little and said soothingly:

"Quite so. Now, m'am. I've had an account of this evening's events from Miss Bellever. A most anxious time for all of you, I'm sure."

"Yes, indeed. It was all so *dramatic*, you know."

"First this to-do between Mr. Serrocold and"—he looked down at a note he had made—"this Edgar Lawson."

"A very odd young man," said Miss Marple. "I have felt all along that there was something wrong about him."

"I'm sure you have," said Inspector Curry. "And then, after that excitement was over, there came Mr. Gulbrandsen's death. I understand that you went with Mrs. Serrocold to see the—er—the body."

"Yes, I did. She asked me to come with her. We are very old friends."

"Quite so. And you went along to Mr. Gulbrandsen's room. Did you touch anything while you were in the room, either of you?"

"Oh no. Mr. Serrocold warned us not to."

"Did you happen to notice, m'am, whether there was a letter or a piece of paper, say, in the typewriter?"

"There wasn't," said Miss Marple promptly. "I noticed that at once because it seemed to me odd. Mr. Gulbrandsen was sitting there at the typewriter so he must have been typing something. Yes, I thought it very odd."

Inspector Curry looked at her sharply. He said:

"Did you have much conversation with Mr. Gulbrandsen while he was here?"

"Very little."

263

"There is nothing especial—or significant that you can remember?"

Miss Marple considered.

"He asked me about Mrs. Serrocold's health. In particular, about her heart."

"Her heart? Is there something wrong with her heart?"

"Nothing whatever, I understand."

Inspector Curry was silent for a moment or two, then he said:

"You heard a shot this evening during the quarrel between Mr. Serrocold and Edgar Lawson?"

"I didn't actually hear it myself. I am a little deaf, you know. But Mrs. Serrocold mentioned it as being outside in the park."

"Mr. Gulbrandsen left the party immediately after dinner, I understand?"

"Yes, he said he had letters to write."

"He didn't show any wish for a business conference with Mr. Serrocold?"

"No."

Miss Marple added:

"You see, they'd already had one little talk."

"They had? When? I understood that Mr. Serrocold only returned home just before dinner."

"That's quite true, but he walked up through the park, and Mr. Gulbrandsen went out to meet him and they walked up and down the terrace together."

"Who else knows this?"

"I shouldn't think anybody else," said Miss Marple. "Unless, of course, Mr. Serrocold told Mrs. Serrocold. I just happened to be looking out of my window—at some birds."

"Birds?"

"Birds," Miss Marple added after a moment or two: "I thought, perhaps, they might be siskins."

Inspector Curry was uninterested in siskins.

"You didn't," he said delicately, "happen to—er—overhear anything of what they said?"

Innocent china blue eyes met his.

"Only fragments, I'm afraid," said Miss Marple gently.

"And those fragments?"

Miss Marple was silent a moment, then she said:

264

"I do not know the actual subject of their conversation, but their immediate concern was to keep whatever it was from the knowledge of Mrs. Serrocold. To spare her—that was how Mr. Gulbrandsen put it, and Mr. Serrocold said, 'I agree that it is she who must be considered.' They also mentioned a 'big responsibility' and that they should, perhaps, 'take outside advice.'"

She paused.

"I think, you know, you had better ask Mr. Serrocold himself about all this."

"We shall do so, m'am. Now there is nothing else that struck you as unusual this evening?"

Miss Marple considered.

"It was all so unusual if you know what I mean——"

"Quite so. Quite so."

Something flickered into Miss Marple's memory.

"There was one rather unusual incident. Mr. Serrocold stopped Mrs. Serrocold from taking her medicine. Miss Bellever was quite put out about it."

She smiled in a deprecating fashion.

"But that, of course, is such a little thing . . ."

"Yes, of course. Well, thank you, Miss Marple."

As Miss Marple went out of the room, Sergeant Lake said:

"She's old, but she's sharp . . ."

CHAPTER X

LEWIS SERROCOLD came into the office and immediately the whole focus of the room shifted. He turned to close the door behind him, and in doing so he created an atmosphere of privacy. He walked over and sat down, not in the chair Miss Marple had just vacated, but in his own chair behind the desk. Miss Bellever had settled Inspector Curry in a chair drawn up to one side of the desk, as though unconsciously she had reserved Lewis Serrocold's chair against his coming.

When he had sat down, Lewis Serrocold looked at the two police officers thoughtfully. His face looked drawn and tired. It was the face of a man who was passing through a severe ordeal, and it surprised Inspector Curry a little because, though Christian Gulbrandsen's death must undeniably have been a shock to Lewis Serrocold, yet Gulbrandsen had not been a close friend or relation, only a rather remote connection by marriage.

In an odd way, the tables seemed to have been turned. It did not seem as though Lewis Serrocold had come into the room to answer police questioning. It seemed rather that Lewis Serrocold had arrived to preside over a court of inquiry. It irritated Inspector Curry a little.

He said briskly:

"Now, Mr. Serrocold——"

Lewis Serrocold still seemed lost in thought. He said with a sigh: "How difficult it is to know the right thing to do."

Inspector Curry said:

"I think *we* will be the judges as to that, Mr. Serrocold. Now about Mr. Gulbrandsen, he arrived unexpectedly, I understand?"

"Quite unexpectedly."

"You did not know he was coming."

"I had not the least idea of it."

"And you have no idea of why he came?"

Lewis Serrocold said quietly:

"Oh yes, I know why he came. He told me."

"When?"

"I walked up from the station. He was watching from the house and came out to meet me. It was then that he explained what had brought him here."

"Business connected with the Gulbrandsen Institute, I suppose?"

"Oh no, it was nothing to do with the Gulbrandsen Institute."

"Miss Bellever seemed to think it was."

"Naturally. That would be the assumption. Gulbrandsen did nothing to correct that impression. Neither did I."

"Why, Mr. Serrocold?"

Lewis Serrocold said slowly:

"Because it seemed to both of us important that no hint should arise as to the real purpose of his visit."

"What was that real purpose?"

Lewis Serrocold was silent for a minute or two. He sighed.

"Gulbrandsen came over here regularly twice a year for meetings of the trustees. The last meeting was only a month ago. Consequently he was not due to come over again for another five months. I think, therefore, that anyone might realise that the business that brought him must definitely be urgent business, but I still think that the normal assumption would be that it *was* a business visit, and that the matter, however urgent—would be a Trust matter. As far as I know, Gulbrandsen did nothing to contradict that impression—or thought he didn't. Yes, perhaps that is nearer the truth—he thought he didn't."

"I'm afraid, Mr. Serrocold, that I don't quite follow you."

Lewis Serrocold did not answer at once. Then he said gravely:

"I fully realise that with Gulbrandsen's death—which was murder, undeniably murder, I have got to put all the facts before you. But frankly, I am concerned for my wife's happiness and peace of mind. It is not for me to dictate to you, Inspector, but if you can see your way to keeping certain things from her as far as possible I shall be grateful. You see, Inspector Curry, Christian Gulbrandsen came here expressly to tell me that he believed my wife was being slowly and cold-bloodedly poisoned."

"What?"

Cury leaned forward incredulously.

Serrocold nodded.

"Yes, it was, as you can imagine, a tremendous shock to me. I had had no suspicion of such a thing myself, but as soon as Christian told me, I realised that certain symptoms my wife had complained of lately were quite compatible with that belief. What she took to be rheumatism, leg cramps, pain, and occasional sickness. All that fits in very well *with the symptoms of arsenical poisoning.*"

"Miss Marple told us that Christian Gulbrandsen asked her about the condition of Mrs. Serrocold's heart?"

"Did he now? That is interesting. I suppose he thought that a heart poison would be used since it paved the way to a sudden death without undue suspicion. But I think myself that arsenic is more likely."

"You definitely think, then, that Christian Gulbrandsen's suspicions were well founded?"

"Oh yes, I think so. For one thing, Gulbrandsen would hardly come to me with such a suggestion unless he was fairly sure of his facts. He was a cautious and hard-headed man, difficult to convince, but very shrewd."

"What was his evidence?"

"We had no time to go into that. Our interview was a hurried one. It served only the purpose of explaining his visit, and a mutual agreement that nothing whatever should be said to my wife about the matter until we were sure of our facts."

"And whom did he suspect of administering poison?"

"He did not say, and actually I don't think he knew. He *may* have suspected. I think now that he probably did suspect—otherwise why should he be killed?"

"But he mentioned no name to you?"

"He mentioned no name. We agreed that we must investigate the matter thoroughly, and he suggested inviting the advice and co-operation of Dr. Galbraith, the Bishop of Cromer. Dr. Galbraith is a very old friend of the Gulbrandsens and is one of the trustees of the Institute. He is a man of great wisdom and experience and would be of infinite help and comfort to my wife if—if it was necessary to tell her of our suspicions. We meant to rely on his advice as to whether or not to consult the police."

"Quite extraordinary," said Curry.

"Gulbrandsen left us after dinner to write to Dr. Galbraith. He was actually in the act of typing a letter to him when he was shot."

"How do you know?"

Lewis said calmly:

"Because I took the letter out of the typewriter. I have it here."

From his breast pocket, he drew out a folded typewritten sheet of paper and handed it to Curry.

The latter said sharply:

"You shouldn't have taken this, or touched anything in the room."

"I touched nothing else. I know that I committed an unpardonable offence in your eyes in moving this, but I had

268

a very strong reason. I felt certain that my wife would insist on coming into the room and I was afraid that she might read something of what is written here. I admit myself in the wrong, but I am afraid I would do the same again. I would do anything—*anything*—to save my wife unhappiness."

Inspector Curry said no more for the moment. He read the typewritten sheet.

> *Dear Dr. Galbraith. If it is at all possible, I beg that you will come to Stonygates as soon as you receive this. A crisis of extraordinary gravity has arisen and I am at a loss how to deal with it. I know how deep your affection is for our dear Carrie Louise, and how grave your concern will be for anything that affects her. How much can we keep from her? Those are the questions that I find so difficult to answer.*
>
> *Not to beat about the bush, I have reason to believe that that sweet and innocent lady is being slowly poisoned. I first suspected this when——*

Here the letter broke off abruptly.

Curry said:

"And when he had reached this point Christian Gulbrandsen was shot?"

"Yes."

"But why on earth was this letter left in the typewriter?"

"I can only conceive of two reasons—one, that the murderer had no idea to whom Gulbrandsen was writing and what was the subject of the letter. Secondly—he may not have had time. He may have heard someone coming and only had just time to escape unobserved."

"And Gulbrandsen gave you no hint as to whom he suspected—if he did suspect anyone?"

There was, perhaps, a very slight pause before Lewis answered.

"None whatever."

He added, rather obscurely:

"Christian was a very fair man."

"How do you think this poison, arsenic or whatever it may be—was or is being administered?"

"I thought over that whilst I was changing for dinner and it seemed to me that the most likely vehicle was some medicine, a tonic, that my wife was taking. As regards food, we all partake of the same dishes and my wife has nothing specially prepared for her. But anyone could add arsenic to the medicine bottle."

"We must take the medicine and have it analysed."

Lewis said quietly:

"I already have a sample of it. I took it this evening before dinner."

From a drawer in the desk he took out a small corked bottle with a red fluid in it.

Inspector Curry said with a curious glance:

"You think of everything, Mr. Serrocold."

"I believe in acting promptly. To-night, I stopped my wife from taking her usual dose. It is still in a glass on the oak dresser in the Hall—the bottle of tonic itself is in the dining-room."

Curry leaned forward across the desk. He lowered his voice and spoke confidentially and without officialdom.

"You'll excuse me, Mr. Serrocold, but just *why* are you so anxious to keep this from your wife? Are you afraid she'd panic? Surely, for her own sake, it would be as well if she were warned."

"Yes—yes, that may well be so. But I don't think you quite understand. Without knowing my wife Caroline, it would be difficult. My wife, Inspector Curry, is an idealist, a completely trustful person. Of her it may truly be said that she sees no evil, hears no evil, and speaks no evil. It would be inconceivable to her that anyone could wish to kill her. But we have to go farther than that. It is not just 'anyone.' It is a case—surely you see that—of someone possibly very near and dear to her . . ."

"So that's what you think?"

"We have got to face facts. Close at hand we have a couple of hundred warped and stunted personalities who have expressed themselves often enough by crude and senseless violence. But by the very nature of things, none of *them* can be suspect in this case. A slow poisoner is someone living in the intimacy of family life. Think of the people who are here in this house; her husband, her daughter, her granddaughter, her granddaughter's husband, her stepson whom she regards as her own son, Miss Bellever, her devoted companion and friend of many years. All very near and dear to her—and yet the suspicion must arise—is it one of them?"

Curry said slowly:

"There *are* outsiders——"

"Yes, in a sense. There is Dr. Maverick, one or two of the staff are often with us, there are the servants—but frankly, what possible motive could they have?"

Inspector Curry said:

"And there's young—what is his name again—Edgar Lawson?"

"Yes. But he has only been down here as a casual visitor just lately. He has no possible motive. Besides, he is deeply attached to Caroline—just as everyone is."

"But he's unbalanced. What about this attack on you to-night?"

Serrocold waved it aside impatiently.

"Sheer childishness. He had no intention of harming me."

"Not with these two bullet holes in the wall? He shot at you, didn't he?"

"He didn't mean to hit me. It was play-acting, no more."

"Rather a dangerous form of play-acting, Mr. Serrocold."

"You don't understand. You must talk to our psychiatrist, Dr. Maverick. Edgar is an illegitimate child. He has consoled himself for his lack of a father and a humble origin by pretending to himself that he is the son of a celebrated man. It's a well-known phenomenon, I assure you. He was improving, improving very much. Then, for some reason, he had a set-back. He identified me as his 'father' and made a melodramatic attack, waving a revolver and uttering threats. I was not in the least alarmed. When he had actually fired the revolver, he broke down and sobbed and Dr. Maverick took him away and gave him a sedative. He'll probably be quite normal to-morrow morning."

"You don't wish to bring a charge against him?"

"That would be the worst thing possible—for him, I mean."

"Frankly, Mr. Serrocold, it seems to me he ought to be

under restraint. People who go about firing off revolvers to bolster up their egos——! One has to think of the community, you know."

"Talk to Dr. Maverick on the subject," urged Lewis. "He'll give you the professional point of view. In any case," he added, "poor Edgar certainly did not shoot Gulbrandsen. He was in here threatening to shoot *me*."

"That's the point I was coming to, Mr. Serrocold. We've covered the outside. Anyone, it seems, could have come in from *outside*, and shot Mr. Gulbrandsen, since the terrace door was unlocked. But there is a narrower field *inside* the house, and in view of what you have been telling me, it seems to me that very close attention must be paid to that. It seems possible that, with the exception of old Miss—er —yes, Marple, who happened to be looking out of her bedroom window, no one was aware that you and Christian Gulbrandsen had already had a private interview. If so, Gulbrandsen may have been shot to prevent him communicating his suspicions to you. Of course it is too early to say as yet what other motives may exist. Mr. Gulbrandsen was a wealthy man, I presume?"

"Yes, he was a very wealthy man. He has sons and daughters and grandchildren—all of whom will probably benefit by his death. But I do not think that any of his family are in this country, and they are all solid and highly respectable people. As far as I know, there are no black sheep amongst them."

"Had he any enemies?"

"I should think it most unlikely. He was—really, he was not that type of man."

"So it boils down, doesn't it, to this house and the people in it? Who from *inside* the house could have killed him?"

Lewis Serrocold said slowly:

"That is difficult for me to say. There are the servants and the members of my household and our guests. They are, from your point of view, all possibilities, I suppose. I can only tell you that, as far as I know, everyone except the servants was in the Great Hall when Christian left it, and whilst I was there, nobody left it."

"Nobody at all?"

"I think"—Lewis frowned in an effort of remembrance

272

—"oh yes. Some of the lights fused—Mr. Walter Hudd went to see to it."

"That's the young American gentleman?"

"Yes—of course I don't know what took place after Edgar and I came in here."

"And you can't give me anything nearer than that, Mr. Serrocold?"

Lewis Serrocold shook his head.

"No, I'm afraid I can't help you. It's—it's all quite inconceivable."

Inspector Curry sighed. He said: "Mr. Gulbrandsen was shot with a small automatic pistol. Do you know if anyone in the house has such a weapon?"

"I have no idea, I should think it most unlikely."

Inspector Curry sighed again. He said:

"You can tell the party that they can all go to bed. I'll talk to them to-morrow."

When Serrocold had left the room, Inspector Curry said to Lake:

"Well—what do you think?"

"Knows—or thinks he knows, who did it," said Lake.

"Yes. I agree with you. And he doesn't like it a bit . . ."

CHAPTER XI

I

GINA greeted Miss Marple with a rush as the latter came down to breakfast the next morning.

"The police are here again," she said. "They're in the library this time. Wally is absolutely fascinated by them. He can't understand their being so quiet and so remote. I think he's really quite thrilled by the whole thing. I'm not. I hate it. I think it's horrible. Why do you think I'm so upset? Because I'm half Italian?"

"Very possibly. At least perhaps it explains why you don't mind showing what you feel."

Miss Marple smiled just a little as she said this.

"Jolly's frightfully cross," said Gina, hanging on Miss

Marple's arm and propelling her into the dining-room. "I think really because the police are in charge and she can't exactly 'run' them like she runs everybody else.

"Alex and Stephen," continued Gina severely, as they came into the dining-room where the two brothers were finishing their breakfast, "just don't care."

"Gina dearest," said Alex, "you are most unkind. Good morning, Miss Marple. I care intensely. Except for the fact that I hardly knew your Uncle Christian, I'm far and away the best suspect. You do realise that, I hope."

"Why?"

"Well, I was driving up to the house at about the right time, it seems. And they've been checking up on things, and it seems that I took too much time between the lodge and the house—time enough, the implication is, to leave the car, run round the house, go in through the side door, shoot Christian and rush out and back to the car again."

"And what were you really doing?"

"I thought little girls were taught quite young not to ask indelicate questions. Like an idiot, I stood for several minutes taking in the fog effect in the headlights and thinking what I'd use to get that effect on a stage. For my new 'Limehouse' ballet."

"But you can tell them that!"

"Naturally. But you know what policemen are like. They say 'thank you' very civilly and write it all down, and you've no idea *what* they are thinking except that one does feel they have rather sceptical minds."

"It would amuse me to see you in a spot, Alex," said Stephen with his thin, rather cruel smile. "Now, *I'm* quite all right! I never left the Hall last night."

Gina cried, "But they couldn't possibly think it was one of *us*!"

Her dark eyes were round and dismayed.

"Don't say it must have been a tramp, dear," said Alex, helping himself lavishly to marmalade. "It's so hackneyed."

Miss Bellever looked in at the door and said:

"Miss Marple, when you have finished your breakfast, will you go to the library?"

"You again," said Gina. "Before any of us."

She seemed a little injured.

"Hi, what was that?" asked Alex.

"Didn't hear anything," said Stephen.

"It was a pistol shot."

"They've been firing shots in the room where Uncle Christian was killed," said Gina. "I don't know why. And outside too."

The door opened again and Mildred Strete came in. She was wearing black with some onyx beads.

She murmured good morning without looking at anyone and sat down.

In a hushed voice she said:

"Some tea, please, Gina. Nothing much to eat—just some toast."

She touched her nose and eyes delicately with the handkerchief she held in one hand. Then she raised her eyes and looked in an unseeing way at the two brothers. Stephen and Alex became uncomfortable. Their voices dropped to almost a whisper and presently they got up and left.

Mildred Strete said, whether to the universe or Miss Marple was not quite certain, "Not even a black tie!"

"I don't suppose," said Miss Marple apologetically, "that they knew beforehand that a murder was going to happen."

Gina made a smothered sound and Mildred Strete looked sharply at her.

"Where's Walter this morning?" she asked.

Gina flushed.

"I don't know. I haven't seen him."

She sat there uneasily like a guilty child.

Miss Marple got up.

"I'll go to the library now," she said.

Lewis Serrocold was standing by the window in the library.

There was no one else in the room.

He turned as Miss Marple came in and came forward to meet her, taking her hand in his.

"I hope," he said, "that you are not feeling the worse for the shock. To be at close quarters with what is undoubtedly murder must be a great strain on anyone who has not come in contact with such a thing before."

Modesty forbade Miss Marple to reply that she was, by now, quite at home with murder. She merely said that life in St. Mary Mead was not quite so sheltered as outside people believed.

"Very nasty things go on in a village, I assure you," she said. "One has an opportunity of studying things there that one would never have in a town."

Lewis Serrocold listened indulgently, but with only half an ear.

He said very simply: "I want your help."

"But of course, Mr. Serrocold."

"It is a matter that affects my wife—affects Caroline. I think that you are really attached to her?"

"Yes, indeed. Everyone is."

"That is what I believed. It seems that I am wrong. With the permission of Inspector Curry, I am going to tell you something that no one else as yet knows. Or perhaps I should say what only one person knows."

Briefly, he told her what he had told Inspector Curry the night before.

Miss Marple looked horrified.

"I can't believe it, Mr. Serrocold. I really can't believe it."

"That is what I felt when Christian Gulbrandsen told me."

"I should have said that dear Carrie Louise had not got an enemy in the world."

"It seems incredible that she should have. But you see the implication? Poisoning—slow poisoning—is an intimate family matter. It must be one of our closely-knit little household——"

"If it is *true*. Are you sure that Mr. Gulbrandsen was not mistaken?"

"Christian was not mistaken. He is too cautious a man to make such a statement without foundation. Besides, the police took away Caroline's medicine bottle and a separate sample of its contents. There was arsenic in both of them— and arsenic was not prescribed. The actual quantitative tests will take longer—but the actual fact of arsenic being present is established."

"Then her rheumatism—the difficulty in walking—all that——"

"Yes, leg cramps are typical, I understand. Also, before you came, Caroline has had one or two severe attacks of a gastric nature—I never dreamed until Christian came——"

He broke off. Miss Marple said softly: "So Ruth was right!"

"Ruth?"

Lewis Serrocold sounded surprised. Miss Marple flushed.

"There is something I have not told you. My coming here was not entirely fortuitous. If you will let me explain—I'm afraid I tell things so badly. Please have patience."

Lewis Serrocold listened whilst Miss Marple told him of Ruth's unease and urgency.

"Extraordinary," he commented. "I had no idea of this."

"It was all so vague," said Miss Marple. "Ruth herself didn't know why she had this feeling. There must be a reason—in my experience there always is—but 'something wrong' was as near as she could get."

Lewis Serrocold said grimly:

"Well, it seems that she was right. Now, Miss Marple, you see how I am placed. Am I to tell Carrie Louise of this?"

Miss Marple said quickly: "Oh no," in a distressed voice, and then flushed and stared doubtfully at Lewis. He nodded.

"So you feel as I do? As Christian Gulbrandsen did. Should we feel like that with an ordinary woman?"

"Carrie Louise is *not* an ordinary woman. She lives by her trust, by her belief in human nature—oh dear, I am expressing myself very badly. But I do feel that until we know who——"

"Yes, that is the crux. But you do see, Miss Marple, that there is a risk in saying nothing——"

"And so you want me to—how shall I put it?—watch over her?"

"You see, you are the only person whom I can trust," said Lewis Serrocold simply. "Everyone here *seems* devoted. But are they? Now your attachment goes back many years."

277

"And also I only arrived a few days ago," said Miss Marple pertinently.

Lewis Serrocold smiled.

"Exactly."

"It is a very mercenary question," said Miss Marple apologetically. "But who exactly would benefit if dear Carrie Louise were to die?"

"Money!" said Lewis bitterly. "It always boils down to money, doesn't it?"

"Well, I really think it must in this case. Because Carrie Louise is a very sweet person with a great deal of charm, and one cannot really imagine anyone disliking her. She couldn't, I mean, have an *enemy*. So then it does boil down, as you put it, to a question of money, because as you don't need me to tell you, Mr. Serrocold, people will quite often do anything for money."

"I suppose so, yes."

He went on: "Naturally Inspector Curry has already taken up that point. Mr. Gilfoy is coming down from London to-day and can give detailed information. Gilfoy, Gilfoy, Jaimes and Gilfoy are a very eminent firm of lawyers. This Gilfoy's father was one of the original trustees, and they drew up both Caroline's will and the original will of Eric Gulbrandsen. I will put it in simple terms for you——"

"Thank you," said Miss Marple gratefully. "So mystifying the law, I always think."

"Eric Gulbrandsen, after endowment of the College and his various fellowships and trusts and other charitable bequests, and having settled an equal sum on his daughter Mildred and on his adopted daughter Pippa (Gina's mother), left the remainder of his vast fortune in trust, the income from it to be paid to Caroline for her lifetime."

"And after her death?"

"After her death it was to be divided equally between Mildred and Pippa—or their children if they themselves had predeceased Caroline."

"So that in fact it goes to Mrs. Strete and to Gina."

"Yes. Caroline has also quite a considerable fortune of her own—though not in the Gulbrandsen class. Half of this she made over to me four years ago. Of the remaining amount, she left ten thousand pounds to Juliet Bellever, and the rest equally divided between Alex and Stephen Restarick, her two stepsons."

"Oh dear," said Miss Marple. "That's bad. That's very bad."

"You mean?"

"It means everyone in the house had a financial motive."

"Yes. And yet, you know, I can't believe that any of these people would do murder. I simply can't. . . . Mildred is her daughter—and already quite well provided for. Gina is devoted to her grandmother. She is generous and extravagant, but has no acquisitive feelings. Jolly Bellever is fanatically devoted to Caroline. The two Restaricks care for Caroline as though she were really their mother. They have no money of their own to speak of, but quite a lot of Caroline's income has gone towards financing their enterprises—especially so with Alex. I simply can't believe either of those two would deliberately poison her for the sake of inheriting money at her death. I just can't believe any of it, Miss Marple."

"There's Gina's husband, isn't there?"

"Yes," said Lewis gravely. "There is Gina's husband."

"You don't really know much about him. And one can't help seeing that he's a very unhappy young man."

Lewis sighed.

"He hasn't fitted in here—no. He's no interest in or sympathy for what we're trying to do. But after all, why should he? He's young, crude, and he comes from a country where a man is esteemed by the success he makes of life."

"Whilst here we are so very fond of failures," said Miss Marple.

Lewis Serrocold looked at her sharply and suspiciously.

She flushed a little and murmured rather incoherently:

"I think sometimes, you know, one can overdo things the other way. . . . I mean the young people with a good heredity, and brought up wisely in a good home—and with grit and pluck and the ability to get on in life—well, they are really, when one comes down to it—the sort of people a country *needs*."

Lewis frowned and Miss Marple hurried on, getting pinker and pinker and more and more incoherent.

"Not that I don't appreciate—I do indeed—you and Carrie Louise—a really noble work—real compassion—and one should have compassion—because after all it's what people *are* that counts—good and bad luck—and much more expected (and rightly) of the lucky ones. But I do think sometimes one's sense of proportion—oh, I don't mean *you*, Mr. Serrocold. Really I don't know *what* I mean —but the English *are* rather odd that way. Even in war, so much prouder of their defeats and their retreats than of their victories. Foreigners never can understand why we're so proud of Dunkirk. It's the sort of thing they'd prefer not to mention themselves. But we always seem to be almost embarrassed by a victory—and treat it as though it weren't quite nice to boast about it. And look at all our poets! The Charge of the Light Brigade, and the little *Revenge* went down in the Spanish Main. It's really a very odd characteristic when you come to think of it!"

Miss Marple drew a fresh breath.

"What I really mean is that everything here must seem rather peculiar to young Walter Hudd."

"Yes," Lewis allowed. "I see your point. And Walter has certainly a fine war record. There's no doubt about his bravery."

"Not that that helps," said Miss Marple candidly. "Because war is one thing, and everyday life is quite another. And actually to commit a murder, I think you do need bravery—or perhaps, more often, just conceit. Yes, conceit."

"But I would hardly say that Walter Hudd had a sufficient motive."

"Wouldn't you?" said Miss Marple. "He hates it here. He wants to get away. He wants to get Gina away. And if it's really money he wants, it would be important for Gina to get all the money before she—er—definitely forms an attachment to someone else."

"An attachment to someone else," said Lewis, in an astonished voice.

Miss Marple wondered at the blindness of enthusiastic social reformers.

"That's what I said. Both the Restaricks are in love with her, you know."

"Oh, I don't think so," said Lewis absently.

He went on:

"Stephen's invaluable to us—quite invaluable. The way he's got those lads coming along—keen—interested. They gave a splendid show last month. Scenery, costumes, everything. It just shows, as I've always said to Maverick, that it's lack of drama in their lives that leads these boys to crime. To dramatise yourself is a child's natural instinct. Maverick says—ah yes, Maverick——"

Lewis broke off.

"I want Maverick to see Inspector Curry about Edgar. The whole thing is so ridiculous really."

"What do you really know about Edgar Lawson, Mr. Serrocold?"

"Everything," said Lewis positively. "Everything, that is, that one needs to know. His background, upbringing—his deep-seated lack of confidence in himself——"

Miss Marple interrupted.

"Couldn't Edgar Lawson have poisoned Mrs. Serrocold?" she asked.

"Hardly. He's only been here a few weeks. And anyway, it's ridiculous! Why should Edgar want to poison my wife? What could he possibly gain by doing so?"

"Nothing material, I know. But he might have—some *odd* reason. He *is* odd, you know."

"You mean unbalanced?"

"I suppose so. No, I don't—not quite. What I mean is, he's all *wrong*."

It was not a very lucid exposition of what she felt. Lewis Serrocold accepted the words at their face value.

"Yes," he said with a sigh. "He's all wrong, poor lad. And he was showing such marked improvement. I can't really understand why he had this sudden set-back . . ."

Miss Marple leaned forward eagerly.

"Yes, that's what I wondered. If——"

She broke off as Inspector Curry came into the room.

CHAPTER XII

I

LEWIS SERROCOLD went away, and Inspector Curry sat down
and gave Miss Marple a rather peculiar smile.

"So Mr. Serrocold has been asking you to act as watch
dog," he said.

"Well, yes," she added apologetically: "I hope you don't
mind——"

"*I* don't mind. I think it's a very good idea. Does Mr.
Serrocold know just how well qualified you are for the
post?"

"I don't quite understand, Inspector."

"I see. He thinks you're just a very nice elderly lady who
was at school with his wife." He shook his head at her.
"We know you're a bit more than that, Miss Marple, aren't
you? Crime is right down your street. Mr. Serrocold only
knows one aspect of crime—the promising beginners. Makes
me a bit sick, sometimes. Daresay I'm wrong and old-
fashioned. But there are plenty of good decent lads about,
lads who could do with a start in life. But there, honesty has
to be its own reward—millionaires don't leave trust funds
to help the worthwhile. Well—well, don't pay any attention to me. I'm old-fashioned. I've seen boys—and girls—
with everything against them, bad homes, bad luck, every
disadvantage, and they've had the grit to win through.
That's the kind I shall leave my packet to, if I ever have
one. But then, of course, that's what I never shall have.
Just my pension and a nice bit of garden."

He nodded his head at Miss Marple.

"Superintendent Blacker told me about you last night.
Said you'd had a lot of experience of the seamy side of
human nature. Well now, let's have your point of view.
Who's the nigger in the woodpile? The G.I. husband?"

"That," said Miss Marple, "would be very convenient
for everybody."

Inspector Curry smiled softly to himself.

"A G.I. pinched my best girl," he said reminiscently. "Naturally, I'm prejudiced. His manner doesn't help. Let's have the amateur point of view. Who's been secretly and systematically poisoning Mrs. Serrocold?"

"Well," said Miss Marple judicially, "one is always inclined, human nature being what it is, to think of the *husband*. Or if it's the other way round, the wife. That's the first assumption, don't you think, in a poisoning case?"

"I agree with you every time," said Inspector Curry.

"But really—in this case——" Miss Marple shook her head. "No, frankly—I can *not* seriously consider Mr. Serrocold. Because you see, Inspector, he really *is* devoted to his wife. Naturally he would make a parade of being so—but it isn't a parade. It's very quiet, but it's genuine. He loves his wife, and I'm quite certain he wouldn't poison her."

"To say nothing of the fact that he wouldn't have any motive for doing so. She's made over her money to him already."

"Of course," said Miss Marple primly, "there are other reasons for a gentleman wanting his wife out of the way. An attachment to a young woman, for instance. But I really don't see any signs of it in this case. Mr. Serrocold does not act as though he had any romantic preoccupation. I'm really afraid," she sounded quite regretful about it, "we shall have to wash him out."

"Regrettable, isn't it?" said the Inspector. He grinned. "And anyway, he couldn't have killed Gulbrandsen. It seems to me that there's no doubt that the one thing hinges on the other. Whoever is poisoning Mrs. Serrocold killed Gulbrandsen to prevent him spilling the beans. What we've got to get at now is who had an opportunity to kill Gulbrandsen last night. And our prize suspect—there's no doubt about it—is young Walter Hudd. It was he who switched on a reading lamp which resulted in a fuse going, thereby giving him the opportunity to leave the Hall and go to the fuse box. The fuse box is in the kitchen passage which opens off from the main corridor. It was during his absence from the Great Hall that the shot was heard. So that's suspect No. 1 perfectly placed for committing the crime."

"And suspect No. 2?" asked Miss Marple.

"Suspect 2 is Alex Restarick, who was alone in his car between the lodge and the house and took too long getting there."

"Anybody else?" Miss Marple leaned forward eagerly—remembering to add: "It's very kind of you to tell me all this."

"It's not kindness," said Inspector Curry. "I've got to have your help. You put your finger on the spot when you said 'Anybody else?' Because there I've got to depend on *you*. You were there, in the Hall last night, and you can tell me *who left it* . . ."

"Yes—yes, I ought to be able to tell you. . . . But can I? You see—the circumstances——"

"You mean that you were all listening to the argument going on behind the door of Mr. Serrocold's study."

Miss Marple nodded vehemently.

"Yes, you see we were all really very frightened. Mr. Lawson looked—he really did—quite demented. Apart from Mrs. Serrocold, who seemed quite unaffected, we all feared that he would do a mischief to Mr. Serrocold. He was shouting, you know, and saying the most terrible things—we could hear them quite plainly—and what with that and with most of the lights being out—I didn't really notice anything else."

"You mean that whilst that scene was going on, anybody could have slipped out of the Hall, gone along the corridor, shot Mr. Gulbrandsen and slipped back again?"

"I think it would have been possible . . ."

"Could you say definitely that anybody was in the Great Hall the whole time?"

Miss Marple considered.

"I could say that Mrs. Serrocold was—because I was watching her. She was sitting quite close to the study door, and she never moved from her seat. It surprised me, you know, that she was able to remain so calm."

"And the others?"

"Miss Bellever went out—but I think—I am almost sure—that that was *after* the shot. Mrs. Strete? I really don't know. She was sitting behind me, you see. Gina was over by the far window. I *think* she remained there the whole time but of course I cannot be sure. Stephen was at

284

the piano. He stopped playing when the quarrel began to get heated——"

"We mustn't be misled by the time you heard the shot," said Inspector Curry. "That's a trick that's been done before now, you know. Fake up a shot so as to fix the time of a crime, and fix it wrong. *If* Miss Bellever had cooked up something of that kind (far fetched—but you never know) then she'd leave as she did, openly, after the shot was heard. No, we can't go by the shot. The limits are between when Christian Gulbrandsen left the Hall to the moment when Miss Bellever found him dead, and we can only eliminate those people who were known not to have had opportunity. That gives us Lewis Serrocold and young Edgar Lawson in the study, and Mrs. Serrocold in the Hall. It's very unfortunate, of course, that Gulbrandsen should be shot on the same evening that this schemozzle happened between Serrocold and this young Lawson."

"Just unfortunate, you think?" murmured Miss Marple.

"Oh? What do you think?"

"It occurred to me," murmured Miss Marple, "that it might have been *contrived*."

"So that's your idea?"

"Well, everybody seems to think it very odd that Edgar Lawson should quite suddenly have a relapse, so to speak. He'd got this curious complex, or whatever the term is, about his unknown father. Winston Churchill and Viscount Montgomery—all quite likely in his state of mind. Just any famous man he happened to think of. But suppose somebody puts it into his head that it's Lewis Serrocold who is really his father, that it's Lewis Serrocold who has been persecuting him—that he ought by rights to be the Crown Prince as it were of Stonygates. In his weak mental state he'll accept the idea—work himself up into a frenzy, and sooner or later will make the kind of scene he did make. And what a wonderful cover *that* will be! Everybody will have their attention fixed on the dangerous situation that is developing—especially if somebody has thoughtfully supplied him with a revolver."

"Hm, yes. Walter Hudd's revolver."

"Oh yes," said Miss Marple, "I'd thought of that. But

you know, Walter is uncommunicative and he's certainly sullen and ungracious, but I don't really think he's *stupid*."

"So you don't think it's Walter?"

"I think everybody would be very relieved if it *was* Walter. That sounds very unkind, but it's because he is an outsider."

"What about his wife?" asked Inspector Curry. "Would she be relieved?"

Miss Marple did not answer. She was thinking of Gina and Stephen Restarick standing together as she had seen them on her first day. And she thought of the way Alex Restarick's eyes had gone straight to Gina as he had entered the Hall last night. What was Gina's own attitude?

11

Two hours later Inspector Curry tilted back his chair, stretched himself and sighed.

"Well," he said, "we've cleared a good deal of ground."

Sergeant Lake agreed.

"The servants are out," he said. "They were together all through the critical period—those that sleep here. The ones that don't live in had gone home."

Curry nodded. He was suffering from mental fatigue.

He had interviewed physio-therapists, members of the teaching staff, and what he called to himself the "two young lags," whose turn it had been to dine with the family that night. All their stories dovetailed and checked. He could write them off. Their activities and habits were communal. There were no lonely souls among them. Which was useful for the purposes of alibis. Curry had kept Dr. Maverick, who was, as far as he could judge, the chief person in charge of the Institute, to the end.

"But we'll have him in now, Lake."

So the young doctor bustled in, neat and spruce and rather inhuman looking behind his pince-nez.

Maverick confirmed the statements of his staff, and agreed with Curry's findings. There had been no slackness, no loophole in the College impregnability. Christian Gulbrandsen's death could not be laid to the account of the

286

"young patients," as Curry almost called them—so hypnotised had he become by the fervent medical atmosphere.

"But patients are exactly what they are, Inspector," said Dr. Maverick with a little smile.

It was a superior smile, and Inspector Curry would not have been human if he had not resented it just a little.

He said professionally:

"Now as regards your own movements, Dr. Maverick? Can you give me an account of them?"

"Certainly. I have jotted them down for you with the approximate times."

Dr. Maverick had left the Great Hall at fifteen minutes after nine, with Mr. Lacy and Dr. Baumgarten. They had gone to Dr. Baumgarten's rooms, where they had all three remained discussing certain courses of treatment until Miss Bellever had come hurrying in and asked Dr. Maverick to go to the Great Hall. That was at approximately half-past nine. He had gone at once to the Hall and had found Edgar Lawson in a state of collapse.

Inspector Curry stirred a little.

"Just a minute, Dr. Maverick. Is this young man, in your opinion, definitely a mental case?"

Dr. Maverick smiled the superior smile again.

"We are all mental cases, Inspector Curry."

Tomfool answer, thought the Inspector. He knew quite well *he* wasn't a mental case, whatever Dr. Maverick might be!

"Is he responsible for his actions? He knows what he is doing, I suppose?"

"Perfectly."

"Then when he fired that revolver at Mr. Serrocold it was definitely attempted murder."

"No, no, Inspector Curry. Nothing of *that* kind."

"Come now, Dr. Maverick. I've seen the two bullet holes in the wall. They must have gone dangerously near to Mr. Serrocold's head."

"Perhaps. But Lawson had no intention of killing Mr. Serrocold or even of wounding him. He is very fond of Mr. Serrocold."

"It seems a curious way of showing it."

287

Dr. Maverick smiled again. Inspector Curry found that smile very trying.

"Everything one does is intentional. Every time you, Inspector, forget a name or a face it is because, unconsciously, you *wish* to forget it."

Inspector Curry looked unbelieving.

"Every time you make a slip of the tongue, that slip has a meaning. Edgar Lawson was standing a few feet away from Mr. Serrocold. He could easily have shot him dead. Instead, he missed him. Why did he miss him? Because he *wanted* to miss him. It is as simple as that. Mr. Serrocold was never in any danger—and Mr. Serrocold himself was quite aware of that fact. He understood Edgar's gesture for exactly what it was—a gesture of defiance and resentment against a universe that has denied him the simple necessities of a child's life—security and affection."

"I think I'd like to see this young man."

"Certainly if you wish. His outburst last night has had a cathartic effect. There is a great improvement to-day. Mr. Serrocold will be very pleased."

Inspector Curry stared hard at him, but Dr. Maverick was serious as always.

Curry sighed.

"Do you have any arsenic?" he asked.

"Arsenic?" The question took Dr. Maverick by surprise. It was clearly unexpected. "What a very curious question. Why arsenic?"

"Just answer the question, please."

"No, I have no arsenic of any kind in my possession."

"But you have some drugs?"

"Oh certainly. Sedatives. Morphia—the barbiturates. The usual things."

"Do you attend Mrs. Serrocold?"

"No. Dr. Gunter of Market Kimble is the family physician. I hold a medical degree, of course, but I practise purely as a psychiatrist."

"I see. Well, thank you very much, Dr. Maverick."

As Dr. Maverick went out, Inspector Curry murmured to Lake that psychiatrists gave him a pain in the neck.

"We'll get on to the family now," he said. "I'll see young Walter Hudd first."

Walter Hudd's attitude was cautious. He seemed to be studying the police officer with a slightly wary expression. But he was quite co-operative.

There was a good deal of defective wiring in Stonygates —the whole electric system was very old-fashioned. They wouldn't stand for a system like that in the States.

"It was installed, I believe, by the late Mr. Gulbrandsen when electric light was a novelty," said Inspector Curry with a faint smile.

"I'll say so! Sweet old feudal English and never been brought up to date."

The fuse which controlled most of the lights in the Great Hall had gone, and he had gone out to the fuse-box to see about it. In due course he got it repaired and came back.

"How long were you away?"

"Why that I couldn't say for sure. The fuse-box is in an awkward place. I had to get steps and a candle. I was maybe ten minutes—perhaps a quarter of an hour."

"Did you hear a shot?"

"Why no, I didn't hear anything like that. There are double doors through to the kitchen quarters and one of them is lined with a kind of felt."

"I see. And when you came back into the Hall, what did you see?"

"They were all crowded round the door into Mr. Serrocold's study. Mrs. Strete said that Mr. Serrocold had been shot—but actually that wasn't so. Mr. Serrocold was quite all right. The boob had missed him."

"You recognise the revolver?"

"Sure I recognised it! It was mine."

"When did you see it last?"

"Two or three days ago."

"Where did you keep it?"

"In the drawer in my room."

"Who knew that you kept it there?"

"I wouldn't know who knows what in this house."

"What do you mean by that, Mr. Hudd?"

"Aw, they're all nuts!"

"When you came into the Hall, was everybody else there?"

"What d'you mean by everybody?"

"The same people who were there when you went to repair the fuse."

"Gina was there . . . and the old lady with white hair—and Miss Bellever. . . . I didn't notice particularly—but I should say so."

"Mr. Gulbrandsen arrived quite unexpectedly the day before yesterday, did he not?"

"I guess so. It wasn't his usual routine, I understand."

"Did anyone seem upset by his arrival?"

Walter Hudd took a moment or two before he answered: "Why no, I wouldn't say so."

Once more there was a touch of caution in his manner.

"Have you any idea why he came?"

"Their precious Gulbrandsen Trust I suppose. The whole set-up here is crazy."

"You have these 'set-ups' as you call it, in the States."

"It's one thing to endow a scheme, and another to give it the personal touch as they do here. I had enough of psychiatrists in the Army. This place is stiff with them. Teaching young thugs to make raffia baskets and carve pipe-racks. Kids' games! It's sissy!"

Inspector Curry did not comment on this criticism. Possibly he agreed with it.

He said, eyeing Walter carefully:

"So you have no idea who could have killed Mr. Gulbrandsen?"

"One of the bright boys from the College practising his technique, I'd say."

"No, Mr. Hudd, that's out. The College, in spite of its carefully produced atmosphere of freedom, is none the less a place of detention and is run on those lines. Nobody can run in and out of it after dark and commit murders."

"I wouldn't put it past them! Well—if you want to fix it nearer home, I'd say your best bet was Alex Restarick."

"Why do you say that?"

"He had the opportunity. He drove up through the grounds alone in his car."

"And why should he kill Christian Gulbrandsen?"

Walter shrugged his shoulders.

"I'm a stranger. I don't know the family set-ups. Maybe

290

the old boy had heard something about Alex and was
going to spill the beans to the Serrocolds."

"With what result?"

"They might cut off the dough. He can use dough—
uses a good deal of it by all accounts."

"You mean—in theatrical enterprises?"

"That's what he calls it?"

"Do you suggest it was otherwise?"

Again Walter Hudd shrugged his shoulders.

"I wouldn't know," he said.

CHAPTER XIII

I

ALEX RESTARICK was voluble. He also gestured with his
hands.

"I know, I know! I'm the ideal suspect. I drive down
here alone and on the way to the house, I get a creative fit.
I can't expect you to understand. How should you?"

"I might," Curry put in drily, but Alex Restarick swept
on.

"It's just one of those things! They come upon you
there's no knowing when or how. An effect—an idea—and
everything else goes to the winds! I'm producing *Limehouse
Nights* next month. Suddenly—last night—the set-up was
wonderful. . . . *The* perfect lighting. Fog—and the headlights cutting through the fog and being thrown back—
and reflecting dimly a tall pile of buildings. Everything
helped! The shots—the running footsteps—and the chug-
chugging of the electric power engine—could have been a
launch on the Thames. And I thought—that's it—but what
am I going to use to get just these effects?—and——"

Inspector Curry broke in.

"You heard shots? Where?"

"Out of the fog, Inspector." Alex waved his hands in
the air—plump well-kept hands. "Out of the fog. That
was the wonderful part about it."

"It didn't occur to you that anything was wrong?"

"Wrong? Why should it?"

"Are shots such a usual occurrence."

"Ah, I knew you wouldn't understand! The shots fitted into the scene I was creating. I *wanted* shots. Danger—opium—crazy business. What did I care what they were really? Backfires from a lorry on the road? A poacher after rabbits?"

"They snare rabbits mostly round here."

Alex swept on:

"A child letting off fireworks? I didn't even think about them *as*—shots. I was in Limehouse—or rather at the back of the stalls—looking at Limehouse."

"How many shots?"

"I don't know," said Alex petulantly. "Two or three. Two close together, I do remember that."

Inspector Curry nodded.

"And the sound of running footsteps, I think you said? Where were they?"

"They came to me out of the fog. Somewhere near the house."

Inspector Curry said gently:

"That would suggest that the murderer of Christian Gulbrandsen came from *outside*."

"Of course. Why not? You don't really suggest, do you, that he came from inside the house?"

Still very gently, Inspector Curry said:

"We have to think of everything."

"I suppose so." said Alex Restarick generously. "What a soul-destroying job yours must be, Inspector! The details, the times and places, the pettifogging *pettiness* of it. And in the end—what good is it all. Does it bring the wretched Christian Gulbrandsen back to life?"

"There's quite a satisfaction in getting your man, Mr. Restarick."

"The Wild Western touch!"

"Did you know Mr. Gulbrandsen well?"

"Not well enough to murder him, Inspector. I had met him, off and on, since I lived here as a boy. He made brief appearances from time to time. One of our captains of industry. The type does not interest me. He has quite a collection, I believe, of Thorwaldsen's statuary——" Alex

292

shuddered. "That speaks for itself, does it not? My God, these rich men!"

Inspector Curry eyed him meditatively. Then he said: "Do you take any interest in poisons, Mr. Restarick?"

"In poisons? My dear man, he was surely not poisoned first and shot afterwards. That would be too madly detective story."

"He was not poisoned. But you haven't answered my question."

"Poison has a certain appeal. . . . It has not the crudeness of the revolver bullet or the blunt weapon. I have no special knowledge of the subject, if that is what you mean."

"Have you ever had arsenic in your possession?"

"In sandwiches—after the show? The idea has its allurements. You don't know Rose Glidon? These actresses who think they have a name! No, I have never thought of arsenic. One extracts it from weed killer or flypapers, I believe."

"How often are you down here, Mr. Restarick?"

"It varies, Inspector. Sometimes not for several weeks. But I try to get down for week-ends whenever I can. I always regard Stonygates as my true home."

"Mrs. Serrocold has encouraged you to do so?"

"What I owe Mrs. Serrocold can never be repaid. Sympathy, understanding, affection——"

"And quite a lot of solid cash as well, I believe?"

Alex looked faintly disgusted.

"She treats me as a son, and she has belief in my work."

"Has she ever spoken to you about her will?"

"Certainly. But may I ask what is the point of all these questions, Inspector? There is nothing wrong with Mrs. Serrocold."

"There had better not be," said Inspector Curry grimly.

"Now what can you possibly mean by that?"

"If you don't know, so much the better," said Inspector Curry. "And if you do—I'm warning you."

When Alex had gone Sergeant Lake said:

"Pretty bogus, would you say?"

Curry shook his head.

"Difficult to say. He may have genuine creative talent. He may just like living soft and talking big. One doesn't know. Heard running footsteps, did he? I'd be prepared to bet he made that up."

"For any particular reason?"

"Definitely for a particular reason. We haven't come to it yet, but we will."

"After all, sir, one of those smart lads may have got out of the College buildings unbeknownst. Probably a few cat burglars amongst them, and if so——"

"That's what we're meant to think. Very convenient. But if that's so, Lake, I'll eat my new soft hat."

I I

"I was at the piano," said Stephen Restarick. "I'd been strumming softly when the row blew up. Between Lewis and Edgar."

"What did you think of it?"

"Well—to tell the truth I didn't really take it seriously. The poor beggar has these fits of venom. He's not really loopy, you know. All this nonsense is a kind of blowing off steam. The truth is, we all get under his skin—particularly Gina, of course."

"Gina? You mean Mrs. Hudd? Why does she get under his skin?"

"Because she's a woman—and a beautiful woman, and because she thinks he's funny! She's half Italian, you know, and the Italians have that unconscious vein of cruelty. They've no compassion for anyone who's old or ugly, or peculiar in any way. They point with their fingers and jeer. That's what Gina did, metaphorically speaking. She'd no use for young Edgar. He was ridiculous, pompous, and at bottom fundamentally unsure of himself. He wanted to impress, and he only succeeded in looking silly. It wouldn't mean anything to her that the poor fellow suffered a lot."

"Are you suggesting that Edgar Lawson is in love with Mrs. Hudd?" asked Inspector Curry.

Stephen replied cheerfully:

"Oh yes. As a matter of fact we all are, more or less! She likes us that way."

"Does her husband like it?"

294

"He takes a dim view. He suffers, too, poor fellow. The thing can't last, you know. Their marriage, I mean. It will break up before long. It was just one of these war affairs."

"This is all very interesting," said the Inspector. "But we're getting away from our subject, which is the murder of Christian Gulbrandsen."

"Quite," said Stephen. "But I can't tell you anything about it. I sat at the piano, and I didn't leave the piano until dear Jolly came in with some rusty old keys and tried to fit one to the lock of the study door."

"You stayed at the piano. Did you continue to play the piano?"

"A gentle obligato to the life and death struggle in Lewis's study? No, I stopped playing when the tempo rose. Not that I had any doubts as to the outcome. Lewis has what I can only describe as a dynamic eye. He could easily break up Edgar just by looking at him."

"Yet Edgar Lawson fired two shots at him."

Stephen shook his head gently.

"Just putting on an act, that was. Enjoying himself. My dear mother used to do it. She died or ran away with someone when I was four, but I remember her blazing off with a pistol if anything upset her. She did it at a night club once. Made a pattern on the wall. She was an excellent shot. Quite a bit of trouble she caused. She was a Russian dancer, you know."

"Indeed. Can you tell me, Mr. Restarick, who left the Hall yesterday evening whilst you were there—during the relevant time?"

"Wally—to fix the lights. Juliet Bellever to find a key to fit the study door. Nobody else, as far as I know."

"Would you have noticed if somebody did?"

Stephen considered.

"Probably not. That is, if they just tiptoed out and back again. It was so dark in the Hall—and there was the fight to which we were all listening avidly."

"Is there anyone you are sure *was* there the whole time?"

"Mrs. Serrocold—yes, and Gina. I'd swear to them."

"Thank you, Mr. Restarick."

Stephen went towards the door. Then he hesitated and came back.

"What's all this," he said, "about arsenic?"

"Who mentioned arsenic to you?"

"My brother."

"Ah—yes."

Stephen said:

"Has somebody been giving Mrs. Serrocold arsenic?"

"Why should you mention Mrs. Serrocold?"

"I've read of the symptoms of arsenical poisoning. Peripheral neuritis, isn't it? It would square more or less with what she's been suffering from lately. And then Lewis snatching away her tonic last night. Is *that* what's been going on here?"

"The matter is under investigation," said Inspector Curry in his most official manner.

"Does she know about it herself?"

"Mr. Serrocold was particularly anxious that she should not be—alarmed."

"Alarmed isn't the right word, Inspector. Mrs. Serrocold is never alarmed. . . . Is that what lies behind Christian Gulbrandsen's death? Did he find out she was being poisoned—but how could he find out? Anyway, the whole thing seems most improbable. It doesn't make sense."

"It surprises you very much, does it, Mr. Restarick?"

"Yes, indeed. When Alex spoke to me I could hardly believe it."

"Who, in your opinion, would be likely to administer arsenic to Mrs. Serrocold?"

For a moment a grin appeared upon Stephen Restarick's handsome face.

"Not the usual person. You can wash out the husband. Lewis Serrocold's got nothing to gain. And also he worships that woman. He can't bear her to have an ache in her little finger."

"Who then? Have you any idea?"

"Oh yes. I'd say it was a certainty."

"Explain, please."

Stephen shook his head.

"It's a certainty psychologically speaking. Not in any other way. No evidence of any kind. And you probably wouldn't agree."

Stephen Restarick went out nonchalantly, and Inspector Curry drew cats on the sheet of paper in front of him.

He was thinking three things, A, that Stephen Restarick thought a good deal of himself; B, that Stephen Restarick and his brother presented a united front; and C, that Stephen Restarick was a handsome man where Walter Hudd was a plain one.

He wondered about two other things—what Stephen meant by "psychologically speaking" and whether Stephen could possibly have seen Gina from his seat at the piano. He rather thought not.

III

Into the Gothic gloom of the library, Gina brought an exotic glow. Even Inspector Curry blinked a little at the radiant young woman who sat down, leaned forward over the table and said expectantly, "Well?"

Inspector Curry, observing her scarlet shirt and dark green slacks, said drily:

"I see you're not wearing mourning, Mrs. Hudd?"

"I haven't got any," said Gina, "I know everyone is supposed to have a little black number and wear it with pearls. But I don't. I hate black. I think it's hideous, and only receptionists and housekeepers and people like that ought to wear it. Anyway Christian Gulbrandsen wasn't really a relation. He's my grandmother's stepson."

"And I suppose you didn't know him very well?"

Gina shook her head.

"He came here three or four times when I was a child, but then in the war I went to America, and I only came back here to live about six months ago."

"You have definitely come back here to live? You're not just on a visit?"

"I haven't really thought," said Gina.

"You were in the Great Hall last night, when Mr. Gulbrandsen went to his room?"

"Yes. He said good night and went away. Grandam asked if he had everything he wanted and he said yes—

297

that Jolly had fixed him up fine. Not those words, but that kind of thing. He said he had letters to write."

"And then?"

Gina described the scene between Lewis and Edgar Lawson. It was the same story that Inspector Curry had by now heard many times, but it took an added colour, a new gusto, under Gina's handling. It became drama.

"It was Wally's revolver," she said. "Fancy Edgar's having the guts to go and pinch it out of his room. I'd never have believed he'd have the guts."

"Were you alarmed when they went into the study and Edgar Lawson locked the door?"

"Oh no," said Gina, opening her enormous brown eyes very wide. "I loved it. It was so ham, you know, and so madly theatrical. Everything Edgar does is always ridiculous. One can't take him seriously for a moment."

"He did fire the revolver, though?"

"Yes. We all thought then that he'd shot Lewis after all."

"And did you enjoy that?" Inspector Curry could not refrain from asking.

"Oh no, I was terrified, then. Everyone was, except Grandam. She never turned a hair."

"That seems rather remarkable."

"Not really, She's that kind of person. Not quite in this world. She's the sort of person who never believes *anything* bad can happen. She's sweet."

"During all this scene, who was in the Hall?"

"Oh we were all there. Except Uncle Christian of course."

"Not *all*, Mrs. Hudd. People went in and out."

"Did they?" asked Gina vaguely.

"Your husband, for instance, went out to fix the lights."

"Yes. Wally's great at fixing things."

"During his absence, a shot was heard, I understand. A shot that you all thought came from the Park?"

"I don't remember that. . . . Oh yes, it was just after the lights had come on again and Wally had come back."

"Did anyone else leave the Hall?"

"I don't think so. I don't remember."

"Where were you sitting, Mrs. Hudd?"

"Over by the window."

"Near the door to the library?"

"Yes."

"Did you yourself leave the Hall at all?"

"Leave? With all the excitement? Of course not."

Gina sounded scandalised by the idea.

"Where were the others sitting?"

"Mostly round the fireplace, I think. Aunt Mildred was knitting and so was Aunt Jane—Miss Marple, I mean—Grandam was just sitting."

"And Mr. Stephen Restarick?"

"Stephen? He was playing the piano to begin with. I don't know where he went later."

"And Miss Bellever?"

"Fussing about, as usual. She practically never sits down. She was looking for keys or something."

She said suddenly:

"What's all this about Grandam's tonic? Did the chemist make a mistake in making it up or something?"

"Why should you think that?"

"Because the bottle's disappeared, and Jolly's been fussing round madly looking for it, in no end of a stew. Alex told her the police had taken it away. Did you?"

Instead of replying to the question, Inspector Curry said:

"Miss Bellever was upset, you say?"

"Oh! Jolly always fusses," said Gina carelessly. "She likes fussing. Sometimes I wonder how Grandam can stand it."

"Just one last question, Mrs. Hudd. You've no ideas yourself as to who killed Christian Gulbrandsen and why?"

"One of the queers did it, I should think. The thug ones are really quite sensible. I mean they only cosh people so as to rob a till or get money or jewellery—not just for fun. But one of the queers—you know, what they call mentally maladjusted—might do it for fun, don't you think? Because I can't see what other reason there could be for killing Uncle Christian except fun, do you? At least I don't mean fun, exactly—but——"

"You can't think of a motive?"

"Yes, that's what I mean," said Gina gratefully. "He wasn't robbed or anything, was he?"

"But you know, Mrs. Hudd, the College buildings were locked and barred. Nobody could get out from there without a pass."

"Don't you believe it," Gina laughed merrily. "Those boys could get out from anywhere! They've taught me a lot of tricks."

"She's a lively one," said Lake when Gina had departed. "First time I've seen her close to. Lovely figure, hasn't she. Sort of a foreign figure, if you know what I mean."

Inspector Curry threw him a cold glance. Sergeant Lake said hastily that she was a merry one. "Seems to have enjoyed it all, as you might say."

"Whether Stephen Restarick is right or not about her marriage breaking up, I notice that she went out of her way to mention that Walter Hudd was back in the Great Hall before that shot was heard."

"Which according to everyone else, isn't so?"

"Exactly."

"She didn't mention Miss Bellever leaving the Hall to look for keys, either."

"No," said the Inspector thoughtfully, "she didn't . . ."

CHAPTER XIV

I

MRS. STRETE fitted into the library very much better than Gina Hudd had done. There was nothing exotic about Mrs. Strete. She wore black with an oynx brooch, and she wore a hairnet over carefully arranged grey hair.

She looked, Inspector Curry reflected, exactly as the relict of a Canon of the Established Church should look—which was almost odd, because so few people ever did look like what they really were.

Even the tight line of her lips had an ascetic ecclesiastical flavour. She expressed Christian Endurance, and possibly Christian Fortitude. But not, Curry thought, Christian Charity.

Moreover it was clear that Mrs. Strete was offended.

"I should have thought that you could have given me *some* idea of when you would want me, Inspector. I have been forced to sit round waiting all the morning."

It was, Curry judged, her sense of importance that was hurt. He hastened to pour oil on the troubled waters.

"I'm very sorry, Mrs. Strete. Perhaps you don't quite know how we set about these things. We start, you know, with the less important evidence—get it out of the way, so to speak. It's valuable to keep to the last a person on whose judgment we can rely—a good observer—by whom we can check what has been told us up to date."

Mrs. Strete softened visibly.

"Oh I see. I hadn't quite realised . . ."

"Now you're a woman of mature judgment, Mrs. Strete. A woman of the world. And then this is your home—you're the daughter of the house, and you can tell me all about the people who are in it."

"I can certainly do that," said Mildred Strete.

"So you see that when we come to the question of who killed Christian Gulbrandsen, you can help us a great deal."

"But is there any question? Isn't it perfectly obvious who killed my brother?"

Inspector Curry leant back in his chair. His hand stroked his small neat moustache.

"Well—we have to be careful," he said. "You think it's obvious?"

"Of course. That dreadful American husband of poor Gina's. He's the only stranger here. We know absolutely nothing about him. He's probably one of these dreadful American gangsters."

"But that wouldn't quite account for his killing Christian Gulbrandsen, would it? Why should he?"

"Because Christian had found out something about him. That's what he came here for so soon after his last visit."

"Are you sure of that, Mrs. Strete?"

"Again it seems to me quite obvious. He let it be thought his visit was in connection with the Trust—but that's nonsense. He was here for that only a month ago. And nothing of importance has arisen since. So he must have come on some private business. He saw Walter on his last visit, and he may have recognised him—or perhaps made inquiries about him in the States—naturally he has agents all over the world—and found out something really damaging. Gina is a very silly girl. She always has been. It is just

301

like her to marry a man she knows nothing about—she's always been man mad! A man wanted by the police, perhaps, or a man who's already married, or some bad character in the underworld. But my brother Christian wasn't an easy man to deceive. He came here, I'm sure, to settle the whole business. Expose Walter and show him up for what he is. And so, naturally, Walter shot him."

Inspector Curry, adding some out-sized whiskers to one of the cats on his blotting pad, said:

"Yes—es."

"Don't you agree with me that that's what *must* have happened?"

"It could be—yes," admitted the Inspector.

"What other solution could there be? Christian had no enemies. What I can't understand is why you haven't already arrested Walter?"

"Well, you see, Mrs. Strete, we have to have evidence."

"You could probably get that easily enough. If you wired to America——"

"Oh yes, we shall check up on Mr. Walter Hudd. You can be sure of that. But until we can prove motive, there's not very much to go upon. There's opportunity, of course——"

"He went out just after Christian, pretending the lights had fused——"

"They did fuse."

"He could easily arrange that."

"True."

"That gave him his excuse. He followed Christian to his room, shot him and then repaired the fuse and came back to the Hall."

"His wife says he came back before you heard the shot from outside."

"Not a bit of it! Gina would say anything. The Italians are never truthful. And she's a Roman Catholic, of course."

Inspector Curry side-stepped the ecclesiastical angle.

"You think his wife was in it with him?"

Mildred Strete hesitated for a moment.

"No—no, I don't think that." She seemed rather disappointed not to think so. She went on: "That must have been partly the motive—to prevent Gina's learning the truth about him. After all, Gina is his bread and butter."

"And a very beautiful girl."

"Oh yes. I've always said Gina is good looking. A very common type in Italy, of course. But if you ask me, it's *money* that Walter Hudd is after. That's why he came over here and has settled down living on the Serrocolds."

"Mrs. Hudd is very well off, I understand?"

"Not at present. My father settled the same sum on Gina's mother as he did on me. But of course she took her husband's nationality (I believe the law is altered now) and what with the war and his being a Fascist, Gina has very little of her own. My mother spoils her, and her American aunt, Mrs. Van Rydock, spent fabulous sums on her and bought her everything she wanted during the war years. Nevertheless, from Walter's point of view, he can't lay his hands on much until my mother's death, when a very large fortune will come to Gina."

"And to you, Mrs. Strete."

A faint colour came into Mildred Strete's cheek.

"And to me, as you say. My husband and myself always lived quietly. He spent very little money except on books —he was a great scholar. My own money has almost doubled itself. It is more than enough for my simple needs. Still one can always use money for the benefit of others. Any money that comes to me, I shall regard as a sacred trust."

"But it won't be in a Trust, will it?" said Curry, wilfully misunderstanding. "It will come to you absolutely."

"Oh yes,—in that sense. Yes, it will be mine absolutely."

Something in the ring of that last word made Inspector Curry raise his head sharply. Mrs. Strete was not looking at him. Her eyes were shining, and her long thin mouth was curved in a triumphant smile.

Inspector Curry said in a considering voice:

"So in your view—and of course you've had ample opportunities of judging—Master Walter Hudd wants the money that will come to his wife when Mrs. Serrocold dies. By the way, she's not very strong, is she, Mrs. Strete?"

"My mother has always been delicate."

"Quite so. But delicate people often live as long or longer than people who have robust health."

"Yes, I suppose they do."

"You haven't noticed your mother's health failing just lately?"

"She suffers from rheumatism. But then one must have something as one grows older. I've no sympathy with people who make a fuss over inevitable aches and pains."

"Does Mrs. Serrocold make a fuss?"

Mildred Strete was silent for a moment. She said at last:

"She does not make a fuss herself, but she is used to being made a fuss of. My stepfather is far too solicitous. And as for Miss Bellever, she makes herself positively ridiculous. In any case, Miss Bellever has had a very bad influence in this house. She came here many years ago, and her devotion to my mother, though admirable in itself, has really become somewhat of an infliction. She literally tyrannises over my mother. She runs the whole house and takes far too much upon herself. I think it annoys Lewis sometimes. I should never be surprised if he told her to go. She has no tact—no tact whatever, and it is trying for a man to find his wife completely dominated by a bossy woman."

Inspector Curry nodded his head gently.

"I see . . . I see . . ."

He watched her speculatively.

"There's one thing I don't quite get, Mrs. Strete. The position of the two Restarick brothers?"

"More foolish sentiment. Their father married my poor mother for her money. Two years afterwards he ran away with a Yugoslavian singer of the lowest morals. He was a very unworthy person. My mother was soft-hearted enough to be sorry for these two boys. Since it was out of the question for them to spend their holidays with a woman of such notorious morals, she more or less adopted them. They have been hangers-on here ever since. Oh yes, we've plenty of spongers in this house, I can tell you that."

"Alex Restarick had an opportunity of killing Christian Gulbrandsen. He was in his car alone—driving from the Lodge to the house—what about Stephen?"

"Stephen was in the Hall with us. I don't approve of Alex Restarick—he is getting to look very coarse, and I imagine he leads an irregular life—but I don't really see him as a murderer. Besides, why should he kill my brother?"

"That's what we always come back to, isn't it?" said Inspector Curry genially. "What did Christian Gulbrandsen know—about someone—that made it necessary for that someone to kill him?"

"Exactly," said Mrs. Strete triumphantly. "It *must* be Walter Hudd."

"Unless it's someone nearer home."

Mildred said sharply:

"What did you mean by that?"

Inspector Curry said slowly:

"Mr. Gulbrandsen seemed very concerned about Mrs. Serrocold's health whilst he was here."

Mrs. Strete frowned.

"Men always fuss over mother because she looks fragile. I think she likes them to! Or else Christian had been listening to Juliet Bellever."

"You're not worried about your mother's health yourself, Mrs. Strete?"

"No. I hope I'm sensible. Naturally mother is not young——"

"And death comes to all of us," said Inspector Curry. "But not ahead of its appointed time. That's what we have to prevent."

He spoke meaningly. Mildred Strete flared into sudden animation.

"Oh it's wicked—wicked. No one else here really seems to care. Why should they? I'm the only person who was a blood relation to Christian. To mother, he was only a grown-up stepson. To Gina, he isn't really any relation at all. But he was my own brother."

"Half brother," suggested Inspector Curry.

"Half brother, yes. But we were both Gulbrandsens in spite of the difference in age."

Curry said gently:

"Yes—yes, I see your point . . ."

Tears in her eyes, Mildred Strete marched out. Curry looked at Lake.

"So she's quite sure it's Walter Hudd," he said. "Won't entertain for a moment the idea of its being anybody else."

"And she may be right."

"She certainly may. Wally fits. Opportunity—and motive. Because if he wants money quick, his wife's mother would have to die. So Wally tampers with her tonic, and Christian Gulbrandsen sees him do it—or hears about it in some way. Yes, it fits very nicely."

He paused and said:

"By the way, Mildred Strete likes money. . . . She mayn't spend it, but she likes it. I'm not sure why. . . . She may be a miser—with a miser's passion. Or she may like the power that money gives. Money for benevolence, perhaps? She's a Gulbrandsen. She may want to emulate Father."

"Complex, isn't it?" said Sergeant Lake, and scratched his head.

Inspector Curry said:

"We'd better see this screwy young man Lawson, and after that we'll go to the Great Hall and work out who was where—and if—and why—and when. . . . We've heard one or two rather interesting things this morning."

It was very difficult, Inspector Curry thought, to get a true estimate of someone from what other people said.

Edgar Lawson had been described by a good many different people that morning, but looking at him now, Curry's own impressions were almost ludicrously different.

Edgar did not impress him as "queer" or "dangerous," or "arrogant" or even as "abnormal." He seemed a very ordinary young man, very much cast down and in a state of humility approaching that of Uriah Heep's. He looked young and slightly common and rather pathetic.

He was only too anxious to talk and to apologise.

"I know I've done very wrong. I don't know what came over me—really I don't. Making that scene and kicking up such a row. And actually shooting off a pistol. At Mr. Serrocold too, who's been so good to me and so patient, too."

He twisted his hands nervously. They were rather pathetic hands, with bony wrists.

"If I've got to be had up for it, I'll come with you at once. I deserve it. I'll plead guilty."

"No charge has been made against you," said Inspector Curry crisply. "So we've no evidence on which to act. According to Mr. Serrocold, letting off the pistol was an accident."

"That's because he's so good. There never was a man as good as Mr. Serrocold! He's done everything for me. And I go and repay him by acting like this."

"What made you act as you did?"

Edgar looked embarrassed.

"I made a fool of myself."

Inspector Curry said dryly:

"So it seems. You told Mr. Serrocold in the presence of witnesses that you had discovered that he was your father. Was that true?"

"No, it wasn't."

"What put that idea into your head? Did someone suggest it to you?"

"Well, it's a bit hard to explain."

Inspector Curry looked at him thoughtfully, then said in a kindly voice:

"Suppose you try. *We* don't want to make things hard for you."

"Well, you see, I had rather a hard time of it as a kid. The other boys jeered at me. Because I hadn't got a father. Said I was a little bastard—which I was, of course. Mum was usually drunk and she had men coming in all the time. My father was a foreign seaman, I believe. The house was always filthy, and it was all pretty fair hell. And then I got to thinking, suppose my Dad had been not just some foreign sailor, but someone important—and I used to make up a thing or two. Kid stuff first—changed at birth—really the rightful heir—that sort of thing. And then I went to a new school and I tried it on once or twice hinting things. Said my father was really an Admiral in the Navy. I got to believing it myself. I didn't feel so bad then."

He paused and then went on:

"And then—later—I thought up some other ideas. I used to stay at hotels and told a lot of silly stories about being a fighter pilot—or about being in Military Intelligence. I got all sort of mixed up. I didn't seem able to stop telling lies.

"Only I didn't really try to get money by it. It was just swank so as to make people think a bit more of me. I didn't want to be dishonest. Mr. Serrocold will tell you—and Dr. Maverick—they've got all the stuff about it."

Inspector Curry nodded. He had already studied Edgar's case history and his police record.

"Mr. Serrocold got me clear in the end and brought me down here. He said he needed a secretary to help him—and I did help him! I really did. Only the others laughed at me. They were always laughing at me."

"What others? Mrs. Serrocold?"

"No, not Mrs. Serrocold. She's a lady—she's always gentle and kind. No, but Gina treated me like dirt. And Stephen Restarick. And Mrs. Strete looked down on me for not being a gentleman. So did Miss Bellever—and what's she? She's a paid companion, isn't she?"

Curry noted the signs of rising excitement.

"So you didn't find them very sympathetic?"

Edgar said passionately:

"It was because of me being a bastard. If I'd had a proper father they wouldn't have gone on like that."

"So you appropriated a couple of famous fathers?"

Edgar blushed.

"I always seem to get to telling lies," he muttered.

"And finally you said Mr. Serrocold was your father. Why?"

"Because that would stop them once for all, wouldn't it? If *he* was my father they couldn't do anything to me?"

"Yes. But you accused him of being your enemy—of persecuting you."

"I know——" He rubbed his forehead. "I got things all wrong. There are times when I don't—when I don't get things quite right. I get muddled."

"And you took the revolver from Mr. Walter Hudd's room?"

Edgar looked puzzled.

"Did I? Is that where I got it?"

"Don't you remember where you got it?"

Edgar said:

"I meant to threaten Mr. Serrocold with it. I meant to frighten him. It was kid stuff all over again."

Inspector Curry said patiently:

"How did you get the revolver?"

"You just said—out of Walter's room."

"You remember doing that now?"

"I must have got it from his room. I couldn't have got hold of it any other way, could I?"

"I don't know," said Inspector Curry. "Somebody—might have given it to you?"

Edgar was silent—his face a blank.

"Is that how it happened?"

Edgar said passionately:

"I don't remember. I was so worked up. I walked about the garden in a red mist of rage. I thought people were spying on me, watching me, trying to hound me down. Even that nice white-haired old lady. . . . I can't understand it all now. I feel I must have been mad. I don't remember where I was and what I was doing half the time!"

"Surely you remember who told you Mr. Serrocold was your father?"

Edgar gave the same blank stare.

"Nobody told me," he said sullenly. "It just came to me."

Inspector Curry sighed. He was not satisfied. But he judged he could make no further progress at present.

"Well, watch your step in future," he said.

"Yes, sir. Yes, indeed I will."

As Edgar went, Inspector Curry slowly shook his head.

"These pathological cases are the devil!"

"D'you think he's mad, sir?"

"Much less mad than I'd imagined. Weak-headed, boastful, a liar—yet a certain pleasant simplicity about him. Highly suggestible I should imagine . . ."

"You think someone did suggest things to him?"

"Oh yes, old Miss Marple was right there. She's a shrewd old bird. But I wish I knew who it was. He won't tell. If

309

we only knew that. . . . Come on, Lake, let's have a thorough reconstruction of the scene in the Hall."

"That fixes it pretty well."

Inspector Curry was sitting at the piano. Sergeant Lake was in a chair by the window overlooking the lake.

Curry went on:

"If I'm half-turned on the piano stool, watching the study door, I can't see you."

Sergeant Lake rose softly and edged quietly through the door to the library.

"All this side of the room was dark. The only lights that were on were the ones beside the study door. No, Lake, I didn't see you go. Once in the library, you could go out through the other door to the corridor—two minutes to run along to the oak suite, shoot Gulbrandsen and come back through the library to your chair by the window.

"The women by the fire have their backs to you. Mrs. Serrocold was sitting *here*—on the right of the fireplace, near the study door. Everyone agrees she didn't move and she's the only one who's in the line of direct vision. Miss Marple was here. She was looking past Mrs. Serrocold to the study. Mrs. Strete was on the left of the fireplace— close to the door out of the Hall to the lobby, and it's a very dark corner. She *could* have gone and come back. Yes, it's possible."

Curry grinned suddenly.

"And I could go." He slipped off the music stool and sidled along the wall and out through the door. "The only person who might notice I wasn't still at the piano would be Gina Hudd. And you remember what Gina said: 'Stephen was at the piano to begin with. *I don't know where he was later.*'"

"So you think it's Stephen?"

"I don't know who it is," said Curry. "It wasn't Edgar Lawson or Lewis Serrocold or Mrs. Serrocold or Miss Jane Marple. But for the rest——" He sighed. "It's probably the American. Those fused lights were a bit too convenient—

310

a coincidence. And yet, you know, I rather like the chap. Still, that isn't evidence."

He peered thoughtfully at some music on the side of the piano. "Hindemith? Who's he? Never heard of him. Shostakovitch! What names these people have." He got up and then looked down at the old-fashioned music stool. He lifted the top of it.

"Here's the old-fashioned stuff. Handel's Largo. Czerny's Exercises. Dates back to old Gulbrandsen, most of this. 'I know a lovely Garden'—Vicar's wife used to sing that when I was a boy——"

He stopped—the yellow pages of the song in his hand. Beneath them, reposing on Chopin's Preludes, was a small automatic pistol.

"Stephen Restarick," exclaimed Sergeant Lake joyfully.

"Now don't jump to conclusions," Inspector Curry warned him. "Ten to one that's what we're meant to think."

CHAPTER XV

I

MISS MARPLE climbed the stairs and tapped on the door of Mrs. Serrocold's bedroom.

"May I come in, Carrie Louise?"

"Of course, Jane dear."

Carrie Louise was sitting in front of the dressing table, brushing her silvery hair. She turned her head over her shoulder.

"Is it the police? I'll be ready in a few minutes."

"Are you all right?"

"Yes, of course. Jolly insisted on my having my breakfast in bed. And Gina came into the room with it on tiptoe as though I might be at death's door! I don't think people realise that tragedies like Christian's death are much less shock to someone old. Because one knows by then how anything may happen—and how little anything really matters that happens in this world."

311

"Ye—es," said Miss Marple dubiously.

"Don't you feel the same, Jane? I should have thought you would."

Miss Marple said slowly:

"Christian was murdered."

"Yes . . . I see what you mean. You think that *does* matter?"

"Don't you?"

"Not to Christian," said Carrie Louise simply. "It matters, of course, to whoever murdered him."

"Have you any idea who murdered him?"

Mrs. Serrocold shook her head in a bewildered fashion.

"No, I've absolutely no idea. I can't even think of a reason. It must have been something to do with his being here before—just over a month ago. Because otherwise I don't think he would have come here suddenly again for no particular reason. Whatever it was must have started off then. I've thought and I've thought, but I can't remember anything unusual."

"Who was here in the house?"

"Oh! the same people who are here now—yes, Alex was down from London about then. And—oh yes, Ruth was here."

"Ruth?"

"Her usual flying visit."

"Ruth," said Miss Marple again. Her mind was active. Christian Gulbrandsen and Ruth? Ruth had come away worried and apprehensive, but had not known why. Something was wrong was all that Ruth could say. Christian Gulbrandsen had also been worried and apprehensive, but Christian Gulbrandsen had known or suspected something that Ruth did not. He had known or suspected that someone was trying to poison Carrie Louise. How had Christian Gulbrandsen come to entertain those suspicions? What had he seen or heard? Was it something that Ruth also had seen or heard but which she had failed to appreciate at its rightful significance? Miss Marple wished that she knew what it could possibly have been. Her own vague hunch that it (whatever it was) had to do with Edgar Lawson seemed unlikely since Ruth had not even mentioned him.

She sighed.

"You're all keeping something from me, aren't you?" asked Carrie Louise.

Miss Marple jumped a little as the quiet voice spoke. "Why do you say that?"

"Because you are. Not Jolly. But everyone else. Even Lewis. He came in while I was having my breakfast, and he acted very oddly. He drank some of my coffee and even had a bit of toast and marmalade. That's so unlike him, because he always has tea and he doesn't like marmalade, so he must have been thinking of something else—and I suppose he must have forgotten to have his own breakfast. He does forget things like meals, and he looked so concerned and preoccupied."

"Murder——" began Miss Marple.

Carrie Louise said quickly:

"Oh I know. It's a terrible thing. I've never been mixed up in it before. You have, haven't you, Jane?"

"Well—yes—actually I have," Miss Marple admitted.

"So Ruth told me."

"Did she tell you that last time she was down here?" asked Miss Marple curiously.

"No, I don't think it was then. I can't really remember." Carrie Louise spoke vaguely, almost absent-mindedly.

"What are you thinking about, Carrie Louise?"

Mrs. Serrocold smiled and seemed to come back from a long way away.

"I was thinking of Gina," she said. "And of what you said about Stephen Restarick. Gina's a dear girl, you know, and she does really love Wally. I'm sure she does."

Miss Marple said nothing.

"Girls like Gina like to kick up their heels a bit." Mrs. Serrocold spoke in an almost pleading voice. "They're young and they like to feel their power. It's natural, really. I know Wally Hudd isn't the sort of man we imagined Gina marrying. Normally she'd never have met him. But she did meet him, and fell in love with him—and presumably she knows her own business best."

"Probably she does," said Miss Marple.

"But it's so very important that Gina should be happy."

Miss Marple looked curiously at her friend.

"It's important, I suppose, that everyone should be happy."

"Oh yes. But Gina's a very special case. When we took her mother—when we took Pippa—we felt that it was an experiment that had simply got to succeed. You see, Pippa's mother——"

Carrie Louise paused.

Miss Marple said:

"Who was Pippa's mother?"

Carrie Louise said: "Eric and I agreed that we should never tell anybody that. She never knew herself."

"I'd like to know," said Miss Marple.

Mrs. Serrocold looked at her doubtfully.

"It isn't just curiosity," said Miss Marple. "I really—well—*need* to know. I can hold my tongue, you know."

"You could always keep a secret, Jane," said Carrie Louise with a reminiscent smile. "Dr. Galbraith—he's the Bishop of Cromer now—he knows. But no one else. Pippa's mother was Katherine Elsworth."

"Elsworth? Wasn't that the woman who administered arsenic to her husband? Rather a celebrated case."

"Yes."

"She was hanged?"

"Yes. But you know it's not at all sure that she did it. The husband was an arsenic eater—they didn't understand so much about those things then."

"She soaked flypapers."

"The maid's evidence, we always thought, was definitely malicious."

"And Pippa was her daughter?"

"Yes. Eric and I determined to give the child a fresh start in life—with love and care and all the things a child needs. We succeeded. Pippa was—herself. The sweetest, happiest creature imaginable."

Miss Marple was silent a long time.

Carrie Louise turned away from the dressing table.

"I'm ready now. Perhaps you'll ask the Inspector or whatever he is to come up to my sitting-room. He won't mind, I'm sure."

314

Inspector Curry did not mind. In fact he rather welcomed the chance of seeing Mrs. Serrocold on her own territory.

As he stood there waiting for her, he looked round him curiously. It was not his idea of what he termed to himself "a rich woman's boudoir."

It had an old-fashioned couch and some rather uncomfortable looking Victorian chairs with twisted woodwork backs. The chintzes were old and faded but of an attractive pattern displaying the Crystal Palace. It was one of the smaller rooms, though even then it was larger than the drawing-room of most modern houses. But it had a cosy rather crowded appearance with its little tables, its bric-a-brac, and its photographs. Curry looked at an old snapshot of two little girls, one dark and lively, the other plain and staring out sulkily on the world from under a heavy fringe. He had seen that same expression that morning. "Pippa and Mildred" was written on the photograph. There was a photograph of Eric Gulbrandsen hanging on the wall, with a gold mount and a heavy ebony frame. Curry had just found a photograph of a good-looking man with eyes crinkling with laughter who he presumed was John Restarick when the door opened and Mrs. Serrocold came in.

She wore black, a floating and diaphanous black. Her little pink and white face looked unusually small under its crown of silvery hair, and there was a frailness about her that caught sharply at Inspector Curry's heart. He understood at that moment a good deal that had perplexed him earlier in the morning. He understood why people were so anxious to spare Caroline Louise Serrocold everything that could be spared her.

And yet, he thought, she isn't the kind that would ever make a fuss . . .

She greeted him, asked him to sit down, and took a chair near him. It was less he who put her at her ease than she who put him at his. He started to ask his questions and she answered them readily and without hesitation. The failure

315

of the lights, the quarrel between Edgar Lawson and her husband, the shot they had heard . . .

"It did not seem to you that the shot was in the house?"

"No, I thought it came from outside. I thought it might have been the backfire of a car."

"During the quarrel between your husband and this young fellow Lawson in the study, did you notice anybody leaving the Hall?"

"Wally had already gone to see about the lights. Miss Bellever went out shortly afterwards—to get something, but I can't remember what."

"Who else left the Hall?"

"Nobody, so far as I know."

"Would you know, Mrs. Serrocold?"

She reflected a moment.

"No, I don't think I should."

"You were completely absorbed in what you could hear going on in the study?"

"Yes."

"And you were apprehensive as to what might happen there?"

"No—no, I wouldn't say that. I didn't think anything would really happen."

"But Lawson had a revolver?"

"Yes."

"And was threatening your husband with it?"

"Yes. But he didn't mean it."

Inspector Curry felt his usual slight exasperation at this statement. So she was another of them!

"You can't possibly have been sure of that, Mrs. Serrocold."

"Well, but I was sure. In my own mind, I mean. What is it the young people say—putting on an act? That's what I felt it was. Edgar's only a boy. He was being melodramatic and silly and fancying himself as a bold desperate character. Seeing himself as the wronged hero in a romantic story. I was quite sure he would never fire that revolver."

"But he did fire it, Mrs. Serrocold."

Carrie Louise smiled.

"I expect it went off by accident."

Again exasperation mounted in Inspector Curry.

"It was not an accident. Lawson fired that revolver twice—and fired it at your husband. The bullets only just missed him."

Carrie Louise looked startled and then grave.

"I can't really believe that. Oh yes"—she hurried on to forestall the Inspector's protest—"of course I have to believe it if you tell me so. But I still feel there must be a simple explanation. Perhaps Dr. Maverick can explain it to me."

"Oh yes, Dr. Maverick will explain it all right," said Curry grimly. "Dr. Maverick can explain anything. I'm sure of that."

Unexpectedly Mrs. Serrocold said:

"I know that a lot of what we do here seems to you foolish and pointless, and psychiatrists can be very irritating sometimes. But we *do* achieve results, you know. We have our failures, but we have successes too. And what we try to do is *worth* doing. And though you probably won't believe it, Edgar is really devoted to my husband. He started this silly business about Lewis's being his father because he wants so much to have a father like Lewis. But what I can't understand is why he should suddenly get *violent*. He had been so very much better—really practically normal. Indeed he has always seemed normal to me."

The Inspector did not argue the point.

He said: "The revolver that Edgar Lawson had was one belonging to your granddaughter's husband. Presumably Lawson took it from Walter Hudd's room. Now tell me, have you ever seen *this* weapon before?"

On the palm of his hand he held out the small black automatic.

Carrie Louise looked at it.

"No, I don't think so."

"I found it in the piano stool. It has recently been fired. We haven't had time to check on it fully yet, but I should say that it is almost certainly the weapon with which Mr. Gulbrandsen was shot."

She frowned.

"And you found it in the piano stool?"

"Under some very old music. Music that I should say had not been played for years."

"Hidden, then?"

317

"Yes. You remember who was at the piano last night?"

"Stephen Restarick."

"He was playing?"

"Yes. Just softly. A funny melancholy little tune."

"When did he stop playing, Mrs. Serrocold?"

"When did he stop? I don't know."

"But he did stop? He didn't go on playing all through the quarrel."

"No. The music just died down."

"Did he get up from the piano stool?"

"I don't know. I've no idea what he did until he came over to the study door to try and fit a key to it."

"Can you think of any reason why Stephen Restarick should shoot Mr. Gulbrandsen?"

"None whatever," she added thoughtfully: "I don't believe he did."

"Gulbrandsen might have found out something discreditable about him."

"That seems to me very unlikely."

Inspector Curry had a wild wish to reply:

"Pigs may fly but they're very unlikely birds." It had been a saying of his grandmother's. Miss Marple, he thought, was sure to know it.

III

Carrie Louise came down the broad stairway and three people converged upon her from different directions, Gina from the long corridor, Miss Marple from the library, and Juliet Bellever from the Great Hall.

Gina spoke first.

"Darling!" she exclaimed passionately. "Are you all right? They haven't bullied you or given you third degree or anything?"

"Of course not, Gina. What odd ideas you have! Inspector Curry was charming and most considerate."

"So he ought to be," said Miss Bellever. "Now, Cara, I've got all your letters here and a parcel. I was going to bring them up to you."

"Bring them into the library," said Carrie Louise.

All four of them went into the library.

Carrie Louise sat down and began opening her letters. There were about twenty or thirty of them.

As she opened them, she handed them to Miss Bellever, who sorted them into heaps, explaining to Miss Marple as she did so:

"Three main categories. One—from relations of the boys. Those I hand over to Dr. Maverick. Begging letters I deal with myself. And the rest are personal—and Cara gives me notes on how to deal with them."

The correspondence once disposed of, Mrs. Serrocold turned her attention to the parcel, cutting the string with scissors.

Out of the neat wrappings there appeared an attractive box of chocolates tied up with gold ribbon.

"Someone must think it's my birthday," said Mrs. Serrocold with a smile.

She slipped off the ribbon and opened the box. Inside was a visiting card. Carrie Louise looked at it with slight surprise.

"With love from Alex," she read. "How odd of him to send me a box of chocolates by post on the same day he was coming down here."

Uneasiness stirred in Miss Marple's mind.

She said quickly:

"Wait a minute, Carrie Louise. Don't eat one yet."

Mrs. Serrocold looked faintly surprised.

"I was going to hand them round."

"Well, don't. Wait while I ask—— Is Alex about the house, do you know, Gina?"

Gina said quickly: "Alex was in the Hall just now, I think."

She went across, opened the door, and called him.

Alex Restarick appeared in the doorway a moment later.

"Madonna darling! So you're up. None the worse?"

He came across to Mrs. Serrocold and kissed her gently on both cheeks.

Miss Marple said:

"Carrie Louise wants to thank you for the chocolates."

Alex looked surprised.

"What chocolates?"

"These chocolates," said Carrie Louise.

"But I never sent you any chocolates, darling."

"The box has got your card in," said Miss Bellever.

Alex peered down.

"So it has. How odd. How very odd. . . . I certainly didn't send them."

"What a very extraordinary thing," said Miss Bellever.

"They look absolutely scrumptious," said Gina, peering into the box. "Look, Grandam, there are your favourite Kirsch ones in the middle."

Miss Marple gently but firmly took the box away from her. Without a word she took it out of the room and went to find Lewis Serrocold. It took her some time because he had gone over to the College—she found him in Dr. Maverick's room there. She put the box on the table in front of him. He listened to her brief account of the circumstances. His face grew suddenly stern and hard.

Carefully, he and the doctor lifted out chocolate after chocolate and examined them.

"I think," said Dr. Maverick, "that these ones I have put aside have almost certainly been tampered with. You see the unevenness of the chocolate coating underneath? The next thing to do is to get them analysed."

"But it seems incredible," said Miss Marple. "Why, everyone in the house might have been poisoned!"

Lewis nodded. His face was still white and hard.

"Yes. There is a ruthlessness—a disregard——" he broke off. "Actually I think all these particular chocolates are Kirsh flavouring. That is Caroline's favourite. So, you see, there is knowledge behind this."

Miss Marple said quietly:

"If it is as you suspect—if there is—poison—in these chocolates, then I'm afraid Carrie Louise will have to know what is going on. She must be put upon her guard."

Lewis Serrocold said heavily:

"Yes. She will have to know that someone wants to kill her. I think that she will find it almost impossible to believe."

CHAPTER XVI

I

" 'Ere, Miss. Is it true as there's an 'ideous poisoner at work?"

Gina pushed the hair back from her forehead and jumped as the hoarse whisper reached her. There was paint on her cheek and paint on her slacks. She and her selected helpers had been busy on the backcloth of the Nile at Sunset for their next theatrical production.

It was one of these helpers who was now asking the question. Ernie, the boy who had given her such valuable lessons in the manipulations of locks. Ernie's fingers were equally dexterous at stage carpentry, and he was one of the most enthusiastic theatrical assistants.

His eyes now were bright and beady with pleasurable anticipation.

"Where on earth did you get that idea?" asked Gina indignantly.

Ernie shut one eye.

"It's all round the dorms," he said. "But look 'ere, Miss, it wasn't one of *us*. Not a thing like that. And nobody wouldn't do a thing to Mrs. Serrocold. Even Jenkins wouldn't cosh *her*. 'Tisn't as though it was the old bitch. Wouldn't 'alf like to poison 'er, I wouldn't."

"Don't talk like that about Miss Bellever."

"Sorry, Miss. It slipped out. What poison was it, Miss? Strickline, was it? Makes you arch your back and die in agonies, that does. Or was it Prussian acid?"

"I don't know what you're talking about, Ernie."

Ernie winked again.

"Not 'alf you don't! Mr. Alex it was done it, so they say. Brought them chocs down from London. But that's a lie. Mr. Alex wouldn't do a thing like that, would he, Miss?"

"Of course he wouldn't," said Gina.

"Much more likely to be Mr. Baumgarten. When he's giving us P.T. he makes the most awful faces, and Don and I think as he's batty."

"Just move that turpentine out of the way."

Ernie obeyed, murmuring to himself:

"Don't 'arf see life 'ere! Old Gulbrandsen done in yesterday and now a secret poisoner. D'you think it's the same person doing both? What 'ud you say, Miss, if I told you as I know oo it was done 'im in?"

"You can't possibly know anything about it."

"Coo, carn't I neither? Supposin' I was outside last night and saw something."

"How could you have been out? The College is locked up after roll call at seven."

"Roll call. . . . I can get out whenever I likes, Miss. Locks don't mean nothing to me. Get out and walk around the grounds just for the fun of it, I do."

Gina said:

"I wish you'd stop telling lies, Ernie."

"Who's telling lies?"

"You are. You tell lies and you boast about things that you've never done at all."

"That's what you say, Miss. You wait till the coppers come round and arsk me all about what I saw last night."

"Well, what did you see?"

"Ah," said Ernie, "wouldn't you like to know?"

Gina made a rush at him and he beat a strategic retreat. Stephen came over from the other side of the theatre and joined Gina. They discussed various technical matters and then, side by side, they walked back towards the house.

"They all seem to know about Grandam and the chocs," said Gina. "The boys, I mean. How do they get to know?"

"Local grapevine of some kind."

"And they knew about Alex's card. Stephen, surely it was very stupid to put Alex's card in the box when he was actually coming down here."

"Yes, but who knew he was coming down here? He decided to come on the spur of the moment and sent a telegram. Probably the box was posted by then. And if he hadn't come down, putting his card in would have been quite a good idea. Because he does send Caroline chocolates sometimes."

He went on slowly:

"What I simply can't understand is——"

322

"Is why anyone should want to poison Grandam," Gina cut in. "I know. It's *inconceivable*! She's so adorable—and absolutely everyone *does* adore her."

Stephen did not answer. Gina looked at him sharply.

"I know what you're thinking, Steve!"

"I wonder."

"You're thinking that Wally—doesn't adore her. But Wally would never poison anyone. The idea's laughable."

"The loyal wife!"

"Don't say that in that sneering tone of voice."

"I didn't mean to sneer. I think you *are* loyal. I admire you for it. But darling Gina, you can't keep it up, you know."

"What do you mean, Steve?"

"You know quite well what I mean. You and Wally don't belong together. It's just one of those things that doesn't work. He knows it too. The split is going to come any day now. And you'll both be much happier when it has come."

Gina said:

"Don't be idiotic."

Stephen laughed.

"Come now, you can't pretend that you're suited to each other or that Wally's happy here."

"Oh, I don't know what's the matter with him," cried Gina. "He sulks the whole time. He hardly speaks. I—I don't know what to do about him. Why can't he enjoy himself here? We had such fun together once—everything was fun—and now he might be a different person. Why do people have to change so?"

"Do I change?"

"No, Steve darling. You're always Steve. Do you remember how I used to tag round after you in the holidays?"

"And what a nuisance I used to think you—that miserable little kid Gina. Well, the tables are turned now. You've got me where you want me, haven't you, Gina?"

Gina said quickly:

"Idiot." She went on hurriedly, "Do you think Ernie was lying? He was pretending he was roaming about in the fog last night, and hinting that he could tell things about the murder. Do you think that might be true?"

323

"True? Of course not. You know how he boasts. Anything to make himself important."

"Oh I know. I only wondered——"

They walked along side by side without speaking.

The setting sun illumined the west façade of the house. Inspector Curry looked towards it.

"Is this about the place where you stopped your car last night?" he asked.

Alex Restarick stood back a little as though considering.

"Near enough," he said. "It's difficult to tell exactly because of the fog. Yes, I should say this was the place."

Inspector Curry stood looking round with an appraising eye.

The gravelled sweep of drive swept round in a slow curve, and at this point, emerging from a screen of rhododendrons, the west façade of the house came suddenly into view with its terrace and yew hedges and steps leading down to the lawns. Thereafter the drive continued in its curving progress, sweeping through a belt of trees and round between the lake and the house until it ended in the big gravel sweep at the east side of the house.

"Dodgett," said Inspector Curry.

Police Constable Dodgett, who had been holding himself at the ready, started spasmodically into motion. He hurled himself across the intervening space of lawn in a diagonal line towards the house, reached the terrace, went in by the side door. A few moments later the curtains of one of the windows were violently agitated. Then Constable Dodgett reappeared out of the garden door, and ran back to rejoin them, breathing like a steam engine.

"Two minutes and forty-two seconds," said Inspector Curry, clicking the stop watch with which he had been timing him. "They don't take long, these things, do they?"

His tone was pleasantly conversational.

"I don't run as fast as your constable," said Alex. "I presume it *is* my supposed movements you have been timing?"

"I'm just pointing out that you had the opportunity to do murder. That's all, Mr. Restarick. I'm not making any accusations—as yet."

Alex Restarick said kindly to Constable Dodgett, who was still panting:

"I can't run as fast as you can, but I believe I'm in better training."

"It's since 'aving the bronchitis last winter," said Dodgett.

Alex turned back to the Inspector.

"Seriously, though, in spite of trying to make me uncomfortable and observing my reactions—and you must remember that we artistic folk are oh! so sensitive, such tender plants!"—his voice took on a mocking note—"you can't really believe I had anything to do with all this? I'd hardly send a box of poisoned chocolates to Mrs. Serrocold and put my card inside, would I?"

"That might be what we are meant to think. There's such a thing as a double bluff, Mr. Restarick."

"Oh, I see. How ingenious you are. By the way, those chocolates *were* poisoned?"

"The six chocolates containing Kirsch flavouring in the top layer were poisoned, yes. They contained aconitine."

"Not one of my favourite poisons, Inspector. Personally, I have a weakness for curare."

"Curare has to be introduced into the bloodstream, Mr. Restarick, not into the stomach."

"How wonderfully knowledgeable the police force are," said Alex admiringly.

Inspector Curry cast a quiet sideways glance at the young man. He noted the slightly pointed ears, the un-English Mongolian type of face. The eyes that danced with mischievous mockery. It would have been hard at any time to know what Alex Restarick was thinking. A satyr—or did he mean a faun? An overfed faun, Inspector Curry thought suddenly, and somehow there was an unpleasantness about that idea.

A twister with brains—that's how he would sum up Alex Restarick. Cleverer than his brother. Mother had been a Russian or so he had heard. "Russians" to Inspector Curry were what "Bony" had been in the early days of the nineteenth century, and what "the Huns" had been in the early twentieth century. Anything to do with Russia was bad in Inspector Curry's opinion, and if Alex Restarick had murdered Gulbrandsen he would be a very satisfactory criminal. But unfortunately Curry was by no means convinced that he had.

Constable Dodgett, having recovered his breath, now spoke.

"I moved the curtains as you told me, sir," he said. "And I counted thirty. I noticed that the curtains have a hook torn off at the top. Means that there's a gap. You'd see the light in the room from outside."

Inspector Curry said to Alex:

"Did you notice light streaming out from that window last night?"

"I couldn't see the house at all because of the fog. I told you so."

"Fog's patchy, though. Sometimes it clears for a minute here and there."

"It never cleared so that I could see the house—the main part, that is. The gymnasium building close at hand loomed up out of the mist in a deliciously unsubstantial way. It gave a perfect illusion of dock warehouses. As I told you, I am putting on a Limehouse Ballet and——"

"You told me," agreed Inspector Curry.

"One gets in the habit, you know, of looking at things from the point of view of a stage set, rather than from the point of view of reality."

"I daresay. And yet a stage set's real enough, isn't it, Mr. Restarick?"

"I don't see exactly what you mean, Inspector."

"Well, it's made of real materials—canvas and wood and paint and cardboard. The illusion is in the eye of the beholder, not in the set itself. That, as I say, is real enough, as real behind the scenes as it is in front."

Alex stared at him.

"Now that, you know, is a *very* penetrating remark, Inspector. It's given me an idea."

"For another ballet?"

"No, not for another ballet. . . . Dear me, I wonder if we've all been rather stupid?"

The Inspector and Dodgett went back to the house across the lawn. (Looking for footprints, Alex said to himself. But here he was wrong. They had looked for footprints very early that morning and had been unsuccessful because it had rained heavily at 2 a.m.). Alex walked slowly up the drive, turning over in his mind the possibilities of his new idea.

He was diverted from this, however, by the sight of Gina walking on the path by the lake. The house was on a slight eminence, and the ground sloped gently down from the front sweeps of gravel to the lake, which was bordered by rhododendrons and other shrubs. Alex ran down the gravel and found Gina.

"If you could black out that absurd Victorian monstrosity," he said, screwing up his eyes, "this would make a very good Swan Lake, with you, Gina, as the Swan Maiden. You are more like the Snow Queen though, when I come to think of it. Ruthless, determined to have your own way, quite without pity or kindliness or the rudiments of compassion. You are very, *very* feminine, Gina dear."

"How malicious you are, Alex dear!"

"Because I refuse to be taken in by you? You're very pleased with yourself, aren't you, Gina? You've got us all where you want us. Myself, Stephen, and that large simple husband of yours."

"You're talking nonsense."

"Oh no, I'm not. Stephen's in love with you, I'm in love with you, and Wally's desperately miserable. What more could a woman want?"

Gina looked at him and laughed.

Alex nodded his head vigorously.

"You have the rudiments of honesty, I'm glad to see. That's the Latin in you. You don't go to the trouble of pretending that you're not attractive to men—and that you're terribly sorry about it if they are attracted to you. You like having men in love with you, don't you, cruel Gina? Even miserable little Edgar Lawson!"

Gina looked at him steadily.

She said in a quiet serious tone:

"It doesn't last very long, you know. Women have a much worse time of it in the world than men do. They're more vulnerable. They have children, and they mind—terribly— about their children. As soon as they lose their looks, the men they love don't love them any more. They're betrayed and deserted and pushed aside. I don't blame men. I'd be the same myself. I don't like people who are old or ugly or ill or who whine about their troubles or who are ridiculous like Edgar, strutting about and pretending he's important and worthwhile. You say I'm cruel? It's a cruel world! Sooner or later it will be cruel to *me*! But now I'm young and I'm nice looking and people find me attractive." Her teeth flashed out in her peculiar warm sunny smile. "Yes, I enjoy it, Alex. Why shouldn't I?"

"Why indeed?" said Alex. "What I want to know is what you are going to do about it. Are you going to marry Stephen or are you going to marry me?"

"I'm married to Wally."

"Temporarily. Every woman should make one mistake matrimonially—but there's no need to dwell on it. Having tried out the show in the provinces, the time has come to bring it to the West End."

"And you're the West End?"

"Indubitably."

"Do you really want to marry me? I can't imagine you married."

"I insist on marriage. *Affaires*, I always think, are so very old-fashioned. Difficulties with passports and hotels and all that. I shall *never* have a mistress unless I can't get her any other way!"

Gina's laugh rang out fresh and clear.

"You do amuse me, Alex."

"It is my principal asset. Stephen is much better looking than I am. He's extremely handsome and very intense which, of course, women adore. But intensity is fatiguing in the home. With me, Gina, you will find life entertaining."

"Aren't you going to say you love me madly?"

"However true that may be, I shall certainly not say it. It would be one up to you and one down to me if I did.

No, all I am prepared to do is to make you a businesslike offer of marriage."

"I shall have to think about it," said Gina, smiling.

"Naturally. Besides, you've got to put Wally out of his misery first. I've a lot of sympathy with Wally. It must be absolute hell for him to be married to you and trailed along at your chariot wheels into this heavy family atmosphere of philanthropy."

"What a beast you are, Alex!"

"A perceptive beast."

"Sometimes," said Gina, "I don't think Wally cares for me one little bit. He just doesn't notice me any more."

"You've stirred him up with a stick and he doesn't respond? Most annoying."

Like a flash Gina swung her palm and delivered a ringing slap on Alex's smooth cheek.

"Touché!" cried Alex.

With a quick deft movement he gathered her into his arms and before she could resist, his lips fastened on hers in a long ardent kiss. She struggled a moment and then relaxed . . .

"Gina!"

They sprang apart. Mildred Strete, her face red, her lips quivering, glared at them balefully. For a moment the eagerness of her words choked their utterance.

"Disgusting . . . disgusting . . . you abandoned beastly girl . . . you're just like your mother. . . . You're a bad lot. . . . I always knew you were a bad lot . . . utterly depraved . . . and you're not only an adulteress—you're a murderess too. Oh yes, you are. I know what I know!"

"And what do you know? Don't be ridiculous, Aunt Mildred."

"I'm no aunt of yours, thank goodness. No blood relation to you. Why, you don't even know who your mother was or where she came from! But you know well enough what my father was like and my mother. What sort of a child do you think they would adopt? A criminal's child or a prostitute's probably! That's the sort of people they were. They ought to have remembered that bad blood will tell. Though I daresay that it's the Italian in you that makes you turn to *poison*."

"How dare you say that?"

"I shall say what I like. You can't deny now, can you, that somebody tried to poison mother? And who's the most likely person to do that? Who comes into an enormous fortune if mother dies? You do, Gina, and you may be sure that the police have not overlooked that fact."

Still trembling, Mildred moved rapidly away.

"Pathological," said Alex. "Definitely pathological. Really *most* interesting. It makes one wonder about the late Canon Strete . . . religious scruples, perhaps? . . . Or would you say impotent?"

"Don't be disgusting, Alex. Oh I hate her, I hate her, I hate her."

Gina clenched her hands and shook with fury.

"Lucky you hadn't got a knife in your stocking," said Alex. "If you had, dear Mrs. Strete might have known something about murder from the point of view of the victim. Calm down, Gina. Don't look so melodramatic and like Italian Opera."

"How dare she say I tried to poison Grandam?"

"Well, darling, *somebody* tried to poison her. And from the point of view of motive you're well in the picture aren't you?"

"Alex!" Gina stared at him, dismayed. "Do the police think so?"

"It's extremely difficult to know what the police think. . . . They keep their own counsel remarkably well. They're by no means fools, you know. That reminds me——"

"Where are you going?"

"To work out an idea of mine."

CHAPTER XVII

I

"You say somebody has been trying to *poison* me?"

Carrie Louise's voice held bewilderment and disbelief.

"You know," she said, "I can't really believe it . . ."

She waited a few moments, her eyes half closed.

Lewis said gently, "I wish I could have spared you this, dearest." Almost absently she stretched out a hand to him and he took it.

Miss Marple, sitting close by, shook her head sympathetically.

Carrie Louise opened her eyes.

"Is it really true, Jane?" she asked.

"I'm afraid so, my dear."

"Then everything——" Carrie Louise broke off.

She went on:

"I've always thought I knew what was real and what wasn't. . . . *This* doesn't seem real—but it is. . . . So I may be wrong everywhere. . . . But who could want to do such a thing to me? Nobody in this house could want to—*kill* me?"

Her voice still held incredulity.

"That's what I would have thought," said Lewis. "I was wrong."

"And Christian knew about it? That explains it."

"Explains what?" asked Lewis.

"His manner," said Carrie Louise. "It was very odd, you know. Not at all his usual self. He seemed—upset about me —and as though he was wanting to say something to me— and then not saying it. And he asked me if my heart was strong? And if I'd been well lately? Trying to hint to me, perhaps. But why not say something straight out? It's so much simpler just to say straight out."

"He didn't want to—cause you pain, Caroline."

"Pain? But why—— Oh I see . . ." Her eyes widened. "So *that's* what you believe. But you're wrong, Lewis, quite wrong, I can assure you of that."

Her husband avoided her eyes.

"I'm sorry," said Mrs. Serrocold after a moment or two. "But I can't believe anything of what has happened lately is true. Edgar shooting at you. Gina and Stephen. That ridiculous box of chocolates. It just isn't *true.*"

Nobody spoke.

Caroline Louise Serrocold sighed.

"I suppose," she said, "that I must have lived outside reality for a long time. . . . Please, both of you, I think I would like to be alone. . . . I've got to try and understand. . . ."

Miss Marple came down the stairs and into the Great Hall to find Alex Restarick standing near the large arched entrance door with his hand flung out in a somewhat flamboyant gesture.

"Come in, come in," said Alex happily and as though he were the owner of the Great Hall. "I'm just thinking about last night."

Lewis Serrocold, who had followed Miss Marple down from Carrie Louise's sitting-room, crossed the Great Hall to his study and went in and shut the door.

"Are you trying to reconstruct the crime?" asked Miss Marple with subdued eagerness.

"Eh?" Alex looked at her with a frown. Then his brow cleared.

"Oh *that*," he said. "No, not exactly. I was looking at the whole thing from an entirely different point of view. I was thinking of this place in the terms of the theatre. Not reality, but artificiality! Just come over here. Think of it in the terms of a stage set. Lighting, entrances, exits. Dramatis Personæ. Noises off. All very interesting. Not all my own idea. The Inspector gave it to me. I think he's rather a cruel man. He did his best to frighten me this morning."

"And did he frighten you?"

"I'm not sure."

Alex described the Inspector's experiment and the timing of the performance of the puffing Constable Dodgett.

"Time," he said, "is so very misleading. One thinks things take such a long time, but really, of course, they don't."

"No," said Miss Marple.

Representing the audience, she moved to a different position. The stage set now consisted of a vast tapestry covered wall going up to dimness, with a grand piano up L. and a window and window seat up R. Very near the window seat was the door into the library. The piano stool was only about eight feet from the door into the square lobby which led to the corridor. Two very convenient exits! The audience, of course, had an excellent view of both of them . . .

But last night, there had been no audience. Nobody, that is to say, had been facing the stage set that Miss Marple was now facing. The audience, last night, had been sitting with their backs to that particular stage.

How long, Miss Marple wondered, would it have taken to slip out of the room, run along the corridor, shoot Gulbrandsen and come back? Not nearly so long as one would think. Measured in minutes and seconds a very short time indeed . . . .

What had Carrie Louise meant when she had said to her husband: "So *that's* what you believe—but you're wrong, Lewis!"

"I must say that that was a very penetrating remark of the Inspector's," Alex's voice cut in on her meditations. "About a stage set being real. Made of wood and cardboard and stuck together with glue and as real on the unpainted as on the painted side. 'The illusion,' he pointed out, 'is in the eyes of the audience.'"

"Like conjurers," Miss Marple murmured vaguely. "*They do it with mirrors* is, I believe, the slang phrase."

Stephen Restarick came in, slightly out of breath.

"Hullo, Alex," he said. "That little rat, Ernie Gregg—I don't know if you remember him?"

"The one who played Feste when you did Twelfth Night? Quite a bit of talent there, I thought."

"Yes, he's got talent of a sort. Very good with his hands too. Does a lot of our carpentry. However, that's neither here nor there. He's been boasting to Gina that he gets out at night and wanders about the grounds. Says he was wandering round last night and boasts he saw something."

Alex spun round.

"Saw what?"

"Says he's not going to tell! Actually I'm pretty certain he's only trying to show off and get into the limelight. He's an awful liar, but I thought perhaps he ought to be questioned."

Alex said sharply: "I should leave him for a bit. Don't let him think we're too interested."

"Perhaps—yes, I think you may be right there. This evening, perhaps."

Stephen went on into the library.

Miss Marple, moving gently round the Hall in her character of mobile audience, collided with Alex Restarick as he stepped back suddenly.

Miss Marple said, "I'm so sorry."

Alex frowned at her, said in an absent sort of way:

"I beg your pardon," and then added in a surprised voice: "Oh, it's *you*."

It seemed to Miss Marple an odd remark for someone with whom she had been conversing for some considerable time.

"I was thinking of something else," said Alex Restarick. "That boy Ernie——" He made vague motions with both hands.

Then, with a sudden change of manner, he crossed the Hall and went through the library door, shutting it behind him.

The murmur of voices came from behind the closed door, but Miss Marple hardly noticed them. She was uninterested in the versatile Ernie and what he had seen or pretended to see. She had a shrewd suspicion that Ernie had seen nothing at all. She did not believe for a moment that on a cold raw foggy night like last night, Ernie would have troubled to use his lockpicking activities and wander about in the Park. In all probability he never *had* got out at night. Boasting, that was all it had been.

"Like Johnnie Backhouse," thought Miss Marple, who always had a good storehouse of parallels to draw upon selected from inhabitants of St. Mary Mead.

"I seen you last night," had been Johnnie Backhouse's unpleasant taunt to all he thought it might affect.

It had been a surprisingly successful remark. So many people, Miss Marple reflected, have been in places where they are anxious not to be seen!

She dismissed Johnnie from her mind and concentrated on a vague something which Alex's account of Inspector Curry's remarks had stirred to life. Those remarks had given Alex an idea. She was not sure that they had not given her an idea, too. The same idea? Or a different one?

She stood where Alex Restarick had stood. She thought to herself, "This is not a real hall. This is only cardboard and canvas and wood. This is a stage scene . . ." Scrappy phrases flashed across her mind. "Illusion——" "In the eyes of the

334

audience." "*They do it with mirrors . . .*" Bowls of goldfish
. . . yards of coloured ribbon . . . vanishing ladies. . . . All the
panoply and misdirection of the conjurer's art. . . .

Something stirred in her consciousness—a picture—something that Alex had said . . . something that he had described
to her . . . Constable Dodgett puffing and panting . . .
Panting . . . Something shifted in her mind—came into
sudden focus . . .

"Why of *course*!" said Miss Marple. "*That* must be it . . ."

CHAPTER XVIII

I

"Oh, Wally, how you startled me!"

Gina, emerging from the shadows by the theatre, jumped
back a little, as the figure of Wally Hudd materialised out of
the gloom. It was not yet quite dark, but had that eerie half
light when objects lose their reality and take on the fantastic
shapes of nightmare.

"What are you doing down here? You never come near
the theatre as a rule."

"Maybe I was looking for you, Gina. It's usually the best
place to find you, isn't it?"

Wally's soft, faintly drawling voice held no special insinuation, and yet Gina flinched a little.

"It's a job and I'm keen on it. I like the atmosphere of
paint and canvas, and back stage generally."

"Yes. It means a lot to you. I've seen that. Tell me, Gina,
how long do you think it will be before this business is all
cleared up?"

"The inquest's to-morrow. It will just be adjourned for a
fortnight or something like that. At least, that's what
Inspector Curry gave us to understand."

"A fortnight," said Wally thoughtfully. "I see. Say three
weeks, perhaps. And after that—we're free. I'm going back
to the States then."

"Oh! but I can't rush off like that," cried Gina. "I couldn't
leave Grandam. And we've got these two new productions
we're working on——"

"I didn't say '*we.*' I said *I* was going."

Gina stopped and looked up at her husband. Something in the effect of the shadows made him seem very big. A big, quiet figure—and in some way, or so it seemed to her, faintly menacing. . . . Standing over her. Threatening—what?

"Do you mean"—she hesitated—"you don't want me to come?"

"Why, no—I didn't say that."

"You don't care if I come or not? Is that it?"

She was suddenly angry.

"See here, Gina. This is where we've got to have a show-down. We didn't know much about each other when we got married—not much about each other's backgrounds, not much about the other one's folks. We thought it didn't matter. We thought nothing mattered except having a swell time together. Well, stage one is over. Your folks didn't—and don't—think much of me. Maybe they're right. I'm not their kind. But if you think I'm staying on here, kicking my heels, and doing odd jobs in what I consider is just a crazy set-up—well, think again! I want to live in my own country, doing the kind of job I want to do, and can do. My idea of a wife is the kind of wife who used to go along with the old pioneers, ready for anything, hardship, unfamiliar country, danger, strange surroundings. . . . Perhaps that's too much to ask of you, but it's that or nothing! Maybe I hustled you into marriage. If so, you'd better get free of me and start again. It's up to you. If you prefer one of these arty boys—it's your life and you've got to choose. But I'm going home."

"I think you're an absolute *pig*," said Gina. "I'm enjoying myself here."

"Is that so? Well, I'm not. You even enjoy murder, I suppose?"

Gina drew in her breath sharply.

"That's a cruel wicked thing to say. I was very fond of Uncle Christian. And don't you realise that someone has been quietly poisoning Grandam for months? It's horrible!"

"I told you I didn't like it here. I don't like the kind of things that go on. I'm quitting."

"If you're allowed to! Don't you realise you'll probably be arrested for Uncle Christian's murder? I hate the way Inspector Curry looks at you. He's just like a cat watching

a mouse with a nasty sharp-clawed paw all ready to pounce.
Just because you were out of the Hall fixing those lights,
and because you're not English, I'm sure they'll go fastening
it on you."

"They'll need some evidence first."

Gina wailed:

"I'm frightened for you, Wally. I've been frightened all
along."

"No good being scared. I tell you they've got nothing on
me!"

They walked in silence towards the house.

Gina said:

"I don't believe you really want me to come back to
America with you . . ."

Walter Hudd did not answer.

Gina Hudd turned on him and stamped her foot.

"I hate you. I hate you. You are horrible—a beast—a cruel
unfeeling beast. After all I've tried to do for you! You want
to be rid of me. You don't care if you never see me again.
Well, I don't care if *I* never see *you* again! I was a stupid
little fool ever to marry you, and I shall get a divorce as soon
as possible, and I shall marry Stephen or Alexis and be much
happier than I ever could be with you. And I hope you go
back to the States and marry some horrible girl who makes
you really miserable!"

"Fine!" said Wally. "Now we know where we are!"

11

Miss Marple saw Gina and Wally go into the house
together.

She was standing at the spot where Inspector Curry had
made his experiment with Constable Dodgett earlier in the
afternoon.

Miss Bellever's voice behind her made her jump.

"You'll get a chill, Miss Marple, standing about like that
after the sun's gone down."

Miss Marple fell meekly into step with her and they
walked briskly through the house.

"I was thinking about conjuring tricks," said Miss Marple.

"So difficult when you're watching them to see how they're done, and yet, once they are explained, so absurdly simple. (Although, even now, I can't imagine how conjurers produce bowls of goldfish!) Did you ever see the Lady who is Sawn in Half—*such* a thrilling trick. It fascinated me when I was eleven years old, I remember. And I never could *think* how it was done. But the other day there was an article in some paper giving the whole thing away. I don't think a newspaper should do that, do you? It seems it's not one girl —but *two*. The head of the one and the feet of the other. You think it's one girl and it's really two—and the other way round would work equally well, wouldn't it?"

Miss Bellever looked at her with faint surprise.

Miss Marple was not often so fluffy and incoherent as this. "It's all been too much for the old lady," she thought.

"When you only look at one side of a thing, you only see one side," continued Miss Marple. "But everything fits in perfectly well if you can only make up your mind what is reality and what is illusion." She added abruptly, "Is Carrie Louise—all right?"

"Yes," said Miss Bellever. "She's all right. But it must have been a shock, you know—finding out that someone wanted to kill her. I mean particularly a shock to *her*, because she doesn't understand violence."

"Carrie Louise understands some things that we don't," said Miss Marple thoughtfully. "She always has."

"I know what you mean—but she doesn't live in the real world."

"Doesn't she?"

Miss Bellever looked at her in surprise.

"There never was a more unworldly person than Cara——"

"You don't think that perhaps——" Miss Marple broke off, as Edgar Lawson passed them, swinging along at a great pace. He gave a kind of shamefaced nod, but averted his face as he passed.

"I've remembered now who he reminds me of," said Miss Marple. "It came to me suddenly just a few moments ago. He reminds me of a young man called Leonard Wylie. His father was a dentist, but he got old and blind and his hand used to shake, and so people preferred to go to the son. But the old man was very miserable about it, and moped, said he was no good for anything any more, and Leonard who was very soft-hearted and rather foolish, began to pretend he drank more than he should. He always smelt of whisky and he used to sham being rather fuddled when his patients came. His idea was that they'd go back to the father again and say the younger man was no good."

"And did they?"

"Of course not," said Miss Marple. "What happened was what anybody with any sense could have told him would happen! The patients went to Mr. Reilly, the rival dentist. So many people with good hearts have no sense. Besides, Leonard Wylie was so unconvincing. . . . His idea of drunkenness wasn't in the least like real drunkenness, and he overdid the whisky—spilling it on his clothes, you know, to a perfectly impossible extent."

They went into the house by the side door.

CHAPTER XIX

INSIDE the house, they found the family assembled in the library. Lewis was walking up and down, and there was an air of general tension in the atmosphere.

"Is anything the matter?" asked Miss Bellever.

Lewis said shortly: "Ernie Gregg is missing from roll call to-night."

"Has he run away?"

"We don't know. Maverick and some of the staff are searching the grounds. If we cannot find him we must communicate with the police."

"Grandam!" Gina ran over to Carrie Louise, startled by the whiteness of her face. "You look ill."

"I am unhappy. The poor boy . . ."

Lewis said: "I was going to question him this evening as to whether he had seen anything noteworthy last night. I have the offer of a good post for him and I thought that after discussing that, I would bring up the other topic. Now——" he broke off.

Miss Marple murmured softly:

"Foolish boy. . . . Poor foolish boy . . ."

She shook her head, and Mrs. Serrocold said gently:

"So *you* think so too, Jane . . .?"

Stephen Restarick came in. He said, "I missed you at the theatre, Gina. I thought you said you would——Hullo, what's up?"

Lewis repeated his information, and as he finished speaking, Dr. Maverick came in with a fair-haired boy with pink cheeks and a suspiciously angelic expression. Miss Marple remembered his being at dinner on the night she had arrived at Stonygates.

"I've brought Arthur Jenkins along," said Dr. Maverick. "He seems to have been the last person to talk to Ernie."

"Now, Arthur," said Lewis Serrocold, "please help us if you can. Where has Ernie gone? Is this just a prank?"

"I dunno, sir. Straight, I don't. Didn't say nothing to me, he didn't. All full of the play at the theatre he was, that's all. Said as how he'd had a smashing idea for the scenery, what Mrs. Hudd and Mr. Stephen thought was first class."

"There's another thing, Arthur. Ernie claims he was prowling about the grounds after lock-up last night. Was that true?"

"'Course it ain't. Just boasting, that's all. Perishing liar, Ernie. *He* never got out at night. Used to boast he could, but he wasn't that good with locks! He couldn't do anything with a lock as *was* a lock. Anyway 'e was in larst night, that I do know."

"You're not saying that just to satisfy us, Arthur?"

"Cross my heart," said Arthur virtuously.

Lewis did not look quite satisfied.

"Listen," said Dr. Maverick. "What's that?"

A murmur of voices was approaching. The door was flung open and looking very pale and ill, the spectacled Mr. Baumgarten staggered in.

He gasped out: "We've found him—*them*. It's horrible . . ."

He sank down on a chair and mopped his forehead.

Mildred Strete said sharply:

"What do you mean—found *them*?"

Baumgarten was shaking all over.

340

She closed her eyes.

"To-morrow"—Miss Marple hesitated—"I shall have to try and talk to Inspector Curry—if he'll listen . . ."

CHAPTER XXI

INSPECTOR CURRY said rather impatiently:

"Yes, Miss Marple?"

"Could we, do you think, go into the Great Hall."

Inspector Curry looked faintly surprised.

"Is that your idea of privacy? Surely in here——"

He looked round the study.

"It's not privacy I'm thinking of so much. It's something I want to show you. Something Alex Restarick made me see."

Inspector Curry, stifling a sigh, got up and followed Miss Marple.

"Somebody has been talking to you?" he suggested hopefully.

"No," said Miss Marple. "It's not a question of what people have said. It's really a question of conjuring tricks. They do it with mirrors, you know—that sort of thing—if you understand me."

Inspector Curry did not understand. He stared and wondered if Miss Marple was quite right in the head.

Miss Marple took up her stand and beckoned the Inspector to stand beside her.

"I want you to think of this place as a stage set, Inspector. As it was on the night Christian Gulbrandsen was killed. You're here in the audience looking at the people on the stage. Mrs. Serrocold and myself and Mrs. Strete, and Gina and Stephen—and just like on the stage there are entrances and exits and the characters go out to different places. Only you don't think when you're in the audience where they are *really* going to. They go out 'to the front door' or 'to the kitchen' and when the door opens you see a little bit of painted backcloth. But *really* of course they go out to the wings—or the back of the stage with carpenters and electricians, and other characters waiting to come on—they go out—to a different world."

343

"I don't quite see, Miss Marple——"

"Oh, I know—I daresay it sounds very silly—but if you think of this as a play and the scene is 'the Great Hall at Stonygates'—what exactly is *behind* the scene?—I mean— what is back stage? The *terrace*—isn't it?—the terrace *and a lot of windows opening on to it.*

"And that, you see, is how the conjuring trick was done. It was the trick of the Lady Sawn in Half that made me think of it."

"The Lady Sawn in Half?" Inspector Curry was now quite sure that Miss Marple was a mental case.

"A most thrilling conjuring trick. You must have seen it— only not really one girl but two girls. The head of one and the feet of the other. It looks like one person and is really two. And so I thought it could just as well be *the other way about. Two* people could be really one person."

"Two people really one?" Inspector Curry looked desperate.

"Yes. Not for long. How long did your constable take in the Park to run to this house and back? Two minutes and forty-five seconds, wasn't it? This would be less than that. Well under two minutes."

"What was under two minutes?"

"The conjuring trick. The trick when it wasn't two people but one person. In there—in the study. We're only looking at the visible part of the stage. Behind the scenes there is the terrace and a *row of windows.* So easy when there are two people in the study to open the study window, get out, run along the terrace (those footsteps Alex heard), in at the side door, shoot Christian Gulbrandsen and run back, and during that time, the other person in the study does both voices so that we're all quite sure there are *two* people in there. And so there were most of the time, but not for that little period of under two minutes."

Inspector Curry found his breath and his voice.

"Do you mean that it was *Edgar Lawson* who ran along the terrace and shot Gulbrandsen? Edgar Lawson who poisoned Mrs. Serrocold?"

"But you see, Inspector, *no one has been poisoning Mrs. Serrocold at all.* That's where the misdirection comes in. Someone very cleverly used the fact that Mrs. Serrocold's sufferings from arthritis were not unlike the symptoms of arsenical poisoning. It's the old conjurer's trick of forcing a card on you. Quite easy to add arsenic to a bottle of tonic—quite easy to add a few lines to a type-written letter. But the *real* reason for Mr. Gulbrandsen's coming here was the most likely reason—something to do with the Gulbrandsen Trust. Money, in fact. Suppose that there had been embezzlement —embezzlement on a very big scale—you see where that points? To just one person——"

Inspector Curry gasped: "Lewis Serrocold?" he murmured incredulously.

"*Lewis Serrocold . . .*" said Miss Marple.

CHAPTER XXII

PART of letter from Gina Hudd to her aunt Mrs. Van Rydock:

——*and so you see, darling Aunt Ruth, the whole thing has been just like a nightmare—especially the end of it. I've told you all about this funny man Edgar Lawson. He always was a complete rabbit—and when the Inspector began questioning him and breaking him down, he lost his nerve completely and scuttled like a rabbit. Just lost his nerve and ran—literally ran. Jumped out of the window and round the house and down the drive and then there was a policeman coming to head him off, and he swerved and ran full tilt for the lake. He leaped into a rotten old punt that's mouldered there for years and pushed off. Quite a mad senseless thing to do, of course, but as I say he was just a panic-stricken rabbit. And then Lewis gave a great shout and said "That punt's rotten," and raced off to the lake too. The punt went down and there was Edgar struggling in the water. He couldn't swim. Lewis jumped in and swam out to him. He got to him but they were both in difficulty because they'd got among the reeds. One of the Inspector's men went in with a rope round him but he got entangled too and they had to pull him in. Aunt Mildred said "They'll drown—they'll*

345

drown—they'll both drown . . ." in a silly sort of way, and
Grandam just said "Yes." I can't describe to you just how
she made that one word sound. Just "YES" and it went
through you like—like a sword.

Am I being just silly and melodramatic? I suppose I am.
But it did sound like that . . .

And then—when it was all over, and they'd got them
out and tried artificial respiration (but it was no good),
the Inspector came to us and said to Grandam:

"I'm afraid, Mrs. Serrocold, there's no hope."

Grandam said very quietly:

"Thank you, Inspector."

Then she looked at us all. Me longing to help but not
knowing how, and Jolly, looking grim and tender and
ready to minister as usual, and Stephen stretching out his
hands, and funny old Miss Marple looking so sad, and
tired, and even Wally looking upset. All so fond of her
and wanting to do SOMETHING.

But Grandam just said "Mildred." And Aunt Mildred
said "Mother." And they went away together into the
house, Grandam looking so small and frail and leaning on
Aunt Mildred. I never realised, until then, how fond of
each other they were. It didn't show much, you know, but
it was there all the time.

Gina paused and sucked the end of her fountain pen. She
resumed:

About me and Wally—we're coming back to the States
as soon as we can . . .

CHAPTER XXIII

"WHAT made you guess, Jane?"

Miss Marple took her time about replying. She looked
thoughtfully at the other two—Carrie Louise thinner and
frailer and yet curiously untouched—and the old man with
the sweet smile and the thick white hair. Dr. Galbraith,
Bishop of Cromer.

The Bishop took Carrie Louise's hand in his.

"This has been a great sorrow to you, my poor child, and a great shock."

"A sorrow, yes, but not really a shock."

"No," said Miss Marple. "That's what I discovered, you know. Everyone kept saying how Carrie Louise lived in another world from this and was out of touch with reality. But actually, Carrie Louise, it was reality you were in touch with, and not the illusion. You are never deceived by illusion like most of us are. When I suddenly realised that, I saw that I must go by what *you* thought and felt. You were quite sure that no one would try to poison you, you couldn't believe it—and you were quite right *not* to believe it, because it wasn't so! You never believed that Edgar would harm Lewis—and again you were right. He never *would* have harmed Lewis. You were sure that Gina did not love anyone but her husband—and that again was quite true.

"So therefore, if I was to go by you, all the things that *seemed* to be true were only illusions. Illusions created for a definite purpose—in the same way that conjurers create illusions, to deceive an audience. We were the audience.

"Alex Restarick got an inkling of the truth first because he had the chance of seeing things from a different angle—from the outside angle. He was with the Inspector in the drive, and he looked at the house and realised the possibilities of the windows—and he remembered the sound of running feet he had heard that night, and then the timing of the constable showed him what a very short time things take to what we should imagine they would take. The constable panted a lot, and later, thinking of a puffing constable, I remembered that Lewis Serrocold was out of breath that night when he opened the study door. He'd just been running hard, you see . . .

"But it was Edgar Lawson that was the pivot of it all to me. There was always something wrong to me about Edgar Lawson. All the things he said and did were exactly right for what he was supposed to be, but he himself wasn't right. Because he was actually a normal young man playing the part of a schizophrenic—and he was always, as it were, a little larger than life. He was always theatrical.

"It must have all been very carefully planned and thought

347

out. Lewis must have realised on the occasion of Christian's last visit that something had aroused his suspicions. And he knew Christian well enough to know that if he suspected he would not rest until he had satisfied himself that his suspicions were either justified or unfounded."

Carrie Louise stirred.

"Yes," she said. "Christian was like that. Slow and painstaking, but actually very shrewd. I don't know what it was aroused his suspicions but he started investigating—and he found out the truth."

The Bishop said: "I blame myself for not having been a more conscientious trustee."

"It was never expected of you to understand finance," said Carrie Louise. "That was originally Mr. Gilroy's province. Then, when he died, Lewis's great experience put him in what amounted to complete control. And that, of course, was what went to his head."

The pink colour came up in her cheeks.

"Lewis was a great man," she said. "A man of great vision, and a passionate believer in what could be accomplished— with money. He didn't want it for himself—or at least not in the greedy vulgar sense—he did want the power of it—he wanted the power to do great good with it——"

"He wanted," said the Bishop, "to be God." His voice was suddenly stern. "He forgot that man is only the humble instrument of God's will."

"And so he embezzled the Trust funds?" said Miss Marple.

Dr. Galbraith hesitated.

"It wasn't only that . . . ."

"Tell her," said Carrie Louise. "She is my oldest friend."

The Bishop said:

"Lewis Serrocold was what one might call a financial wizard. In his years of highly technical accountancy, he had amused himself by working out various methods of swindling which were practically foolproof. This had been merely an academic study, but when he once began to envisage the possibilities that a vast sum of money could encompass, he put these methods into practice. You see, he had at his disposal some first-class material. Amongst the boys who passed through here, he chose out a small select band. They were boys whose bent was naturally criminal,

348

who loved excitement and who had a very high order of intelligence. We've not got nearly to the bottom of it all, but it seems clear that this esoteric circle was secret and specially trained and were later placed in key positions, where, by carrying out Lewis's directions, books were falsified in such a way that large sums of money were converted without any suspicion being aroused. I gather that the operations and the ramifications are so complicated that it will be months before the auditors can unravel it all. But the net result seems to be that under various names and banking accounts and companies Lewis Serrocold would have been able to dispose of a colossal sum with which he intended to establish an overseas colony for a co-operative experiment in which juvenile delinquents should eventually own this territory and administer it. It may have been a fantastic dream——"

"It was a dream that might have come true," said Carrie Louise.

"Yes, it might have come true. But the means Lewis Serrocold adopted were dishonest means, and Christian Gulbrandsen discovered that. He was very upset, particularly by the realisation of what the discovery and the probable prosecution of Lewis would mean to you, Carrie Louise."

"That's why he asked me if my heart was strong, and seemed to worried about my health," said Carrie Louise. "I couldn't understand it."

"Then Lewis Serrocold arrived back from the North and Christian met him outside the house and told him that he knew what was going on. Lewis took it calmly, I think. Both men agreed they must do all they could to spare you. Christian said he would write to me and ask me to come here, as a co-trustee, to discuss the position.

"But of course," said Miss Marple, "Lewis Serrocold had already prepared for this emergency. It was all planned. He had brought the young man who was to play the part of Edgar Lawson to the house. There was a real Edgar Lawson —of course—in case the police looked up his record. This false Edgar knew exactly what he had to do—act the part of a schizophrenic victim of persecution—and give Lewis Serrocold an alibi for a few vital minutes.

"The next step had been thought out too. Lewis's story

that you, Carrie Louise, were being slowly poisoned—when one actually came to think of it there was only Lewis's story of what Christian had told *him*—that, and a few lines added on the typewriter whilst he was waiting for the police. It was easy to add arsenic to the tonic. No danger for you there —since he was on the spot to prevent you drinking it. The chocolates were just an added touch—and of course the original chocolates weren't poisoned—only those he substituted before turning them over to Inspector Curry."

"And Alex guessed," said Carrie Louise.

"Yes—that's why he collected your nail parings. They would show if arsenic actually had been administered over a long period."

"Poor Alex—poor Ernie."

There was a moment's silence as the other two thought of Christian Gulbrandsen, of Alexis Restarick, and of the boy Ernie—and of how quickly the act of murder could distort and deform.

"But surely," said the Bishop, "Lewis was taking a big risk in persuading Edgar to be his accomplice—even if he had some hold over him——"

Carrie shook her head.

"It wasn't exactly a hold over him. Edgar was devoted to Lewis."

"Yes," said Miss Marple. "Like Leonard Wylie and his father. I wonder perhaps if——"

She paused delicately.

"You saw the likeness, I suppose?" said Carrie Louise.

"So you knew that all along?"

"I guessed. I knew Lewis had once had a short infatuation for an actress, before he met me. He told me about it. It wasn't serious, she was a gold-digging type of woman and she didn't care for him, but I've no doubt at all that Edgar was actually Lewis's son . . ."

"Yes," said Miss Marple. "That explains everything . . ."

"And he gave his life for him in the end," said Carrie Louise. She looked pleadingly at the Bishop. "He did, you know."

There was a silence and then Carrie Louise said:

"I'm glad it ended that way . . . with his life given in the hope of saving the boy. . . . People who can be very good can be very bad, too. I always knew that was true about Lewis. . . . But—he loved me very much—and I loved him."

"Did you—ever suspect him?" asked Miss Marple.

"No," said Carrie Louise. "Because I was puzzled by the poisoning. I knew Lewis would never poison me and yet that letter of Christian's said definitely that someone *was* poisoning me—so I thought that everything I thought I knew about people must be wrong . . ."

Miss Marple said: "But when Alex and Ernie were found killed. You suspected then?"

"Yes," said Carrie Louise. "Because I didn't think anyone else but Lewis would have dared. And I began to be afraid of what he might do next . . ."

She shivered slightly.

"I admired Lewis. I admired his—what shall I call it—his goodness? But I do see that if you're—good, you have to be humble as well."

Dr. Galbraith said gently:

"That, Carrie Louise, is what I have always admired in you—your humility."

The lovely blue eyes opened wide in surprise.

"But *I'm* not clever—and not particularly good. I can only admire goodness in other people."

"Dear Carrie Louise," said Miss Marple.

EPILOGUE

"I THINK Grandma will be quite all right with Aunt Mildred," said Gina. "Aunt Mildred seems much nicer now —not so peculiar, if you know what I mean?"

"I know what you mean," said Miss Marple.

"So Wally and I will go back to the States in a fortnight's time."

Gina cast a look sideways at her husband.

"I shall forget all about Stonygates and Italy and all my girlish past and become a hundred per cent American. Our son will be always addressed as Junior. I can't say fairer than that, can I, Wally?"

"You certainly cannot, Kate," said Miss Marple.

Wally, smiling indulgently at an old lady who got names wrong, corrected her gently:

"Gina, not Kate."

But Gina laughed.

"She knows what she's saying! You see—she'll call *you* Petruchio in a moment!"

"I just think," said Miss Marple to Walter, "that you have acted very wisely, my dear boy."

"She thinks you're just the right husband for me," said Gina.

Miss Marple looked from one to the other. It was very nice, she thought, to see two young people so much in love, and Walter Hudd was completely transformed from the sulky young man she had first encountered into a good-humoured smiling giant . . ."

"You two remind me," she said, "of——"

Gina rushed forward and placed a hand firmly over Miss Marple's mouth.

"No, darling," she exclaimed. "Don't say it. I'm suspicious of these village parallels. They've always got a sting in the tail. You really are a wicked old woman, you know."

Her eyes went misty.

"When I think of you, and Aunt Ruth and Grandam all being young together. . . . How I wonder what you were all like! I can't imagine it somehow . . ."

"I don't suppose you can," said Miss Marple. "It was all a long time ago . . ."

THE END